Also by Michelle Sagara West

Cast in Shadow *

The Sundered Series*
Into the Dark Lands
Children of the Blood
Chains of Darkness, Chains of Light

The Sacred Hunt Duology**
Hunter's Oath
Hunter's Death

The Sun Sword Series**
The Broken Crown
The Uncrowned King
The Shining Court
Sea of Sorrows
The Riven Shield
Sun

*As Michelle Sagara
**As Michelle West

Lady
— OF —
Mercy

BOOK THREE OF
THE SUNDERED

Michelle Sagara West

BENBELLA BOOKS, INC.
Dallas, Texas

Copyright © 1993 by Michelle Sagara West

First BenBella Books Edition September 2006

BenBella Books
6440 N. Central Expressway, Suite 617
Dallas, TX 75206
www.benbellabooks.com
Send feedback to feedback@benbellabooks.com

Cover design by Mondolithic
Frontmatter Design and Composition by John Reinhardt Book Design
Printed by Victor Graphics, Inc.

Printed in the United States of America
10 9 8 7 6 5 4 3 2 1

Library of Congress Cataloging-in-Publication Data

Sagara West, Michelle, 1963–
    Lady of Mercy / Michelle Sagara West.—1st BenBella Books ed.
        p. cm.—(The sundered ; bk. 3)
    ISBN 1-932100-92-X
    I. Title. II. Series: Sagara West, Michelle, 1963–   . Sundered ; bk. 3.
    PR9199.3.S156L33 2006
    813'.6—dc22

                                                        2006015749

Distributed by Independent Publishers Group
To order call (800) 888-4741
www.ipgbook.com

For special sales contact Yara Abuata at yara@benbellabooks.com

prologue

Lord Vellen's return to the capital was not a happy occasion,
nor was it particularly grand or open. Had he desired such obvious fanfare, he would have been denied the choice.

All of his Swords—the four taken that he had most trusted—
were dead, and the Servants who had come at God's behest were
dispersed. Yet somehow the First of the Enemy remained. As
did Sargoth.

"It is God's game," Sargoth had said. "Do not question it."
But no ruler of the Greater Cabal took well to external orders.

Travel at the hands of the Second of the Sundered was unpleasant and best forgotten quickly—but it brought him immediately to the heart of his house, without any of his rivals' spies
the wiser for it. His rooms were as he had left them, perfectly
manicured and completely secure. There were, no doubt, house
guards posted at the doors—and they would have their surprise
soon enough.

But he was weary and sought the comfort of sleep. His arm
was useless, and any attempt to call upon the powers of his birth
caused pain—an echo of the burning. The slave—that cursed
child—had been his downfall; all of Lord Vellen's attention had
been focused on the First Servant and the known half blood.

He pulled back the covers without ringing for his attendant
slaves. Weakened, he would be shamed by their presence; it was
more than he was willing to undergo. But he had to think clearly,
even if he was so weak that standing proved difficult. Weeks had
passed, and those, taught and sheltered as he had been by the
Second of the Sundered, had made his position in the Greater
Cabal tenuous. The balance of power was a game that he had

1

mastered well—but even a master must be present for a majority of the moves.

Tomorrow he would send for a doctor; tomorrow he would discover just how long his recovery would be—and just how much time Lord Torvallen would have to plot and build a base from which to attempt the high seat of the Greater Cabal.

Tonight he would dream of the death of a slave, a woman, and the Lord of the Empire.

> *To Vellen of Damion, seat of the Greater Cabal, High Priest and Lord of the Karnari:*
> *Light King takes four. The game isn't over yet.*
> *Renar of Marantine.*

Lord Vellen's hands trembled in the dark silence of his bedchamber. He laid the note carefully upon the thick, soft counterpane and gazed at it; his face was still and betrayed nothing of what he felt, although none were there to remark upon it.

The curtains were drawn, denying light and day. An empty crystal decanter lay on the bed table beside fresh-cut flowers, quill, and inkstand.

He had survived. He had barely survived.

His eyes silvered, although he knew this precious use of energy was vain and impulsive, and the edges of the parchment caught orange light and fire as his magic reigned. No heat burned the counterpane; no flame touched anything but the words of a foe that Lord Vellen had never quite managed to trap.

Corval was dead; Stillonius, too, had met assassin's blade. Of the twelve members of his cabal, these two had been firmly and completely owned by Vellen. In two short weeks, Renar of Marantine had struck a quiet and efficient blow to the power structure that made Vellen's word law: Morden of Farenel and Sorval of Kintassus had been "voted" upon as replacements in Vellen's absence.

In his weakened condition, unable to travel beyond the perimeter of his rooms, Vellen had had little choice but to sign the official document. He had kept a measured and steady correspondence with Lord Valens, delicately skirting around the issue of both his health and his presence at meetings of the full cabal.

He pushed himself up against the headboard and grimaced in

pain. The white-fire that had struck him still burned and scarred his insides; he could not move at all without betraying this.

And he knew, clearly, where this strike had come from. He had looked up, before the fire took even that ability away from him, to see the slave that he had once kept for the Lord of the Empire. The slave's revenge was not yet complete, and in the darkness, Lord Vellen vowed that it would never become so.

But a boy and a disinherited prince of Marantine had achieved a goal that Vellen had thought impossible for any outside of the political Greater Cabal to achieve.

Grimacing, he fell back and slid into the cool sheets. The Second of the Sundered had not seen fit to supply him with any information of the happenings of the battle; he had come into the preternaturally still hall to teleport Vellen away from the scene of battle without speaking a word.

Vellen was too proud to ask, and besides, he maintained his own small force to hunt out information, stationed just outside of the castle, in the village of the Vale. Two days had passed, by a count admittedly not as reliable as it usually was; Lord Vellen expected a report and waited with patience that had become ingrained but never pleasant.

He let the shadows hide his gaunt, pale face for a few minutes longer before reaching for the bellpull and tugging it softly. There was work to do, letters to be dictated.

chapter
one

The Swords were ready for battle. The castle of the Lord of the
Empire loomed in the near distance, a monument of great,
carved stone and high towers—a banner not perturbed or moved
by the wind on the open hillock.

Not three hundred yards from the Vale's village, in the cover
provided by thin trees and goldenrod grown too high from a
plenitude of rain and sun, the four men kept watch. They were
dressed simply and hadn't seen use of razors or water for a four-
day—but they no longer looked bored or irritated. Like a brand,
the clash of white and red in the night sky two evenings past had
burned itself into their eyes, a harbinger of doom or war that the
blood understood well, even if the mind did not.

Although they wore no chain and no black surcoats, and attended no high priest, they bore arms that were perfectly crafted.
They were Swords; Malanthi, all.

They had seen the nightwalkers drifting through the wrought-
iron gates of the castle. Servants of the the Dark Heart. What
had drawn the four here, they did not know. Nor were they
certain they wanted to.

But they were not bored; indeed, even if they had been relieved of their long duty, they would have had trouble sleeping.

The sky was the color of firelight reflected in tears; light,
misted orange. Sara rose with the dawn, in silence and mourning. Someone tended to her; she drank the water of Lernan's
wound and found it both sweet and bitter to her taste.

"Sara?"

4

She coughed, pushed the hand away, and murmured something only half-distinct.

"Almost two days," was the quiet reply. "We're in the garden house. Shed," Darin added as he looked at the rough walls. "I haven't gone back outside. I left yesterday morning to try to find the Lord, but I—there's a spell on the ground around the castle. Bethany said it was dangerous. I didn't cross it. I tried calling him, but he didn't answer. And all the slaves are gone."

He tilted a cup to her lip; she swallowed, and once again felt the warmth and tingling of Lernan's Gift. It was almost more than she could bear. Gently, she eased herself to sitting.

"I'm fine," she whispered. "I—have to go outside."

He offered her a hand—and a shoulder when her weight proved unstable. She stood, leaning against him until Lernan's healing offered her body strength enough to stand on its own. Then she opened the door and walked into the pink sky, the open garden. She shuddered as she passed beneath the wide door's frame.

"What's wrong?"

"There's a magic on this outbuilding. It's—I don't know what it is. But it's not mine. Not ours."

Before Darin could press her for more, Bethany spoke quietly into his mind's ear. *Leave her for the moment, Initiate.*

But—but if there's a spell on the shed, shouldn't we do something about it?

Bethany offered momentary silence, as she often did—the pause for breath before the answer. *No,* she said at last. *I do not think we need to fear it. It was for our protection, I think; it kept us hidden from our Enemy's detection.*

He looked at Sara's drawn, pale face; he saw the shudder that stretched across her shoulders and arms. *She doesn't think so.*

Perhaps. But you will not ask her.

She remembered everything.

She saw, in the sunset and the low morning haze, a flicker of lids over a blood-drenched face. She arrived again a moment too late and let loose her power—her line's gift—in an empty display of anger, of pain, of betrayal.

Belfas was dead. Not even the body remained, and she knew that there had been no ceremony for him, no easing of the way. She hoped that the Bridge had been open to him and that the

Beyond held nothing of war or its memories to torment him. Nothing of war, and nothing of her.

She saw the back of a young boy, started, and then relaxed—if the slight easing of her shoulders and jaw could be called that. Darin stood, elbows against the stone lip of Lernan's Gifting, eyes on the surface of the gently moving waters. His fingers, smooth and bloodless, skirted the water; his lips moved, and his fair, pale hair bobbed lightly as he rocked. He was writing something that no other eyes would see.

Darin was of Culverne. Culverne lay across the continent. Keranya's words echoed quietly in the air, where only she could hear them. It had been five years since the fall of Line Culverne—only five. Not four hundred.

A hundred bitter questions pressed against the tight line of her lips, which were closed against their utterance. She looked out at the garden; her eyes followed the smooth and perfect line of the hedges and wending trail of all manner of flowers, only a few of which she knew by name. She caught the scent of roses and saw that they were white—the color of mourning, of passage. She looked again at Darin. Now was not the time for questions, and she doubted that he could answer even a fraction of them, even if it were.

She knew where she was, although the forest and the Lady's trees had been cleared completely away, and no trace remained of the path, once familiar and oft traveled, to the Gifting—the Gifting that Elliath had kept and preserved in its long battle.

They had lost it, and she would abandon it again. There was no choice.

She was quiet as she walked to the inner gates that kept the garden from the rest of the castle; quiet as she bent down to retrieve what Gervin, slavemaster no longer, had left for her keeping.

There was a weapon, a sword a little longer than those she had trained with, and a shield and armor; there was food, snares, and two bedrolls; there was even a small tent which would serve both her and Darin well.

"Sara?" She heard the soft pad of quick, light steps as Darin left the well and approached her turned back.

"It's morning," she said quietly. "We should leave now, while we have the chance." Swallowing, she continued.

"Lord—Lord Darclan gave us time, but only that. The priests will probably come, if the lord was injured or—or killed."

"Can't we check?"

"No." The word was quick and clear—too quick. As if realizing this, Sara added, "The ward on the grounds would make it very difficult—and we . . . we can't risk the power. Not now. Trust me, Darin. It's best this way."

He nodded, hearing her words clearly, and misunderstanding the shakiness with which they were delivered. He had been told, by both Gervin and Lord Darclan, that they would have to flee the castle and perhaps Mordantari itself.

Lady Sara slid quickly out of her dress, and, before Darin could blush or offer his aid, found her way into the tunic and trousers that Gervin had also seen fit to provide. They were plain, but not coarse; even though they were simple, no observer would have mistaken them for mere slave's wear. Padding followed, as did armor. She buckled leather into place and girded herself with her weapon.

"Should I change, too?"

"Yes. But keep the clothing anyway. It's fine, a little too fancy, and not very practical—but we may need it, in time."

He began to change, and she, to rearrange the backpacks. When she was done, she lifted the heavier one with quiet authority and slid it onto her shoulders. It felt strange. It had been years since she'd traveled with one. Darin's grunting drew her attention, and she turned with almost a sigh.

She walked over, held out both hands, and caught the straps of his pack before they crossed at the back. He flushed a little; it added color to his cheeks, to the fairness of his face. "Sorry, Sara," he muttered, as he turned and held his arms out behind his back.

She was familiar with the gesture. It cut; it cut deeply. "Don't be afraid to ask me for help."

He would remember that, later. That, and the expression on her face.

Two others watched the castle from without, aware of the Swords, although they were not aware of each other. One was an older man who carried his age like a mantle of authority or a symbol of wisdom. He wore a brown robe, one simple and unadorned by any threads or embroidery that spoke of rank or office. The hood at the back was pulled up and rested just above the line of salt-and-pepper brows; a twined rope girded his midsection and hung to his knees. A pack lay at his feet and a staff beside it—one of gnarled wood that would stretch to just past his shoulder when carried. He stood almost in plain sight, certainly more so than the Swords—but none noticed or remarked on his presence.

He was a man of many talents and many dangers—and the moment that he had been planning for, even hoping for, was about to come to pass.

Indeed, as he watched the gates he hardly seemed to breathe at all.

The last man waited, better hidden and more silent than any of the others. He watched the Swords, and he watched the gate; it would have been hard to say which garnered more of his attention. He was not old, but not in the first bloom of youth either; lines had been etched into the corners of his eyes, but whether it was due to smiling or frowning was impossible to divine. His face was smooth and perfectly expressionless beneath the dark, deep brown of his hair. There was a scar across his forehead, and another across his cheek—but they were faint, like the trace of an old web that's been all but removed.

His arms were crossed; he kept his hands at his sleeves. The sword that he wore hung, sheathed, past his.knee. Yet he, too, was prepared for battle.

"Darin," Sara said softly, "stay behind me."

Her voice, quiet, was nonetheless edged and cold. Darin tilted his head, as if to question her commands, and fell silent at the look on her face, although it was not directed at him. The sweep of lashes closed in a narrowed line over her eyes; those eyes flared green for a second—a fleeting echo of the previous night's battle.

Her sword rang out in the stillness, a raw scrape of steel and light. Following her gaze, he saw four men, villagers by their dress, but far too idle for those of the Vale. They lounged by the roadside, but even at this distance it was obvious to Darin that they, too, held swords—swords that were drawn.

Without a word, he reached—fumbled, really—for Bethany.

She came to his hand, and he leaned on her for strength; he called on her for knowledge.

A thin, murky thread of light, almost invisible in the greater brilliance of sun and clear sky, streaked across the distance that separated them from the four that waited.

Before it reached them, it died, cut off abruptly.

"Malanthi," Darin whispered.

Sara nodded quietly, her eyes a green sheen, her jaw a rigid, square line. "Swords."

"Should we go back?" He looked over his shoulder; the road behind them was clear.

"No," Sara said softly. "I can't."

"Then maybe we should get off the road?" His eyes darted to trees, but even the suggestion was made doubtfully; the Swords were close. As if his words were beacons, they began to move forward—not running, not precisely, but walking at a very quick pace.

Sara stopped, planting her feet slightly apart in the flat dirt road. Her pack hit the ground and rocked to a stop. She reached for the shield that rested atop it and shrugged her forearm through its leather straps. The handgrip was caught and held in whitening fingers. The shield's rounded contours fell just below her hips. It had been years since she had held either sword or shield; there had been little call for either in Rennath.

Years? Centuries.

She wondered, briefly, if she would be up to the fight. There were four men, each taller and larger than she, and each was carrying a sword with a greater reach than hers. No doubt they were in practice with those weapons. At least they carried no bows. The Swords were an arrogant group of men, skilled at their arms and vicious in their service to the Church of the Dark Heart—but even they had standards. Ranged combat, the kill from a distance, was a measure of last resort. After all, what good was a kill if you couldn't feel the death?

At twenty feet, they stopped. She held her place, aware of Darin's presence—and Bethany's power—at her back.

"Excuse me, ma'am," the foremost Sword said, pointing slightly with his weapon. "We'd like a few words with you, if it won't take you out of your way." He smiled congenially—which is to say that his teeth flashed in an even line between his parted lips. His was a square face, gentled by a long forehead, full cheeks, and short, soft hair. But his eyes never relaxed—and they never really left Sara's weapon.

Damn. Damn it. Sara tightened her grip, both on sword and shield. She had hoped that the Swords might somehow take her presence at face value—a common woman in the Empire didn't really know much of the use of weapons, and even if she had one, would probably not know how to use it. Stupidity was an advantage that she wasn't going to be offered here.

"What," she said evenly, "did you want to know?"

"You came from the castle." He took another step forward, and the three behind him fanned out at his back in a half circle of glinting steel. "We just want to ask you about the events of two nights past."

"Ask, then. But stay your ground." She pulled her sword up until the flat rested very lightly against her shoulder.

He didn't stop; she didn't expect him to. He had all of the advantage that numbers, size, and, to his mind, rank provided. He had no reason at all to heed her quiet request.

"Here isn't really the best place for such a discussion; it's very open." Another step, slow and carefully placed. His eyes were dark brown—she could see them very clearly now; they were as sharp to her eyes as his breathing, tense and short, was to her ears.

"You know that the Lord of Mordantari doesn't always appreciate the importance of his Church or its agents." His smile died suddenly; his voice lost even the patina of friendliness that had, after all, soothed no one. "You'll both come with us to the village."

"Mordantari?" Her reply was almost dreamy, so peculiar was the tone. "Is that what he calls it now? *The peace of the dead?*"

A frown rippled subtly down the Sword's face, a sudden unease exposed to the light. He started forward, sword at ready, even as she raised and lowered her arms. Her free hand danced in the air more quickly than his feet against the ground; her lips moved soundlessly.

But her eyes, her eyes were the most terrible thing of all to the Sword who was several years her elder. He had never seen such an ugly, all-encompassing shade of green. And he had never, for all of his lessons and studies prior to attaining his rank, felt the Greater Ward.

Light seared the insides of his skin. The pain was great enough that he forgot, for full seconds, the use of the counterward. He heard the shouts to his left and right as he brought his own hands up in the gesture and the call.

The fire increased; the light grew brighter. He lost the words and the rhythm of the ward as Bethany joined her power to Sara's.

But he saw, through the haze, the quick dart of his enemy's lunge. He brought his sword up, as a reflex, and felt it clang against hers. She swore; he smiled grimly and struggled to gain his feet before realizing that he'd never lost them.

At his back, he heard footsteps retreating. He shut them out; they were not his concern. She was. He wanted her death, more than he'd wanted anything in his life. In this Sword, of the four, the blood was still very strong.

Sara felt his shields flare to life; she saw the faint pink glow of the two other Swords as they also drew close. She called upon her power as Sarillorn and moved quickly and concisely. Her physical shield she thrust to the side in a low block, but her light she held out before her at the strongest of the three. Her sword, the third of her weapons, moved in a perfect harmony to her two defenses.

She felt the blood call; her body tingled with its imperative. For the first time in years, she gave in to it, joining her skill to the dance of the red and the white, the Dark and the Light.

There was no longer any reason to hold back. Belfas was dead. The Lady was dead. The line had been consumed by history; what was there to hope for now?

Her anger was her direction and her commander. Bethany's light flared white and warm, a pillar to her right. She heard a scream start—and ended it viciously and absolutely with an instinctive thrust to the side. In the midst of white light came crimson blood.

But it had been four years since she'd wielded a weapon, and Telvar's words and warnings returned to her too late. Never let anger guide your tactics. Curt, short, true. Her blood flowed next as the point of a sword disappeared into her left thigh. And her blood, as it flowed, was also red.

There was hardly any pain at all, the call to battle was still so strong. But the wound was a heavy warning, and a cold one. She pulled her rage in and pushed it aside, seeing her two remaining enemies clearly. She called on her healing skill to block the wound; it answered, slowing the flow of the blood, but no more.

She was not foolish enough to take the time to tend it. Instead, she used her power to bolster the Greater Ward. She saw the square, fair face of the Sword, made mottled and ugly by his blood's desire, and knew that she saw a mirror of her own expression.

Here, then, was her advantage. She was quit of the call for the moment; he was not. But his remaining ally was hesitant, almost distant. She took a slow step back, brought herself to a stop against Darin, and threw out the remainder of her power until it was almost a visible aurora.

For a moment the Swords stood, suspended. Then they gathered their own, lesser, powers around them like mantles and charged forward, like any inexperienced sixth might have done, bereft of leadership.

They were almost easy to kill, and she did so as quickly as possible. She couldn't bear to feel the call of their pain as an aftereffect of her victory.

Darin was ash gray and silent as the last Sword died. His fingers were wrapped around Bethany, and he leaned against her for support, as if suddenly old enough to require it.

Initiate, she said, and her voice was cool, *this is a war, not a fable.*

I know.

He heard the ghost of her sigh; it was an impatient one. *Tend your lady, then. She is injured, but alive, and may require your assistance.*

Nodding, he swallowed, and stepped over the outstretched hand that curled, wet and thumbless, inches away from his feet. "Sara?"

"I'm sorry," she said, as she turned. She had already run a tight strip of cotton across her thigh, but the blood had come clean through. "It's been too long. I was careless."

"Do you need any help?"

"Not yet. I can walk; I didn't break any bones."

"Bethany can—"

"I think you need her." Her eyes, as they glanced briefly off his, were dark and tired. She looked very much like a warrior priest—an old one. He couldn't argue with her, and Bethany didn't insist on it.

"Come on, Initiate. One of the four went running somewhere, and we'd better be gone when he returns. He won't come back alone." She started down the road, her stride only slightly off—and not at all slowed.

"Where are we going?"

"To the Lady's Woodhall."

Erliss of Mordechai was not a comfortable priest. Nor was he particularly happy, and to make matters worse, he had no appropriate way to vent his spleen—not within the confines of the village of the Vale in the domains of Mordantari. Mordantari belonged to the near-mythical Lord of the Empire. Twice in the history of the Dark Heart's Church, high priests had attempted to intervene in Mordantari affairs, seeking perhaps good lands and the influence owning them would bring. Neither of the two survived, and their deaths had been in no wise a private affair. Their bodies had been conveyed, by means magical and not well understood, to the center square of the High City in Malakar. Enough remained of their faces, and the fingers that bore their signatory rings, to identify them. And of course, the stories had spread.

Erliss of Mordechai had been far too young to see the last priest disposed of, but the lesson and the story had traveled down from Lord Mordechai to all of his clan: Do not interfere in the matters of Mordantari. It will bring ill fortune upon us all.

The words came back, sharp and clear, as he sat stiffly in a winged chair in the cramped little living area that passed as a room for travelers. It was wood-walled and mud-sealed, with windows that weren't even glassed in—and were small, at that. The ceilings near the fireplace were low and ugly, and the decor—what there was of it—was laughable. In any other village, he and his attendant slaves would have merely requisitioned use of the reigning noble's manor—usually some small officiant to the Church itself. There were none in the Vale.

Vellen, he thought, as he rose for the thirteenth time to walk in a circle over a rug made up of braided rags—rags!—*there had best be worthwhile information here.*

But of course there was, information and more, all of a highly valuable nature. Why else would Lord Vellen, first of the Karnari, holder of the high seat of the Greater Cabal, make his trek here in secrecy and silence? Why else would he travel with so small and unimpressive a party of Swords—without even slaves in attendance?

And where is Lord Vellen now? he asked himself darkly. *Has he escaped cleanly and left us to the Lord of the Empire?*

Erliss ran a hand through dark, perfect hair. A man who sought power was wise to counsel himself in the ways of patience; he had been told this many times as he struggled out of his youth. As always, it was a particularly painful trial to follow that advice.

But patience was willing to reward him, this one time. The knock came.

He forced himself to walk slowly to the door; he forced his hand to lift the latch and pull it open with a casual strength. He even forced himself to remain silent as the Sword fell to one knee beneath the door's frame.

"Lord Erliss."

"Rise," the lord responded, "and give me your news. Have you sighted Lord Vellen?"

"No, Lord," was the quiet response. But the tense, stretched look of the Sword's mouth promised worthwhile information anyway. He rose at the priest's command and entered the room as Erliss stepped back.

"What news, then?"

"Two people left the castle by the front gates. They came down the road toward the Vale. One was a woman, one a boy."

"And?"

"We tried to stop them. To interrogate them."

"Openly?"

The Sword cringed at the edge in the single word. "There was no observer, lord." He bowed his head. "They—resisted."

"Where are they now?"

"I don't know."

"Pardon?"

"The woman—she—" he swallowed. "She had a sword."

Lord Erliss' eyes narrowed. "There were four of you."

"Yes, lord. But she also—she had the Enemy's magic."

Lord Erliss was still a young man; at twenty and one years of age, he had not the wisdom or the controlled, silent power of his older cousin, Lord Vellen of Damion. His dark eyes widened in astonishment; the line of his brows rose and vanished beneath his hair. *"What?"*

"She—I think she cast the Greater Ward. Her eyes were of the Light. Captain Sanderston attacked."

"Did he kill her?"

"I hope so."

"Idiot!" Erliss spun so quickly on his feet that the Sword jumped back and dropped into a defensive stance. "You had best hope he has not. This—this is what Lord Vellen bid us watch for." Erliss breathed deeply and more regularly. Yes, even though no one had thought to mention a woman, this was obviously the reason that Lord Vellen had left him in the village.

The Sword fell again to one knee, in a silence that was not the product of fear alone. For he had seen the green light in this woman's eyes, and had felt the sting and call of the Enemy. Lord Erliss had not.

"Quickly—get the others. All of them. Meet me on the northernmost edge of the village and be prepared to lead us to her."

The Sword nodded grimly. His feet barely touched the ground as he leaped up to do his Lord's bidding. His Lord smiled openly as the door swung back on its hinges.

Lord Vellen had lied, both to the nobility, which was a minor crime, and to the Greater Cabal, which was not. He had stated, for the record of the Church and the Karnari, that all of the lines were destroyed. Erliss wanted to shout with inappropriate glee. This woman, this single enemy, was quite possibly worth the high seat of the Greater Cabal to the man who could both capture and play her properly.

Oh yes, Erliss well understood why Vellen had come in swiftness and secrecy, daring the anger of the Lord of the Empire. She was a sign of his failure. And if Erliss could, without intervention, bring her back to Malakar, she would serve as the sign of his success. What, with this knowledge and proof of it at hand, could he not receive from Lord Vellen? Perhaps he would ask for a place in the Greater Cabal—at the youngest age in history. Perhaps he would be forced to . . . disagree with his

cousin, and take his acquired possession to Benataan, Lord Torvallen—Lord Vellen's greatest rival for the high seat, and second
of the Karnari.

The plans were pleasant and had such a ring of authority to
them that Erliss of Mordechai was happy for the first time in
almost a month.

Darin was afraid now. All of the glory and glow of victory
had been burned away by the weak red light, the cold, straight
steel, and the final, sudden deaths of the Swords. He knew who
the Swords must have served. He knew that the priests would
follow. And he knew that Sara was tired, nearly exhausted—she
didn't have any power left for another battle; she hadn't even
used the power she did have to heal her wound. Surely, surely
they would be caught, and he would once again serve as slave
in House Damion. Maybe this time, he'd be forced to watch
Sara's death on the altars at the quarters and carry her blood in
the silver pail only to spill it carefully along the grooves of the
Damion crest.

But it wasn't just the Church, the priests, or Lord Vellen that
frightened him. It was the look, burned into memory, that had
twisted Sara's face as she'd killed the Swords.

The sun was up—how could it be so high already? He felt its
bite on the back of his neck. He felt naked and completely
helpless as he followed the bends the road took. His neck developed a kink because he was constantly looking over his
shoulder, even though Bethany told him—and sharply—that it
only slowed them down.

But at least Sara walked with quiet strength and purpose. He
paced her well and tried not to notice the ugly red blotch at her
thigh. At least the wound had closed somewhat; the blood no
longer left a visible trail upon the ground.

She stopped after walking for an endless amount of time and
squinted into the darkness of forested land to their right. The
undergrowth was meager here, although weeds sprang up at any
crack of sunlight that showed through open branches.

"Here," she said softly. She turned back and touched his
shoulder. Even through his tunic he could feel her fingers: they
were icy; they shook. "It isn't going to be an easy passage—but
it won't be much longer, either. Come on." Her hair had slipped

out of her back-knot; strands of it ran across her pale cheeks like dried blood.

"Sara?"

"Yes?"

"What is the Lady's Woodhall?"

"It is," she replied, as she turned and began to navigate between the trees, "the hall that the Lady of Elliath dwelled in. She created it with her blood and Lernan's magic. It was her castle, her private retreat."

He scrambled to keep up with her as the shadows fell upon his upturned face, darkening his hair and his eyes. And he listened as she told the tale of the Woodhall and its creation; listened in a way that he would never have done as a student of Line Culverne, in the teaching halls of the Grandmother. Her words, soft and distant, flowed in the cadence of a teacher's voice. For a moment he felt safe as he pulled images from her words: the great, white height of the Lady's arches, the towering walls, the plain, majestic hallways. Sara said they would reach it soon, and perhaps, in that magical, unearthly realm, they might be safe.

He was not to find out that evening. An hour's march into the forest, Lady Sara stopped walking. Her brow rippled, and her eyes narrowed; she teetered on knees as she gazed out into a sea of great trunks. "I think," she said quietly, "that I must call a rest."

Darin had just enough time to catch her before her eyes rolled up and her legs collapsed beneath her.

chapter
two

Erliss of Mordechai was quiet; among the Mordechai clan this was considered a bad sign. The Swords that served him had been handpicked by Lord Vellen—he didn't trust them to follow all of his orders, but that was not his concern.

Adorning the wide, rough road that led from the village toward the borders of Mordantari were three bodies. Where blood had pooled into the dirt, the ground was wet and heavy. He walked, taking no care to avoid them; death was a part of his province, and the bringing of death, his duty; he would have made a poor priest if such painless deaths as these gave him any feeling of discomfort. Still, his thick face was dark, and his forehead gathered in lines that would, through the years, become etched there. If he survived that long.

"You said," he murmured, to the Sword who had brought them here, "that there were only two. A woman and a child."

"Yes, Lord."

Erliss knelt in the dirt, taking care to avoid the worst of the mess. He reached out, touched cold, slack skin, and pushed. Muscles, locked in death's grip, resisted a moment before he stopped. "You."

"Lord." A Sword stepped forward. He had a hand on the pommel of his sword and, although he stood in formal stance, did not remove it. Captain Sanderston was a vicious fighter who now lay dead—too cleanly dead.

"Take up the watch. You," Erliss said, pointing almost at random, "join him. If anyone else seeks to leave the castle, do not interfere. Watch or follow. Is that clear?"

"Lord."

18

"Good. Go, now."

Erliss rose, leaving the captain behind. Sanderston had, after all, failed. Burial and other such niceties were not the proper concern of a priest. "You two—get your mounts. Follow the road." He bit down on the rest of the words; the Swords were already running in crisp, even steps. The sound of his voice barely had the time to die out into stillness.

A woman. A boy. He shook his head. These deaths must have occurred minutes after the Sword—the only one with brains of the four—had left to bring the report to his commanding priest. The danger the woman presented had been real in theory and report; now, he felt it fully as a fact against which he had no desire to argue.

He had to know where she was running.

He had to think, and he felt, truthfully, that there was little time for it.

"Lord?"

"What?"

"Priest Tarantas wishes to speak with you."

Tarantas? Just what he needed. Gritting his teeth, he glared at the Sword who had interrupted his reverie with such unwelcome news. "Who informed Tarantas of our whereabouts?"

The Sword heard the death in the question without any reaction at all. There was no time for an answer; the aged Priest Tarantas was already upon them.

Erliss greeted him with poorly concealed ill-humor. "Ah, Tarantas. Is it not rather early for you to be abroad?"

"It's early," the old priest replied. But early or no, he was still dressed in the out-of-place black robes that marked him as full priest. Even in the Vale, he chose to announce himself with very little care for subterfuge or silence. His hair was long and pale, streaked black by artifice rather than any lingering youth, and his fingers, slightly bent with time—not labor—ran through the thin, long line of his beard. It, too, was peppered white, but it shone without tangle or knot; he attended it well. "But it seems that early or no, I am required." He glanced sideways at Erliss. "Lord Vellen gave me explicit instructions, Erliss."

No doubt. "And those?"

"I have made a study of Mordantari's history. You would find it quite interesting—had you any talent for academia." He turned before Erliss could reply and began to examine the bodies. This he did while maintaining a fastidious distance; if his body was aged, his eyes were still quite capable—and he recognized death when he saw it.

"Your point?"

"House history, Erliss. These lands, claimed by the Lord of the Empire, were once the seat of all resistance to God's power. They were ruled by the Lady of Elliath—you might remember her?"

"Tarantas." Erliss' stiff face was quite grim. Although Tarantas was of the lesser nobility, in an unlanded house, he was also under Vellen's command, and to argue openly with him was to question the leader of the Greater Cabal. Erliss was a cousin, but family blood flowed freely between relations; this had always been the case.

Tarantas shrugged elegantly. "She was the First of the Enemy, and hers was the first line to fall to the Lord of the Empire."

"Your point?"

"She dared the veils of the future; we do not know how long she walked, or how far she saw. But we have heard that she foresaw a path that would lead to the end of our reign."

Erliss shrugged, his face dark. "She's dead."

"But her work remains, or so we believe. You said that this was done by a woman and a young boy?"

He had said no such thing, but was too annoyed to play word games.

"Ah. Good. You saw the fires two evenings past. You did see them?"

"Yes."

"There was a power in the air that has not been seen in the Empire since the fall of Culverne. There was a power there, quite strong, quite old. I think that power"—and he glanced down at the hem of his robe as it brushed across a stiff face— "was responsible for these deaths."

"Really?" Erliss said, but the acid edge of his sarcasm was lost upon the old priest.

"And now, we have the last wonderful task at hand. The Lady had a fortress unlike any you or I have ever seen. We have studied, have searched, have struggled to find its location—but we have always failed."

"How surprising."

That hit; Tarantas' fingers stopped their steady stroke of beard. His eyes, rather dark, glanced off Erliss', and his jaw squared. "Do go on, Tarantas."

"Very well." The old man glanced off into the trees, his eyes darting from light bark to brown, casting about in the shadows as if for answers. "It was in Mordantari that the Lady's fortress was hidden. And I believe that today, we might at last have our answers."

"Our answers?"

"Come, come, Erliss. I know what you seek, and it does not concern me. But you do not have my knowledge of our ancient Enemy's power. I know how to look for it and how to catch it sleeping. I know how to sense its use. Do you think to just track your quarry, she a fox and you the dogs? A greater discovery awaits us both."

"Greater?"

Tarantas leaned forward and grabbed Erliss' forearms. The Swords stiffened, but their Lord gave no word. "I can lead you to the woman, if she wields the power I think she does. You are young—you have always circled around Malakar. You know the game of the houses, but I know the war of the lines." He looked up, eyes almost misted. "I fought them on the fields long ago."

Erliss managed to keep the contempt off his face as he considered Tarantas' words. He could not understand why his cousin had seen fit to force the scholar's presence upon their mission— but he grudgingly admitted to himself that Vellen had never been a fool. He looked down at the dead, looked up at the priest, and made his choice.

"Very well. If you can find her, you will be well rewarded."

"Oh, indeed," Tarantas said, as his fingers slid off the sleeves of Erliss' fine shirt. "Now let me concentrate. Do not interrupt me." He swept his long, grand sleeves back and raised his bare hands high. His fingers danced across the stage of the empty air until his arms pulled them back into a wide, crossed arc.

Erliss recognized the Greater Ward. More than that, he recognized the dance of blood-magic that rippled around the old priest's frame, a fire brought suddenly to life.

"Tarantas," he hissed, "where did you get such power?" He already knew the answer, but asked in hope of receiving an intelligent reply.

"In the Vale," the old man answered. "Now, silence!"

In the Vale. Erliss' face lost its ruddy, darkened anger. Tarantas had performed rites on a villager of the Vale. In Mordantari. The young priest wanted to scream in shock and outrage at the foolishness of his elder. He also wanted to flee. He did neither. "You," he said quietly to the closest Sword present. "Lord."

"Find Tarantas' residence and make sure that it is . . . clean. Be prepared to move out, quickly. We will follow the old man's lead for the present. When we have what we want, it would be expedient to offer him to the Lord of the Empire, should the villager's death be reported. Understood?"

The Sword smiled. "Lord."

"Good. Warn the watch."

She dreamed.

She walked in a land of shadow and a darkness that was black to her only because her senses could not explain the color otherwise. Beneath her feet the ground curved in awkward, unnatural formation like a living thing. It shied away from the touch of her step, creating large holes that would half swallow her before spitting her out. Behind and ahead, the landscape never varied; it was, to her eyes, the essence of all that was ugly.

She walked alone, threading her way over the terrain, searching for something. She did not know what it was, but it was important—for no other reason would she walk these domains.

Her eyes could see no living thing, but the blackness was hard to penetrate, thicker than fog or shadow or starless night. She looked down to see that she was translucent, almost a ghost.

Perhaps she had finally earned her death—and her fate in the halls of Judgment. But even as she thought it, she shook her head, knowing it was wrong. She had to find something, but it was not Judgment.

And then, as she continued her endless walk, she heard it: a long, bitter wailing that seemed to come from all around her. Some voice, but it was altered perhaps by shadow to have no hint of humanity in it. She began to tingle as the cry passed through her, piercing the ghostly fabric of her otherworld flesh. She felt the call of her blood waken to a pain so large it could not be contained in the folds of rippling darkness that held her.

As if pulled, she began to run across the landscape, leaping over trenches that opened malevolently in midstride.

Twice more the scream rang through the air, drawn across the silence like a serrated knife. This, this is what she was seeking; she could feel the certainty push away all doubt. This pain, so in need of easing, had brought her across the barrier between the mortal plane and this dark world. It was real, and it made her feel more substantial, more solid.

But still, when she looked at herself, she was a ghostly shadow of light, ringed with the faintest hint of green—the heritage of troubled peace that came with her blood.

If I bleed here at all.

The thought was in earnest; she knew that her blood had somehow brought her here in its search for pain, but she wondered what she could do in her present form, should she find what she was seeking.

What agony could so distort a voice? What circumstance could strip it bare of anything human but pain itself?

She moved quickly, more surely, and this time the ground that she walked on proved less treacherous. And that worried her. The whole landscape was alive, and its intent was anything but beneficial; of this she was certain.

"You can never be certain of anything, Erin."

That voice . . . She turned around, slowly, the feel of hair rising along her neck.

"We were certain of you, but you betrayed us."

Her eyes could make out only darkness, shades of it leavened by something that was not quite light. But memory was no stranger to her; although the voice was distorted and strangely distant, she knew it well.

"Belfas?"

The ground buckled soundlessly beneath her; the voice was gone, an echo too weak to remain.

"Belfas—if you are here—show yourself. Please."

"There's nothing to show, Erin."

But even as the disembodied voice spoke, a light began to grow in front of her; white, muddied by the currents of darkness that seemed to pass for air. It stopped its progress before it claimed a distinct shape, but to Erin's otherworld eyes it looked vaguely human.

"Belfas—are you truly here?"

Laughter, then. Bitter, ancient laughter. It was so cold, she barely recognized it.

She didn't want to. "You can't be here. It's just a . . . a—"
"—figment of your imagination? I wish it were. But indeed,
Erin, I'm here. We all are. Bound." Again, there was the bitter,
cold laughter—something Befas would not have been capable of
when she had known him.
"Wouldn't I? You didn't find us in time to know, Erin. If I'd
seen you before I died, you might have heard worse."
"Why are you here now?" She took a step back from the
light, raising her arms to shield her eyes. It made no difference;
she could see through them into the gray and the darkness.
"To listen to the laughter of the Twin Hearts, Erin. To listen
to the tears of—"
Once again the wailing cut the air, obliterating the last of
Belfas' bitter words.
"No. No. I won't believe that of you. I won't—"
"And what did you leave us to believe, Erin? You doomed
Kandor and the rest of your line, with your choice. You doomed
us—"
"Peace, Belfas. Or truth."
The first voice fell silent beneath the pale music of the sec-
ond. And Erin began to weep, ghost tears along an insubstantial
cheek. If the ground had been solid, she would have knelt, but
her knees locked her into a standing position.
"Little one. It has been long, although this place knows no
time. I would have spared you this." Kandor of Lernan, the
Third Servant of the Bright Heart, also called the darkness home.
And as he spoke, another light grew in the darkness, but it
was bright, shining palely against the colorless cold. Only as
she stared did Erin notice the trace of gray along its forming
limbs. The Third of Lernan had survived through the millennia
of a war that had started before the body of the world had
formed—to come to this place, this moment, this taint.
"Yes, Sarillorn. This place will affect even one such as I.
And the children of the Lady are not so strong. Do not weep for
us, not while there is hope."
"Hope?" The tears fell, and Erin let them. "What hope?
You are all dead; you're gone. The Lady is dead. The lines lost."
And Belfas . . . the change in him, the anger—he was not the
same person she had once risked the fires to save. The fires
might have been a better death than this.
More than words carried thought here; Belfas spoke to her as

if all her fears were on display. "I would rather have died there, consumed by red-fire, than exist in this darkness. Erin—*why?*" And in the bitterness of those last two words, Erin found a type of peace. Belfas had allowed the pain to show through his anger; something of him remained, and it called her quietly and wordlessly. She reached out and was surprised when her hands touched something that seemed solid.

It moved—he moved—away from her, and she followed, but slowly.

"Enough. It doesn't matter why."

"Ah, Belfas"—she reached out, this time making her grip a sure one—"you could never lie well and never at all to me."

"Once, Erin. Once that was true. Until you proved how loyal you were to the line."

The words stung almost physically, but she held tight to the formless shape. In the miasma of mottled dark, she began to test the use of her power, sending it out through translucent hands. It came, albeit slowly; she could see it trembling down her arms to her fingertips; she could almost watch it as it raced, like a stream, through the fine veins beneath her skin.

The formless light before her began to take shape; as true a shape as Erin's own. A face coalesced, growing stronger as the light of Elliath fueled it. And the face was familiar, if the expression was not. The pointed, slightly hooked nose; the pale, half-kempt hair; the high, wide cheekbones; and the firmness of jaw—these things Erin remembered well.

"Belfas."

Almost unaware of her, he looked down, dead eyes taking in the stretch of firm arms and legs, the light that flared outward from a bare chest.

"How?" He turned, not to Erin, but to the image of Kandor of Lernan.

"Truly, Initiate, I do not know."

"Belfas?"

This time he turned, and she could see the pale echo of his once-bright eyes search hers thoroughly. His face was hard, unforgiving.

"Why, Erin? Why?"

A loud, bitter cry returned to fill the air. Erin willed herself to disregard it. Out of habit, she drew a deep breath, although her lungs did not require it.

"I lived with him for four years." She knew it was not enough. He waited. "I—I watched him change, Belfas. Until that night he never broke his word."

"How can you know that?"

She couldn't. Nor could she answer the accusation in his eyes; she turned her face away. "You didn't see him. You couldn't know. He stopped walking, Belfas. He let me do as much as I could to help the people of Rennath—"

"It would have helped them more if he had died there, Erin. You know that!"

"Maybe." But if Belfas had never been able to lie to Erin, she, too, had been unable to lie to him. And a lie would have been a comfort to her. "I don't know! I don't know anymore. Just at the time—at that one time—I couldn't just watch him be destroyed . . . not even by you. I—Belfas, we were rited."

"Lord of Light, Erin."

Belfas stepped forward, and the ground that opened beneath him had no effect. He reached out, catching her face between his trembling hands. The anger drained out of him, leaving only a pale shock.

"You loved him."

She wondered if he could feel the tears as they left her eyes and traveled over his fingers.

"Kandor."

"Belfas."

"It's not possible, is it?" His voice was raw with something akin to hope; here, after so long, was the truth—the explanation that would drive away all the pain and the anger. "It must have been some sort of spell—he must have cast it over her when she was too weak to resist! We know she was his captive. She couldn't have loved him on her own!"

Kandor was silent while Belfas spoke; silent when the lingering question began to lose its trace of hope.

"Erin," Belfas said quietly, "are you still alive?"

She thought the question odd until she remembered the very last time she had seen him. She nodded.

"Then how can you be here?"

"I don't know. I didn't come here to find you."

It was the wrong answer. "Then why?"

Another cry wracked the landscape. Question and answer

flickered through Belfas' eyes, one after another, until at last he turned to Kandor, who remained silent throughout.

"I understand." He drew away from Sara. "Though you would not, or could not, explain, I understand it. Erin . . ."

"Yes?"

"Do you know where you are?"

She shook her head. As did Kandor, but for different reasons. The Servant stepped forward.

"Little one, Sarillorn, you must go on; if not now, then soon."

"And what of you? What of the others?"

He paused, perplexed at the question she did not ask aloud. Sighing, he nodded, and one by one, dim shapes took form, pale, slightly glowing, and voiceless in the shadow. Wordless, Sara went to each and lent them the strength of her Light, like a sculptor drawing form out of shapeless rock. And when she finished, tired and drawn, she stood surrounded again by those who had once been her companions on the field.

And the youngest, an adult of a few years, stepped forward, hands outstretched. Her voice was a shadow, a ringing sibilance of whisper.

"I understand, Erin. If no one else does, I do. I saw—I saw what you saw in him. I don't think the price we pay is a fair one, or a just one—but I know why you asked it. I cannot forgive it, but understanding it helps."

A ghost of a sigh echoed in Erin's ears, the rustle of wind through leaves; Kandor's wordless comment.

Belfas, standing slightly apart from his line-mates, looked through her—at something she couldn't see, but could guess at. "Truly, Erin, you are of the living. The brightest of our number."

She cringed at the phrasing he used—one of the superlatives given to the Sarillar or Sarillorn of the Line Elliath. But there was no mockery in his voice now, and only a trace of the bitterness that would never leave it.

"Can you hear it, Erin?"

She nodded; her very skin tingled with the pain of the call. "Do you know what it is?"

"Yes." He shook his head softly before she could ask the question, and it died on her lips.

"It called us, too; called what was left of our spirit—our

blood—in the dark plane. We came, as you came, with just as little choice. We are all still slaves to the blood.''

"You never used to think of it as slavery.''

"Nor you. But you will, Erin.''

The chill bitterness of his words disturbed her, and she changed the subject. "Can you help—whatever it is?''

He laughed, and in the laughter Sara heard his anger blossom again, with its sharp, cruel edges unfurling in the darkness. But it was an echo; it lingered quietly in the air before dying away.

"No. Even if I would help it—and I would only do so if the blood gave me no choice—I can't. Listen carefully, Erin. Listen well.''

She knew he spoke not of his own voice, and again turned her ears outward. The ground shuddered, bucking her.

"Not that way, Sarillorn. You must listen with more than a priestess' ear. Be open, Erin. Let the sound pass through you.''

"I—''

"Don't worry about the darkness; I don't think it would touch you; it can't yet, and you won't be here for long enough to lose your protection against it.''

"But the cry—''

"It belongs here.''

And she heard again the anger and bitterness in his voice. "I brought you to this.'' She said it to herself, not really caring if he heard it.

"Yes.''

"I'll answer the call. I don't care if it's stupid. I don't care if it's dangerous.'' She brought her hands to her face, but they were useless; translucent, they blocked out no darkness, no light.

He was silent a long time, his face inscrutable. And then he said, almost against his will, "Erin, you were always the strongest of our number; the brightest, even before you were made Sarillorn. I remember the day that we fought side by side in Kanara against the Malanthi border raiders. I remember the pain of the red-fire so clearly here''—he shuddered—''but now that you're here I also remember what followed. I still see your face through the fire, Lady. I still see the pain you endured—knowing that you would have to—to bring me back whole. I see your expression, and it brings back the light.''

Erin watched in silence, remembering as he remembered. She had saved his life, bringing her lifeblood and her whitefire to him where without he would have perished. She had become Adult on the fields, amidst the ruins of a fallen city's walls. Because Belfas needed her. And she had saved him for this. She wanted to run, but dared not. Prayed that he would finish speaking and leave her in the silence.

He shook himself forcefully, opened his mouth, then closed it. Opened it again and then began to speak anew. "And I still see it in you now: The power of Elliath and the power of our mortal determination. Sometimes I think I know you: I see you as the instrument of the First Servant; a tool of darkness and death. It's easier than . . . than other thoughts.

"But now that you're here, I still see all that I always saw in you; feel all that I always felt.

"I've plotted against you all these years; I dreamed of what I'd do when we met in the Halls of Judgment. I've hated you more than I could ever hate our Enemy."

Listening to the venom in his words, Sara found herself strangely moved. She was not afraid as she brought her hand up. He backed away before she could touch him.

"I hated you Erin. When I saw you in Rennath—do you remember the first night I came to your rooms?"

She nodded, unable to speak. She remembered it, as all else, well.

"I was so happy to see you alive! I could have revealed our presence there just shouting for joy!"

The anger and pain that lashed out at her were too much to contain in the stillness; she darted forward before he could step away and caught him in the cool green power of her embrace.

Belfas, Belfas, she mouthed, half cradling him as her power flowed outward; she had no strength left for voice.

"And then—in the hall—when we'd paid so high a price for our attempt—when we'd spilled our own blood . . ." He tried to pull away, but halfheartedly.

"I didn't know." She forced the words out, knowing them for truth, knowing that it didn't matter. "I didn't know that he'd break—"

"How could he do anything else? Erin, dammit, he's the *First Servant!*" But he stilled in her arms as she rocked him.

After a while she said, "Do the others feel the same way?"

And Teya's youthful voice filled the air around her.

"Yes, Sarillorn."

Erin cringed at the accusation that Teya's tone made of the honorific—an honorific that she had ceased to deserve centuries past. "Please, don't call me that. Please."

Teya smiled softly; the expression was not gentle. "We have all felt what Belfas feels, Carla, Rein, and I. But not as strongly. We had our lives to lose; we had our trust to lose. But we never lost our—"

"Erin."

She knew what he was going to say. She placed her hands against his lips to still the words; her eyes opened and misted in a plea that had only one expression. "Belfas."

He had no mercy; she deserved none. "I never loved anyone as much as I loved you." And his insubstantial arms wrapped themselves around her insubstantial form, and she wept, wishing for the first time that Belfas could offer her a lie that she could believe; his truth was too devastating. Her power flowed outward to him, and he drank it in until they looked, to the eyes of their watchers, like one light searing itself into the blackness all around them. She would not call the Light back, and it wrapped itself around her former comrade, as gentle and all-encompassing as a shroud over a loved one.

And as she opened herself up, fully, to the mirror of Belfas' pain, she felt another pain shoot *through* her. It was wordless, silent, and strong; it was stronger than the cry that had first drawn her to this place. It was too deep for tears, too wide for mortal expression to contain. Against her will, she found her grip on Belfas weakening; try as she might, her insubstantial fingers lingered only moments longer before pulling away. The call was stronger than any she had ever felt.

Years of practice fell away, absorbed by darkness and the spirits who bore witness to her silent struggle. She began to step forward as the plane shifted. *No.*

"Erin," Belfas said, his voice a whisper in her ear.

She turned to see his pale face and shadowed eyes.

"It's the answer to all your questions. You have to go. And I can't go with you." But he reached out anyway; ghostly fingers passed through ghostly hair.

She didn't want to leave him; even in darkness, he was all that remained of her home. But she walked anyway.

"It's the blood," he whispered, resignation in his voice. "Will you come back?"

She looked back; she saw the edges of his face as they wavered between anger, fear, and pain. "Yes." But before the single word died out, he was gone—as were the rest of his companions, her dead line-mates.

She stood completely alone. Fear touched her then, but it was not by fear that the Lernari were ruled.

Very well. Whoever you are, you've called me. I'll answer as I can.

Controlling the urge to look backward, she took a firm step forward, and then another, the large walls that loomed suddenly high serving as blinders to the darkness. She felt the thing that had summoned her. Clear, raw, almost overwhelming in its intensity. It surrounded her like a halo, twisting her mind until she stumbled from the contact. She looked around, and could see, faint and glimmering, beads of fine, red mist. They were gone as soon as her naked eye touched them, but memory held the image.

"Where are you?"

No answer. It didn't matter; she hadn't really expected one. She continued to walk, with no idea of how much distance she had covered; she had little choice.

The walls began to change. The oily slickness of their surface, pockmarked by a grotesque parody of color, began to harden. Erin didn't notice this at first; the change was too subtle, too slow. But the air around her grew chill until she trembled with the cold. She wrapped her arms around her shoulders, bent her head, and continued forward.

She stopped as her eyes caught sight of her legs. They were solid. They were pale, shining with a hint of the green light that heralded her kinship with the lines, but undeniably solid. She untwined her arms and looked at her hands; these, too, looked somehow more solid. More mortal.

Then she turned, slowly, actual hair rising along the white of her neck, to look at the tunnel that contained her. It was black—true black, with flecks of gray. It looked like rock on a blasted, barren landscape.

Some battle must have been fought here, she thought, remembering the sites of some of the greatest Malanthi-Lernari clashes.

They had a similar look—were it not for the sky, she might have guessed that she was on the plain of Merthor.

The rock opened up as the tunnel neared its end. Sara took firm, solid steps, feet brushing dry ground with a dull thud. She stopped at the pass' mouth, hands slightly curved, body tensed with readiness to make a dive should it prove necessary.

Here, she thought. *You couldn't have made yourself more clear. Come. I'm ready.*

And she gave herself over to the needs of the blood. Pain filled her; raw and alien. Almost unaware of her surroundings, she came forward, hands outstretched, green eyes glazed and immobile. It didn't matter that the pain was something strange and incomprehensible; it was there, and she was a healer born to be its salve.

Her fingers brushed against something. It was cold, hard, but smooth as steel—and it burned like red-fire. She cried out once, and stumbled backward, hands dancing to no effect in the red of the sky. She had an instant to cradle her hand before the call surged through her open mind, jerking her unsteadily to her feet.

She walked forward again, thinking of fire, knowing what it would be like to walk into a pain that strong; she had done so for Belfas. And she knew, as she had known then, that she would not choose otherwise. She conjured up images of Elliath, images of the Grandfather of her line, images of battle, sound, and smell, to steady her in her task.

Her hand crept slowly forward. Contact. Her nerves screamed out, and she bit her lip, pushing her hand forward to pass beyond whatever barrier had been erected against her coming.

Something shot up to grip her hand, crushing her fingers inward. Her eyes snapped open to an inky, dense mist. A tendril of it lay curled like a bracelet around her knuckles.

She started to pull away and felt it: the pain that had drawn her emanated from this—whatever it was. The cold ice that shot through her veins came from here as well.

She did what she could to pull free, but it held her tightly. She could not move forward; she could not move back. Closing her eyes, she did the only thing that she could: She sent her power outward, twisting her fingers around so that she could touch the tendril.

Green flared in the blackness; green, healing power—not the white purity of Elliath wrath. She had enough self-control to choose. It left in a rush, blood from a wound that no eyes could see, and none not healer-born could understand. Her free hand came up and she gripped the tendril more firmly. Power flared in the clearing; the rocks at her feet began to melt into a slimy ooze.

"Damn it, I'm trying to help you!" Slowly, the rocks reformed, swallowing the chaos with a strong, steady shape.

And then it hit her. Loss. A loss so strong that even the image of Belfas, weeping in her arms, faded into nothing. Wordless, she reached out, trying to gather the mist into her arms, to meld with it—her comfort, her peace, for its pain. Her power fled outward, strongly and steadily, more quickly than it had ever gone. Her knees gave beneath her; she was made dimly aware of this fact when something cut into the flesh of her leg as she fell.

Too soon, she had nothing left to give. The taste of pain left her with the last of her blood's power, and she opened her eyes once more.

Cradled in her arms lay the form of a silent, sleeping man. His hair, matted and dark, concealed his features; Sara could see a pale glint of white, but no more. She moved gingerly into a sitting position, trying not to jostle him. But the movement itself caused him to stir. His arms, supple and quick, wrapped themselves around her waist.

"Shhhh. It's all right." She began to brush his hair back, gently and slowly. Her hands trembled with even this effort, but although stripped of her power, she still had much to give. She had been the Sarillorn of Elliath. He stirred again as her fingers made contact with his cheek.

Beneath her fingers, the corners of his mouth curved into the semblance of a smile. A rigid smile, cold and controlled—so subtle that Sara might have missed it. It reminded her of—

No.

With a quick, sharp start, she pulled back. Arms tightened around her waist, and the man's head twisted suddenly to one side. His eyes snapped open.

Green eyes met blackness.

No. No.

Paralyzed, she sat gazing down at the pale face of the First of Malthan.

"Sara?"

His voice was weak, a pale echo of what it had once been. She tried to pull his arms away.

"Sara." The word twisted into her, and her arms tightened automatically.

No. NO. With one vicious tug, she pulled away. Rolling, she got unsteadily to her feet.

He tried to follow, swaying as he stood unsteadily. "Lady?" One pale arm reached outward, hand up and open. "Lady . . ." She heard everything in that word, a loneliness and longing too old and too strong for a mortal to contain. She stopped, staring at the outstretched hand, remembering all of the times he had comforted her, playing through her hair or catching her tears as they fell.

Green met black again, and in the slowly dissolving landscape she thought she caught a glistening at the corner of his eyes. She started forward a step and then stopped, for his hands were suddenly red, a deep, brilliant crimson. Of red-fire. Or blood.

Wordless, she turned again, forcing herself to deny the strength of her heritage, the ability to comfort. She was bitterly aware that only her exhaustion allowed her to do so—at any other time the call would have jerked her forward. Unbidden, Belfas' words came back to her.

She squared her jaw. *I am no slave.*

"I have betrayed my line to you once, First of the Enemy. I shall never do so again."

She began to run.

"Sara . . ."

The ground twisted at her feet, becoming once again the flesh of the otherworld; the meeting place of the Servants of Malthan with their Dark Heart.

A dark, shattered wail followed her into the daylight.

"Sara?" Darin peered down anxiously at her face, his nose two inches away from hers. He held a small canteen to her lips, and she drank; she was parched. "Are you all right?"

She rose, stumbling against the nearest tree. Her hands touched bark and moss as she righted herself.

"Sara, are you all right?"

"Yes." A wan smile crept across her lips; it was broken before it caught. "I was stupid," she said, as she gazed down at the injury. "It's been too long since I've fought. Telvar would've killed me." Her hand slid suddenly down to her sword; she shook an instant before she found the hilt. Then she nodded, as if satisfied, and began to walk again.

"What are you doing?" Darin ran over and slid an arm beneath her shoulders, bracing himself to take some of her weight. She wasn't too heavy, and he knew that she wouldn't allow herself to be.

"Walking," she answered quietly. "We aren't there yet."

"You can't walk! Sara—you just collapsed! You've been unconscious for at least half an hour."

"That long?" Her face grew pale and more grim. "Then we can't wait, and we can't rest. We don't have any choice. Those Swords weren't here alone; they never travel without priests. We can't meet them yet, Darin. We've got to find the Woodhall."

He swallowed. He wanted her to rest and regain her power; only then would she be able to properly heal her leg. But he never wanted to be in the power of a priest of the Enemy again. Shaking, he held the weight she let him carry, and they began to traverse the forest.

Belfas was dead.

Glimmering over the red of early morn, she could see the liquid sheen across his open eyes. His eyes, already shadowed, already dimming.

Everywhere she walked, she felt his dying presence. Those trees, growing greener with sunlight, might have shaded them while they practiced, swords in hand, Erin the better, always the better, of the two. Those mosses, those wildflowers, those fallen logs—any might have been a place where she and Belfas went for privacy, on the occasions when he could convince her that a day of rest was called that for a reason.

Elliath's holdings had been here, across these miles of thick, strange forest, with these trees that had changed in shape and size and color. The shadowed light taunted her cheeks with its gaudy splash between leaves and branches; insects blurred across air, buzzing happily and audibly in their flashes of incandescent color. She knew these; her line's death was writ large around her in the things that remained alive.

Every so often she would look at Darin's bowed head or bent back and then look again more closely. All that she remembered had closed around her tightly, and she knew now who he reminded her of.

Those that were dead.

Years had passed since she'd walked the forest this way. The pack at her shoulder held snares and dry supplies; there was a water flask at her hip, twin to the one Darin wore. Bedrolls, a small tent, a few utensils—all of these had been provided. But not only these. A sword, longer than she was used to, two daggers, and her robes had also been left at the gate. By Gervin.

He, too, was dead.

It should have been me.

Why didn't you take me?

The answer was too hard to accept.

chapter
three

"Well?" Lord Erliss' *tone was brittle and chilly; it gave voice* to his impatience and anxiety, where mere words did not.

Tarantas smiled almost beatifically. "Yes. There is one. That person has the strongest taint of our Enemy's blood that I have yet felt. It will be dangerous."

"That," Erliss said, as he relaxed marginally, "is not for you to decide."

The Swords waited the outcome of the discussion in silence— and at a crisp attention usually reserved for the formal sacrifices of the year's quarters. Erliss was young enough to demand this detail and powerful enough to get it—just.

The silence stretched thinly; Erliss waited for Tarantas to continue, and the older man waited for Erliss to ask. Tarantas won the quiet contest.

"Where is that one?"

"He or she has only just started to move again." He turned around to gaze northward.

"And has he visited this fortress that you seek?"

A white brow rose a fraction over Tarantas' left eye. "Of course not. Power such as that—the opening of the portal—I could feel without casting my nets. But I do not think it the boy; the woman is the more likely of the two. And we do not know the capacities of either; don't think in terms of one alone."

Erliss found the trees overhead oppressive and annoying; he glared up at them, then wheeled around to study the expressions that lined the faces of his Swords. "Can we move, then?" He asked at last.

"Do you wish to warn them early?" the priest asked, rising

from the soft ground and adjusting his beard's fall. "No? Good.
I have done what I can to obscure our presence—but it will be
sought, I assure you. They are on the move, Lord Erliss, but
they travel slowly. I think, when next they stop, we will have
time to properly prepare."

"Very well," the young lord said, as he slid his hands behind
his back and clasped them, hard. "We will wait. But Tarantas?"

"Don't lose them," the old man said. He had heard it at least
thirty times since he had begun to trace the path.

Orvas blossoms pushed white heads up through the shadowed
undergrowth. They were fresh and new, and no season's change
would dim their brilliant color. A scent, clinging to breeze,
brushed past Darin and his lady as they walked.

"Sara?"

"Yes?"

"We could stop for a bit. I could brew orvas leaves, or try."
He started to bend, and she caught his shoulders, straightening
them into a stand. "But it'd help."

"After the Woodhall." She looked over her shoulder, and
then back. "Something feels wrong; I'm not sure what. But if I
had to guess, I'd say that the priests have been warned. We have
almost no time."

"But wouldn't they have been here by now?"

It was the right question, but the wrong time to say it; her
brow rippled, and her face became set. She started to walk
forward; he struggled to keep up with her speed. But he cringed
as her feet passed almost clumsily over the orvas blossoms,
crushing the occasional petal and whole flower. She didn't seem
to notice.

Orvas blossoms became less rare, and where the trees at the
road's edge had been dark and uniform in height, bark, and
color, the trees in the forest's heart were different. They were
no less lofty, no less aged—but they were silver-barked, with
golden leaves and white, full flowers; and although their leaves
were just as wide and greedy with the sun's light, the forest floor
beneath them was bright with greens and blues and little shocks
of color.

"The Lady's trees," Sara whispered, looking up. Her body
shivered once and then her muscles relaxed.

Darin grunted; she suddenly weighed a lot more. "The Lady?"

"Of Elliath," she answered—and then looked at his upturned face; her own tightened again for a moment, but this time it passed. "Not of Mercy, Darin. She was the first of the Servants of the Bright Heart."

"I know her," he said, although it had been five years or more since he'd last heard the name. "She built the walls of Dagothrin with the power of God. She promised that they'd never be taken from without."

"Dagothrin?"

"The city. I lived there."

"Then it fell."

They lapsed into silence as the flowers grew whiter and the trees more majestic. And that silence held pain, but as they walked, Darin felt the warmth and peace of the Lady's forest; the soothing silence that hinted at sleeping life, and the fragrance of the blossoms that crowned the Lady's trees. As those trees continued to grow in age and number, he felt as if he were stepping backward in time, into a different season, where the height of summer had not yet given way to the golds and the reds of autumn.

He thought it would be pleasant to walk, just walk, in these woods forever. He thought that they might be proof against the darkness and the Enemy's many priests, no matter what Sara might say. He thought many, many things.

But they vanished when he saw the Tree.

It rose on a trunk the width of many men and towered into the sky. No mortal spires, he was certain, could ever rise so gracefully or powerfully upward. Even the lowest of the tree's many branches, thicker than his chest, stood twice or three times his height above the ground—and flowers of gold and white, perfect, and untroubled by even breeze, bloomed everywhere. The bark of the tree was gold with flecks of brown; it was almost smooth to the touch.

Everywhere that he looked, he could see the faint trace of pale, green light. It reminded him of the Gifting.

"This is it," Sara said softly. "The Lady's Woodhall." She pulled herself away from Darin's support and managed not to stumble.

"But it's—it's only a tree."

"It's a door, a gate." She took a step forward. Her fingers she spread out against the smooth bark; she mouthed words too quick and fleeting for Darin to catch. "But here I must go on alone."

"Alone?"

She nodded almost sadly. "The Hall won't grant you entrance, Darin. You're not of my blood—and more important, not of the blood of the Lady." She began to lift her arms to either side and let them drop. Turning, she gave Darin a fierce, quick hug.

"You'll be safe enough here—I've never heard of any harm coming to the lines in the Lady's wood." She released him and turned to face the tree again. "If I could, I'd take you with me. I—" Shaking her head, she walked forward and wrapped her arms around the tree's large trunk.

At least, that's what she appeared to do. But even as Darin watched, he saw her *melt* into the wood itself—as if the tree were slowly opening up to swallow her. He started forward, half in alarm, and was halted by Bethany's voice.

No, Darin. This is not for you. Do not risk yourself to the spells of the Lady—there would be no contest.

But she—

I know. Yet she does what she must. If she must be alone, there is no safer place in the lands for her to be so. Have faith, Initiate.

Darin stopped moving, but only barely. He wanted to tell Bethany that it was not for her safety that he feared. The priests were about in the forest, searching or waiting, or maybe both. He would rather have dared the Lady's spell than wait outside, alone. He didn't tell Bethany; he knew that it would not change the fact that he would not be allowed to enter the Hall. Instead, he pulled the staff from its place at his back and took a seat on the forest floor, facing the tree.

And as he watched it, he felt what Sara must have felt the first time she had seen the doors to the Woodhall. He let his vision be absorbed by the great Tree until he could see nothing else. And he felt the peace of the Lady touch him with its precarious fingers.

Erin was certain her teeth had come through her lower lip. She was also certain that she must be splayed out against the marbled floor of the Lady's Hall; her stomach was still spinning from the awkward transition. She was very surprised when she opened her eyes and found herself standing—or wobbling—on two feet.

The last time wasn't this bad. She stretched out one arm and felt a wall beneath her open palm. *Of course not, idiot. The last time the Lady waited.* Grimly she forced herself to stand apart from the wall. She hadn't the time for the luxury of confusion.

Looking ahead, she saw the long, arched hallway before her— a standing monument to the will of the Lady and the power of Lernan's Gifting. The ceiling was about twenty feet above the ground, and it easily dwarfed her, although she was certain that had she been forced to crouch under a ceiling of dubious height, she would still feel no less dwarfed. Things magical were here; things of the blood that she could never hope to duplicate and that would never be made again. A familiar tingle traced itself along her spine, causing her to shudder. Line Elliath calling its own.

Turning, she looked hard at the one thing that had remained the same: the trunk of the Lady's Tree. It did not seem out of place surrounded by cold stone and marble. In the odd, pale glow of the hall, it, too, seemed a monument to the Lady—and one no less hard than the walls around it.

Latham was not here to guide her, not here to await her return. He would not come again, but his ghost stood watch in her memory. Darin waited instead.

The walk down the hall was eerie. Her steps rang in the silence, as they had done twice before. But now she was alone, no Lady to follow, and no direction laid out for her.

Not that she needed one. There were no branching paths from this long hall and no doors to tempt her away from the final destination that lay at its end: the Lady's garden. The hall seemed to go on forever, but she realized it for illusion—or perhaps fear. If she had ever hoped to come home to Elliath, this was not the manner that she had envisaged. Although they were long dead, she felt the eyes of her line upon her and felt their anger, their sense of betrayal, at all that she had done against them. Not for this had she been made Sarillorn of the line; not for this had she become the vessel for the ancient power of the first matriarch. It would have been better for all concerned if the power had traveled through the line as crown, or staff, or ring, the way it did with any other line. That way, had the power been misused, it could have been passed on, either by will or force, to one less likely to fail it.

Now, with the destruction of the Lady of Elliath, there was no way that the power of the forebears of the line could be handed down. The power was locked within her blood, and when she died, it would die with her—lost forever to the mortal world. Not that it mattered. Who was left to pass it down to? Silent, she cursed the Lady's choice. But not so dearly or deeply as she did her own.

The hall ended, gradually opening out into the garden that Erin remembered. She stepped onto the narrow path, assailed by the fragrance of a hundred different blossoms. Taking a deep breath, she allowed her wonder to show—for this was indeed the garden of her memory. The centuries that had passed had wrought no changes here. More than at any other time, she felt awe at the power of the Servants of Lernan. That the hall had remained untouched by tracery of dust or cobweb did not surprise her; the hall was a dead, solid thing. But these flowers, these plants and smallish trees—they were of the living, and what lived, changed. That was a maxim of all the lines.

On impulse, she bent down to touch a petal of a large violet flower. It was cool but not cold. She snapped it in two and a thin trickle of sap beaded unevenly across the tear. The flowers were indeed alive. Half-ashamed, she tucked the half petal into a pocket and continued to walk toward the garden's center.

She became aware that she approached it when she heard the musical tinkle of water striking water—the fountain of the Lady's garden. The flowers gave way before her as she stepped onto a patterned patch of stone and marble-work—one that interlocked seamlessly beneath her booted foot. And in front of her, the fountain flowed. Clear, small streams of water fell from either hand of the statue in its center.

Erin lost control of her knees for a moment, and they folded beneath her.

In the middle of the fountain, the piece of sculpture that she had once seen as vague and unformed was now a precise, alabaster cast. She knew the lines of the face, with its narrow nose and squared chin. She knew the shape of its rounded eyes, and the way the white, stone hair flowed around its high cheekbones. The only thing that she did not recognize was its expression; a thing halfway between peace and pain—caught and frozen by the hands of the master sculptor that had designed this hall.

The Lady of Elliath.

She rose again, and stumbled toward it, until she stood at the edge of the water looking into a mirror that bleached all color from her.

Erin of Elliath, the last Sarillorn of the line, looked back at her, face unreadable, expression the only thing that was not exact. Even the details of what she wore now were correct.

Wordlessly she removed her boots and socks. Placing them in a haphazard pile beside the fountain she rolled up her pant legs and took one firm step in. She wasn't sure why, but she wanted to actually touch the statue—to wring some sort of answer out of it.

And as her foot hit the water, a brilliant glow engulfed her. It was warm and light, but not blinding. She heard the voice that she most and least wanted to hear, but the words, at first, made no sense.

"Forgive me, Erin. Forgive God."

"Forgive *you*?" She wheeled around, searching for a glimpse of the figure that had always accompanied the voice, wondering if Stefanos—First of the Sundered—had been too confident of his victory and his work. Her heart quickened with hope.

"Forgive me if you can." The voice continued as if it had not been interrupted. "Our time is short, although the essence of my garden will preserve yours for a while."

"Lady, please—"

"I am no longer here. If I had had the chance, or the courage to risk it, I would have conversed with you in times past—but I made my choice, whether fairly or not, and it is only an echo that you hear now, caught and trapped as my garden is, by the power of Lernan. I can only ask again that you forgive me. When I have finished speaking thus, I will take the field against the First of the Enemy—and, child, I shall not survive it. By my choice, and by the vision and hope of God, I will perish.

"This cowardice, it is such a human thing. I am almost ashamed of it. And I have little enough time to be ashamed."

The voice paused, and Erin clenched her fists; the Lady was gone, as dead to her as the rest of the line. Hope's birth was short and bright—but its death lingered. She listened, afraid to lose a single word of the Lady's last message to her.

"Some years after the awakening of the Twin Hearts—and the first of our many sacrifices—the Servants of Lernan found a way to discern the difference between time present and time to be; we lost one of our number to this discovery—the veils of time tore him from the grip of the merely present, and we could not call him back. We are not human, child, and the ties that bind us to mortal time are few; we knew that we could not use this odd form of travel and magic without too much of a risk.

"We had fought long and hard against the Servants of the Enemy and their Malanthi children, but the ranks of the Enemy seemed to swell and grow, even as ours dwindled. I, and three others whom you have never met, went to the meeting place of Lernan, and spoke with Him. Long and bitter were our words, for if we are not human, there is something of the mortal understanding within us—and those that were dying were the children and grandchildren of our blood.

"Thus was the Gifting of Lernan granted. Two Servants it cost us, and we paid that price willingly, that our children might have recourse other than death to defend our mutual goals. And so we fought again, some hundred of your years, but although the rate of our loss was less, the Malanthi still gained ground.

"I went alone to Lernan, to speak with Him again. We spoke long, and the words were painful. For He is God, but His hand could do nothing to stem our losses—nothing beyond the Gifting. But still . . . Ah. . . ."

The voice stopped a moment as Erin bowed her head. When it resumed, it was harsher.

"After that meeting, I made my first attempt to see through the veils that tie the present, like a blindfold, around us. Years I labored in my Woodhall, for I had not the mage-craft of some of the Servants, but I would not ask them to go where the First of their number would not—and I would not ask them to pay the price.

"The price . . . ah, Sarillorn, forgive me."

Again the voice fell silent for a moment. Erin's hands hung slack at her sides as she waited for it to continue.

"I found my first answer: the time and place of my death—and its manner. Perhaps if I had stopped then, you would not be here with such just cause against me. But I could not, or would not, stop. I chose the death, accepted it, and the lines of the future hardened around my choice. I looked beyond my

death, to see our lands fall inevitably to the hands of the Enemy
and his minions. And I looked beyond that still.

"To see you, Sarillorn. To see you here."

Again silence. But the bitterness of it was Erin's alone. She
couldn't understand why the Lady's tone held sorrow, but no
anger.

"Much was not clear to me, and I retraced my steps, traversing present and future and past alike to find better answers.
Forgive me," the Lady said again.

"Forgive you?" Erin said numbly again. "For what, Lady?
It was my choice that has brought us here."

But the voice continued, unbroken by Erin's tortured words.

"I saw the death of your mother."

Erin went white.

"I saw the vow that you would make should your mother's
death take place. I knew of the death in you that would make
you Lernan's Hope, and the hope of the future generations. I
am sorry. Many years I searched for a way to avoid that death—
for Kerlinda was my daughter, my youngest. But choice—and
the luxury of it—was not mine."

Erin's eyes clamped shut. She saw again her mother's still,
devastated body. *I saw your mother's death.* . . . Understanding
was far more painful than the question had been. Silence closed
in upon her, constricting her throat; she struggled against it,
destroying its fabric with a single word.

"Sorry?" Her voice tore into the hall's stillness. She struck
out and hit the statue at the fountain's center. It didn't even give
her the satisfaction of scraping her hand; it was smooth and cold.
In a sudden fury she brought her fists down and sent water
splashing chaotically out to the tiled ground. The voice of the
Lady was silent a few moments, as if, three centuries ago, she
had expected no less.

When she spoke again, it was worse.

"Child, there is much to forgive. Do you understand now
why I spoke to you of cowardice? We all, high or low, have our
fears—and you are the worst of mine.

"For I saw more.

"I saw your meeting with the First Servant of the Enemy. I
saw what the outcome of that meeting would be. I could not
speak of it to your comrades—but to Kandor, I did. Because I
had seen that I would, and I had seen what his choice would be.

He is most human of our number, although far from last, and he could not, for our sake, believe in the harsh path our hope had to take.

"I saw your choice as well.

"I would have told you—believe that—but in one of the reckonings, I did, and you left off your course. Now I tell you because I cannot see as clearly what happens after this. I do not know if it is because I have not the power, or because the First of the Enemy has begun his own Sight, or if my absence blurs the future."

She fell silent again. Erin shook, drawing her arms tightly around her chest, and sinking into the water.

"I spoke of my vision to God. I can go where He cannot go, but I cannot understand all of His working. And Lernan said that in you, and in your choices, so hard and so painful, lay our only hope for an end to this ancient conflict—for an end to Malthan, and through that his church and his rule."

"An *end*? He rules the whole damned world!"

"And so we chose.

"But there is more, child. You slept for over three hundred years, bound by the First Servant to darkness. And you did not age or wither in this time. Erin—you will not age. Not while Stefanos lives. Your comrades—Belfas, Rein, Teya, and Carla—paid blood-price for your youth. And Kandor, unhuman, unchanging, cemented this. You are tied, through them, to the Lord of the dark plane. And they are tied to you until the moment of your death releases them."

Erin looked up, her chin skimming the edge of the water. Her face was ashen. She realized then what she had avoided even suspecting: that her dream had been no figment of troubled subconscious. The friends that she had loved and betrayed in life continued to be betrayed *by* her life. They were trapped, without hope of waking, in the nightmare realm of darkness.

For one wild moment she wanted to have an end to it. She searched around frantically for some weapon, some means of killing herself—and freeing those five she had trapped by the cruelty of her choice.

"*Why?*"

Sarillorn, you have changed.

His voice. Stefanos' words. Here.

She gave a choked scream and put her hands to her ears—

shutting her eyes so that she would not have to see the expression on Stefanos' face once more. His look of surprise, of fear, and of a slowly building, implacable determination. His work, the work of the darkness he served, the Enemy he was bound to.

"No! Not for me!" She twisted in the water as if invisible hands had wrenched at her insides, going through the curtain of fragile flesh to do so.

The Lady spoke again—bitter comfort.

"Sarillorn. I am sorry."

"How *could* you? They trusted you! *I* trusted you! How could you *use* us this way?" She struggled to her feet, dripping wet, the knot in her throat too tight for tears.

And once again, as if she had seen it—and she probably had, Erin thought bitterly—the Lady's disembodied voice said, "For the only hope of a true end to our conflict. Do not think that I do not know how much our lands will suffer—have suffered—from the only choice I have. But I must look beyond myself, and my kin—to the future of the rest of humanity.

"You accepted, by your vows within the circle, the burden of responsibility—whatever the cost. Each of us, making that vow or hearing it, pray that the cost will be measured in our lives alone—that price, all of the line's kin are willing to pay. You are not the strongest of your line, except in power. And you must pay the same price that I have paid—not the sacrifice of your life, which for you especially would have been easy, but the sacrifice of that which you have loved.

"Forgive me, Sarillorn. Forgive me, child of my blood. But there was no other path. And even this one is only the fragile hope of the First of Lernan and her troubled God. I cannot even be of aid to you when you need it most; I cannot share the burden that I have forced upon shoulders that may prove too mortal to bear it. Daughter . . ."

Again the voice trailed off, and for a moment Erin feared that it, too, had left her. She felt trapped by the Lady's Hall, trapped by the Lady's choice, and trapped by the God that she had sought solace from all her life.

She tried not to think of her mother's death. She tried not to think of the last time she had seen Belfas, with his red wet face. She tried hardest not to think of how it could have been avoided but for the duplicity of those whom she had trusted.

Is this how you felt, Belfas? she thought bitterly. *Is this what*

*you remember of me? That you loved me, that you trusted me—
and that I failed you?*

"*Lernan!* God, why?"

It was not Lernan who answered. "Erin, I have little left to say.

"I have made a map for you; you will need it. The lands have changed. Marked especially, in gold outline, is the former boundary of the Culverne holdings. For Culverne, unlike for either you or I, it is not too late. If I guess correctly—and if you do not choose to abandon my hope entirely—your road lies through those lands. They are recently conquered, and they still remember our touch.

"I have also preserved a sword for you. It is light, but hard and sharp. I have seen your sword-work, and believe that it will prove worthy of your skill. Last, there is the fruit of the garden—my garden. It is made by the same magic that sustains the Eyes of God, and it will hold you in your journeys. More I cannot offer. Nor can I tell you what you must do to free the land—but I can offer you this: The seed of the Enemy's destruction has already been sown, and you carry it within you. What fruit I hope it will yield, you already know.

"Take these, dearest of daughters."

The voice faltered, and then continued.

"I have spent too long in the mortal lands; it hurts me—I never knew how much it could hurt. In the Final Judgment, it is you who will judge me, and I who will abide by your decision.

"Ah. The First Servant is on the field now and waiting for me. My time here is done. I go now, to peace. I pray that you find yours in a different way—and that it not be as Pyrrhic a victory as mine.

"Forgive me . . ."

The light ebbed, and Erin stood alone. She stepped woodenly out of the fountain. The water ran off her to lie at her feet. Ignoring it, she walked over to her boots and found them in a pile beside a gray pack. She lifted it automatically and found it rather heavy. Numb fingers undid the ties, and when she lifted its flap, she found the first of the Lady's gifts: a rolled piece of ivory parchment.

She did not open it. Beneath the rolled map there were a variety of round gold-tinged objects: the third of the Lady's gifts. She forced herself to ignore the urge to throw them away.

Instead, she mechanically put on her socks and her boots, not minding that her feet were still damp from the fountain. She swung the pack over her shoulder and noticed, beneath it, a sword in a scabbard.

Slowly she leaned over to pick it up. The handle and pommel of the sword were wrought in a pale silver color, and they gleamed in the light of the garden. All along the scabbard, in gold work and etching, were seven linked circles and some type of rune that she could not read. Nor did she take the time to try to. She knew what it said.

For the Responsibility of Power.

It was Gallin's sword. Gallin, the greatest hero that the Lernari had ever known. And the being who had crafted it lay dead these three centuries.

In one lightning move, she pulled the sword out of the scabbard, hearing the faint whisper of metal against metal. The blade seemed to leave a lingering trail across the air as she tested its balance and weight, a signature, in ink made of light.

"What you made, Lady," she said bitterly, "you made well." Again she felt the urge to have an end to this horrible, endless game. The edge of the sword was sharp and unblooded. She brought it close, and closer still to her throat, until she could feel the edge of it against the skin of her neck.

And then she put it down. She would take blood-vow to end the work of the Enemy and his First Servant. Death before that was not an option—not through suicide. She swung the sword about in a tight, sharp circle, her wrist flipping back with a surprising elasticity. Three times she circled the flashing blade about her body, and as the third arc ended, she opened her mouth on a silent syllable. At long last, and too late, the Sarillorn of Elliath was going to join the war again. But this time she did not intend to leave it—not alive.

The sword went back into its scabbard, and she belted it around her waist. Even as she did so, she noted that the flowers in the garden were beginning to wither. The spell that had kept them safe from time had done its purpose. Erin of Elliath, last of her line, had received the Lady's final message.

She walked out of the garden and back toward the great hall. Ahead of her, she could see the glowing Tree grow larger with each step she took. She felt alone, sullied and scarred by what she had found. Even the gifts of the Lady couldn't change that.

Grimly she walked up to the Tree, free from the awe that had always been inspired by it before. She held her arms out, to catch it in a final embrace—and to be free of it forever.

Even as she did so, she heard the Lady's voice one last time. "Erin, child, my love goes with you."

She couldn't even raise the strength to express the bitter, dark laugh that lurked beneath her clenched throat. Without a backward glance, she walked out the door of the Lady's Woodhall, never to return.

The fact that she walked without limp, or any sign of injury, escaped her notice for the moment; only later would she remember the golden glow that had warmed her before the ice had truly set.

The first person she saw was Darin. He stood, hands bound together in plain sight. His face was white, except where it was purpled by bruising and a trace of blood. His shirt was torn, and the dark soil of the Lady's wood clung to his hair and clothing. But worst of all were his eyes; they were flat, almost lifeless—and when they met hers, although they flickered briefly, they did not change.

The Swords, though, they had expressions. As did the priest—the two priests—that were visible in the clearing. Black robes, black armor, and the solid gray of steel formed a half circle of attendance before the Lady's Woodhall. It encircled Darin, who stood, bound more by fear, Erin judged, than by the simple ropes that restrained him.

"Well met," the older priest said quietly. He even took pains to bow, and the gesture was not meant as an insult. It angered her anyway. "You must be of Elliath blood. We thought all of your line dead, centuries past." He ran his fingers through his beard as he straightened. "This"—he raised one hand—"must be the famous Woodhall of the long-dead Lady. We've searched for it before, you know." His smile deepened; his expression took the aspect of his God. "Thank you for leading us to it."

"Enough, Tarantas," the younger priest said. He was not so finely dressed as the older man and did not bother with the conceit of a beard that would be, at best, sparse. But he carried himself with the impatience of power. Erin knew him for the leader. He nodded to his Swords. She counted fifteen in all. "Take her. We don't have time for pleasantries."

"You realize," she replied, shifting her sword as she met Erliss of Mordechai's eyes, "that I can't allow that."

"We realize that it wouldn't be your first choice." He gestured, again without relying on words to form a command, and one Sword, weapon drawn, came to stand behind Darin. He lifted his sword; it glinted where it caught the light. Its shadow fell halfway between Darin's shoulder and neck. "If you fight, we'll kill the boy."

She looked for some sign from Darin; some acknowledgment of his fate. She searched in vain. He lowered his head, exposing his neck as if he could expect nothing better than a clean strike.

"I see," she said softly. Once or twice before, she had been in a very similar circumstance. And war had its mandate. If they killed Darin, they killed the last of Line Culverne. But if they did not, and that because she surrendered, they would shortly kill the last of both lines. Without fight, and without loss to themselves.

I'm sorry, Darin. She raised her sword as she steadied herself against the back of the tree; the effects of the transition were still with her.

And then the head of the Sword exploded. His weapon fell, unblooded by all save he, and his body toppled stiffly forward, knocking Darin off his feet.

Lord Erliss wheeled, his eyes wide and then narrow.

"It isn't her power!" Tarantas cried. "It isn't the magic of the Enemy!"

chapter
four

Erin barely had time to react before the Sword closest to her fell, clutching his neck. Wire, weighted on either side by small, dense balls, was tightly wrapped around his throat. And a very, very small portion of that throat had been exposed.

"Kill her!" the young priest shouted, in a voice that seemed to have grown more distant. She didn't dare look beyond the men that now circled to see where their leader lay.

When the second Sword fell, she had no time to see the manner of his injury. Gallin's sword moved her hand with an almost-tangible will; it was weightless, almost supple, for all that it was a southern blade. She saw its legendary signature—the flash and spread of green light across the air—and wondered if the Swords could see it, too, before they met its edge. She almost expected to hear a voice, some sign of Gallin, but in this she was disappointed.

They tried to force her from the tree to open ground, where they could attack more easily, and with greater numbers. They chose the west to concentrate their drive, and she defended as heavily as possible against attacks from that quarter. It quickly grew impossible; where two men had stood against her, with the advantage of height and distance, a third, and then a fourth, came to join them.

And in such close quarters, the speed afforded by light armor became much less of an advantage than the protection afforded by chain. She was fast, yes—she had always been among the fastest in any unit she had served—but she had no room to maneuver and had no shield with which to block.

She called light; it came, sealing the two glancing blows she had taken. She called fire, and it, too, came—but where it touched the Malanthi, it caused only pain, not death, only giving her a second's respite, rather than a reprieve. These were weak of blood, these enemies, almost completely gray. Only the most powerful of all light could serve as a weapon against them—and she needed that power to heal herself if she was to continue her fight.

Sweat beaded her brow, but at least the Lady's greatest Tree sheltered her from the worst of the sunlight. She was tiring too quickly. A sword sneaked in at her side; she pivoted on her feet and caught its edge with her armor. In battle, she had never felt so closely pressed.

She would die here, she felt certain of it; she would die alone, with no comrades and no other warriors of her once-great line, her once-great God. At last.

And then, without warning, she felt the pressure of the Swords' lessen. She spared a glance up and saw someone new enter the fray, brandishing a sword as if it were a hat, and he in the middle of a flowery bow.

"Take that, scoundrels! Quake in fear!"

She almost laughed out loud.

"Have no—mmph—fear, Lady!" The black-clad man said. "We'll be—urk—out of this in a minute." Through some quirk of luck, he actually managed, albeit clumsily, to parry the weapons that his—and her—enemies raised against him. His shoulders seemed to shake as he tried to brace himself for their weight and ended up teetering back on his feet.

"Don't talk!" she shouted back, breaking one of her former weaponsmaster's cardinal rules. "Fight!" If he could. Suddenly, she was no longer alone; some strange, dramatic young oaf, from God alone knew where, had chosen to enter battle, on her side. And if she couldn't kill the two that she fought against, she wouldn't be in time to rescue him.

For one second, her sword was in midswing. A heartbeat later, another explosion tore through the air. Her blade, trailing light and danger, passed harmlessly over what remained of the Sword's head. There was no blood; no bits of flesh or bone were left to rain down upon her. Ashes, the acrid smell of cooked meat, and the black smoke of burned fat were all that remained of the Sword's face. His body fell. She dodged it, and put an end to the Sword that stood spellbound in shock.

And then there was silence.

The odd, loud stranger stood, arms crossed, face wreathed in an obviously self-congratulatory smile. At his feet lay two Swords; neither moved. And both were charred beyond recognition.

There, in the shadows of leaved canopies, she could see tufts of white hair and the wreckage of a priest's robe. All around, in armor that was smeared red or black, lay what remained of the Swords. She counted carefully and hoped that her memory was up to the task.

Fifteen. One priest. That left only one unaccounted for.

"Well, Lady," the stranger said loudly. "It appears that I arrived in good time." He lifted his sword and swung it back into the scabbard that hung too low on his waist. Or at least he tried. He narrowly avoided splitting his thigh open the first time.

She moved as if he hadn't spoken; her feet were light upon orvas, grass, and moss—and careful, as she vaulted over the great roots of the tree. The young priest who had obviously been this squad's leader was nowhere in sight.

They had a moment's respite, then. She used it to find Darin. It wasn't that hard; he lay beneath the headless body of the first man to fall. Darin hadn't moved at all; a careless observer might have taken him for one of the dead.

Erin was not careless. "Darin?" She turned him over gently and cut away at the ropes that bound his hands.

He opened his eyes, looked up at her wordlessly, and then threw his arms around her neck, not minding the blood or the sweat or the smoke smell. She held him, but briefly. "We won."

"Indeed," the stranger said, "we did. Say, did this belong to the antiquated old priest?"

They both turned to watch as the man began an exaggerated hobble toward them, digging the staff of Culverne into the dirt to emphasize his mime.

Darin was unamused. He let go of Erin at once, got unsteadily to his feet, and then stomped off across the ground. "No," he said, grabbing it firmly and yanking it out of the man's hands. "It doesn't."

"Well, it certainly doesn't belong to you, boy. And there's no need to be so rude." The man frowned, and Erin got her first real chance to study his features.

He was of her height, perhaps an inch or two taller; it was

hard to tell—he wore boots with heels that had obviously been constructed to increase his . . . stature. They were finely made and well designed—but completely out of place in the village of the Vale. His face was pale as well—and smooth. If he had been in any real battles in his life, Erin was certain that he'd managed to avoid being anything but a lucky archer. His chin was pronounced, his hair a sandy, wavy profusion of colors that changed with the light; now, in the shade, it made him look like a red-tinted mouse with dark, wide eyes. And his nose was almost perfect. She would have liked such a patrician profile at one point in her life.

"Were you responsible for that?" she asked bluntly, pointing to the headless corpse that had served as Darin's shield.

"That?" He wrinkled his nose in distaste. "Of course not. What do you take me for? A priest?"

"A priest couldn't have such an effect," another voice said. And a figure in brown robes stepped out from the line of trees that faced the Woodhall. Even Erin started; her hearing—the pride of the unit scout—had detected nothing of his presence. She tensed; her weapon arm rose to ready without any concentration on her part.

The man lifted his arms in perfect unison and very carefully pulled down the cowl he wore; it fell neatly, a frame for the thin line of his jaw. His eyes were gray, his skin the color brought by too much sunlight. His hair was white and thin. He wore no beard, and his hands were ringless and firm as they fell once again to his sides.

"Lady," he bowed. "I am Trethar. I have been waiting for you."

Erin waited for him to rise; minutes stretched past. Finally, she realized that he waited her word. More minutes passed as she stared in surprise at the peak of his skull. Darin elbowed her gently, and she started; she hadn't been aware that he stood quite so close.

"Rise," she whispered.

He did, the faintest hint of a smile across his lips. "Indeed, I have waited for a long time. Well met."

"How did you do—that?"

"Wait? Ah, no. The Sword? I will tell you all, Lady. But I think that this is not the best place for it." He glanced up at the lowest branches of the Lady's Tree. "Once, maybe. Not now."

"Well, I certainly agree with that. But don't you think this 'wait' is rather too convenient?" The short black-clad stranger had chosen a less-grand tree to lounge against. As he spoke, he examined his fingernails closely.

The man who had named himself Trethar frowned. "Convenient? You haven't been under my geas, then. And I note that I, at least, have identified myself."

"Oh," the stranger said, standing suddenly at attention. "I did forget myself, didn't I?"

"I don't imagine," Trethar replied, disapproval deepening the lines of his face, "that it happens often."

"Not very, no. Lady, I am often called Robert in these parts. Well, not these parts precisely, but close enough."

"Robert of?" Erin replied. She wondered if his bow could be performed by a less-agile person without causing spinal damage; his nose nearly scraped the moss.

"Of? Oh—you want a house name, I imagine. I fear I shall have to disappoint you. I am Robert. And you?"

She took a deep breath and used the excuse of sheathing her sword to give her space to think. It wasn't enough, so she walked over to the base of the Lady's Tree and picked up her pack, sliding it over her shoulder with an ease that years of luxury had done nothing to dispel. She adjusted the straps quietly as her hands shook. *And I?*

"Erin," she said at last. "Only Erin."

"Well, then, Lady Erin—I do think the old man is right. We'd best move; we were too slow to stop one of the priests, and we wish to disappoint him upon his return."

They walked as quickly as possible, and the Lady's wood seemed to open to grant them passage as they moved. The road would have been smoother and easier to traverse. No one had suggested they take it.

Darin held Bethany tightly in one hand; the other he used to push aside thin branches and tallish weed. But he kept missing these because his eyes wandered to Sara's back. She formed the lead of their line, he came second, the loud, incessant chatterer came third, and the brown-robed old man pulled up the rear. He wanted to ask her why she had called herself Erin. Maybe she didn't trust these two, although they had saved her life. And his own.

He slapped his shoulder, narrowly missed the mosquito that perched there waiting to draw blood, and grunted as a branch then scraped the underside of his jaw.

No, he didn't think it was lack of trust. But he didn't understand it, either. There were other things to worry about, and maybe because they were so large, he chose to focus on the simple question of a name instead.

"It was magic," Erin said quietly, as she took a seat around the dying fire. The flames were low and small, enough to make a dinner by, but not enough to provide real warmth. The fire was dwindling into embers now, which was a comfort; it cast few shadows.

"Yes," Trethar said. He had eaten rather sparsely, as if afraid of depleting supplies.

Erin's forehead creased in a frown. "But how?"

"How?" He bent forward; his hands came to rest, palms flat, against his knees. His face was cowled by shadow, his expression remote. What he looked at, while his eyes stayed stationary upon the orange wood, no one could have said. Perhaps history. "How much do you know of the Origin?" he asked at length.

"I know of the awakening of the Dark and the Light. I know of their war and the eventual change of their bodies. I know of the Servants and their children."

He nodded his quiet approval, and for just a moment, beneath the black canopy of branches and starlight, Erin felt as if she had earned the approbation of her teachers in Elliath. "But what do you know of mortal history?"

She was silent.

"Don't feel ashamed of the ignorance. It was common among your kind." Had he been one of her teachers, he would have gone on to lecture her in some idiosyncratic way; she waited for him to begin to drum his knees and lap in impatience. But he was perfectly still as he met her eyes. "It is varied and long. The development of the lines mirror each other, from beginning to end; not so with the history of the gray kin.

"But yes, I know this is not the time. Let me just say that I've studied human history for many years, and my teachers have all been unusual." He smiled. "I am Trethar. I've been watching for you for most of my adult life."

"Me?"

"Yes, Lady." He smiled again. "Not all of the people in
Elliath perished at the hands of the Enemy's army. Three or four
of your teachers, and many more of your servers, escaped into
Lernan's lands. Because they were nonblooded, they couldn't
be easily—or magically—tracked."

"And the rest?" Erin asked. Her voice was soft, quiet.

"They perished."

She nodded grimly. "I'm sorry. Please continue." Her eyes
had grown wide and dark.

"One of these was a teacher who had worked long with a—a
Master Latham of Line Elliath. His name was Carlentin; he had
a great and curious mind, and he had spent years studying the
line, even as he was teaching its children. Blood-magic fascinated him; the very idea of the Hand of God, reachable only by
the Servants, did the same.

"We do not know or fully understand what happened over
the next twenty years; our records are not . . . written. It was
too dangerous a risk.

"Do you find it cold?"

Erin shrugged. "Not really."

"Ah. Well, I'm an older man; I do." He gestured, and suddenly a shape rose in the gathering darkness outside of the camp-
fire's ring. As it approached, Erin saw that it was a log—no,
two. Before she could speak, they joined the ashes of the fire.
Trethar gestured again, harshly, and they became flame and
warmth. "Better. Where was I?

"Ah. Yes. Carlentin chanced, in his studies, upon the magics
that I have just used. Those, and more. It was an arduous task;
it took most of his life in the doing, and when he had called his
first weak fire, he was far too old to travel. But no other person
could have achieved it. He was brilliant. He opened the gate to
the fire first; we always start with that when we find another who
will be a fitting brother of our order. There are not many; the
power that we gather can't be openly used—or else our primary
mission would be endangered. That mission is—"

"What did he teach in Elliath?" She asked it as if the rest of
his words had not reached her at all.

"He taught history—but not in the school halls. No, he
worked instead with those members of your line who would deal
with kings and princes, cities, taxes, and towns."

There had always been visiting dignitaries who were off-limits to the children. Erin did not remember Carlentin, but that in itself was not surprising.

"Now, Carlentin was not obsessed only with knowledge; he also hated the Darkness—he had seen too much of its work at the fall of Elliath to ever forget that. He turned his skills to the teaching of those he trusted to combat the Enemy.

"It was Carlentin, and his teachings, that brought me here—although others of my brethren dwell in different cities across the Empire, each waiting for a sign."

"But why are they looking for Sara?" Darin asked, as he rolled Bethany between his cold hands. All eyes turned to look at him, and he blushed. "Umm, Erin, I mean."

Trethar raised an eyebrow. "Carlentin learned much of Elliath business, by both observation and careful questioning of the servers. And he knew two important things: that Erin of Elliath had been chosen as the Sarillorn of the line, and that the Lady of Elliath had traveled beyond the veils. Ah—the veils of the present."

Darin's brow creased, and he opened his mouth to ask. But Bethany answered before the question escaped. "Oh. Well, that still doesn't answer the question."

"Not directly. But he knew, of course he knew, when the Sarillorn was taken. A whole village of people had witnessed her bargain with the First Servant of the Enemy; they had even lived to bear the news to the next town.

"And he knew, from those very few slaves who escaped the Empire, that something dire and strange was occurring. You see, they spoke, many of them, of a . . . Lady of Mercy.

"The priests perhaps did not place enough importance upon the reports of those slaves—it's impossible to say. Perhaps they could not conceive of a Sarillorn of Line Elliath as consort to the Lord of the Empire. But Carlentin did. Still, it meant nothing.

"Until the fall of Elliath. We do not know how he observed it, but we're certain he would not have, had he had Elliath blood; they hunted for that."

Erin's palms were opened by her fingernails.

Trethar took a breath and then continued. "You see, Lady," he said, in a most apologetic tone of voice, "the First of the Enemy spoke of you—or rather, said that he had sheltered Elliath blood. Sheltered and nurtured, I believe."

She closed her eyes. "Go on."

"Carlentin thought nothing of that—until, once again through the lips of those who'd escaped the Empire, he began to hear tales of the Lady of Mercy. You see, she had disappeared, much to the grief of her people—but it had been promised that she would come again, at the time of her people's greatest need, when hope was at its nadir.

"We assumed this to be acceptable to the Lord of the Empire; there are the monuments and the statues that were erected against the strict wishes of the Church, and there are other signs.

"So. Carlentin assumed, rightly I now see, that that Lady was you. And when Culverne fell, we began our search in earnest. Twenty of our number are in Rennath, the old capital, listening and watching.

"I alone of our brethren came to Mordantari. And I—even with my mortal eyes—saw the sign in the skies. Red and white, Lady. The return of the Light.

"And I offer you my magic, my magery, and its skills, if you will have them." He bowed his head, and the flames leaped high.

Darin sat still, Bethany clutched in his white hands. Robert sat slack-jawed, his expression so open it was almost farcical. Trethar was quiet, peaceful. All three watched Erin closely.

"Thank you," she said. "In the days to come, you'll have to tell me more of the history you know. But it's late," she added quickly, before anyone could interrupt. "Robert—do you have a bedroll and tenting?"

"Of course I do, Lady, do you think I would travel without them? Why any—"

"Good. We rise just before first light."

Blackness, like velvet with fangs, closed around her. She saw it, but it failed to be important—it couldn't be; the pain here was too strong. The screams were liquid and heavy; they filled her; she was their perfect vessel. And she walked. She did not want to walk.

They came, companions to her trek, whiter, somehow clearer, than they had been the last time she'd seen them. Belfas, no longer brother, Kandor, Teya, Rein, and Carla. They were ghosts, and like ghosts in children's stories, they were pinned and trapped by some evil fortune to a dark and ugly place.

By some evil choice.

"I'm sorry," she said, aware that the words were inadequate, but unable to offer anything else. "Belfas, I can't change the choice I made. I can't change the fact of your deaths, but I can change"—and here she gestured widely—"your prison. Please, give me just a little more time." She thought of Stef—of him. Her own pain grew, becoming an anchor against his.

"What is the First to you now?" Kandor asked, a curious edge to his voice.

"Enemy." The word was so cold and so final that no hint of warmth, or a past without that ice, existed in it.

"You feel his call."

"Don't you?" she countered, angry. Guilt made her voice harsh and rough.

"Yes," he answered softly, and turned to gaze into the blackness. "But I feel yours as well, Sarillorn. And his is easily the stronger of the two."

She sucked in her breath, as if at a sudden blow; his words were sharp and pointed, and she had no defense against them.

"Good," she said abruptly. "He—he deserves to suffer."

Belfas reached out with a hand of mist; his fingers pressed into her shoulders, falling beneath the outline of her flesh. At once, he flared with her warmth and her power. "Do you hate him?"

There were no tears. "Yes."

"You always thought you knew everything, Erin." He shook his head, but his lips were curled into a hard smile. "We feel his pain, but we've got nothing to offer it. We four weren't healers, and Kandor—can't help."

She wanted to tell them all, then. *The Lady knew, Belfas; she knew—she condemned you to this.* But the words froze on her lips. It was truth, yes—but would it help them to know it? No matter what, it had still been Erin's choice that had doomed them.

But the Lady had known. She struggled a few minutes more.

"I went to the Woodhall today," she whispered at last, turning away from them all. "And I discovered that the Lady of Elliath knew what I would do to you all. She knew it, Belfas. She *saw.* She could have stopped you. She didn't."

The silence was eerie and horrible.

"She could have told me," Erin continued, her voice uneven

and rough. "Could have warned me. I would never have made that choice. Never."

"But you did."

She wheeled to face Belfas, hands outstretched, palms up. "But I believed him!" Silence again, then. Silence and an aura of waiting.

"Sarillorn," Kandor said, and his voice was very heavy. "Did you find aught else?"

"I found Gallin's sword." She let the Lady go for the moment. "I have one country to liberate, if I can. I have one Enemy to fight." She wheeled suddenly and lurched forward, hands reaching in reflex for pain to heal. No. Gritting her teeth, she continued.

"Fight, then, and with our blessing," Kandor said quietly. "But, child, perhaps the First Servant loved you as much as his nature allowed."

She laughed darkly. "Loved me? He was able to kill the Lady, the lines, and God alone knows how many innocent people— because of *my* choice. Because I believed that he loved me. Maybe"—she bowed her head briefly—"I believed it because I wanted so badly for it to be true. But I—I valued it above my vows to the line and my responsibilities. Now, I'm the last of my line, Darin's the last of his—and the Gifting of God is in the Enemy's land. He is my enemy now and will be until either the lands are free again or I am dead."

Her head shot up suddenly, to view the darkness ahead of her with a bitter fury. "Do you hear me?" she shouted.

Kandor tried to interrupt her, but she shook him off.

"I pledge blood-vow! I shall destroy all that you have built!"

"Sarillorn, do not—blood-vow is binding in life. Do not lightly—"

"Lightly?" She gave him a wild, angry laugh, and he looked long and hard at her face before turning away.

"Erin." Belfas, and only Belfas, could have brought her back. "We've been here a long time, but now that you've come—now that we almost understand, we'll wait. The Lady called you Lernan's Hope."

"God's hope?" Erin gave a dark laugh. "Do any of you know what it was? Perhaps the Lady did, but she left me no word." She laughed again, and the five standing before her looked around uneasily. "Will you tell me what it is that I must do?"

Kandor spoke. "You are to end the reign of the Enemy. How, I do not know. But I know that the Lady believed, with God, that your path was the only one that would lead to peace for your world. She saw correctly, I believe. The First of the Enemy—"

"Don't speak to me of him. I won't listen."

"Erin."

She met Belfas' gentle word with a rawness that caused him to flinch.

"He betrayed you. I betrayed you. The Lady—" She swallowed convulsively. "Where's your anger now that I've found mine? Where is it now?" She laughed again, and then brought her hands to her face.

Memory colored the pale light of the hair that fell into his ghostly eyes; she could see it through the bars of her fingers.

"I—Erin, if she had told us, we'd never have believed it; we'd have gone anyway. It wouldn't have hurt less." He looked young. "But it helps to know that we didn't die for nothing. She knew it—and our deaths, they must serve the line."

"I can't accept that we were given no choice."

"Sarillorn," Kandor interrupted, in a soft voice that was not at all gentle, "you were given a choice."

"Yes," she answered starkly, but she barely seemed to hear him. "Belf—my mother—she could have saved my mother . . ."

Belfas touched her; her power ebbed again.

She stared at him for a moment before pulling away.

The landscape was screaming. Pain, heavy and seductive, crawled through the air, a call to her blood. She felt, at that moment, that she would never answer the call of this blood again; it had been, after all, the Lady's blood passed down through a generation. And then she forgot that; forgot all but the source of it: Stefanos.

With stark determination, she fought her way into the light of the dawn, and lay exhausted and trembling beneath the folds of her bedroll. Only then did her fury recede enough to allow her the grace of self-contempt. She knew that her vow was binding—and made it again, to confirm in reality the determination of dream. She knew what the First Servant had done and understood some of his methods in the doing of it. She knew that thousands, hundreds of thousands, had been lost—either immediately or through the debilitation of slavery—at his dictate. She knew who he served and knew what the Enemy demanded.

And she knew that she would keep, unswerving, to the course she had set for herself.

But knowing it didn't ease the ache that threatened to immobilize her.

A part of her missed him.

And she loathed it freely.

She only prayed that now that she had made the only *right* choice, she would sleep a mercifully dreamless sleep, with no hint of light or dark to trouble her. She wasn't surprised when the prayer went unanswered.

"Master."

Second of my Servants.

"The fortress of the Enemy has been destroyed."

The landscape slithered, all fluid, colorless darkness. It stilled slowly. *Are you certain?*

"As certain as I can be where the workings of the Enemy are concerned. What we sensed and sought for these hundred human years we can no longer feel."

Then you were correct. This human half blood is the one you have watched for; the one my enemy called hope.

"Yes, master." Sargoth paused.

The Heart of the Darkness waited, and time passed, moving so far beneath him that it did not even merit his notice.

"I do not wish to question your decision, Lord."

Silence then, dark and intangible. It was the only silence that Sargoth hated; he could pry no answers from it to satisfy his endless curiosity, and stood waiting, just another victim of ignorance.

"If she is the one that I and the others of your Servants have watched for, perhaps she is not one with whom we wish to toy. The First of the Enemy was of greater power than I, and if she saw a danger to us in this half blood, then there is a danger present."

The landscape rumbled with the thoughts of the Dark Heart and the accursed, incomprehensible silence. It pained Sargoth; he understood more than any single being, immortal or otherwise, yet he still could not pierce the wall that either of the Twin Hearts stood behind to comprehend them clearly.

How much more, he thought bitterly to himself, *must I learn before I truly know all?* It was his one desire, and he was certain Malthan knew it.

I cannot see a danger in the form of a half blood, no matter what power she claims. The Servants of my Enemy were tainted by his weakness; what destruction can they wreak? If there is a danger, it is small. I will not lose this chance to sweeten the sending of my First.

"Yes, Lord. I shall not speak of it again."

Good. Fingers of darkness wreathed the ethereal shadow of the Second of Malthan. *How do you proceed?*

"As can be expected."

This half blood is mortal.

Sargoth smiled coldly. "Yes, Lord." He did not explain the source of his mirth further, and the Dark Heart did not press him; it was not the amusement of the Second of his Servants that carried his interest now.

"The human visited the fortress of the Enemy's First. We do not know what she did there"—his voice fell a moment in irritation—"but we believe she received some message of succor from her dead ancestor. The binding that held the fortress was released; it is gone. We will never know the manner of its creation."

Sargoth, do not lose her.

"No, Lord. Even as we speak, one of your followers is making ready to receive her."

chapter
five

Erliss of Mordechai had been left with three Swords and two
slaves—hardly a fitting party for a lord of his station. At any
other time, justifiable anger would have consumed his attention—but he did not have the leisure for it now. Later, in the
comparative safety of Malakar, with a host of house guards as
a wall between his person and any physical threat, he would
plan his revenge.

Now, his retreat firmly under way, he planned his meeting
with his elder cousin. Lord Vellen of Damion was every inch a
Karnar; any whiff of failure, no matter how reasonable the excuse, was usually cause for someone's death. Erliss had always
taken great care, when operating under Lord Vellen's directives,
not to merit that death. Until now.

Because of one woman and one useless slave.

At least now, outside the boundaries of Mordantari, he was
free to requisition the use of proper manors and inns. He could
not completely take advantage of it at the moment—the speed
of travel did not allow it—but at least he always had a large bed,
a warm fire, and real food. Travel in the provinces was usually
the best way to feel one's power at an early age, and Erliss, as
had most of the young nobles, had done so often.

He did not enjoy it now.

He had even been forced, by circumstance and a hazy understanding of all that was at stake, to speak with the provincial
priests and warn them of the possible coming of two runaway
slaves: one woman, dressed outlandishly as some sort of soldier,
and one boy on the threshold of adulthood. He made them sound
almost harmless, which fooled none of his listeners, but he made

absolutely certain that they had no understanding of the issues and complexities of her presence. Because that, of course, was proprietary information for which, if spread, Vellen would certainly, and justifiably, kill.

The capital was a ten-day away, and he had already ridden three different horses to ground. That would come out of Church coffers. If he survived his meeting with the head of the Greater Cabal.

Darin had rarely traveled outside of the city before, but the one long trek he had made across the Empire made the strangeness of the forest quite serene. Sleep had come slowly and been fitful at best, and even before the sun had peaked the treetops, he was up and dressed. Sara was quietly about the business of breakfast, and he did what he could to help her.

"Are the others awake?" she asked, as she poked at the fire. Orange light limned her arms and face, highlighting the shadows beneath her eyes. Something about her looked very, very different—and only after minutes of staring at her as she worked did Darin realize what it was. Her auburn hair, long and straight, had been pulled and plaited in the warrior's braid. Not that the warrior's braid had been common in Line Culverne at the time of its fall, but Darin had seen the statues and tapestries of a bygone age, and he knew the look well. She wore her armor, and her sword—her strange, runed sword, with its trail of light that burned the eye—hung at her side.

He could no longer imagine her as the Lady of castle Darclan, with her long, simple dresses and her love of gardens and sunlight and outdoor lunches. Gone was any hint of the doctor in the infirmary who had tended to the complaints of slaves, minor or serious.

And gone was any hint of the softness about her eyes when she looked up at her Lord.

She had called herself Erin. He thought he understood why her name had suddenly changed. He opened his mouth to call her, and shut it again.

Waking their new companions would be less strange.

Trethar of the Brotherhood, as he had named himself, was awake before Darin reached his tent. Early morn was obviously no stranger to the man, and without the shadows and eerie hint of dying firelight echoing from his face, he seemed normal, older, and less mysterious. His brown robes blended in perfectly with the morning greens and golds.

"Good morning, Darin," he said, inclining his head slightly. "The Lady is already up?" The smell of breakfast cooking came on the air, and his eyes brightened considerably. "I see she is."

"I'll wake Robert," Darin replied, as he watched Trethar turn. The older man was obviously used to a life led away from the comfort of roads, inns, or manor houses. Darin would learn it as well.

As he approached the one-man tent that Robert used, he discovered that Robert snored loudly.

"Robert," he said, as he lifted the tent's flap a foot. "Robert." Then, more loudly, "Robert!"

"Mmrphle?"

"Wake up. Breakfast's ready."

"Hmmmm."

Darin poked his head into the tent; the disarrayed strands of jet-black hair were caught above the line of the bedroll. Robert, presumably beneath them, was a large, curled lump. "Robert— you've got to wake up. We want to leave as quickly as possible."

The pale face of the slight man peered out of the protection of covers. One eyelid pried itself open, and shut again, much more quickly. "Lower the flap!"

Surprised, Darin did as ordered, and in a few moments, Robert peered cautiously out again. "Boy, do you have any idea what time it is?"

"Six, I think."

"Then go away and come back again at a respectable hour." Robert's head disappeared into the tent again.

Darin was silent for a moment, more in shock than anything else. He backed out of the tent and threw a helpless gaze in Erin's direction. "He's sleeping."

Her eyes went round, and for a moment she stopped moving. "Pardon?"

Trethar rose. "We'll wake him, then."

"He doesn't—he says he's not ready to wake up."

"Pardon?" There was an unsubtle difference between Trethar's use of the word and Erin's. Hers held Darin's surprise. His held an obvious annoyance. He stalked over to the tent—the only one that had not yet been taken down and packed away.

"Stand aside." It was the voice of a man used to being obeyed, and Darin moved quickly to one side.

Trethar knelt in the undergrowth and grass, steadied his hands, and then began to pull the tent pegs out of the ground. Robert's head appeared again before the tent had completely collapsed.

"Is this behavior necessary, my good sir? It's really too early to—"

"Get up!" the old man replied, his voice just shy of a shout. Gone was the near-serene austerity of an aged member of a secret order. "Now!"

"Uh, sir?" Darin said quietly, as Robert's head disappeared into the crumpling tent. "He did help to save our lives . . ."

"That he did," Trethar replied, with steely amiability. "That's why the tenting isn't ash now." He turned neatly on heel and headed toward breakfast. "But you'll note that he didn't come up with much of an explanation as to why he was there at all."

Everything about Robert was loud. From the moment he crawled out of the shapeless structure that had been a tent, that was obvious. Gone were the subdued, dark shades of the previous day; he wore a brilliant shirt—a *lace* shirt, of all things—and a jacket that was so deep a green, the forest paled beside it. His boots folded up in a heavy leather roll just short of his knees, and he wore the most garish hat that Darin had ever seen: a wide-brimmed monstrosity with three dyed feathers that hung wayward over the side. There was no way that a hat such as that would survive a trek through the forest.

"Does anyone have a mirror?"

Everyone stared at him. It was Trethar who answered the question. "A mirror? Young man, where exactly do you think we're going?"

"West, I'd imagine," Robert answered. "I take it that's a no, then. Well, I'll make do." He drew an exaggerated breath, sat down squarely between Darin and Erin, and reached for a bowl. "Twin Hearts, what *is* this?"

Trethar's brow darkened considerably. In the days and weeks to follow, it would become a common sight. "Breakfast."

"I see," Robert said. He tried a smile that stretched his face poorly. "Well, Lady—I thank you for your . . . efforts."

* * *

He never seemed to stop talking. Darin swung a branch out of the side of his face and sucked in breath when its needles scratched his cheek. The ground was damp and soft, but the forest floor held life where the sun managed to squeeze through the high treetops. Here and there, various mushrooms grew beneath low leaves where the earth was most damp. Sara—no, Erin—had shown him what to look for to discern edibility.

The fungus underfoot wasn't edible. He briefly considered picking it anyway and sliding it into Robert's food.

". . . and as I was saying, the Swords are much better trained in the capital, you know."

He longed to escape Robert's endless tirade—he had long since ceased to listen to any of it—but he didn't quite trust Trethar not to do something drastic. Trethar's patience with Robert had worn so thin by their third day of travel that it was nonexistent.

"Boy, are you listening to me?"

"Yes, Robert," Darin said, sighing heavily. It was midday, and they wouldn't stop to rest for at least three hours, so he had no easy escape. But he wondered, as he walked, how Robert had managed to be at exactly the right place and right time. Listening to the man babble had worn away any belief that Darin had in his competence.

If Erin hadn't sworn that she'd seen him in useful action . . . Never mind.

They traveled through the morning rays of stiff, sweeping light; walked while the sun on high managed to catch their skin in its unfaltering light; and marched until the day finally began its retreat. All this they did under forest cover. Erin would not risk the roads.

She foraged, and Trethar surprised them all by being quick and sure with his aid. He was able to set snares almost as well as she, and he had an uncanny knack for finding edible roots and mushrooms. Darin could find berries easily enough—he looked for birds clustered around a particular bush.

To no one's surprise, Robert did not prove useful in the forest. But he did guard their campsite against predators, and at least his eye, when he was on watch, was keen.

On the fifth day, they found a small lake, and happily took turns washing and basking in the sun. Darin was troubled by blackflies and mosquitos—but Robert's fair skin was the more delectable target. He gave up rather quickly, and as usual, rather volubly.

On the sixth day, while Darin scrounged around the forest floor hunting for edible mushrooms, Trethar came to speak.

"Darin," he said quietly.

Darin turned his cheek to white bark and looked up. "Trethar?"

"I think we should speak, while we have time for it." He offered Darin a hand, and Darin took it, standing to his full height.

"About what?"

Firelight crackled suddenly in the palm of Trethar's hand. It danced, a hairsbreadth above the fine-veined older skin, at the whim of its master. Long fingers closed over it, and it vanished; when the hand opened again, a wind left it, calling leaves.

Leaves came in profusion, clustering around the old mage's arms, blending harmoniously with the brown cloth of his sturdy robes. He gestured, short and sharp in the movement; two words left his lips, and the leaves drifted wayward, caught once again by a gravity other than Trethar's.

"Do you understand?" Trethar asked quietly.

Darin could only stare. For the old man's eyes had turned a shade of silver gray that he had seen but twice in his life.

As if aware of the sudden change in Darin's mien, Trethar became perfectly still, perfectly quiet. "Darin?" There was no threat at all in his voice, and no hint of the anger that seemed reserved for Robert alone. Still, Darin fought the surge of panic that closed his throat. Scrambling backward slightly, he reached out for Bethany as she lay strapped across his back.

Initiate. She came.

He's a priest—he's a priest, isn't he?

Her power fled instantly, a green glow of light that was familiar enough to be of comfort and warm enough to dim the chill that had taken him. It went out, circled around the brown-robed mage, and then came back.

Trethar had not moved at all; indeed, he did not seem to see Bethany's light, or Bethany's power.

I do not think he can, she said in her willow's voice. *He does not have the blood.*

You're certain?

As I can be of anything. She paused, waiting for Darin's breath to become regular and steady. *There is a power in him that I do not understand; I feel it, though. It is . . . very strange.*

"Darin, what is wrong?"

"I've—" Darin swallowed. "I've seen that magic before."

Trethar's stillness became the stillness of tension; the single word he spoke carried it all. "Where?"

"In—the high priest of the Greater Cabal. His eyes—they go silver like yours did." It was not all of the answer, but Darin did not mention Lord Darclan.

"The high priest?" Trethar's brows rose up, past the line of his cowl. "Ill news, Darin. When?"

"A week ago, maybe a little more."

Trethar did not move. "That is very, very bad." His face was set in grim, cold lines, and Darin wasn't certain whether the old man was angered or frightened. He didn't ask. "How was it used?"

"He wanted to take my Lady to Malakar. For the—for the ceremonies. He—he attacked our Lord, but we were able to fight free. I—" He swallowed, and fell silent, suddenly unwilling to expose Bethany's presence more than he had already done. "I think he was injured. He might be dead."

"Let us hope, then." Trethar shook his head. "But now, I must talk with you even more urgently. It must be clear that the power I wield is power that *can* be taught to another."

Darin nodded, suddenly unsure of whether or not he wanted to hear the rest.

"I am old, Darin. I will bide with the Lady for as long as I'm able—but I am not the man I once was. In time, the Lady will have to take her fight to the heart of the Empire, if she survives that long. And I will pass from her—but you are young enough to remain.

"I wish you to learn what I have to offer. I wish you"—and he gestured for flame once again—"to do this, and more. You will be my apprentice; my disciple to the brotherhood."

"But—you said there were others. Can't we find them?"

"Yes, in time—but how much time, I can't say. And unless they have taken students, they, too, are older." Trethar stepped forward suddenly, tossing flame aside. He caught Darin's hands, and Bethany fell to the ground, rolling to a stop against the large root of a nearby tree. "If you've the will and the discipline, Darin, you will be a better protector than the most skilled of fighters; you will be fire against the Swords of the Enemy." He looked down at his hands and released Darin. "I'm sorry. Let me leave you to think.

"Give me your answer, if you can, this evening."

Darin nodded; he didn't trust himself to speak.

"And if," Trethar added, with a sudden, wry grin, "Robert lets you get a word in edgewise."

The search for food forgotten, Darin sat with his back against the rough grain of tree bark. Although the summer's colors were splendid in their last burst before autumn change, he saw the world at a distance, in shades of gray. Trethar—already gone half an hour—occupied all of his thoughts; the clearest image before him was not the birds peering through the foliage of the bushes yards away, although he appeared to be observing them. No; he saw fire and wind, caught in large steady hands just beneath silvered, penetrating eyes.

You don't like it, do you? he asked at length, trying to gain a foothold in Bethany's silence.

No, Initiate, I do not.

He waited for her to expound upon her answer; another fifteen minutes passed. *Why?* he said at last.

A human foible, although I am far from human. A glimmer of humor warmed the words, but it was faint and quickly guttered. *I do not understand this power. I have only seen it used twice before, and I do not trust it.*

He could have said the words himself, had he chosen to. Instead, he answered them. *Bethany, if Trethar was an enemy, we would be dead now—or at the very least, captive. Lord Darclan used that power, and he, too, used it in our defense.*

She was silent.

He would never have taught Vellen. I know that. He rose, brushing dirt off the back of his breeches. His small bag was almost empty—and dinner would be called soon. *If I could wield that fire . . .*

What would you do with it?

I'd protect Sara, Erin, I mean. I'd stand beside her in any fight. Even downed as he had been, he had seen the effect of Trethar's explosive magic. The remains of the Sword that had held him still clung to the shirt he had been wearing; no amount of beating it at stream's side could clear the last trace of blood.

And that is all of your concern?

Damn Bethany, anyway, Darin thought irritably. He pulled a small flower out of the dirt and tossed it angrily over his shoulder.

Is that your true motivation, Initiate? she pressed on.

Yes! He opened his mouth in a shout and clamped down on his tongue before the noise filled the clearing, scattering birds. Before he could utter the lie, where any but Bethany might hear it and wonder. *No, then. Are you happy?*

I am satisfied. Go on.

If I had his power, Darin said, as his fingers glanced off another prized mushroom, *I would never fear being a slave again. I could protect myself.*

Her silence held the flavor of thought; deliberation. He had learned to read her silences well, since she offered them so often.

He continued. *I could go back to Marantine—and maybe even to Dagothrin. I might be able to help our people there. I could be the patriarch of Culverne, truly.*

The patriarchs of Culverne—or the matriarchs, for that matter, have never wielded a power other than mine.

And until the city fell, they didn't need to, he answered sharply. *I could help them—I could help myself—I could help Sara.*

Her words drew to a sharp, fine point. *You could be a hero?*

And to that, with the sudden rush of memories the words brought, Darin had nothing to say.

"Where have you been, boy?" Robert asked, as Darin made his way to the campsite. His sleeves—laced, by god, at the cuffs—were rolled halfway up his forearms; it was clear that he had been put to some sort of work, and equally clear that he was disgruntled about it.

"Gathering food," Darin answered quietly.

"Well, next time, I may accompany you. Around here it's been ice and fire." He threw a baleful glance over his velvet—velvet!—covered shoulder. Beyond him, both Erin and Trethar were working in silence.

"I don't think you'd like it much," Darin offered, as he side-stepped the small man. "I spend an awful lot of time close to the ground."

"Well, it couldn't be worse than spending too much close to

those two. The Lady's lovely, Darin—but she's a bit chilly. And the old man?'' Robert snorted in disgust.

"She's had a difficult time," Darin replied defensively, the grip around the mushroom bag growing tense. Robert was enough to try the patience of a saint. He started to walk forward, stopped, and turned to face Robert fully. "Where did you come from, anyway?"

"Oh, I see." Robert drew himself up to his full height, which wasn't much; his chest came out in an unnatural puff, which made him look even more ridiculous. "It's inquisition time."

Darin knew then exactly why his Lady had been chilly. "Look, they're perfectly reasonable questions. You come out of nowhere, in the middle of a forest, just to help save our lives. Wouldn't you want answers if you were us?"

"I'd accept a civil demur, that's for certain."

Why, Darin thought, as he inhaled loudly, did he find that difficult to believe? "Robert—"

"The old man came out of the woods in just the same way, but I don't see him under the line of fire." The pronounced pout annoyed even Darin.

"The 'old man,' as you call him, had an explanation that was halfway reasonable." He knew his voice was beginning to rise, and he forced the last few words down to a conversational level.

"The old man was wielding Bright Heart alone knows what kind of magery! You call his little story *reasonable*?"

"At least he came up with a story—it's more than you've done!"

"I also happened by to help in a rather dangerous fight, if you hadn't noticed—doesn't that deserve something?" Robert's hands hit his hips, and his shirt sleeves flopped downward. "It's—"

"Why don't you just tell us why in the hells you were there?"

"Darin?"

They both spun around at the quiet word. Erin stood two feet away, one hand outstretched.

"Yes?"

"Dinner?"

He started guiltily, then handed her his less-than-full bag. For a moment, his cheeks reddened, and a ghost of a child's embarrassment caused his shoulders to hunch down. He had reacted thus when the Grandmother had caught him arguing in the cloisters with his friends—which was often.

Robert sniffed and began to roll up his sleeves again. "Is there anything else I should wash, Lady?" he said stiffly.

"No thank you, Robert," she replied quietly.

The man flounced off—there was no other word to describe his leave-taking—and she shook her head shortly, a tight smile across her lips.

"Sara?"

She flinched quietly and looked out of slightly bruised eyes. "Darin—please, try to remember not to call me that."

He hung his head. "Erin. I'm sorry; it's hard to remember. Sara's what he—"

"I know. But it isn't my name. What did you want to tell me?"

"You're the Grandmother of Elliath now, you know that?"

She started in surprise, and then the tight smile melted into a real, rueful one. "Was I that awful just now?"

He smiled, too. "Not awful. Robert's . . . difficult." Leaning forward, he lowered his voice to a whisper. "Do you think he's an enemy?"

"Robert?" She said the name slowly, then shook her head. "No. I don't know why. I trust him to want to help us; I don't trust him to be of help. And I think I only want his story because he won't give it. Childish, isn't it?"

"No—if we don't know why he was there, we don't know whether or not we can trust him."

"Oh, I don't know about that," she said, as she turned back to the small fire, "there's nothing about him that seems dangerous to me—and I've met a lot of enemies, declared or otherwise, in my life."

"I don't like priests," Robert said quietly, after dinner had been finally set aside. It was not yet dark, but the air was already chilly; autumn was coming too quickly to the lands, and they would be traveling north and west. None of them were prepared for the harshness of winter travel.

Trethar grimaced. "None of us do."

"Look, old man—do you want the story, or no?" Suddenly, Robert had the unwavering attention of all three of his traveling companions. He hardly preened at all.

"Go on," Erin said softly, and almost gently.

"I'm used to a better life than this," he said, encompassing the clearing with an airy wave of the hand. "I had everything, as did my family."

Darin bridled at the disdain in the words and tried not to feel angry at the implied insult they carried. He felt Bethany's quiet approbation for his attempt and settled back to sitting. Trethar's brow was a single, pale line, but Erin did not seem moved at all to anger.

"We lost it to Lord Vellen of House Damion." Gone was the flamboyance of tone that would have made a drama of Robert's anger. Even his usual frenetic gestures were lost to the hypnotic gaze of the fire and the coming darkness. "We were all trained," he continued, his voice low, "in many arts. I'm not sure the lady would approve at all, but there you have it." He raised his head and grinned briefly at Erin, but the smile dimmed before it had started.

"Lord Vellen came here, with such a small party it was obvious he traveled in secrecy and haste." He reached back and cupped his neck in his fingers; slowly he began to massage the tension out of it. "I followed.

"I've done all I can to harry the Karnar in the years since my family's downfall. This seemed to be another opportunity." His fingers stopped their motion and fell away as he raised his neck. It was to Erin he spoke, not to Darin or Trethar. "I'd kill him slowly, given the opportunity."

No one hearing those words could doubt their truth. "But I found little information, either here or in the village, and I decided to wait until he left the castle.

"I saw you leave, and you, Darin. I saw the altercation with the Swords." His eyes narrowed in the thinness of his face. "And I saw how quickly you killed them. You're trained to it, aren't you?"

Erin shrugged. "Yes."

"Given the choice of following you, or waiting for Lord Vellen, I chose to wait. Until the young priest came, with many, many more of his Swords. They did something, I'm not sure what, and then began to track you.

"This time, given the choice of waiting or following, I chose to follow. And there you have it; I was ready when you arrived—

from the tree-side." There was a question in his voice. Erin did not choose to answer it. Instead, she asked one of her own. "What was your house?"

Bitterly, he smiled. "It is dead now, Lady. I would rather leave it nameless."

"And if we would rather hear the name?" Trethar suddenly said.

"I would consider it quite rude, as I have stated my preference." Robert gazed back at the mage with a touch of haughty defiance.

"We won't ask further, then," Erin said, raising a hand to forestall Trethar. "But, Robert—thank you for telling us this."

His shoulders relaxed, and his face took on the jaunty, haughty mask of his daytime self. Erin sat back, stealing a glance at him out of the corner of her eyes. Although he was odd, she almost believed him. Almost.

Only when Erin and Robert had retreated for the evening did Darin dare to speak. By mutual consent, silent at that, he and Trethar had chosen to keep their vigil by the dying fire. Darin squinted to bring the lines of the mage into sharper relief; saw that the dark brown of his robes looked like draped shadow in the darkness. He had not spoken with Bethany since that afternoon, but as always she was with him, riding his thoughts like a passenger that can give guidance, but not orders, to its carriage.

Trethar spoke first. "Have you given thought to my offer?"

Darin nodded.

"And what is your answer, young Darin?"

"I have to know more," Darin said quietly. "I have to know how it works. There are only—were only—two magics, and they both needed blood. I can't study with you if—if the source of your power is—is wrong."

"Wrong?" Trethar smiled suddenly, his teeth a pale glint. "The source of my power knows no right, no wrong. Is a sword ethical? Is a bow evil?" He inclined his head slightly, but did not move at all.

My move, Darin thought. "No."

"That's how it is with my mage-craft. And how it will be with you. There are no gods to dictate the use of the craft; we choose it. The high priest elects to use it in a way that glorifies his own power; you might choose to use it to strengthen your cause. It has no mind for *right* or *wrong*."

"But the Enemy's priest uses it," Darin said, echoing the heart of Bethany's concern.

Trethar snorted. "And their Swords use swords. What of it? You don't disavow the use of steel, do you?" His voice conveyed movement, but he sat absolutely still, his eyes trained on Darin as a crossbow might be in the hands of a wary guard.

"No."

"Darin, I do not promise the use of this magic will be easy; the power has its own voice. You'll learn this. But you have to trust me." He raised one hand slowly and held it, level with his eyes, palm toward Darin. Fire, so often called by the mage to make a point, limned his fingers with a gentle glow. "It wants to burn, you see," he said conversationally. "And I exert will to refuse it. This, you'll also learn."

Do you trust this man? Bethany asked quietly.

I—I think so. "Why do I have to trust you?"

"Because, Darin, in order to teach you in the quickest and most efficient way, I must also touch your mind."

"W-What?"

"There are pathways the mind must travel to reach the source of my power. We don't have years, Darin, but months, I think, before your lady needs all that you can give her. I can help you learn quickly, judging by the shape of your summoning." Now he rose, unfolding slowly. "I want very much to help you learn this, but trust cannot be forced; if you don't choose to give it, I can't help. Will you learn?" He held out a hand; it was the one that wore the glove of flame.

Darin heard the muted whisper of Bethany's voice; she urged caution; she feared the unknown. But she gave advice; as she had promised, she made no attempt to force his decision. After all, neither of them understood this strange, new magic, and they both saw a possibility in it. He took a breath, dragged air across his dry throat, and spoke. Until the word left his mouth, he himself wasn't sure what it would be. "Y-Yes."

"Then take my hand."

"It's burning!"

"Do you trust me, Darin?"

Darin nodded. And then he stared at the hand, knowing it suddenly for a test of resolve. Swallowing, he reached out; his hand shook. Fire had touched him once before, and he bore the brand of Damion because of it.

But worse than fire had happened under the house of that brand. He could stand fire, now. Closing his eyes, he reached out and suddenly clamped his fingers around Trethar's hand. It was cool and dry to the touch. Darin opened his eyes gingerly and saw that the fire still burned—but it was a halo that surrounded and warmed their locked hands. After a few seconds, Darin looked up to meet the eyes of the brown-robed mage.

"Very good," Trethar said quietly. "You've courage, Darin. Now, sleep. Tomorrow is the first day of your apprenticeship."

At midnight, the moon a slim white face above the trees, only three of the tents were occupied. The occupant of the fourth, dressed in black, moved silently around the camp site. He carried no light and stopped often, but his movements were catlike in their grace and surety. He seemed small, almost slight, and he never stood long enough in one place to cast the moon's shadow wide.

He found the tent he sought in the darkness and hesitated a moment at its side; his breath, as everything else about him, was silent. He bowed his head, and then quietly drew the flaps of Darin's tent open.

Darin didn't stir, although there was a risk of it, as Robert reached over his sleeping body. His hand hesitated; his uncertainty was shown by his sudden stillness. Doubt? Too much of it.

With a decisive movement, Robert reached out and grabbed the staff of Culverne. His grip, though firm, was gentle as he levered it quietly away from Darin's side.

The moon was quarter-cut, and in its slender light, he raised the staff and ran his fingers down its sides, staring at it, eyes narrowed in question. Minutes passed in his silence; he dropped the staff, point to ground, and let it rest against his shoulder. He let it carry his weight for a simple step or two, and then lifted it again, holding it inches away from his eyes.

Then, when his inspection was done, he crept back to Darin's tent, and once again lifted the flaps, causing no more sound than a passing breeze might. He laid the staff down, once again, at Darin's side, then let a sliver of light touch Darin's legs.

A flash of teeth, too painful to be a smile, cut the shadows of his face for a moment. Then he stepped aside and left, with no one the wiser about his visit. No one but Bethany, whose voice he would not have heard, even had it been raised.

And Erin slept in the safety of her tent—but walked and dreamed in the darkness that the world didn't touch. The lands moved about her, dissonant with pain that was not her own; she crossed the bridge it made, but fought it in sorrow and anger both.

chapter
six

Lord Vellen of Damion, heir to the Damion title, leader of the Greater Cabal, could not call or touch the power of his heritage; it came weakly and caused pain before it could be shaped and used. He could not preside over ceremonies given for the nobility and had to hand that duty, in trust, to Benataan Lord Torvallen, the second of the Karnari—his rival for the seat of the Empire's power. It had not gone unnoticed or unmarked, and House Damion's fortunes and alliances had grown cool and somewhat shaky.

He could now sit for hours at a stretch, but any walking tired him quickly—and he continued to keep his presence confined to his rooms. The lack of public appearances hurt his power base, but any display of weakness would harm it immeasurably. He bore his confinement with poor grace.

Left alone, he had time to dwell upon the First Servant and the cursed slave that had slipped, at the Lord of the Empire's behest, through his fingers. He should have killed the boy when he'd had the chance and taken the consequences that might have resulted; surely they could not have been worse than this. Yet how could he have known that the boy was of Line Culverne? How could he have known that the First Servant of the Dark Heart would have willingly harbored such a one?

The ringing of the inner bell in his sparse, plain sitting room pulled him from his moody reverie. He sat up in bed and gave the quiet command to enter. A slave shuffled in and dropped gracefully to both knees; he settled his forehead against the deceptively plain design of an ancient rug.

"Lord," the slave said quietly, "Erliss of Mordechai requests an audience."

Vellen exhaled slowly. News; news at last. "Very good. Send a valet and keep Erliss waiting for the half hour. I will see him in my study."

"Will you require refreshments?"

"No."

He knew, of course, the moment he set eyes upon his cousin, that his timing was poor—had he the choice or the chance, he would have retreated immediately to wait for a better time. As it was, all choice had been removed as he met the eyes of Lord Vellen of Damion.

Erliss fell immediately to the posture of supplicant; one knee to ground and forehead to knee. His hands fell to either side of his stiff body as he strove to control his trembling. The last thing he needed now was an overt display of fear.

"Lord," he said steadily, with no reference at all to their kinship. It would have been too great a presumption at the moment, and he had survived by being just cautious enough to recognize a near death when it was present. "Please forgive your servant for interrupting your repose."

"Erliss," Lord Vellen said, in a congenial tone of voice that fooled neither. "I gave you leave to report any news of import at the moment of your arrival in the capital. Rise." Vellen knew, by Erliss' composure, that the news would not be to his liking. But he also knew, as he glanced briefly down at the formal red and black of the Karnar, that he needed Erliss for the moment; his young cousin had ambition enough to make him controllable and as loyal a servitor as one might find in the priesthood. He also had mobility. Of the two, Vellen valued the mobility more highly.

Erliss lifted only his head and met his cousin's pale eyes with his dark ones.

"What do you have to report?"

Not even the slightest of hesitations marred Erliss' reply. He watched his cousin's face like a sparrow watching the hawk's passage. "We saw the signs of battle the evening after your arrival at the castle." Lord Vellen stiffened; Erliss swallowed.

"What signs?"

"The red and white fires in the air; I have never seen either brighter.'' He searched Vellen's face for some sign of displeasure before continuing. "We cannot ascertain what occurred there, Lord—and we did not question." A lie that was expedient; better to say that they had no answers. Erliss disliked to look unintelligent. "What we do know is this: one young woman and her slave left the castle grounds shortly after the battle."

"And?" Pale blue eyes narrowed; the lowering of lids was the only movement that Vellen made.

"We attempted to stop her. Three of our Swords were dead in minutes."

If he expected any sign of surprise, Erliss was to be disappointed. Vellen nodded quietly to himself and raised his fingers, in a steeple, to his chin. "And this slave?"

"The slave?" Erliss froze for a moment, unsure of how to answer the question. Silence reigned before he rose, clumsily, to retrieve the documents that he had carefully composed about the incident. He ruffled through the parchment. "Here. A youth; not tall, but not yet finished growing. Pale hair, pale eyes and complexion. Slight and awkward looking. Slave's clothing; brown tunic—"

Vellen raised a hand. "Enough. Continue with your report."

Erliss did so. He described Tarantas' role in the search for—and discovery of—the woman, and then described, in hazy detail at best, the events that followed.

"Stop. The short man in black. Describe him."

Erliss was no memory-walker to see into and clearly recall the past, but he did what he could. "Reddish hair; dark clothing. Fully grown; younger than you, perhaps, but not by much. Thin face. He moved quickly; he used odd weapons, perhaps thrown daggers."

"Did he name himself?"

"No, Lord."

"And this—this fire, this explosion. Describe it."

Erliss tried, and failed utterly. But he gave enough information for Vellen's satisfaction. "You've told no one about this, of course."

Erliss shook his head.

"Good." He rose from his chair and turned to face the curtained window. "This is a delicate matter, Erliss. I'm sure you understand why. But I believe it can be resolved to my satisfaction—and to our mutual benefit. How long have you studied in the priesthood?''

''Seven years, Lord.''

''A long time, then. I have heard good said of your abilities with blood-power.''

Erliss said nothing, but he lowered his head to hide the sudden flush of pleasure that lined his cheeks.

''There will be . . . a new opening in the Greater Cabal in a month, perhaps less. Should you serve me well, Erliss, that seat will be yours.''

''Lord.''

''But in order to take that seat, you will have to learn the last of the rites. These are not taught to any but the Karnar, and you will not speak of them to anyone—is that clear?'' He called fire suddenly, and it came—an orange cloak that guilded his back without burning him. The fire shivered in the air a moment, and then, the warning made clear, it died. ''I will teach you how to call up the power of God and use it in the Church's behest. It is a gesture of faith in you, Erliss. A gesture of my intent.''

''And how must I serve, Lord?'' Erliss asked, eager and youthful in his impatience.

''You must find and capture—or kill, if capture is impossible—the enemies of the Church. The boy, the woman, and their companions.''

Erliss nodded, and Vellen studied his face in the silence, wondering if he had ever been so transparent and so easily manipulated.

Benataan Lord Torvallen was in a contemplative mood, which was a common occurrence. That it was also a pleasant mood was more rare, but still not unheard of. However, his hands were occupied with a philter of a vintage that was dear enough to be called for only on special occasions.

The occasion was special enough.

He was not a man who disdained finery or elegance to prove some misguided notion of strength or discipline, and his study, with its multiple rooms, each lavishly detailed with only the finest of paintings and small sculptures that the Empire could produce, was testament to his preferences. He dressed well; his shirt was of deep, dark purple, and his jacket, folded carefully over the divan, was turquoise velvet, with a border of gold thread and black lace.

He held, in perfectly manicured hands, two letters: the cause for his celebration. Lord Vellen—momentary leader of the Greater Cabal—had been absent for mere weeks, but his leaving had been perfectly timed; perfectly opportune. The assassination of Corval and Stillonius had left two seats in the Greater Cabal—two seats that had been filled by Lord Morden of Farenel and Lord Sorval of Kintassus.

In the two weeks of privacy, with great care to avoid Vellen's accursed allies and ever-present spies, Lord Torvallen had managed to link the fortunes of these two men with his own goals and rise to power. He considered the makeup of the Greater Cabal with something approaching sublime joy; the seat had never been so closely contested in his tenure.

Of course, the ideal would be Lord Vellen's death—but that was unlikely; and besides, how would he then usher in a new regime? It was the custom of the high seat to give over to God the Karnar that had once been his most powerful mortal agent— and Lord Torvallen briefly relished the thought of Vellen upon the high altar.

Ah, what a grand dream. The fact that it was no longer completely out of reach made it more intense, more intoxicating. Smiling, he ran his fingers through the dark streaked hair that was the Torvallen trademark. His signet ring glittered in the light as he brought his hands to rest, folded neatly, across his chest.

He had Wintare, he had Abranthraxus—and in a very tight game, he had Urturas. Valens—the wily Lord Valens—was open, as always, to question. But he was close now; perhaps another death to tilt the balance, and he would challenge Vellen openly for the seat.

At Erin's behest, they avoided the road entirely as they made their way through Mordantari. They stopped seldom and foraged heavily where they could—but the autumn shades had already fallen like a curtain that would only be lifted by winter. Nights grew chilly, and even the mornings were just this side of frosty.

They lost the entirety of a morning studying the map that Erin had been left by the Lady of Elliath; it had taken more than a week for her to finally pull it out of her pack and accept it as the gift that it was.

"It's old," Trethar said softly, "and I've never seen such parchment in my life." He reached out, and his fingers hovered over the details writ there by an impossibly fine pen. "But it doesn't reflect the Empire, Lady."

"It was made before the Empire existed," she answered quietly. She would not say more, not even when pressed—although only Robert did so.

"I need your help; we need a map that's as detailed as any of us can make it. This," she said, pointing to the northwestern corner of the map, "must be Culverne holdings."

"Marantine," Darin said softly.

"Marantine?" She looked up and met his eyes just before he closed them.

"The name of the kingdom." His grip on Bethany was tight enough to whiten his knuckles. "Are we really going there?"

"Well," Robert answered, before Erin could, "I don't see that we have much choice—where else in the Empire would you suggest? That's at least a new addition—why, I think they even have a resistance of sorts."

"Yes," Erin said, as if Robert had not replied. "Do you know its boundaries?"

"The former ones, you mean?" Robert said again, although the question had clearly been asked of Darin.

"No," she said coldly, turning to face him, "I mean Marantine's boundaries."

"Oh," he answered. It was as close to quiet as he got, and it was bound not to last. "Well, then, in case you hadn't realized, there was a bit of battle there. It's called Illan now, by the Church elite."

"I don't care what the Church calls it." The words came from between teeth clenched so tight it seemed air wouldn't breech them. "Robert, you can help with the drawing of the map—I don't think it needs scaling—or you can go and forage. Now."

He took one look at her face and bent himself to the task of mapping. It came as a great surprise to all of his companions when he proved to be the most useful. The major roads he seemed to know by heart, and even the minor ones that surrounded any of the provincial capitals were ones with which he was familiar.

"But you know, Lady," he said, when his knowledge had mollified her annoyance, "it's going to be a very long walk. Horses—"

"Are out of the question. We can't chance the roads here; they'll be looking for us."

Erin did not feel the cold, and neither did Trethar, the mage of the brotherhood; each had magics to protect them from the worst of the evening's chill. But Darin and Robert were not quite so lucky, and Erin saw this with growing concern. She tried to teach Darin the use of his blood-magic, but it was not a completely easy task, and he was also often called upon by Trethar. He learned the compass spell, but nothing more complicated.

Robert and Darin took to wrapping sleeping blankets around their shoulders in the early morning; the afternoons were warmer, but that would change soon. Food became more difficult to find, and travel slowed considerably as snares were set and watched.

During these days, Darin took his lessons.

"It is not a matter of blood or instinct," Trethar said, as he strode the ground in a circle, his arms clasped tight behind his back. "It is a matter of two things: the key to the gates and the will to control what will come of opening them."

Darin nodded intently; he sat in front of a magical fire, created and held by the mage. This fire was special; it burned nothing, casting no plumes of smoke or wood particles. It was small, but very hot, and when a chill wind gusted by, the flames didn't waver at all.

"Are you listening, Darin?"

"Yes, sir." He brought his head up, tearing his eyes away from the fascination the fire held.

Trethar raised an eyebrow, but did not make his skepticism known with words. "Good. This fire—I call it and it comes. I am its gate; I am its master. When I'm finished with it, it will return." He frowned. "You show a lack of concentration, apprentice."

Darin reddened.

"We do not have the time for it." Two steps brought him to

Darin's side. His eyes grew silver; they reflected firelight and day in an eerie semblance of a Servant's eyes. Darin pulled back and brought his arms up in front of his face as Trethar reached out. The mage stopped at once.

"Darin," he said quietly, "have you reconsidered?"

The voice brought him back. He shook himself—easy, given the chill—and squared his shoulders. "No."

"Then sit still, and sit straight." Trethar stood behind him. "I will be with you; I'll be your guide." So saying, he placed both of his hands on Darin's shoulders.

Darin stiffened as he felt a tingle cut across the base of his spine and bury itself in his neck. He started, and Trethar's fingers relaxed. "I'll stop, if you wish it."

"What is it? What are you doing?"

"I told you," the mage answered gently, kneading the knots of tension out of Darin's shoulders. "I must use my power to study the form and shape of your thought. I will be as much inside your mind as you are."

"Can you—can you hear what I'm thinking?"

"If you think it at me, yes. Only then; my spell watches nothing but the shape of your will, the path to your gate." He murmured a word, a foreign syllable.

Fire covered Darin's chest like a breastplate. It warmed without burning, a reminder of a previous evening, a previous choice. Slowly, Darin relaxed. "Yes," he said quietly.

This time, he did not resist the magic that penetrated his skin and sank down like a stone in water. He relaxed completely and gave his life, and its responsibilities, to the teachings of the mage. Calm and at peace, he listened to the resonant cadences of Trethar's voice.

"Many things were created with the birth of the world; new things, unknown. White-fire and red-fire are only for the light and the dark—but for the gray, there is the fire that burns flesh: tonight we will begin to seek it.

"Look at my fire, Darin. See its shape; hear its voice. Concentrate on it; see nothing else."

Darin did as he was told, or at least he tried. But in the efforts he made, he was sharply constrained; Trethar corrected him even when there was nothing, in Darin's opinion, to correct.

"You don't have an opinion," the brown-robed mage said severely. "You have nothing but the fire."

When the evening call for dinner finally came, Darin was no closer to fire than he had been before he had accepted Trethar's tutelage—yet the mage seemed pleased, or rather, as pleased as he ever got. And Darin had the sharpest headache of his life.

It was Robert with whom Erin argued.

Trethar, for all of his knowledge and testy mannerisms, accepted her word and her direction as if he were born to a higher command; Darin trusted her to know what she was doing. Only Robert, with his irritating flamboyance and self-aggrandizement, ever voiced a contrary thought. Unfortunately, he always voiced these loudly and at a length greater than Erin was used to.

"We cannot continue to travel in the heart of the forest," he said, jabbing at the map laid down over canvas. "We can barely feed ourselves now—we'll starve or freeze before winter has a chance to take hold."

"We aren't in lands known for heavy winter," she replied, for perhaps the tenth time.

"They're certainly heavy enough. We need to find an inn, a place to stay. We need to gain the road."

Erin folded her arms, and her lips thinned. "Why?"

"In case it had escaped your notice, Lady"—his voice was heavy with sarcasm; this was about as subtle as she was certain he knew how to be—"Darin and I are cold."

"Robert—" She bit her lip suddenly. "Yes. I've noticed." The evening carried a chill wind; she could feel it nip at her skin, although her Light kept it at bay. She sat down heavily and looked at the map as if it accused her. "We can't take the road for long; I would prefer that we not take it at all. Darin and I will be noticed."

"Why do they want you, anyway? What have you done?"

She stared at him, her silence the only answer she was willing to give. Secretly, she hoped that he would become disgusted and take his leave—but Erin had never been good with secrets, and her desire was open in the lines of her mouth and the narrowed shape of her eyes.

"Well, never mind. I suppose it doesn't matter. You've said that we're not to worry about food?"

She glanced at her full pack, and her stomach took knots as she thought of the Lady's last gift. But she had trained with the army, and in desperate situations, she was willing to use whatever she could to survive. A very dear price had been paid for it, after all. "Yes. I have food."

He sighed dramatically, and his chest jutted out. It only emphasized his lack of height. "Will you allow us to follow this route? We can come to road here"—he pointed—"and then stay roughly parallel to it. Here"—his finger traced the vellum gently—"is a village of moderate size. You and Darin are visible, yes; I can be less obvious. Let me take leave of you. I know the village well. I can buy what we need, and we can return to the forested land. Here," he continued, "is the edge of the Torvallen River. If we veer, we'll reach a bridge crossing; if we continue in this direction, we'll have to ferry."

"The Torvallen?" she whispered. "Is that what they call it now?"

"After a great imperial house." He looked up and met her eyes; for a second his expression mirrored hers—hard and cold. Then, it was gone—his face was empty of anger or any feeling of substance. "You obviously won't do it for my sake"—his lips turned down in the pout she had come to hate most—"but won't you have some consideration for the poor, freezing boy?"

If she could have taught Darin the use of his blood-magic, she might have said no. As it was, she began to curl the map into a neat cylinder.

"Lady?"

"We parallel the road—we don't travel it." She slid the map into its container. "Is that clear?"

"Oh indeed, indeed," he said, bowing low. "I'm most grateful for your consideration, Lady—I know that it's a most difficult—"

"Good."

"Ah, well, ah . . ." But she had already walked away.

Robert was good to his word. When they found the road, and properly gauged its direction, they retreated together to a spot only a mile in; Robert marked the ground carefully and quite unsubtly. Erin changed his markers—but resisted the temptation that urged her not to inform him of the fact.

If only she felt that he couldn't be trusted—then, she would leave him at once, taking great pains to conceal her presence. But although she disliked his proprietary, spoiled airs, she knew he meant no harm—and though she hated to admit it, his help with the map would probably prove invaluable. He had saved her life, and Darin's, as if they fought a mutual war; surely she could accept a few . . . character quirks? She set snares, and she foraged as they waited upon Robert's return.

But she did so alone, beneath the open skies and the brilliant, dying leaves. Darin and Trethar studied. This disturbed her, but distantly, coolly; she felt almost removed from Trethar's magic. It was a strange magic, to be sure—but if Darin learned this skill, his lack of weapon-play wouldn't make him so easy a target, so vulnerable a liability.

Liability? She shivered, suddenly, as she worked. She wondered where such a dispassionate thought had come from. And she wondered if, when night fell at last, she would sleep in peace and comfort.

Robert returned in two days, bearing food and clothing appropriate to the night's growing chill. Although he knew that Erin and Trethar didn't suffer much by the weather, he had even provisioned them reasonably well.

"If we're ever spotted, or if, as I do suspect," he explained, as he handed Erin her cloak, "we have to take to the road more abruptly than you'd like, you'll both stand out for a mile dressed the way you are. It's *cold*. People freeze. Normal people, that is."

She looked at the cape; it was heavy and seemed sturdy and finely made. Too finely. "Robert—where did you get these?"

But Robert wasn't listening; he'd saved the most magnificent piece of clothing for last. It was a greatcoat of heavy wool, with gold-trimmed edges and leathered cuffs as grand as any Erin had seen before. "And this"—Robert beamed brightly—"is mine."

Speechless, Erin watched him don the coat. He'd taken boots and hats and long wrappers as well—but the coat made those seem insignificant.

"You didn't buy these," she whispered, afraid of what she would say if she found her full voice.

"Ah, well, uh—what makes you ask that?"

"You idiot!" She stalked across the ground and grabbed his coat by its lovely collars. "You—you stole these from a noble house!"

"Not a noble house," he said quickly, attempting to disentangle himself. "A priest's manor."

"You are *never* going anywhere without supervision again. Never!" And she dropped his collars. He stumbled back, righted himself, and stared woefully at Darin. "Why on earth is she so angry?"

Darin only shook his head.

"Then I don't suppose now would be a good time to give her the necklace I, ah, found for her?"

"A very good time," Trethar said, with a completely reposed face. "I'm sure it would be quite cheering."

Not even Robert was that witless.

They continued on, moving to the west and the north as the days grew both shorter and colder. The pace that Erin set was a harsh one, but the threat of discovery by the Enemy's forces made it necessary; none complained but Robert, and after a while, he blended in with the background noises of breathing and walking and wind through the settling trees.

Every few days they would pause while Erin set her snares in a radius from the campsite she had chosen; during those days, Darin would study with Trethar, and Erin, teeth clenched and fingers curled in ever-tightening fists, would learn her history of this world made new at Robert's side.

She discovered the exact date of the fall of Elliath—the first of the seven lines to be conquered and destroyed. That was the hardest lesson, but she accepted it in silence made heavy by the nightmare of sleep. The fall of the remaining six lines seemed thankfully more removed; they became names and dates and faceless dead—as all history had been when she had struggled to learn it in the halls of Elliath.

She found out how the Church operated—that had changed. Now, the Empire was de facto ruled by the Greater Cabal; thirteen high priests who held the rank and title of Karnar. Each province was in turn overseen by a Lesser Cabal, composed of priests, and headed by a high priest; it, too, was composed of thirteen, for the purpose of determining a balance of power in favor of one faction. She also heard a little of the mysterious Lord of the Empire; the shadows and mystery that surrounded his name made her wince.

I could tell you more, she thought, as Robert spoke in his even, long-winded way, but she forbore; it served no purpose to expose herself further to this whimsical, infuriating thief.

When at last he turned to the Lady of Mercy, she was so immune to the strength of words that she barely heard him at all. The shadows of night were calling, and she went because she had little choice but to answer.

There was no sign of the fugitives on the road in Mordantari. There had been no sign at all at the border crossings to either Landsfall or Cordenant, and no caravans of any note had passed their checkpoints either.

Although he concealed it well, Erliss was a very worried man. He looked up from his desk as the last of his Swords finished his long report, and nodded grimly in dismissal. The Sword left with unseemly haste, and Erliss was alone.

Nights had become the dominion of lessons he would and did—kill for, but the days demanded his attention; lack of sleep circled his eyes in bleary gray-toned pink. He had earned his cousin's favor, but he knew well that it was due to necessity—and it could turn at any failure into something less pleasant to consider.

But if he was successful, Lord Vellen had hinted that he might teach Erliss the use of his other magic. Success was something that Erliss wanted very badly.

He glared at the map, with its various negative marks. How could a woman with a sword—a remarkable sight in the Empire—vanish without a trace? And why did it have to be this particular woman?

The need for secrecy made it all the more difficult. Erliss was expressly forbidden to call up either a good-sized contingent of the house guard—for fear that spies would note it, and report it to another house—or the Church Swords, for the same reason. He had few men, and those, dispersed, could not possibly cast a net wide enough.

"Vellen," he said aloud, grinding his teeth, "you ask too much." But that was the privilege of Lord Vellen; the privilege of Erliss was only to serve. He rose and doused the flame of the lamp. The map fell into shadow.

But before he could make ready to depart, one more knock disturbed the room's silence. Frowning, he walked to the door; he expected no callers.

Tantaer, Sword life-sworn to Vellen, stood in the hall. He was muddied and obviously well-traveled; his face was wreathed by lines of exhaustion. In the poor light, the scars from an old political war faded into shadow; his face looked lean but not gaunt, and much younger than its years.

"Tantaer," Erliss said, in some surprise. "I didn't expect you until tomorrow. No, two days hence."

Tantaer nodded. "Forgive me for disturbing you, Lord. I had news which I felt warranted the interruption."

"Come in." Erliss returned once again to the darkened map. With a frown, he lit the oil lamp. "What news?"

"It may be nothing," Tantaer said, although it was obvious that he did not believe it, "but that is for you to judge. There are two roads into Senatare from Landsfall; along the northern route, Priest Kovassen holds the territory."

"Kovassen? I don't know him."

"He is new to the Lesser Cabal there. Young, possibly destined for a better position." Tantaer let his commentary lapse. "Six days ago, in Surres, the town closest to the Landsfall border, a number of items were stolen. We would never have known of them—but two of those items came from the priest's manor."

"What was stolen?"

"Winter wear, Lord. Food, supplies that would indicate travel in the cold. Also, a necklace that belonged to the priest's lady; hard to miss, he says, as it's heavy gold and large rubies."

"And this is unusual?" It was a perfunctory question; Erliss already knew the answer.

"There were no new arrivals in town; the inns don't see much business this close to the edge of storms."

"Six days, you say?"

"Sir." Tantaer nodded. "I've taken the liberty of offering our aid in patrolling the northern road; I left two men behind. The priest is irate enough to consider only the damage done to his pride. We are safe there."

"Thank you, Tantaer. Dismissed."

When the Sword had gone, Erliss allowed his relief to show. He carefully marked his map with the first sure sighting, and then stared at the lines. He knew where they had been, and when—he would never forget their battle—and he now knew, roughly, the distance they had traveled. They were not moving quickly; they almost certainly weren't traveling by road.

Again he cursed the restrictions placed upon his search, but he did so with less venom. For it was clear, from the line drawn between Mordantari and the province of Senatare, which direction the woman traveled in.

She was heading to Illan—the province that had once been guarded by the last of the seven lines to fall.

As the knowledge sank roots and grew firm, his frustration eased. They would find her, and no word would reach the Greater Cabal that Lord Vellen of Damion had failed in his promised conquest of the end of the lines. If he wondered how she had arrived in Mordantari, he quickly put the thought aside; Lord Vellen, holder of the high seat, could deal with the mythical Lord of the Empire should trouble arise.

The first of the snows came. Light and powdery, it rested against bare branch and forest floor in an even shroud of white. The winter wear that Robert had somehow managed to procure—no one, not even Darin, cared to ask how—served them well, for the time being.

But setting snares in heavy winter had not been among the skills that Erin had learned; she had stayed on the southern front for most of her life, and although cold was a factor, it had never been accompanied by snow.

Darin seemed almost comfortable with the weather, although it affected him; his shoulders, as he walked, were drawn in so tightly they shook. She asked him, once, why he didn't call upon Bethany's power to ease the chill. He answered that Bethany's power might be needed for more important battles than simple winter. His voice had cracked in the saying; he was growing into the title of Patriarch. She didn't ask him again.

The food that the Lady of Elliath had provided was—as all that she touched or made had been—of a nature that defied understanding. Trethar found it most curious, and with Erin's reluctant permission, set about studying it in the evenings as his time permitted. His time, of course, coincided with meal times, but Erin was privately relieved when he took one of these oddly hued nuts and left the campfires; it meant that Robert and he were separated, and therefore mostly silent.

But no matter how hard he might study, Trethar did not find answers to the mystery of the Lady's gift; it remained the Lady's gift. When eaten, even in the smallest of quantities, it satisfied. It looked odd to sit around a fire and crack the smooth perfect shells of small golden nuts, with no other sustenance in sight. But the meat and heart of the Lady's gift was a blessing that no one questioned after the first meal. If it was bitter to Erin's taste, she said nothing and made no complaint.

After the fourth snowfall, it was clear that they could no longer travel through forested lands. The imperial roads were, if not clear, still traversable and easy to follow. They were also dangerous, and Erin was reluctant to emerge onto any path on which they might meet people. But they covered less distance daily, and the food supply was dwindling. Money—the coin of the realm, with its stamped swords crossing the relief of a crown—they had in some supply. But it had been Gervin's gift, and one Erin had thought not to use.

"Lady, think," Robert said, for perhaps the twentieth time that evening. "We're barely moving, even with the path that the old man clears for part of the day."

The old man in question narrowed his eyes at a title that seemed to have replaced his name. His brows, frosted with ice from his breath, came together in a creased V. But he did not demur or disagree with the slight thief—which was as much a sign of his approval as he ever willingly granted to Robert.

She wanted to tell them all that she was afraid of the road, afraid of touching the reality of the Empire that spanned the continent in anything other than the dreams that always came. Swallowing, she met the eyes of her three companions and nodded her grudging approval.

But they left her to the night's call when the matter was settled. Robert returned to his snow-enshrouded retreat—fashioned at the direction of Trethar—and Darin settled in for an evening hour with his new teacher.

Erin sat in the stillness, so tired and weary that she almost prayed for a dreamless night.

"They have to be on the road." Lord Vellen shuffled the papers and maps to one side of his desk and stood. The motion was stiff and formal, but it hid much.

"We're spread too thin," Erliss replied, his voice just shy of a whine. "I have our house guards, and your Swords, along the main roads where any traffic moves at all."

"And?"

"Nothing." It was best not to prevaricate. Erliss ran a hand through jet-black hair and looked up. His eyes were darkened and ringed by lack of sleep; his cheeks were hollowed, his skin almost sallow. "But they've only been ordered to sight and follow; fifteen of my men were not enough to stop her in Mordantari."

Lord Vellen frowned and turned back to the desk. At his direct order, a recess to Karnari activity had been called; the Greater Cabal would not sit in official session until the beginning of the next quarter.

But he knew that Benataan Lord Torvallen was already in motion; spies had reported at least six meetings of an "informal" nature that had taken place at the Torvallen estates in the city. The nature of these meetings had been well hidden, but Vellen did not need their minutes to know what Lord Torvallen planned.

"Lord?"

"They must take to the road. You're right, Erliss. We don't have the resources to track them in the provinces—but we do know that they must travel to Illan. Where else can they go?" He did not need to look at the maps again; he had studied them, and he remembered them in detail. "There is only one road to Illan in the winter. They will have to either travel through the capital of Senatare, or around it." If he could but call his power, he would be able to find the woman; her blood-power could not be hidden from his God's. But the power still burned and could not be controlled. Yet. Abruptly he turned and placed a hand upon the flat surface of his desk. "You have progressed well, Erliss. This will be the final test of your studies. Go to Verdann in Senatare. Find them."

Robert took control of the party almost as soon as they found the road again. He was not, and had never been, a woodsman of any note, but the roads he knew well. He talked often and made as much sense as he usually did while he babbled, now at Erin, now at Darin, seldom, if ever, at Trethar. He wore the coat he had procured at the village long past with a dapper pride and a playful elegance that was completely out of place. Trethar found it annoying, but he found almost anything that Robert was prone to do or say annoying.

Robert found the inn on the road with an ease of familiarity that no one had the energy to question—not even Erin. Rooms, real food, and a chance to get truly clean held an allure that long absence had made undeniable.

Robert dealt with the innkeeper; Erin had expected more difficulty in the transactions, but kept silent at Robert's bidding. In the end, the slightly built man held the keys to two rooms—one for his two attendant slaves, and one for he and Erin. Erin listened as he talked, and found herself cringing at the easy way he slid into the demeanor of a housed noble.

She knew better than to even raise a whisper of protest, and weariness helped her to keep her head bowed and her attention focused on ground, the way any slave, no matter how valued, would.

"Come along," Robert said, and she looked up. He handed a key to Darin and gestured again; she followed as he walked down the long hall to the room that would be his. "We have food, or will have food shortly, and I've taken the opportunity to call for a bath for the lot of you." The wrinkled bridge of his nose was no act.

"Why, thank you, Lord," Trethar whispered, in a tight little hiss of a voice.

Robert chose to ignore him, which was just as well; they were not yet out of the innkeeper's field of vision.

When the door to Lord Talspon's quarters—Robert insisted that the house was real, which made Erin less nervous—was opened, Erin knew that they must be the largest set of rooms in the inn. They were well decorated, with two framed paintings of simple country idylls and a vase on each of two low tables. The carpets here were blue and deep. A large fire burned in the grate, coloring the glass of the windows with orange translucent fingers.

"I know it isn't much," Robert said apologetically, "but you can't expect much from a town inn. I think they've done exceptionally well, all things considered."

She turned at the sound of his suddenly unfamiliar voice, her eyes leaving the carpet.

"My dear Lady, are you well?"

She shook herself and smiled. This was just another room, the bed another bed. And Robert, approaching her with his gregarious, and unwelcome, expression of concern was simply

Robert—whoever that happened to be beneath the flamboyant mask he usually wore.

He saw the turning of her expression, more eloquent than any word of warning could have been. With a shrug that was anything but subtle, he turned away and walked over to the wall— and another door, unnoticed until now.

It led into a study, with a large dark desk and yet another fireplace couched within the wall. The leaded glass caught most of her attention; all of the panes were there, and whoever had cleaned them was very good at the job.

"Come," Robert said, "and lay the map out on the desk. There is something we need to discuss."

She nodded, went to her pack, and came back with the tube that contained the Lady's gift. Gently, she eased the parchment out and laid it on the desk. There was a plain, heavy ornament, made in the likeness of the inn's crest, that served as a paperweight for one side of the map; Robert's hand served as the other.

"We are here, give or take a few miles." He jabbed at a silver dot. We want to be"—and his fingers moved north in the lamplight—"here, give or take a few more.

"The road between these two points is, in the winter, the only passable road. I am sorry, as you seem so reluctant to travel this way, but we take the road. It leads to Verdann." Robert paused, obviously expecting some reaction. After a minute, he frowned.

"My dear girl," he said, folding his arms in a sure sign of mild annoyance, "surely you recognize the name by now?"

"Verdann is the capital of Senatare, the northernmost province of the Empire, if you don't include Illan." Her voice was without inflection.

"To be honest, I don't include Marantine, war or no war." Robert bent over the map, studying its lines as they seemed to glitter.

"No," she said quietly. "We don't pass through a large city."

He snorted. Lifted and crossed his arms, letting the map curl up. "Passing around the city is possible on side roads, but those roads are neither patroled—which is good—or cleared at all in the winter; there's also a marked increase in banditry, and the farmers are . . . unfriendly. Besides," he added, drawing himself to his full height, "I *know* the city. Well."

Erin stared at him for a few moments. Her glance was enough to make him bristle, but then again, an early morning was enough to make him bristle.

"We can gain valuable information if we stop there. We can travel freely once we pass the gates, and there's a quarter of the city which, while it may not be suitable for women and children, will hide us quite effectively from any would-be captors. We can get supplies there." He took a step away from the table and let his arms fall to the side. "And we can get passage from Verdann to Dagothrin, the capital of Illan." He took a step back and held out his hands in a poor mimicry of supplication.

And the worst thing about it was that he was probably right. If he knew the city, and could find any information about the occupied state of Culverne, the stopover would be very valuable.

If he knew the city.

But if he didn't . . .

"All right," she heard herself saying. "We'll enter the city."

"Good. I have to leave for the moment to procure supplies. Never fear, though—I shall return in due haste. I never keep a pretty woman—uh, never mind." He walked out of the study in the wake of Erin's silence.

Erin waited in the dying warmth of the room, with fire as her sole companion. She listened for the jaunty step in the hall that would sound his return as he brought those supplies so necessary in the growing cold. Supplies, she mused bitterly, that she herself couldn't safely provide.

She watched the flicker of firelight. It was red, almost too red, as it dwindled. She remembered and shivered abruptly, drawing her arms close. Red was the color of pain, the color of his eyes. It was the color of the blood that bound her life. Beyond her, through the wide slit of heavy open curtains, darkness beckoned, all cold winter night, devoid of the sounds of motion.

For a moment she saw undulating just to one side of the glass the writhing landscape of the Dark Heart.

The door to the suite burst open and Erin flew from it, a pale, half-ethereal shadow. Her feet felt less solid, and they made no noise as they struck ground that seemed shaky and treacherous. She ran to the room that Darin shared with Trethar, and with trembling hands knocked on the door.

Trethar opened it and frowned. "What's happened?" he asked softly. She made no answer.

Darin sat in the center of his cot. The sweat beading his forehead was the only thing that made Erin certain he was still alive. With a wordless little cry she started forward. The motion seemed to pull some invisible string, and Darin's eyes, circled with shadow, fluttered open.

He gave her a wan, happy little smile. "Look, Erin," he said softly. "Look at what I can do."

He raised his hands from their resting place in his lap; cupped between them, like a frail blossom, was a tiny red flame. She stared at it, transfixed.

"Erin? Erin, are you all right?"

chapter
seven

Verdann loomed in the distance, sprawling beyond the open
ground of blanketed farmers' fields, rising steadily upward in a
vain attempt to dominate the sky as it did the countryside. The
walls of the city were high. From a mile off, they could be seen
standing out against the flat farmland; what remained of the city
inside, only approaching it would reveal.

"This," Robert said conversationally as he picked up his
pace, "is the evidence of the effectiveness of Marantine. It is
the only city thus walled in the Empire. The border city." He
looked irritably back when Darin failed to respond.

Trethar murmured something quietly, and Darin looked up.

"Sorry, Robert. What were you saying?"

"That you spend altogether too much time with that ill-
tempered old man. Never mind. It isn't important."

Darin wondered how a grown man could sound so petulant.

"Robert?"

"Lady?"

"Will it be hard to gain entrance?"

"Not now. It's been a number of years since Marantine was
a threat, and besides, I came prepared for this." He fingered
the collars of a jacket that was still fine and noble, even if it had
seen an extraordinary amount of use in the past month.

She nodded and fell silent. Robert stared at her a moment
and then walked briskly toward the city once more, leaving his
imprint in the powdered snow.

True to his word, Robert had come prepared. When the guards
at the gate—and the term *guard* was to be applied advisedly—

103

stopped them, he walked quietly to where they stood. His hands flew around the air, and from the angle of his chin, Erin knew that he was aggrandizing himself. She was thankful she couldn't hear the words, although the mixture of tone and temper carried quite well.

Biting her lip, she forced her hand away from the sword hilt, wondering exactly how it was that Robert had survived his personality. She was certain that every guard on the curtain wall was now staring pointedly at their heads, and she barely managed to maintain an aura of indifference to match her lord's. But as she heard the trill of his annoying, flowery speech lengthen on into a quarter of an hour, she made a note to speak with him. Next time, they would follow her lead.

"Very well, my good men," Robert said loudly, in a tone that conveyed anything but respect, "if you would be so kind?" He brought something out from under his cloak and passed it quickly into the outstretched hand of one of the guards. The clinking of metal against metal was audible, even over Robert's huffing.

The guards nodded in bored indifference and stood aside.

"Don't just stand there gawking," Robert said, irritable once again. "Come on. We've little time to reach an inn before they close the quarter down for the evening."

Erin stood back and let Darin and Trethar precede her.

"And I don't need to say—" Robert began.

"Good. Don't."

The look that passed from Robert to the brown-robed mage was sharp and clear. "—that I can't very well afford to buy off any more of these detestable guards. So we don't want to be caught out past curfew."

"Where are we going?"

"Talking," Robert replied, as Trethar listened expectantly, "will only slow us down."

"Robert, where are we going?"

"Now now, Darin." Robert glanced nervously at the sky; it was already a deep blue.

Darin's eyes darted from building to building, catching the lengthening shadows of garbage and snow in the alleyways. "I lived in Malakar for four years. I know the cities of the Empire. Where are you taking us?"

"Darin, really, I—what are you doing? Twin Hearts, Darin, is that necessary?" He eyed the staff of Culverne with some distaste as it slid out of the restraining strap at Darin's back. With exaggerated care, the slight man brought his fingers up to massage his dimpled forehead. Behind Darin, the sound of metal's hiss could be heard, and Robert wheeled almost too quickly and overbalanced on the ice. He prevented himself from falling.

"Lady, please." His eyes fell to the shimmering blade of the unsheathed sword that adorned Erin's hand. "I assure you, I *know* this city. Would *I* lead you into danger?"

Erin's wary turn of the head was all the answer he needed—and all the answer she gave. He sighed.

"I realize that this is not, perhaps, the most savory part of the city, but I—"

"Where are we going?"

Darin, he might ignore; Trethar he might annoy. To Lady Erin, he gave an answer. "The Red Dog Inn."

"Lead," Erin said softly; the name meant nothing to her. "Lead quickly. We'll follow."

To Darin's surprise, Robert did as bid without a single word. His expression spoke volumes—but Robert rarely left anything to the subtlety of expression alone.

After another ten minutes, no one was concerned with Robert. The buildings around them grew taller and less well kept; the alleys between these buildings grew darker and more frequent. All of the city's shadows seemed to gather here; the stretch of buildings in the dying sun seemed the perfect harbor for them. There was no pretense of civility or finery anywhere in sight, and a soft breeze moved through the streets, carrying with it a smell of old garbage, urine, and decay.

Trethar mumbled a few sharp words to himself—nonmagical words, to Darin's ears, that he wasn't particularly interested in hearing fully. *If we get where we're going safely,* he said to Bethany, as she thrummed in his gloved hand, *I'm going to kill Robert.* Bethany made no response.

Robert stopped abruptly in front of one of several alleys. "Here."

"Here?" Trethar asked, with narrowed eyes. "You lead."

"It's perfectly safe. It will get us out of the streets more quickly; if we don't take the short cut, we've got to circumnavigate another four blocks."

"You lead."

"Nothing is going to happen, old man. Trust me. I've gone through this alley literally hundreds of times."

A small red glow started in Trethar's cupped hands.

"All right," Robert said tartly, "if it makes you feel better, I'm perfectly willing to lead."

The light in Trethar's hands dimmed as Robert stepped into the alley. Erin followed at his heels, brushing past Darin so deftly he hardly had time to misstep. As he recovered, Trethar also dodged in front of him.

"Watch our backs, Darin."

Darin drew his staff closer to his chest and followed his companions. They kept quite close together; if Darin had reached out with his staff, he would have been able to touch Erin's stiff back just beyond Trethar's chest.

"You see?" He heard Robert hiss. "No one's—"

"Evening, Your Lordship."

As one person, they froze. A shadow detached itself from the wall a few feet ahead of Robert. Then another joined the first, and another, and another.

"And what do we have here?"

Robert muttered something quietly.

"Tsk, tsk, Your Lordship. Language like that sets a bad example for us all." The shadow stepped forward, and Darin leaned around Trethar's broad back to try to get a better view. He could make out the outline of a slender man, no more.

"We're on our way to the Red Dog." Robert's voice was subtly changed. "We want no trouble."

"The Red Dog?" The man barked out a terse laugh. "And you don't want trouble?" The laughter, forced, died. After a significant pause, the man's voice became less friendly—and infinitely more honest. "Appears you're in the wrong section of the city."

"Nonetheless," Robert replied, a sudden edge to his voice, "that is where we are headed. I'd suggest that you step out of the way." There was nothing at all flowery in the words; no exaggerated politeness, no aggrieved complaint. He was cool and still—economy had replaced theatrics. For the first time in weeks, Darin remembered clearly how they had first met.

"Not very friendly, is he?" another voice said. A fifth

shadow joined the four. Darin heard the sharp intake of Erin's breath. Frustrated, his fingers tensed around Bethany.

Light? her voice whispered, startling him. He nodded, and a pale green glow filled the alley, robbing it of shadow, but not of menace. He could clearly see that the foremost of their enemies was obviously the leader; his style of dress, while somewhat dirty, was whole and a cut above the rest. Dark leather over the edge of a sweater fell to his midthigh; breeches trailed into worn boots. The man's face was thin, a crescent of white, sided by shadows and hair, as the moon on low ebb. Of the four men, with their scarred, emaciated faces, only one other caught Darin's attention, and held it: the thin, tall man, shivering slightly in the cold, who held a crossbow.

"Isn't that a bit fancy for your line of business?" Robert asked, casually letting his hands fall to his hips.

"Whatever works," the man holding it replied. He lifted it, just as casual in the motion as Robert had been in his shift of position, and centered it on Robert's chest.

"Now, Your Lordship," the leader said, "you should take a lesson from all of this. Wandering the streets of Verdann ain't safe after curfew." His voice lost banter and cruel mirth. "Drop the sword, Lady."

"Why should I?" Erin asked, in a flawlessly reasonable voice. The light in the alley played at her back; Darin could not see her face, but her hair shone like wire in the warrior's braid.

The man holding the crossbow swiveled slightly. His mouth was turned up in a smirk, and one thin brow was raised, almost in disbelief.

She returned his stare. Her grip on the sword slackened. Crouching down, she let the edge of the blade strike the cold ground; it seemed suddenly so sharp it might cut snowflakes.

The man nodded; he had expected no real resistance.

Erin raised her face suddenly, to meet his gaze again. "Not good enough." Her voice was cold and hard. A sudden light burned white in the alley, starting directly in front of the crossbowman's eyes and spreading outward in one brief flash. Darin had time to see the color of the man's eyes—brown—before the light became too harsh and too painful.

For the brief seconds that sight was lost to him, he concentrated on the cries—the screams—of the men who had thought to attack them. They danced around the scuffle of bodies and the sound of metal against metal.

Robert was nowhere in sight. Trethar stood, completely still, his back to one wall. Gripping Bethany tightly, Darin brushed past the older man, shaking off the brown-robed arm that tried to restrain him. He had to reach Erin. He had to help her. Light called its own. "Erin!"

She didn't answer, and the trail of Bethany's gentle green light became just another component of shadow. A loud scream filled the alley. Male. Not Erin's. Darin stepped forward and stumbled over a body that lay facedown in the crushed snow. A foot away from its outstretched hand was a crossbow, the string slack.

"Erin?" Using Bethany as support, he struggled forward again. When he stopped, Bethany supported the whole of his weight.

Even in the darkness, he could see her clearly. There was no one left standing to block his sight. Around her feet, like a terrible tribute, bodies lay at odd angles. Darin was grateful, then, that the light still burned at his vision. He saw no details.

Trethar came to stand behind him. He touched Darin's shoulder with one hand, as if to assure himself that his student was whole. That hand shook. "Did you kill them all?" he asked softly.

Erin turned to face the two of them, her eyes glittering in darkness, all deep and green and light. Darin shuddered, struck suddenly by the wrongness of it—that light, in this place. She walked forward to the body of the man who'd held the crossbow. With one foot, she rolled him over. "Not all."

This close to the body, Darin could see one long shadow across its chest. That was not what caught his eyes, though. The handle of a small dagger protruded neatly from the dead man's throat. Erin shook her head again. "Not all."

Darin glanced at Trethar.

"It's not my dagger, Darin."

A shadow detached itself from an alley wall, moving a little too noisily to be dangerous. "Is it over?" Robert rejoined the quiet trio, pausing for a moment to look at the mess at Erin's feet. The tangle of bodies and new deaths seemed inseparable from the woman who had caused them. "That wasn't necessary," he said softly. "They weren't always like this."

She met his gaze and held it. To Darin's surprise, it was she who eventually looked away. Leaning down, she wiped her blade against a torn jacket—not her own—and neatly sheathed it.

"Come on." Robert turned. "The Red Dog is just around another two corners. We've made enough noise here to assure our safe arrival."

"Robert?"

"Yes, Lady?" he said, without turning back.

"You've forgotten your dagger."

He stopped and turned again, walked forward with a light, measured step. He had to move to get past Erin. As he brushed against her, she tapped his shoulder lightly. He looked at her, the brown of his eyes meeting the green of hers. Then his lips curled mirthlessly.

"Touché," he said softly. With a deftness that spoke of experience, he extracted the small knife from its sheath of flesh. He held it steady, his knuckles white. "Old man."

Trethar bristled slightly, but nodded, too weary for argument.

"Lead them. Take the first right, and the first right again. I shall follow shortly." Robert smiled politely. "You won't be able to miss it—it becomes noisy very quickly. Wait outside for me."

"Lady?" Trethar asked.

She nodded and began to follow his lead. Darin trailed behind them reluctantly. As he rounded the first bend, he stopped and glanced back, pressing his palm flat against cold wood.

Robert rose from his half-kneeling position and looked out toward the mouth of the alley. He drew his arm back as if it were a bowstring, and a hint of moonlight revealed a flying glint. The arm fell back to his side slowly.

The guards were out in the streets; in this quarter of Verdann, they were numerous and went about their duty with every sign of pomp and attentiveness. Carriages, lacquered and decorated with crests of Verdann's noble families, also came and went with some frequency.

Erliss of Mordechai sat in the window seat of his rooms in the Carmillion hotel, watching as night fell. At his back, preparing a hot bath and a light meal, were the slaves he had been allowed to bring with him; they gave directions to the menial help of the Carmillion. Well-dressed and perfectly mannered, these slaves brought a certain respect to their house—that of Damion. In their hands, he could almost relax.

The guards at the gate had proved difficult, and he could not yet ascertain whether his quarry had arrived in the city. But he was certain, given the weather and traveling conditions, that they would have no choice but to seek harbor here. His cousin's Swords—one day, he would have Swords as his personal attendants—were already down in the city proper, hunting for information. With them, or under their surveillance, were two of the slaves that served the house proper.

Seeking refuge, or so they would claim. It was shoddy, but Erliss knew very little about the operations that led to and from Illan. He hoped that his people would find the information that was necessary.

Robert had been right about the noise, which immediately soured Trethar's already unpleasant mood. What he hadn't mentioned was the *smell* of the place, or the look of it, for that matter.

It was flanked by two decrepit tenement buildings; paint of at least three different colors had chipped and cracked to create a pattern visible in the light that the inn shed. No fourth coat would cover it or make it look more appealing; of this Trethar was unhappily certain.

More light might have touched the alley, but one of the windows had been boarded up, and the one intact pane looked half-black. Loud cries, angry shouts, and raucous laughter drifted through the open doors. Wreathed about them came the smell of alcohol and tightly packed bodies.

"He can't be leading us here," Trethar murmured, a mutinous look causing the wrinkles in his brow to furrow. "He wouldn't dare. This isn't an inn—it's a—a—"

"It's the Red Dog," Erin said softly.

"You can't be certain of that, Lady."

She lifted one slim arm to point at a placard that hung crookedly from one chain just above the door. "Read it."

Darin squinted, but could make out nothing on the sign's face. Trethar was not so lucky.

"Why, that foolish—"

"Well, I see you found it. Very good, old man. I'll take over from here." In one hand, Robert swung a small purse.

Trethar spun around. "We can't stay here!"

"Would you prefer the Carmillion or the Majesty?" Robert replied icily. "Or perhaps the Church dungeons?" He raised a hand to stem off Trethar's heated reply. "If I, who am most assuredly used to better, can find it in myself to stay in the Red Dog, you should have no difficulty. Now, if you please?"

Darin caught Trethar's arm as the brown-robed mage began to gesture. "He's been here before," he whispered, eyes pleading. "We have to trust that."

"Just as we trusted the short cut?" Trethar glared at Robert's back. Only when the old man snorted rudely did Darin relax his grip.

Getting past the block of bodies at the door proved more simple than Darin had first thought. People moved, and quickly, when they caught sight of Erin's jacket. In the light, the dark stain took on a vivid, ugly color that only served to heighten the severity of her expression. Her sword was sheathed, but her hand hovered over its pommel, and her eyes sought out every visible corner of the room as if waiting for any excuse to use it again.

Yet she seemed unaware of the attention that she gathered to herself; the noise and the smell, the awkwardness of forced laughter and little wells of uncomfortable silence, were part of a grim backdrop to another person's story: flat and unimportant.

Darin stared at her upturned jaw, and for a moment, he too lost sense of noise and smell; he could see darkness, an endless plain of battle, and Erin alone upon it.

"Verdor! *Verdor!*" If Robert, at his height, was lost in the crowd, his voice was not. "*Verdor!* Where in the hells are you?"

"Coming!" an equally loud voice boomed, from somewhere in the back of the bar. It was a low, strong rumble. Darin wasn't certain that he wanted to see the man that matched it.

And not seeing him wasn't easy. The press of bodies standing around the counter moved slightly back to make room, which was necessary. A large man, taller than many that Darin had seen, made his way out from behind the bar, wiping his hands on a dirty rag. He wore an apron that might once have been white and thick faded trousers that might once have been black. Both were solidly made and had obviously stood some test of time. Light and sweat gleamed off his perfectly bald skull and the open scowl of his teeth. The scowl didn't falter at all as he took note of who had called.

Robert gave a low bow—a markedly less flowery one than was his wont.

"You." Verdor tossed the rag past his shoulder. It hit a customer, obscuring the man's face. Darin wasn't surprised when the customer made no complaint.

Robert took a step backward.

Verdor reached out and grabbed Robert's collar with his fists. The slight build of the thief yielded easily to Verdor's grip.

"Surely you don't still hold *that* against me?" Robert twisted his neck slightly to one side to take note of the distance between his boots and the floor. "I thought we'd squared that nonsense away."

"Nonsense?" Verdor shook Robert, hard. "You didn't stay long enough to see the mess your game made of my bar!" He nodded toward the boarded window.

"Be reasonable, Verdor. I was quite willing to stay. You had me ejected. I might add," Robert said, gritting his teeth as Verdor's grip tightened, "that you also removed all the funding I had with me."

"That went to replace the chairs."

"Ah. Well, I'm sure that—"

Verdor shook Robert again, harder. "What the hell are you doing back here?"

"Well, I—"

"Did you attract your usual quota of guards?"

"I don't—"

"And can you give me one good reason why I shouldn't break your scrawny little neck?"

Robert gave a quirky little smile, not an easy thing to do when breath was so difficult to come by. "Well," he said, with what dignity he could muster, "you had been complaining that things had been too quiet, and I did give you a reason to stop complaining."

The innkeeper lifted Robert another foot off the ground. Erin's hand slid to her sword hilt.

"And besides," Robert added quickly, "if not for me, who would you have to laugh at?"

Verdor made a sound that was halfway between a bark and a growl. With one easy motion, he tossed Robert over the bar's counter, scattering a number of his patrons in the process. Ignoring the sound of clanging tin, Verdor leaned over the wooden counter.

"You owe me forty crowns, half-wit. I expect them by dawn." He straightened out, wiped his hands against his apron, and headed for the side entrance to the bar. There was a scuffling sound, and Robert peered up over the counter's edge.

"Where is he?" he asked.

Darin shrugged and grimaced. "Behind you."

"Wonderful." Robert spun around and began to back up. "Please—nothing that I'd have cause to regret."

This time, the larger man grinned. "You know the rules, half-wit. No customers behind the bar."

The counter cleared immediately, as men clutching tankards dove for cover, unmindful of the fact that what they spilled had been paid for already by their precious coin.

Robert closed his eyes. "Ready when you are." Verdor threw him back across the counter. He rolled along the ground, breaking his fall with his shoulder, and ended up, surprisingly, on his feet. Along the back wall, people who weren't in danger of being hit broke out in spontaneous applause.

Robert ignored them—he rarely ignored attention—and began to fastidiously dust off his jacket. "I keep forgetting what I have to endure," he whispered to a slack-jawed Darin, "every time I come into this place. Just look at this!"

The innkeeper's bark filled the room, and this time Darin identified it as laughter. After a few moments, the crowd in the bar judged it safe to join him.

Robert winced as Verdor once again left his post at the bar. "You'd think," he whispered, "that someone that big could have the decency to move slowly."

Which was all he had time to say. One large hand swung back and gave him a friendly clip on the shoulder—one that sent him staggering into the bar.

"Why are you here, half-wit?"

"For a room or two, actually," Robert replied, righting a three-legged stool. "Given my luck the last time I played at your gambling tables, I thought I'd content myself with that."

"Two rooms?" Verdor frowned. "The girls won't like that much. I'll get enough of an earful just giving you the one."

"That, dear man, you may leave with me. I wouldn't dream of asking you to try to arrange it."

Verdor snorted. "Regular rates, then. If you can manage it."
He snickered. "I know you have such a way with the ladies.
But what about your companions?"

"Ah, yes. These," Robert said, throwing one arm in a wide
circle, "are friends of mine. This is Lorie, this is Mika, and
this is, well, the old man."

Verdor's eyes narrowed as he studied the three. He turned to
Erin and said curtly, "We want no trouble here. At least, no
more than the half-wit can cause."

She nodded. Very slowly, her hand fell away from her sword.

He stared at her pale, drawn face a moment more, then turned.
"Astor!" He waited a few seconds, then brought a fist down
hard on the countertop. "Astor!"

A young man, perhaps two years older than Darin, came
trundling out from behind a swinging door; a glimpse of the
kitchens flashed by before the door came to rest. The young
man's hair was mousy brown and matted with sweat; it was clear
that his clothing was cut from the same bolt, and of the same
vintage, as Verdor's.

"Don't just stand there gawking. Get over here!"

"Yes, sir." Astor came to stand beside Verdor, looking even
smaller than he normally might.

"Take the lady's coat to Marlin. Tell her I want it cleaned."

Astor grimaced, but Verdor didn't notice, which was just as
well. The large man walked gently over to where Erin stood.

"Your coat, Lorie."

Erin drew back a step; she seemed to move slowly, but he
missed as he reached out.

Robert caught the innkeeper's shirt and tugged it firmly.
"Verdor, I really think—"

Verdor's hand shot out and found the neck of Robert's jacket,
although the innkeeper's eyes didn't stray from his new guest.
"Shut up."

Wisely, Robert did as told.

"Lady, your coat, please. I'll have it cleaned. It needs it, by
the look of you." His voice was mild, even friendly. "Have you
eaten?"

Her eyes met his, without ever really seeing them. Silent,
still, and pale, she let his words wash around her and vanish
without stopping to catch a single one.

"She isn't like your girls," Robert said. "Be careful, Verdor.

I'm not sure this is wise. Boy," he added, catching Darin's attention, "what on earth is wrong with her?"

Darin shook his head. "I don't know." He watched as the innkeeper continued his step-and-stop dance, approaching Erin with exactly the same caution one would use to approach an injured animal. At last, when a wall caught her back, Erin stopped moving.

Verdor caught her then, his hands steady but firm as he unfastened the catches of her coat. He frowned. "I thought so." Then he looked up and met her eyes again, as if they were a wall he could almost see over.

"It doesn't hurt," she said.

"It hasn't stopped bleeding," he answered, letting the jacket fall back into place.

"It hasn't? How odd." Her eyes fell to the floor, glancing off the injury as if it didn't merit, or couldn't catch, her attention.

"Come with me, Lorie. I don't think the bar's the best place for you." So saying, he slid his arms beneath her arms and the crook of her knees, swinging her gently off the ground. She stiffened and looked down, half-wild; her shadow cut the floorboards and the smoke. "Don't move, Lorie—we'll get you a doctor."

"I'm a healer," she whispered.

He frowned and pressed a stubbly chin to her pale forehead. The frown deepened, and he gathered her up more tightly against his chest. Turning, he headed for the kitchen.

Darin stepped into his way. "What's—what's wrong?"

"Not now, Mika," Verdor answered, as he attempted to side step the boy in his path.

"Erin?"

She struggled to sit in the uncomfortable chair Verdor's arms made. "Belf?"

He frowned at Darin. "She's been wounded," he said curtly, as he began to forge his way through the crowd. The look on his face caused his patrons to melt to the sides to grant him free passage. Darin shadowed his heels; he had no hope of following otherwise. From the sound of the vague and polite mumbles growing ever distant at his back, Robert and Trethar had discovered this for themselves.

Is it wise to leave them alone? Bethany suddenly asked. Darin froze and almost lost the innkeeper. Then he caught sight of

Erin's legs, dangling over the innkeeper's arm, and that decided him.

They can learn to get along, he answered.

They left the bar quickly, passing through a remarkably clean kitchen and into a larger room. A fire burned cheerily within a stone hearth, flickering off a worn couch and two large armchairs. The orange light looked ugly and thick against the green wool, but it was warm.

Verdor very gently eased Erin out of her coat and set her down upon the couch. "Rest here. All right?"

She nodded and fell back; her hair, like the fire, looked out of place against the green wool of her makeshift bed. Verdor brought blankets and a pillow from the corner of the room, and she lifted her head obligingly—and absently. Her eyes played with the beamed ceiling as if it could be read. She would not let him take her sword. Her lips became a tight, mutinous line when he tried, and he left off quickly.

"Watch her," Verdor said curtly to Darin. He left the room, and Darin huddled at the foot of the couch, doing as ordered. He would have, anyway.

"Erin, what happened?" He whispered.

She turned to look at him, and he shivered; her eyes went beyond him. He had never seen her look so young.

"I'm sorry," she whispered, and turned away.

When Verdor returned, a woman preceded him. She was short and round; her hair was gray around the edges, and her eyes wrinkled at the corners in a way that suggested laughter—or suspicion, as was clearly the case now. She cast a frown at Darin; he returned it with a hesitant smile.

Rolling her eyes, she turned back to Verdor. "What have you agreed to this time?"

"I haven't agreed to anything," he replied. "Marlin—the girl's been wounded. I asked the half-wit—he took his usual short cut."

"And you with more mush than brains volunteered the expense of a doctor, no doubt?" She snorted before he could answer and walked across the room. Darin got out of her way.

Erin's eyes flickered open at the approach of a stranger. They were wide and green, unblinking as a cat's. "I've done the wrong thing again, haven't I?" she whispered. "I always do."

"Who's she talking to?" Marlin asked.

No one answered.

Erin's eyes fell shut again, and a little trail of light could be seen at the corners of her eyes.

"You're a fool, Verdor Mackinson." Marlin stood, a hand on either hip. "A complete and utter fool."

"But she's not like the people we normally see. I think—I think she's Marantine born and bred."

Marlin snorted; a stray strand of hair flew out at right angles to her creased forehead. "That's as may be, but it isn't our problem."

"What do you want me to do?" He spread both of his hands, palm up, in front of her.

She thumped him across the side of his head—quite a distance to reach. "Don't go putting the responsibility on me—why do I always have to play the ogre? You'll do as you damned well please. You always do."

A loud crash, filtered by two doors, came from the bar. Marlin's eyes narrowed, and Darin backed away. Marlin walked over to the fireplace, picked up a poker firmly in her right hand, and turned to her husband. "Feed her then, and send Astor for the doctor. I'll take care of the bar." She stomped over to the door. "And, Verdor?"

"Yes?"

"I'll be a grieving widow if trouble comes of this!"

He didn't have to reply. As soon as she was gone, he winked broadly at Darin. "You see? No trouble."

"But—but—"

"That was nothing. You should see her when she's really angry. I wonder what's happened in the bar?"

Darin had a very bad feeling that he knew. He shrugged weakly. "I don't know," he said, as he resumed his seat by Erin's side. "I was never allowed in a tavern before."

chapter
eight

"Mika, don't you think you should get some sleep?"

Darin stopped rubbing his eyes and tried to stop his mouth, mid-yawn. "You haven't."

"I wake up late." Verdor's smile was a little haggard. "Besides, Lorie doesn't need the two of us. I'm awake anyway."

Darin nodded solemnly and ignored the innkeeper's advice—just as he had for the past two hours. Feed her what she'll eat, the doctor had said, and pray the fever breaks. Darin was praying, when he had the concentration for it. Erin had lapsed from sleep into unconsciousness, and the food that Marlin had made—complaining all the while—had gone from hot chicken soup to a thickening gel.

The wound wasn't bad—or so the doctor had claimed, as he bound it and hid it beneath cotton and linen—but the fever was something to watch for. He had remarked on her apparently weak constitution. Darin didn't understand it. In all the time he'd known her, Erin had never been ill.

"Well, if you won't sleep, why don't you at least rest a bit on the couch? Fire's going, and it's chilly."

Darin nodded again. Erin had been moved, at the doctor's orders, and slept in Astor's room, by the woodstove. Her skin was clammy and her breath very quick and shallow. He had seen her almost this weak only once before—the result of a nightwalker's touch.

But Bethany, pressed against the width of Erin's forehead, had found no trace of such a powerful enemy. She had done her best, with her lambent green light, to bring Darin's Lady some peace.

He did not notice any discernible difference.

Robert and Trethar had been refused entrance. Darin had thought that Trethar meant to cause trouble when Verdor had barred them both from the room, and had barely managed, with Bethany's touch, to calm his teacher.

"Marlin's had enough of you two to shorten your lives," was the innkeeper's explanation. "And I'm in trouble enough as it is."

Robert, knowing Marlin well, had agreed almost meekly—if not quietly—and had gone off, walking rather unsteadily, down the long hall. After a period of time that at least guaranteed some separation between them, Trethar grudgingly followed, his stride perfectly steady in contrast to Robert's.

Darin suddenly raised his head. Verdor smiled. "Lie down, Mika. I'll wake you if anything changes. You have my word."

This time, the innkeeper rose, and, half lifting, half pulling, made certain that Darin was arranged like any valued pillow, upon the old couch.

"But I won't sleep," Darin murmured.

"Of course not."

"... and I'm the one who the doctor delivered his bill to!"

"Hush, Marlin—you'll wake Mika."

Marlin snorted. "I don't understand what's going on with you, Verdor. And I don't like it. Since when have we started to adopt young mercenaries?"

"We don't know that she's anything of the sort."

"Damned well do—one of Candice's young women, I'll wager. What else could she be with a sword like that?"

Darin shrunk down below the back of the couch and tried to cover his head with the blanket. He found Marlin intimidating and didn't want to do anything to attract her attention. Especially not with the fire pokers so close to hand.

"Out with it." There was a rustle of cloth.

Verdor, stubborn, said nothing, as if silence was his way of contesting her. Minutes passed. Marlin won. "You'll have your temper whether I'm right or not," he said, with a heavy sigh. "And you'll think I'm a fool into the bargain."

"True. Which means you've nothing to lose."

"She's lost, and she's sick, Marl."

"And you called her a doctor. Fine. But you're sitting up here as if she were your own daughter—and at that, an infant."

Verdor lapsed into silence again. Darin moved very carefully. He struggled free of the blanket over his head, and then peered over the edge of the couch. Neither Verdor nor Marlin appeared to notice.

Verdor was staring at the tabletop and some reflection there. Marlin was staring at her husband. As Darin watched, her face changed, losing a little of its hardness.

"That's it, isn't it?"

"When I moved her—she called me 'Father.' " He continued to stare at the wood grain.

Marlin put a hand on each of Verdor's broad shoulders. "Love, she doesn't look anything like Caitlin. Nothing about her's the same. She's small, she's weak, she's built like a boy." She shook him, half in frustration, to little effect.

"She's sick, she's wounded, she may be dying." Verdor reached up and caught his wife's plump hands, pressing them more firmly into his shoulders. "Didn't we pray that someone had at least tried to help our girl? Don't you wonder about it even now?"

If he thought that she would pull away, he was mistaken. "I don't wonder anymore. She's dead. We're not."

"Marlin—"

"But you'll do as you do," Marlin said, in a voice so depleted of anger that it sounded almost gentle. "And I'll complain anyway. Now let go of my hands, you oaf. I've work to do."

She pulled away, turned, and left—all so quickly that it seemed one motion, one blur of brown and white. But even in the poor light, Darin thought he had glimpsed tears along her cheeks. He looked across at Verdor; the innkeeper had spread his hands out along the tabletop and stared at the darkness between his fingers, his face blank and his eyes dry.

Darin wanted to say something, but he didn't know what—and he once again sank back into the meager retreat the couch provided. Sometimes, battle felt easier.

Why didn't she say anything? He asked Bethany. *Why didn't I notice?*

You didn't want to face the fact that she'd killed your enemies.
Bethany's voice was so soft it was a whisper.

I knew she'd killed them.

Yes.

He was silent; as still as Verdor had become. At last he said,
She's changing, Bethany. I don't understand why.

You don't like it.

It wasn't a question; Darin answered it as if it were an accusation.

I—she's my friend. He didn't say anything else, but his silence
was uneasy and mutinous at the same time.

Father, look, look—can you see what I can do?

Your father is dead, Erin.

That was the first loss. It had taken months for the words,
mixed with the grim tearlessness of her mother's face, to develop
meaning. But she learned. No father; no one who picked her
up, complaining about her weight; no one to lay out maps along
the surface of the hardwood floor of their dwelling and explain
what all the markers meant, to prepare her for the struggle of
adult life; and no one to still the tears her mother kept hidden
until sundown. The emptiness made itself known, slowly struggling
to fruition.

This was what death meant.

Your mother is dead, child. I'm sorry.

*Your mother is dead, Erin. There isn't anything you could
have done to save her. Can't you accept that?*

Twelve. She had been twelve. The lesson was fully blown and
fully understood before her mother had breathed her last.

*Telvar died a hero's death, Erin. One that all of his line can
be proud of.*

There was no one.

Belfas . . .

No one at all.

She gazed around at darkness that was never still. It was
familiar to her now, no longer alien in its ice and ugly splendor.
She was alone; none of her companions appeared, in their gray-
tinged light, to keep company.

But the screaming, the low, unbroken howl, was calling.
Closing her eyes, she began to make a gesture that suddenly felt
awkward to her hands—a large arc that ended too suddenly in
front of her face. Confused, she tried again, but her otherworld
fingers were numb.

She began to drift forward, leashed by pain that angered her.

She brought her fingers to her ears, although she knew that it would make no difference; her skin was tingling in time with his pain's demands.

She raised her arms again, and again the ward failed. One did not call that light in this darkness. She struggled against the walking and heard his cries grow louder; the ground at her feet felt as if it were buckling.

No! I won't go. She needed an anchor, something to force her steps to still; something to give her weight and substance in the darkness.

And suddenly, she had it. Her eyes snapped open; the darkness was gone. The innkeeper's lined and tired eyes met hers. "Lorie?"

She tried to speak, found no comfort there, and reached out weakly. He said nothing, nothing at all, because he could not clearly see her.

But what he could not see was there nonetheless, pulsing faintly with the signature of her subconscious need: bands of light, strengthening as the minutes passed.

Her hands lacked the strength to maintain a firm grip, but this at least Verdor understood. He tightened his own until the rigid lines of her face seemed to melt into sleep. Even then, she held him invisibly, and the gate of the Dark Heart shut firmly behind them both.

Father . . .

Verdor stood his guard there, ignoring the crick in neck and back. He was a very strong man.

The pillar of fire burned brightly an inch away from the planks of the floor. Although he sat a yard away, Darin could feel it twisting in his hands, as if tethered by an invisible leash that was too thin, and too weak, to hold it. He struggled to call forth more power from the gate that he'd envisioned with Trethar's help, then worked to contain it in the form that he'd decreed.

"Good." Trethar's words could barely be gleaned over the snap of the struggling column. "Very good." Darin was only aware that his teacher had moved when he felt a callused hand touch his shoulder. "You've done much for the day. Rest."

Darin's jaw tensed. It was almost as much work to force the power back through the gate and close it as it was to summon and control it. Still, once the gate was gone, he could relax. He closed his eyes, picturing absence of red and orange light. In the darkness behind his lids he found the process less arduous.

By degrees the fire died, and Darin slumped backward against the wall.

"Very good," Trethar repeated. "Soon you'll be able to call upon the fire, and any other gate that you wish, with ease. You know the way."

Darin didn't feel as if he could spare the energy to argue. He barely grimaced as Trethar touched his forehead. Darin hadn't liked the feeling the first time Trethar had "checked" his progress and only barely endured it now.

"Let your enemies be careful." Trethar smiled. "What your Lady brings with her sword, you'll be able to bring with your will."

Darin forced his eyes open at the words—but not in time to avoid the memory of sword against sword in a dark alley. He could see the flicker of green light against wood and snow and dirt and blood; he could see the odd smile across the lips of someone he loved made strange by carnage. He shuddered, hoping Trethar wouldn't notice.

Trethar noticed nearly everything. "Darin, this isn't a game. It's a war—and you've got to wage it with any means at your disposal. Do you expect to be able to fight without killing? Will you face your enemies with the hope of merely subduing them? And if you somehow manage that, do you expect to be able to convert them?"

Darin shook his head, and Trethar caught him by the shoulders. "Look at me, Darin. You've never killed before. But on the field—wherever that field happens to be—you will either kill or die." He let his hands fall away. "I should be more patient with you. I'd like to say that I would be, if I had more time—but I'm not a patient man.

"Aye, boy, you've come farther than I expected—but I expect better of you yet."

Better. Darin clutched that staff that lay across his legs. *He means more powerful.*

Initiate. Her voice, a whisper, was also a warning.

I'm tired of death, Bethany. I'm tired of thinking about nothing but ways to cause it. I'm tired of thinking about what happens if I can't.

I know. To deal death is not a thing that comes easily to the lines, and you are of them.

He thought of Erin, standing silhouetted against the walls of the cold alley.

Darin.

I know. I know, Bethany.

"Well, what's this then?"

Darin's eyes fluttered open, almost in relief. Trethar's darkened. Neither had heard the metallic click of the doorlatch, or the soft creak of its hinges—but Robert, once revealed, was unsubtle and impossible to miss.

"You aren't thinking of sleep at a time like this, are you? There's still light outside, and I've finished my scouting for the day. We leave in the three-day, but you'll have to depend on me to get us all to the drop point." Robert smiled broadly and swung the door gently shut behind his back. "What do you think of it, Darin?" He lifted the edges of a dark blue coat, one trimmed in gold, with gold-thread buttons and catches.

"I think you're the only person I've ever met that would go out and buy *another* jacket at a time like this."

"Thank you. I always think it's important to look your best— you never know when it might be necessary." His smile dimmed slightly. "How is the Lady?"

"Sleeping. Doctor's orders. Verdor says she's eaten, and sleep's what she needs most."

"And so do we," Trethar said curtly.

Robert graced him with a disdainful side glance and rolled his eyes. "Well, yes, I suppose at your age you do." He grabbed Darin by the arm and dragged him to his feet. Darin caught Bethany before she clattered to the ground. "But Darin and I shall properly sleep when it's darker. We've a good two hours before the market closes for the week, and I've a little funding to ensure that we enjoy ourselves properly. You've been to a city market before?"

Darin nodded quietly. "In Malakar, when we had tasks to run for the house."

"All the better. This one's similar. Not, perhaps, quite as grand—but it'll do quite well for our circumstances. I intend to go. Will you come with me and keep me company?"

"No," Trethar barked.

"Yes," Darin said, at the same moment. He gave Trethar a guilty glance and then looked away.

"Better and better, then." Robert smiled. "Come along, Darin. You can be my attendant."

Darin walked across the room to where his coat was spread against the floor.

"Darin," Trethar said, annoyance obvious in his voice. "I prescribed rest, and going anywhere with this one isn't the way to get it."

"Nonsense, old man. You're running the boy ragged with your talk of gloom and doom. There's not much point to saving one's life if one doesn't have a life to begin with. Now do get out of the way and let us be off."

"Darin, show the sense that he won't. You're wanted, boy, and not just by the local city guards."

Robert snorted. "*They're* wanted, old man. Trust my experience. No one seeing the two of us together is going to notice a mere slave." He reached for Darin's hand. "Now come on, Darin. We've hardly any time at all."

Lord Erliss looked up from his seat by the fire and set his glass aside. He hated the northern climate intensely; the cold penetrated his quarters, even when a fire burned in the odd fireplace in the room's center. He looked out the uncurtained window and frowned; the sky was gray enough that it was hard to judge time quickly.

But an interruption was expected, even welcomed, and he motioned a slave to the door when it came, trying to play Lord of the Manor, and succeeding admirably in his own opinion. The slave rose from his kneeling position and made haste, in complete silence, to follow his master's command.

Captain Steverson walked into the room, dropped to one knee, and bowed his forehead.

"News?"

"Lord." The captain raised his head. "Of the three people you set us to watch, one has shown promise."

"Which one?"

"A metals merchant, caravaned under the crest of House Bordaril."

"Metals merchant?" Erliss knew that House Vanellon was responsible for all of the metals and precious stone trade for the

eastern coast. Everyone knew it; Vanellon was the strongest
merchant house in the Empire, and although it held no Greater
Cabal seats, it was still a force to be reckoned with.

"Lord." The captain nodded. "The only metals merchant
this side of the continent." He waited expectantly, and then
added, "House Vanellon has no trade routes to Illan."

"Not good news, then." Erliss rose and shuffled over to the
window, trying to be still. "What route does he take?"

"She. And she takes the clear road from Verdann to the capital of Illan. The family that owns the mine concession will not
deal with any but her, and as she has dealt fairly and equitably
with Bordaril—the most powerful house in Senatare—no one
has seen fit to press the point."

Erliss picked up his drink again. "Are you sure that she's our
most likely target?"

"Of the three named, she is the only one to have been visited
since our arrival. The woman and the boy did not appear. We
think it unlikely that they will. A slim, short man entered and
left her quarters."

House Bordaril held the high seat of the Lesser Cabal; Erliss
knew at least this much. He also knew that they had a small
standing army, which they often used in times of difficulty to
guard their caravans. The mining concession was the one most
dear to them, and they were likely to give a nominal guard—at
the very least—to any caravan that traveled between Verdann
and Dagothrin.

Wincing as alcohol burned the back of his throat, Lord Erliss
stood. He clapped his hands just so, and held out his arms; two
slaves were at his side at once, tending to his clothing.

"I will need to travel in haste to the consulate from Vanellon.
It is a matter of some import, and I will approach as a humble
equal," he told them. They would make certain his dress was
appropriate.

He did not need to choose his garments; he had said enough.
"See what you can do to hire mercenaries on short notice,"
Erliss said to Lord Vellen's captain. "I'll see what I can do to
offer terms of concession to the only house that would happily
fight Bordaril."

The captain bowed his head to the edge of his knee and then
rose crisply to follow Erliss' new orders.

* * *

For the first time in months, Darin was grateful for the cold. It helped alleviate the effect the press of bodies had, as people huddled in the market square, seeking barter, trade, and warmth. He had thought he would find the market terrifying, for it was in Verdann that he and the last of Culverne's servitors had been forced to part company.

But without the slave line and the Swords as company, without the watchful and angry eye of Lord Vellen of Damion, beneath a winter sky, rather than the peak of summer blue, the market was a completely different place.

"Quite a crowd here, isn't there?" Robert said. He had to raise his voice to be heard, but it attracted no attention; everyone else was shouting as well.

Darin nodded silently.

"I want to show you something before we start losing crowns," Robert said, and caught Darin's arm.

Darin had enough time to catch the odd flicker in Robert's eyes before he was dragged through the crowd. He was glad that he had no money or anything of value anywhere on his person—without the protection of house guards, he would have lost it to a thief. He kept the staff of Culverne drawn tightly to his chest and kept his eyes on his feet. Beneath a fine layer of dirty slush, he could see uneven cobblestones that would be unforgiving to the clumsy.

"This way, Darin. Market center!"

Why Robert bothered to tell him where they were going, since he didn't bother to let go of Darin's arm, Darin didn't know. But he nodded anyway, his attention caught by the echoes of shouts and calls, the scent of winter food, and the flashes of colored cloth at banner height.

"Just past this rail, and we'll be clear of the crowd." Robert dragged him quickly past the last few people and alongside a black iron railing that nearly hit him in the stomach. "Now," Robert said. "Look straight ahead."

But Darin was no longer listening. The wrought-iron fence extended in a small circle, maybe ten feet across. In the center of the circle, on a pedestal no more than a foot high, stood the solitary statue of a woman. Robed in white alabaster, her arms were outstretched, hands up, in either supplication or blessing. Her hair, white as well, fell long, and curled in a hard, cold circle about her shoulders and cheeks. The face that was upturned to the day's light wore an expression of such love and peace that Darin took a step forward, into the rails, as if called.

"She's called the Lady of Mercy," Robert said softly. He waited a moment, while Darin continued to stare. "Don't look at her expression, if you can help it. Look at her face."

But Darin still wasn't listening. *Lady of Mercy.* He drew a breath that was sharp enough to cut, and for an instant, his lips curved in a whistled tune—one that Stev had taught him in House Damion. His eyes prickled in the sunlight—it had to be the sunlight—as he remembered exactly where he'd seen this statue before. It had stood, gray-robed and flesh-colored, exactly so, its expression no less rapt for the fact that it was alive.

"Sara."

Robert's hands fell away. "You see it, then." If he noticed the difference of name, he made no comment. "Darin, who is she?"

Darin shook his head. "Lady of Mercy," he whispered. For just one moment, he had the absurd desire to turn back his sleeves and lift his slave's scar so that the statue could plainly see it.

Bethany?

In the hand of God, she whispered. His spine tingled as her power surged in the silence.

Robert whistled softly. "And we're all on the road to Marantine," he said, clipping Darin's shoulder to break the moment. "Come on."

Darin nodded quietly, then stopped to stare at his companion. He had known Erin for much longer than Robert had—but he would never have recognized the dirt-stained, determined warrior in this statue. If Robert noticed Darin's scrutiny, he gave no sign of it, but he was unusually quiet and kept his own counsel.

A pastry stand, one of three, was their next stop; Robert did all of the barter, and they left it with dry, flaky concoctions cooling in their mouths.

"Not bad," Robert mumbled, around a full mouth. "I've had better, mind. Why, in the capital, I—" He froze suddenly; wind swept crumbs from his lips. Without another word, he grabbed Darin's collar and jerked him out of the thoroughfare and into one of the market's few alleys.

Two stone walls rose on either side, and each had a small

stairway that barely infringed on the open alley space. The doors, small and simple, were obviously not meant for a buyer's use. The buildings were old but well kept, and it was obvious that they were the permanent home of either a very rich merchant or a merchants' consortium. Darin had no time to ask; Robert trotted up the stairs to the building on their left and yanked the door open.

Darin had no choice but to follow; the door closed behind him with an authoritative click.

"Church delegation," Robert said quietly, bowing his head in the direction of Darin's ear. "I really don't feel like meeting a priest today, if it can be at all avoided."

For the second time that day, Darin wasn't listening—at least not to Robert. Another disembodied voice had grabbed his attention.

"And for such a specimen, the starting price is not less than five hundred crowns."

Darin froze, the words and their cadence horribly familiar. He swung his head from side to side in a wild silence and started to edge backward. Robert put an arm firmly around Darin's shoulders.

"Not that way," he whispered, a tight smile strung around his lips. "We'll leave by the front doors." So saying, he began to edge his way into the crowd, glibly uttering arrogant apologies to the people he managed to run into as he did so. It was an art, this making of apologies that somehow managed to be more offensive than plain rudeness, but it was not out of place among the nobles for whom apologies were a pastime for the weak or overpowered.

"Come, come, ladies and gentlemen. Have you ever seen so fine a child? Five hundred crowns for an investment like this is so low that she's almost a gift! Have we no takers among the lot of you? No one with the imagination necessary to think of the hundreds of uses for the girl?"

"Five hundred."

"I see we have a gentleman of inordinate taste. But the rest of you—will you let this man deprive you of the opportunity?"

Darin tried to ignore the rest of the droning speech. He did his best not to see another hand raised, and another amount called out. He turned his face in random directions to avoid looking at the girl on the platform, or at the fine blue silks that hung so ridiculously on her small frame—or at the thin iron bands that covered her small wrists. And most of all not at the shaky, vacant smile that froze the corners of her slightly bruised mouth.

"Darin, don't attract attention."

But he couldn't avoid it. He couldn't avoid remembering the feel of the chains and the eyes of the buyers that clambered into the room in front of the block. He couldn't shake loose from the nervous start each bidder gave him when they looked at him with those bored, acquisitive eyes, even though he had already been reserved for use by House Damion.

"*Sold!* Take your number and come back to the block in an hour."

The girl was led, gently, off stage. Darin felt his knees unlock and began to back away, finally released from a spectacle that was no entertainment.

Robert gave a tiny sigh of relief and began once again to direct Darin toward the doors. A hint of light could be seen between the standing figures that crowded the room in front of it.

"And now, nobles of Verdann, something a little more dangerous." At his back, Darin could hear the clank of chains and a few muffled grunts. He wanted to cover his ears as he walked to the door—but he didn't dare. Robert was right; he had probably already attracted unwanted attention.

"Take a good look at the size of this man. Fresh from Illan and only half broken."

The words meant very little to Darin. Robert stopped and swiveled, bringing his hand up to signal a halt. Darin dared to glance up and he saw that Robert's mouth was set in an unfamiliar line. In dread, Darin turned to once again face the auction block.

On it, standing stiffly, was a large man. He was probably about thirty, which was generally considered too old for a slave to be of much use. His hair hung in an ugly, uneven fashion, and his face had one scar, still red, across the left cheek. His chest was also similarly marked—which was easy to see. It was completely bare.

No tame slave this, as Darin could see by the size of the chains that ran around his arms, ankles, and throat. But the shadows under his eyes marked a fatigue and a pain that showed how close he was to slavery's edge.

"Well, ladies? Wouldn't you like to take a man like this home with you? He's strong as an ox. Look at the muscle on him! This is a man made for strong field work or quarry labor." There was a general chuckle, mostly male, from the audience.

"Boy," Robert said, loudly enough to be clearly heard.

Darin looked up.

"Remain here. I've one short task to run in the market, but I'll be back before the bidding closes."

Darin didn't even dare a protest. Habit forced his head low; habit informed his posture. He didn't even glance to the sides; when he raised his head again, it was to stare at the block—perhaps the only neutral area in the great room.

"Turn around," the auctioneer said.

The man on the block glanced down. Very deliberately, he took the small, short steps necessary to show his back to the audience.

"The caravan had a little trouble with him—they were forced to remove his tongue. Everything else is intact. The asking price is only two hundred crowns. Two hundred crowns will guarantee this slave to the right purchaser. Who will bid two hundred crowns?"

"For an unbroken slave?" A faceless man shouted from the audience. Darin let him remain faceless.

The auctioneer gave a broad, dark smile.

"To the right master, that wouldn't be a problem."

Once again the chuckle rose like a dark wave.

"Lord Kellem, you've never bought bad stock from us. Will you take him on? Two hundred crowns for strength that is rarely seen in the Empire. I imagine with just the right training, you could make him a slavemaster without compare."

"Two hundred, then."

"Lord Kellem is willing to take him on. Are there any others? Two twenty-five is the asking price; two twenty-five."

"Turn him around again, if you can."

The auctioneer nodded, and once again the slave turned to face the crowd, taking his slow, short steps. The chains rankled every inch of the way.

"He's half-tame, I'll wager. Two twenty-five."

"A perceptive buyer. Lord Osserann? Ah yes, I thought I recognized you. Lord Kellem, for a pittance of twenty-five crowns, will you lose your sport? Two fifty will guarantee it."

There was a silence for a moment, and then a curt, crisp yes. "A wise man indeed. Two seventy-five. Two seventy-five." The silence was louder. "Lord Osserann, take a good look at him. Two seventy-five takes him from Lord Kellem." The silence lengthened, and the auctioneer's tone made it clear that he thought the game at an end. "Very well. Two fifty once."

Darin looked furtively to either side, trying to catch a glimpse of Robert.

"Two fifty twice."

He heard a commotion that came from the back of the room. "Two fifty—"

"Three hundred!" A voice boomed out. Darin relaxed as he recognized it for Robert's. Then the sum penetrated his mind. Three hundred crowns? He began to move in the direction of Robert's voice, keeping his head bent and his eyes upon the ground.

"Three hundred?" The auctioneer's voice held genuine surprise—and genuine pleasure. Both were rare. "Three hundred is the bid. Do I hear—"

"Three twenty-five."

"Three fifty."

There was silence, and then a tall slim man stepped out of the crowd and headed toward the block. Darin could see him clearly as he entered his field of vision. He was robed in crimson velvet, with dark black boots and an equally black hat. Across his back—and most probably his chest, although Darin couldn't see it—was the regalia of House Kellem. He'd seen it only twice in his life—but he remembered it.

"Three hundred and seventy-five."

"Four hundred."

Lord Kellem's head swiveled to the side, giving Darin a good look at the hawkish profile. The lord's eyes narrowed. "I don't believe I know your house."

And Robert stepped into view, as if the block were his stage. He wore a cloak of velvet as well, and Darin's throat tightened. *Please*, he prayed silently, *please don't let us be caught.* He remembered clearly the last time that Robert had brought new finery into their midst. Robert only shrugged.

"I recognize it, Lord Kellem. House Montan; the money is good. Four hundred is the bid. Four hundred and twenty-five?"

Lord Kellem nodded, but his eyes never left Robert.

Robert shrugged again. "Four fifty."

"Lord Kellem?"

The man moved once more, to stand directly in front of the slave on the block. "Four seventy-five."

"Five hundred," Robert said, yawning.

"Five twenty-five."

"I tire of this," Robert said, folding his arms across his chest and leaning into the platform. "Seven hundred."

The minutes of silence that suddenly stretched out were a testimony to the auctioneer's dumbfounded shock. He recovered quickly, but his face was red when he spoke again. "Seven hundred. Seven hundred is the bid."

Lord Kellem looked once at the slave, and once at Robert; it was hard to tell which of the two was a more pointed glare. But he nodded, curtly and forcefully, and strode back into the crowd. With a murmur, it closed around him.

"Take your number and come back when the block has closed," the auctioneer said, once again the smooth-faced man of business. He handed Robert a slip of slightly crumpled paper that shook. "Lord of Montan."

Robert nodded, his face equally businesslike. He also turned and cut neatly through the crowd, stopping as he reached Darin's side. He did not acknowledge the boy; he was wearing a noble demeanor. "We wait."

Darin nodded, chin almost flush against his neck.

And wait they did. It was agony for Darin; he kept his face frozen, unable to stop some of the horror and fear from showing, as, one by one, slaves were led to the bidding block. He recognized, in all of them, a bit of himself.

The auction drew to a close very slowly. Nobles and merchants, satisfied with their purchases, filtered out of the open doors until only a few remained, chits in hand, to speak with the auctioneer and formalize their claim. They were tired or bored except when casting their sidelong glances at Robert; then, their eyes flickered with a curiosity that they knew enough not to express.

Robert waited until most of these remaining nobles had gone. Then he walked to the block and handed a new attendant the small slip in his hand. The man, in simpler dress, and of a less prepossessing size than the auctioneer, glanced at it, raised an

eyebrow, and then barked out an order that was high enough to
carry clearly.

In a few moments, the clanking of chains answered it.

"Didn't bring guards, Lord?"

"No."

"Want an escort, then? For a small fee we can—"

"No."

"Have it your way," the man shrugged, obviously put out by
Robert's terse replies. He stomped to the back of the block and
carefully pulled the screen that separated the selling area from
the hall that led to the holding rooms to one side.

The large giant of a slave was half led and half shoved
down the long corridor behind the block. Two men flanked him,
and one—at a safe distance from the reach of his arms—prodded
his back with a thick wooden pole. His chest had been covered
by a canvas shirt and a thin, padded vest that would probably
protect him from the cold for long enough to be transferred from
the block to a house. Both were off-white and unadorned.

"Enough of that," Robert said irritably. "I want something
left for my own amusement."

As if this were a signal, the auctioneer, having completed the
transaction that had occupied his attention, now turned.

"Ah, Lord Montan." He held out one hand, and after a de-
liberate hesitation, Robert took it. "A good purchase. If anyone
can deal with this barbarian, I'm certain it's you. Would have
been a pity to let Kellem have him—wouldn't have been much
of use left." He held out an open palm.

Without a word of acknowledgment, Robert deposited a small
cloth sack into the man's hand. "It's more than coin is worth."

The auctioneer didn't take Robert at his word—which was to
be expected. He opened the drawstrings of the small black bag
and smiled to himself.

"We will have to have them appraised, if you'd care to wait."

"I would not."

"Ah." The auctioneer bowed awkwardly. "Well, the account can be settled with Montan, one way or another. A pleasure doing business with you."

Robert made no reply. Instead, he turned to the guards.
"Remove the ankle chains."

"Aye, Lord. And the rest as well."

Robert raised an eyebrow.

"Cost of chains wasn't covered." The man gave an unpleasant smile. "You'd best hurry. You might want the help of the market guards, and they'll be gone in a quarter."

Shrugging, Robert turned and began to lead the way. After a few moments, the large slave followed. The auctioneer watched them go.

"Something strange about that," he muttered to himself. His round hands caught hold of the jewel pouch, and he gave a philosophical sigh. "Still, it's none of my bother."

It had been a good day.

chapter
nine

Robert's mood stayed grim and "noble" as he traversed the market square. His jaw was a tight, angular clamp, and the little muscles of his neck, visible over the cloak's odd collar, twitched. He had never been a quiet man, and Darin found the ice of his silence unnerving.

The crowds had thinned, and the boards were already being raised in the stalls; the flags would be the last thing to come down. Together, Darin, Robert, and the nameless giant joined the steady stream of traffic that was leaving by the west market gate.

Only when those gates, with their guards and their flow of people, had been left far behind, did Robert speak.

"Curfew's coming. We'd best move quickly. As usual, we're in the wrong part of town for it."

They quickened their pace, until the building facades surrounding them once again melted into tenements, snow, and garbage.

Darin stared at Robert's stiff back, then turned to glance at the man he thought of as the giant. The giant's hair was unevenly shorn—not, Darin thought, a matter of choice—and hung in lanky, dark locks about his long face. The scar across his cheek was new, but there were older ones there as well along the line of his jaw.

But he walked steadily, even proudly; his dark eyes were fixed to Robert's back as if something there mesmerized him. Darin thought he could see the hint of a smile about the giant's lips. It was hard to tell.

* * *

They went in silence to the Red Dog, and if there were any
thieves in the alley, they kept their distance from the giant and
the people he escorted. The bar itself was near empty, and Verdor was nowhere in sight, although Astor could be seen cleaning
mugs and scrubbing at burns in the counter. He looked up as
they entered and waved his hello.

Robert grunted and stalked past.

"What's the matter with him?" Astor said to Darin.

Darin shrugged. "He spent seven hundred crowns in the market today." Astor's eyes went round. "On the big man," Darin
added hastily, already regretting the reply.

"Bet there's going to be trouble," Astor replied cheerfully.
"He always is."

Darin didn't think the comment funny at all. He scurried
through the bar and up the stairs in Robert's, and in the giant's,
wake. They headed to the room Robert occupied, and waited
while he opened the door. The giant entered first, and as Darin
moved to follow, Robert blocked his entrance.

"Darin," he said, bowing, "I'm terribly sorry to have caught
you up in this mess. I can't imagine the slave block was a pleasant experience, and I can assure you it wasn't what I intended."
Before Darin could speak, Robert continued. "But this matter—
it doesn't really concern you. I have to discuss a few things with
an old friend, and I think it's best they remain private."

The door was shut in his face before Darin thought to tell
Robert that the giant couldn't discuss anything; he didn't have a
tongue. He knocked at the door, but Robert chose not to answer
it, and the doors were surprisingly thick enough to muffle words,
if not tone.

"Robert, I think you've had enough."

Robert didn't even glance up. He was a thief, after all, and if
his eyes were caught and held by gold, what of it? The gold was
good, even if it was only liquid. Amber fluid danced on the rim
of his cup and disappeared quickly down his own mouth. He
winced as the alcohol burned at the back of his throat.

Darin was surprised he could feel it at all.

"Astor," Robert said, pronouncing each syllable distinctly.
"Another of the same."

Astor glanced hesitantly at him and then nodded curtly. The
bar was too busy for more. After a few minutes, a similar glass

was clunked down. The liquid eddied in a brief little tide. Robert didn't give it time to still.

"Robert, I really think you've had enough."

Darin glanced nervously from side to side, seeing shoulders and bar stools occupied by men that he'd rather not speak to, let alone be trapped in a crowded room with. His second night on the floor of a bar hadn't done much to improve his opinion of it. It smelled bad, it was too stuffy, and it was full of loud and boisterous people, every one of them outweighing him—that is, if you didn't count Astor, who stayed behind the safety of the counter.

Robert sent the contents of the ninth glass the way of the eighth. The empty shot glass was placed beside the others; they formed a neat, clear testament to a good evening's work.

"Robert."

This time, he deigned to notice Darin's presence. His smile was quirky and unfamiliar; it stretched too tightly across his features, like a mask that didn't quite fit.

"You know, Darin," he said, with perfect enunciation, "you're beginning to remind me overmuch of my oldest brother Gregory. Astor, get me another of the same." He reached into his pockets, pulled out two gold crowns, and casually slapped them onto the counter for emphasis.

The idea of a brother to Robert had never occurred to Darin, and anyway, it wasn't important now. "Robert, you—"

"Gregory always insisted on parenting me in the most ineffective of fashions. Why don't I just pretend you're Gregory? I haven't had this conversation in years." He placed his hands against the counter and suddenly shoved the glasses to the side.

"I don't—"

"Gregory, why is it that just because you don't know how to have fun, you insist on making certain that none of the rest of us do?"

"This isn't fun, Robert. You've had too much."

"No, no, no. That isn't the way it's supposed to go. You're supposed to say, 'Fun is not a thing that should ever outweigh the good of Marantine, Robert. We are representatives of and to our people, and as such are expected to put on a good face.' "

Robert gave a jerky little laugh. Like his expression, the sound didn't fit; it was too thin and hollow.

"Then I say, '*You* are a representative of Marantine, Gregory.' And you say, 'Don't be facetious.' And I say, 'Ask your father.' "

Robert reached over the counter and picked up his latest drink. "And you say, 'He's just angry. You shouldn't have accused our uncle publicly.' "

Robert spun suddenly, and alcohol rained down on the counter. "And damn you, Gregory, you self-righteous bastard, *I was right!*"

Darin took a step back at the force of words that he knew he didn't really understand. Robert stopped speaking and almost idly drank what little remained in the glass.

"Damn you all," he said, to no one in particular. "Astor, get me another one."

This time, Astor looked askance at Darin.

"Get me another one, boy. Don't stand there gawking. It's rude, and I hate poor manners."

Astor nodded grimly, but leaned over the counter. "Get Marlin," he whispered to Darin. "She'll take care of him."

Thankful for the opportunity to hand the responsibility to someone who could deal with it, Darin began to pull away from the bar.

Initiate, Bethany suddenly said, *do not leave him here. He is . . . unwise at the moment.* Darin bit his lip and then nodded firmly. He walked up to Robert and caught his arm. Robert frowned and began to pull away, but before Darin could say anything, another pair of hands intervened. Darin looked first at the edge of rough cuffs, then followed the arms up to see the face of the giant.

"Ah, Gerald," Robert said, trying futilely to pull away. "Have you come to join me? How novel. Astor, a drink for my friend. Saurian fire, this time."

The man that Robert had named Gerald—and Darin wondered if that was any more real than "Mika" or "Lorie" had been—shook his head firmly.

"No? A pity. I shall have to drink it myself. A good thing that I don't mind drinking alone."

This time, Gerald didn't bother to shake his head. He shook Robert instead. Hard.

"You never give up, do you?" Robert said bitterly, his lips moving against collars that had ridden up his neck. "The old man's gone. Gregory's dead. The lands are in the hand of a new governor. And you just can't quit.''

Lack of a tongue had nothing to do with the silence that Gerald offered to Robert's anger. Darin was certain of it, perhaps because the giant's face seemed very determined and somehow peaceful.

"Dammit, what do you want? It's over! Don't you understand that, you big oaf? You aren't my keeper anymore. It's gone. It's finished. Just leave me alone. Let me get back to my drinking.''

Velvet sounded strange when ripped. Common, really.

Stranger still was the sight, not the sound, of the water that played around the red rims of Robert's eyes—that, and his expression. Darin looked away, knowing that it was not something that Robert wanted to share with anyone.

Gerald didn't care. He reached out, grabbed Robert under either arm, and lifted him from his stool. Then, the giant swiveled to one side, and he raised an eyebrow in Darin's direction. After a moment, Darin nodded and began to lead the way out of the bar. Gerald had no difficulty following—not even when he had to drag Robert along behind him; Darin moved slowly, stopping to stammer an apology whenever he bumped into someone, which was often.

Robert did not speak at all. He shrank inward, his eyes ringed black now, and hollow. When Gerald set him down, he walked slowly up the stairs, and if his footing was a little uncertain, no one complained.

"What do you want me to say?'' Robert, hands folded tightly across his chest, glared at Gerald.

Gerald did not reply.

"I can't give you answers. I can't give you reasons. I did what I could seven years ago.'' His lips curled briefly in a smile that was no smile at all. "You know what happened afterward.''

Gerald still continued to pin Robert down with his immutable, unblinking stare. Unnoticed, Darin moved around to one side. There, he saw that Gerald's lips were moving slowly. He couldn't tell what the giant was trying to say.

Robert could. "Don't. Don't call me that. I lost the right to that title years ago, and I don't want it back.''

Gerald raised an eyebrow.

"No.''

Deliberately and slowly, the giant raised his right arm and rolled his sleeve back. His lips made no motion; the scar spoke elegantly and starkly for itself.

"I didn't do that for the damned title. You were a friend once, you pompous bastard, and I owed you." He turned on heel and started toward the door. Gerald stopped him.

"Get out of my way."

Gerald shook his head, his face implacable and more impassable than the body that blocked Robert's egress.

"*What do you want from me?*"

Gerald's lips didn't move. Instead, he dropped to one knee and bowed his head, both fluidly and rigidly. At any other time, it might have looked ridiculous—the giant bowing to the bedraggled drunk. But Gerald lent the gesture a powerful dignity that even Robert could not deny.

"Damn you," he said, in an unsteady voice that had less and less to do with alcohol. "I won't accept this. I won't be made responsible for you. It wasn't my fault—I did what I could—and it's no longer my problem!" He spun around, more to escape Gerald's bowed head than Gerald's presence. He reached the door, grabbed the handle, and then stopped, straining against something that Darin couldn't see. At length, he pressed his forehead into the unadorned, stained wood.

"Gerald," he said, deceptively softly, "your tenure is ended. You're free to go wherever you will—back to Illan, forward to the capital, or to Candice and her mercenary corps in Verdann. I don't care. Do you understand?" He spun around again, losing the anchor of the door. "*I don't care.*"

It was obvious that Robert was lying—and obvious, even to Darin, that he wanted that lie to be taken as truth and be left alone. But things were suddenly clearer to Darin, as he watched the silent giant and the man who had bought him free of slavery.

I didn't know, he said to Bethany, as he brought her around and held her, lengthwise, in front of his chest. His hands were trembling; his knuckles white. *I traveled all this way with him— and I didn't know.*

Patriarch of Culverne, she replied, *the Line Culverne was bound to Marantine a century ago, and while the laws of the line's war and the line's struggle remained with the line's leader—they were tied to the Marantine crown.*

You—did you know?

Yes.

Why didn't you tell me?

You didn't ask, she replied, almost tartly. But that faded; now was not a moment for such a game. *He did not see fit to tell you, Initiate. And he is . . . your king.*

What should I do?

You may repeat after me, Darin. No one will know, save you, that the words are not your own.

Darin doubted that very much, but he nodded, and after a moment, fell into a position similar to the one that Gerald held. "Your Majesty," he said, in a shaking voice, "accept our pledge of service, given to you over the staff of Line Culverne, by her patriarch." He bowed his head, and then raised it again, to look upon Renar, the first of Marantine—Prince Renar, the thief and the slight, black shadow of childhood memory and game—as if seeing him truly for the first time.

Gerald's eyebrows rose, but he did not break his position.

"Yes," Darin said quietly. "Line Culverne survived the treachery."

The truly-named prince remained short, red-faced, and be-draggled; if anything, the use of his title, spoken so quietly and so reverently within these cramped little walls, made him lose an inch or two of height. Across his face, several expressions struggled for supremacy, none staying put long enough to be identified by either of the two watchers. His hands, clenching and unclenching, seemed to follow those thoughts. And his thoughts were unreadable, unknowable; if his face was a map, the geography of it was alien and inverted. His eyes, red and white around dark centers, sought out ceiling, wall, and floor, not pausing to notice any of them.

But he didn't seem at all surprised by Darin's declaration. He took a deep breath, straightened out, and faced Gerald. "Rise," he said stiffly.

Only then did Gerald leave the ground; Darin remained as he was—at Bethany's silent urging.

"Open your mouth."

Without hesitation, Gerald did as ordered. Darin turned away at the sight of the stump that retreated behind yellowed teeth.

"This is what your years of service have gained you. This is what the leadership of Maran has given you over to. We—*I*—did not prevent it."

Gerald did not move.

"Close it—I don't need to see any more." Angered, he added, "At least if it had to happen to someone, it happened to you. You never did talk much anyway."

Darin drew a sharp breath; the words, hard and cruel, stung. He opened his mouth to speak, and Bethany bade him be silent.

"I have no home. I have no family. Marantine no longer exists, except as a figment of our imagination. The royal guards have *no* function and no claim to me; I have *no* function and no claim over them—you. And I don't want it. You are dismissed."

Darin rose, then, and Bethany did not seek to stop him.

"Robert—Renar—whoever you really are."

"Patriarch of Culverne," was the quiet reply. The slight man inclined his head.

"If all that is true, where are you going?"

Renar was silent and absolutely still.

"Why did you rescue us? Why have you followed us—or led us—this far? You *know* that we're going to Marantine." He turned Bethany around, changing her from a symbol of supplication and honor to a pointer that he could hit the floor with. "You knew who I was. And you know—you're the only one who knew—who Erin might be. If you don't care, and Marantine isn't your problem, why in the hells are you with us?"

Initiate, Bethany said wryly, *that is hardly the way to address your monarch.*

The sudden twitch of said monarch's lips matched Bethany's tone of voice. "That," he replied, "is none of your concern."

"Don't laugh at me!" Darin said, swinging Bethany around until she wavered a few inches away from Renar's chest. "It's all of our concern. Why do you think we're going? We want to free the kingdom!"

Dark eyes narrowed as Renar spoke again. "You're barely free yourself." His voice was cool, but not loud. "How do you expect to 'free' Marantine? Will you walk in beside your Lady and the old man? Fire a few buildings with some strange sorcery and expect the city to just come apart? Will you wish away the army within Dagothrin's walls? Will you single-handedly destroy the Lesser Cabal that governs with Church might?"

"No. Yes. I don't know! But we'll do something!" Bethany hit the floor sharply as Darin's hands shook.

"You're all fools, then."

"And what are you? You were going to come with us!"

"Yes," he said oddly, crossing his arms and leaning back against the closed door. "But I was going to accompany you as just another stupid fool." His lips lost even the trace of a smile, no matter how condescending. "I wasn't going as the rightful heir to the Maran crown."

"That's what you are."

"Darin," he said, shaking his head. "I'm hubristic and incautious to the point of idiocy—but even I know that it takes more than blood to be a king. I wasn't raised to lead or rule, and if I did, the Bright Heart alone knows how briefly the kingdom would last." He gave a little bow.

"Liar." Darin's cheeks were as red as Renar's.

At this, the uncrowned prince looked up, and Gerald glanced to the side.

"That's not why you won't do it," Darin continued. "You just don't want to feel guilty anymore. You don't want to have to explain why you spent *years* doing *nothing.*"

Initiate! Bethany's voice was cold and hard. *Enough!*

But Renar only smiled bitterly. "This is to be a night for destroying secrets, isn't it?" He bowed again. "Very well, Patriarch and hereditary keeper of the king's conscience." He bowed, and when he rose from it, his face was paled and twisted in a grimace that hovered between pain, distaste, and anger. "You are quite right."

Darin opened his mouth to speak, but found that he suddenly had nothing to say. Shoulders shaking, he lowered Bethany and leaned against her as if the argument had aged him.

"I tried to warn them," Renar continued, almost conversationally. "I was disowned for it. And I will be honest, Patriarch: I was angered." He shrugged, as if the anger were dead, a thing of the past. "You learn fire—but fires have already played in the streets of Dagothrin. Most of the friends that I had there died in them. I have no army to lead into battle; no way of taking even the city."

Gerald stepped forward then, breaking position. He placed one large hand on Darin's shoulder, and one on Renar's. And he shook his head, denying the last of Renar's words. He let go of them both, then reached out to grip Darin's staff midsection. With his free hand, he touched his chest and bowed his head once again.

"What do you mean?" Renar said softly, almost urgently. He crossed the room, opened a drawer in the spare little desk beneath the window, and cursed. No paper. Frustrated, he turned back and met Gerald's gaze.

Deliberately, and very, very slowly, Gerald's lips moved in an exaggerated mime of speech.

Renar's eyes widened for a half second, and then his lips curled in the shadow of a smile. "I'm not to escape either of you, am I?"

Neither Darin nor Gerald answered.

"Gerald, could you reach—could you notify—the remainder of the royal guards and the Marantine army?"

Gerald nodded.

The man who decried the kingship seemed to shrink back a few inches. "Will they all be as foolish as you, do you think?"

Gerald nodded again. Darin held his breath. They both watched the subtle play of expression across Renar's face. The king looked away and began, fastidiously, to remove his overfine jacket. The long tear was, fortunately, down a near-invisible seam; with some little work, it might be repaired.

"You realize that this was hard to come by?" He frowned. "It comes out of your pay, understood?"

Breakfast was a quiet, somber affair; Renar of Marantine had indeed, in spite of all protests, drunk more than was wise the previous evening, and it showed in the puffy shadows of his eyes. Gerald ate well, if slowly, and Darin, himself a little tired from the evening's discussions, was hard put to keep up.

"Is there anything left for me?"

Darin looked up, and his eyes grew round. "Erin!"

Erin smiled, and her eyes, for the first time in nearly two months, were a gentle green that sparkled a little more than the morning light could explain.

"That's Lorie, Mika," Verdor said, smiling just as broadly. He looked tired but well satisfied. Erin's left hand was tucked neatly in the crook of his right arm as they walked together across the dining-room floor.

Verdor snorted as he surveyed the near-empty platters on the table. "I knew it. Good thing I told Astor to cook up something extra, isn't it? Mika, pull out a chair for the lady."

Darin was already doing just that. As she sat, he said, "You—you look better."

"Damndest thing I've ever seen," Verdor replied, before a word could leave Erin's lips. "Just yesterday, I'd've sworn she was on death's door."

"You said she was fine," Darin pointed out.

"Yes. Well." The innkeeper shrugged. "I was right." He walked around the table to where Renar was cringing. "Hello, half-wit!"

"Verdor—please. Can you play the booming giant elsewhere?"

"No," Verdor said, with a nasty grin. "Don't you want my company?" He clapped Renar soundly on the back and, while the thief was busy choking, winked at Erin. She shook her head in mock disapproval.

"Where's Trethar?"

"In the room," Darin replied. "Sleeping, I think. He doesn't like mornings if he can avoid them—we worked late last night."

"And who is this?"

"That," Renar broke in, as he massaged his temples gingerly, "is Gerald. Big as Verdor, but thank the Twin Hearts, that's all they have in common."

Gerald nodded politely.

"So, half-wit," Verdor said jovially, "Lorie says you'll be leaving in a few days."

"A few minutes," Renar muttered under his breath.

"Well, well, well. Friendly this morning, aren't we? I'm beginning to understand why you never bother to look a morning in the face."

Renar had time to draw breath—a deep one which signaled the onset of a lengthy diatribe—and Darin had just time to roll his eyes, before the front doors to the inn flew open, crashing loudly against the wall.

The morning crowd, sparse and for the most part quiet, surged apart in a sudden panic, taking to the walls like ducks to water. Nothing blocked the view to the doorway; nothing got in the way of the Swords that stood in the Red Dog's entrance, framed by the rectangular patch of daylight in the narrow street at their backs.

"What in the hells?" Verdor stood slowly, drawing himself to his full height. Renar was already on his feet. In fact only

Darin, jaw suddenly slack, remained seated at the breakfast table.

Verdor walked past his back, stopping once to gently squeeze his shoulders in a quiet warning. He wiped those hands on his apron, as he often did when annoyed, and stopped five feet away from the intruders.

"May I help you gentlemen?"

"You harbor a man who styles himself Renar of Dagothrin. Bring him now, and no harm will come to you."

"Renar of Dagothrin?" Verdor shrugged. The movement did not look casual. "Don't know him. Do you have a description?"

The Sword tried to look down at Verdor, failed miserably, and forced the tone of his voice to carry the weight of his authority instead. "Short man. Dark hair. Wears a velvet jacket with House Montan insignia."

"A house lord? Here?" Verdor lifted his hands expansively.

Dark eyes met blue ones in a more telling exchange than words alone could provide. The Sword shook his head sharply, walked into the room until he stood less than a foot away from the innkeeper, and gestured his men forward. They came wordless, but not silent, as they passed around both their commander and the innkeeper.

"Fan out. Find him. You four, check the upper rooms."

Erin stood against the back wall, her face pale, her eyes blank. Her hand rested against the hilt of her sword, although she'd not unsheathed it.

Renar was nowhere in sight.

Darin breathed a sigh of relief, but found that he could not relax his grip upon the staff of Culverne. The Swords, however, did not seem interested in either him or Erin. Two of them brushed roughly past, sparing less than a glance for a young boy and a wraithlike woman who was obviously too overwhelmed to cause trouble.

How had they known who Renar was? And how had they known he was here? Darin chewed at his lip. He knew that Renar was not, and would never be, very subtle.

Except for the sound of heavily booted feet and the occasional shouted command, there was no noise in the inn. Fifteen minutes passed. Then another fifteen went by, as the Church guards once again gathered in the center of the bar in two precise lines.

Their surcoats, black with a glittering red trail in the shape of a broken circle, were crisp and new; their chain mail, for chain it was, was well oiled and in good repair. Even the leathered joints at elbows and knees seemed to stand out in the darkness as the work of an expert. Only their helms were questionable; elegance, slenderness, and simplicity of line couldn't hide the fact that they were not very functional. Then again, they didn't have to be; very little challenged the Swords in this, or any other, city.

The captain of this patrol looked grim indeed as he surveyed them. Darin was weak with relief; had he not been seated, he might have fallen. Renar had not been found.

"He can't have left. We've covered all exits. Traynen—did you check with the exterior guard?"

Somebody barked a quick "Yessir" without falling out of line.

"Rooms?"

"Empty, sir. Most of them."

The captain fell silent, and Darin closed his eyes. He didn't pray, not this close to Swords.

"Very well, then."

They were going to leave. Darin's fingers curled in tight fists as he struggled to stop shaking. They were going to leave, without ever noticing him or Erin.

"Bring in Lord Kellem."

One of the Swords turned sharply on heel and exited the inn. Almost as an afterthought, the captain added, "Everyone will remain where they are."

No one even attempted to differ. Where Swords were concerned, silence served best. It was a truth that everyone in the warrens could attest to. The quarterly sacrifices in Verdann were taken from a criminal levy, and not surprisingly, it was a crime to obstruct the justice of the Church or its representatives in any way.

Several heads turned as the door swung open for the second time that morning. The Sword entered and quietly resumed his place in the formation. Following closely behind came a man dressed in a crimson cloak, with burgundy pants topping black leather boots. Emblazoned across his chest in gold thread was a sword, held lengthwise as the horizon for a setting sun.

Lord Kellem.

Darin shuddered, shrinking back. He couldn't prevent himself from turning his head to look at Gerald. The quiet giant gave a barely perceptible nod.

"Lord Kellem." The captain bowed. "The criminal in question does not appear to be within these walls at this time. You have seen—"

"I realize that," Lord Kellem replied distantly. He was already scanning the silent crowd.

"If you could—"

"I will do as I must, Captain. I do not need your advice." He began to walk into the thick of the sparse crowd.

Darin's throat tightened as he realized that Lord Kellem was heading directly toward his table. He tensed, keeping himself very still. But the lord continued to walk in his measured, slow stride; Darin felt the edge of his cloak flutter past his shoulders. He tried very hard to be small and unnoticed and in the end he succeeded; he had not trained so long and learned so many of the lessons of slavery to no avail.

But he felt no real relief as Lord Kellem spoke again. "This one. You, open your mouth."

Gerald looked down at the lord. His only answer was silence and a tight compression of lips.

"Captain, I believe I need your assistance."

The captain started forward, obviously annoyed by the tone of the lord's voice, but just as obviously willing to obey. He had crossed half the distance that separated them when Lord Kellem found that the difference between the station of slave and noble did not eradicate the difference between the stature of the two. A sound that was halfway between a scream and an angry shout was cut off abruptly as he met the captain in midstride.

For a moment the entire room seemed frozen. Then a shocked murmur passed through the crowd—and the ranks of the Swords—like a wave.

Gerald stood in much the same position as he had when Lord Kellem had approached him. His eyes left the stunned Swords only once, to flicker briefly over Darin. His mouth moved, forming one silent word.

That motion, that half-born articulation of lips with no voice, was the key to Darin's legs. The chair struck the ground and rocked to a halt; no one thought to lift it.

Yes. Leave. Darin's eyes darted from side to side. The Swords remained in line until their captain's bark gave them leave to move forward.

"He's no use to us alive—he can't talk. Bring him down, quickly. He's dangerous!" Lord Kellem's face was red with anger.

If they heard Lord Kellem, they showed no signs of it; their progress was slow and measured. There was no pain here, only wary experience and the benefit of years of training.

Darin jumped toward the door that led to the kitchen. He nearly collided with Astor, who was rushing inexplicably *into* the bar, a poker—the family's weapon of choice—tightly in hand.

"What are you doing?" Darin asked.

"My father," Astor replied, his eyes skimming the crowd. "He'll need my help."

"He's—he isn't under attack."

"You don't know my father." The poker was stiff against the boy's leg, a brace or a crutch to his courage, not his stride. Lips moving, he counted the number of Swords to himself; he paled, but he still took a step forward, away from the safety that the kitchen door represented.

Darin almost told him that he'd miscounted. But he stopped, his hand flush against the swinging door, and looked back, ashamed.

Erin still stood with her back pressed firmly against the wooden wall. Her hand gripped the pommel of her sheathed sword.

"Erin!" The force of the whisper scratched the back of his throat.

She didn't seem to hear him. Her eyes, glassy and wide, saw only the Swords of the Church as they closed with Gerald. In the dim light of the bar, their weapons seemed dull—more like clubs than blades. There were five, with three forming up in a secondary line, but they approached Gerald with all the respect due his size. Lord Kellem was not a small man, and Gerald had thrown him, without apparent effort, halfway across the room.

Still, the giant had no weapon and no shield.

"Look here, Captain," Verdor said. Darin couldn't see him. "You've no cause to go assaulting my customers. They've broken no law."

"Shut up."

Verdor made no reply. It seemed that Astor's fear was unfounded. But not for long; from the front of the tavern, the captain gave a surprised and angry shout. Darin knew the sound of a sword being drawn well; he didn't have to see it. Straining for a glimpse anyway, he missed the first flurry of activity that signaled Gerald's defense.

The chairs were oak and heavy; they were no match for a sword, but they were enough of a surprise to knock one man off his feet and to disarm another. Gerald held it easily, unmindful of its weight or shape. His lips curled back in a snarl, and his eyes were wide—but whether he was truly maddened or very clever, Darin couldn't tell.

Bethany found her way into Darin's hands, and he held her like a shield between himself and the chaos of battle. No one appeared to notice. Blades rose in the inn; blades fell. Blood speckled the floor.

Astor screamed.

And Erin, eyes suddenly flashing, drew her sword. It glowed, visible and brilliant, drawing for a moment all unwary eyes. *"No!"*

She lunged forward, light on her feet, and suddenly silent; her eyes were dark but limned with unnatural light. Her blade sliced through air, cutting neatly through black chain link. Darin had hardly seen her move, so fast and sudden was her lunge. Her victim didn't have time to realize that he was dead before she took another, separating a head quite neatly from a throat.

A pretty, useless helmet clattered to the floor and careened to a stop beneath the table. The warm liquid that splashed Darin's cheek brought him to life.

chapter
ten

The blade that had once been Gallin's now sang in the hand of
a different master; Darin could hear its song, and the light along
the edges of steel was cold, hard, and brilliant. The Swords
could see it, too; the aura of the power of its maker was both a
call to battle and a warning to the Dark Heart's distant kin.

Gerald, mute and towering, was left alone to two men as four
of the Church-trained soldiers began to confront this unforeseen
enemy—a slight, pale woman who had barely been worthy of
dismissal.

She reached the man on the right flank, moving low. He was
surprised—seemed surprised—and then he was dead.

Darin watched. He had warned her—and had thought to join
her, somehow, in battle. He couldn't; he had no idea, suddenly,
who it was he wanted to defend. The light in the alley had been
poor, except when she had summoned it; here, everything was
clear. Repelled and fascinated, he could not look away, and he
could not move forward.

Erin struck out at the closest of the Swords, calling the light
she used in battle to blind. The man screamed as her blade
caught in his collarbone—and screamed again as she gave a
vicious twist to free it.

She opened her mouth. Her lips moved. Darin thought she
might utter a battle cry. What she did say, he heard but didn't
understand.

"Father!"

For a moment she stood frozen, eyebrows and mouth curved
into lines of pain and fear. It was a perfect opportunity. The

Sword on the right took it, bringing his blade in to catch her ribs.

She screamed; they stopped at the sound. There was nothing human about it. There was nothing human about the tears that ran down her cheeks as she raised her face. And there was nothing natural about the slender sword arm that flashed outward, inexorably finding flesh targets.

Her lips curled, lending her face a grim, feral smile. Blood spattered upward, coloring her cheeks and brow. Darin took a step back, shielding his eyes. He no longer felt fear for Erin, but of her. He could hear her murmur, unbroken and soft, but couldn't make out the words. When he looked again, she was a moving blur, a pale shadow. At her feet, at her feet . . .

Gagging, he looked away, had to look away. She didn't—she couldn't—need his help.

But Gerald did. The giant was bleeding, and the two men left to face him were whole. The chair proved a good shield in Gerald's hands, but without a weapon to complement it, his fight was almost at an end.

The hands that held the staff of Culverne raised it high. Without a spoken word, Darin called forth Bethany's fire and sent it like a bolt at the foremost of the Swords.

The Sword shifted and cursed, but that was all.

In confusion, Darin called white-fire again, and it came and left, traversing the room to halo the other combatant. Nothing happened.

Bethany! What's wrong? Why isn't it working?

They are human, Darin, or of blood too weak to be burned by our fires. Their choices are gray and not dark.

No. He brought the staff down in trembling hands. *No . . .*

He saw the point of a sword bite deeply into Gerald's thigh. He heard Erin's unnatural cry and looked up without hope. She was advancing quickly to the front of the bar.

Initiate, Bethany said quietly, *she cannot be reached by you.* Wreathed through her words, like a hint of smoke, was fear.

I—Gerald's going to die, Bethany. I have to be able to do something . . .

And he knew, suddenly, what he must do. His hands almost numb, he returned Bethany to the strap at his back. No one seemed to notice him, or to consider him worthy of note. He was grateful for it. He was grateful that he had the opportunity to prove himself worthy of more.

He took a deep breath, blocking out the sounds of the shouts and screams that surrounded him. He made himself an island of calm and dark tranquility, as Trethar had taught him to do.

Fire is best, Darin. That is the gate easiest to reach and to open. Find your path to that door.

He began to bend his mind into the shape necessary to touch fire, to call it forth, and to hold it. The inn receded further and further until he was only conscious of the myriad shades of gray that danced behind his eyelids. Twice he felt the gate within his grasp, and twice it slipped away.

I'm not ready for this, he thought. But he had to be. Sweat beaded his forehead, as it had done many times during his exercises with his elderly mentor. But this time it was not due to exertion alone. His heartbeat felt like the steady drone of drums in his chest. He took another, deeper breath, fighting off his fear.

The third time he touched the gate, he held it.

Slowly, and as carefully as he could, he pulled it open, allowing the rush of warmth and unworldly flame to fill his mind. He retreated before it, keeping the core of his thoughts away from its red touch. It coiled within him like a snake that was only barely contained.

Light and image filled his mind as he opened his eyes.

Gerald still stood, but bore two new gashes across the breadth of his chest. They did not look deep, but a part of Darin knew that Gerald could not continue to suffer even minor wounds; the blood loss would kill him even if the Swords could not.

He raised his hands, focusing the power he held within. His lips opened and fumbled along the sharp edges of the words that Trethar had taught him—the words that honed his focus and control.

And what will your will shape, Darin?

Fire, Trethar.

And fire there was, a sudden blazing blossom that opened around the feet of a Sword—the one closest to Gerald—and snapped ruthlessly shut. The man's screams accompanied the crackle of unnatural flame before he blackened and withered.

Darin did not watch—even distanced as he was, he could not.

Instead, with grim determination, he brought his power to bear upon another armored man.

"Fire!"

The fear of the Swords that had tethered the crowd snapped at the presence of a greater threat. As one man, the gathered crowd began to rush for the closed door of the bar. Glass crashed and scattered, and a small stream of bodies pressed through what was left of Verdor's last window. Not even the Swords were immune to the frenzy that gripped the Red Dog's patrons. Although some held their ground, waiting tensely for orders to follow, many left through the now-open doors, cutting a place through the line with the authority of weapons.

Darin watched them go, although it barely registered. All of his concentration was consumed in fire, in holding fire. Never before had he held it for so long; never before had he given it leave to burn and destroy as it desired.

And it did desire only this; he could feel it, trembling through the gate in his mind, with its increasing urgency and unwelcome demand. It had no voice, no words to express the desire—but this close to Darin, words were not required.

Darin had thought that all of his energy and will would be sapped in the opening and closing of the gate. This had been his experience over the past weeks, and he'd felt a growing pride at the measure of power he was able to summon and send back.

Now he was humbled; his pride at children's tricks deserted him completely. Something trickled down the side of his face and round the corner of his mouth.

The flame began to drift away from the unrecognizable corpse of a man. Inch by inch, it hovered in the air, seeking something else to caress. Only one man remained close to it.

Gerald.

If Darin could have, he would have screamed. His lips locked around a jaw that was trembling with tension. He gestured, his fingers wobbling in the air. The fire continued to move.

No. No!

Panic blurred his concentration, and the fire lapped out as Gerald backed away. Darin knew that if the flame touched Gerald at all, nothing could quench it. He tried to drag the fire back. If Gerald died by flame, it would be a far worse death than the Swords had offered.

Gerald's hands flew up to cover his face. He couldn't know how futile the gesture was.

No!

The flame moved forward again.

Frantically, Darin searched for the thread that bound the flame to the gate he had opened. He caught it, a wisp at the corner of his conscious thought, but could not hold it. It danced away from him with a will of its own. Will.

It's will, Darin. All will. Remember that. You've only your will between you and the fire once you've opened the gate.

Will. Will.

Darin stopped trying to speak. He forced his body to relax, and then, with a shudder, closed his eyes. Gerald's fate was in his hands—but only if he could forget his fear and anxiety could he control the outcome. Darkness descended as he imagined himself taking a great step back from the world. There was no Gerald. There was no bar. There were no frantic, screaming people.

Darin was alone, with only fire; the hunger of flame.

No.

But it was more now than just word or thought—it was physical, a totality. He caught the flame in it and felt its struggle as an outward pressure that sought to disrupt his concentration. Slowly, if time had any meaning here, he began to draw it inward. He did not open his eyes; for a moment, in perfect struggle, he forgot that he had them. There was just the fire that fought him, and his desire to contain it. Black and white.

White and red.

Warmth suffused him; he ignored it. The gate stood open before his inner eye, and he continued to gather the fire, hoarding it, refusing to share its touch with the distant, pale world.

The gate did not resist him. It accepted a return of its fire with a greater ease than Darin could have hoped for had he spare thought for hope. Slowly and surely the flame dwindled inward; the tingle fell away from his arms and legs.

He felt queasy and tired.

The world around him felt as if it were rumbling.

Never mind. There was no fire—of this he was certain. He shook with relief. No, wait. Something was shaking him. He forced his eyes open and forced them to focus.

I've killed a man. Two men.

The thought swirled around the unclean ache of his body. Images of the burned corpses, combined with their very real smell, became a flame of a different kind.

It is not Lernan's way.

It has been, Initiate. To those trained in the warrior way, it has been.

But I killed them . . .

He felt the shaking again. Gerald held him.

Yes, Bethany said, her voice curiously soft, *and this is why:* Gerald, bloodstained and pale—but whole.

Darin smiled up at the giant and surrendered his eyelids to gravity. Or he tried to; Gerald's grip tightened and the shaking grew worse.

"What?" Darin opened his eyes fully, remembering that Gerald couldn't speak. Gerald stared at him for long enough to assure himself that Darin was indeed aware before lifting him and turning him slowly toward the front doors. If any expression graced the giant's face, Darin could not discern it. That worried him.

Worry was transformed as Darin's gaze lingered over the trail of injured and dead men that seemed to lead straight to the door—a poorly made, dearly bought road. Blood colored the path, not ash, and silence and stillness reigned there. He did not want to look.

And then he heard weeping, soft and muted, and thought he understood. "Gerald, put me down."

The large man complied, but caught him swiftly as his knees buckled.

"Can you—do you think you can carry me there?"

Gerald was already in motion. He grimaced slightly and Darin reddened; he had barely returned to the world, and in the distance of fading concentration, he'd completely forgotten the large man's injuries.

But he let himself be carried. Astor would need him—or need Bethany's touch. He couldn't see clearly beyond the bar counter until they were almost at its edge. Then, Astor's back came into view. It was still, stiff. The poker that had been so tightly clutched moments before now lay on the floor. Bloodless.

"Astor."

Astor turned at the sound of his name. Tears blurred his eyes, but he contained them, struggling with water almost as intensely as Darin had struggled with fire moments before.

Confused, Darin looked beyond Astor. There, on the floor, curled tightly around Verdor's body, sat Erin. Her sword lay across his thighs; his apron was wet and sticky.

"Put me down," he told Gerald. This time, he was prepared for the weakness of his legs—enough so that he didn't give in to them.

"She won't—" Astor said, through clenched teeth, "she won't let me near him."

"She's trying to help," Darin answered. But even as the words died he knew that it was a lie. *What's wrong with her?*

Bethany did not answer, but her silence was heavy with knowledge. If he'd had the time, Darin would have argued. Instead, as Bethany was to be no use in one way, he put her to work in another. He set her tip firmly down on the hardwood planks and leaned against her, absorbing support from the contact. Slowly, he made his way toward Erin.

The sword that had been set aside came swinging around, its point to Darin's chest. He had not even seen her touch it.

"Get back!" she snarled, in a voice low and trembling. "Get back! You can't have him!" Her face was white, with a hint of red running down her cheeks. Her eyes, wild, showed no sign of recognition.

Darin stopped, and the sword came slowly down. Without thinking, he brought his staff around as if to challenge her. Light leaped from its rounded tip, a column of white-fire that sped unerring to its target.

It eddied around Erin and Verdor, finding purchase only in her hunched body. Her eyes widened in shock and horror, and she threw up her arms to cover her face. One loud scream touched the air, to fade slowly into sobs.

This time, when Darin started forward, the sword remained where it lay. "Erin?"

She looked up at him, one arm still thrown across Verdor's chest. The fact that she seemed to know him now gave little comfort.

"It's no good," she whispered, fighting for breath. "It's no good. Don't you see? I can't—I can't—" Her fingers curled into small, shaking fists. The rest of the sentence was lost.

Astor came forward and knelt for a moment beside Verdor,

his small hands seeking something at his father's throat. He bowed his head a moment, and then bellowed.

"Mother!"

Darin jumped back as Astor swung around to face him. Tears ran freely down the boy's face.

"Thank the Hearts," he whispered, looking at Darin. "He's—I think he's still alive. Father. Father."

"Still alive?" She shook her head. "No." The light in her eyes was intense; green, but strange and growing wild. "No. I tried to find him." She choked as Darin brought the staff of Culverne around once more. "I dug up his grave. He was dead, Darin."

"No," he replied softly. "It was—a dream, Erin. A bad dream. Come away." The words sounded strange to his ears, and it was a moment before he understood why: Bethany underlay every syllable with the surety and warmth of her experience, her strength—and her voice.

Before Erin could answer, Marlin strode into the bar. Although small and subdued, her presence was in many ways more intimidating than her husband's—everyone noticed.

"Mother!" Astor turned to her.

"Astor—no." A rustle of skirts, and Darin found himself being pushed roughly out of the way. Erin's hold on the innkeeper tightened, but she left the sword lying as Marlin approached. If Marlin thought anything odd about the way Erin held on to her injured husband, she said nothing; there wasn't time for it. She knelt, pushing Erin's sticky hair aside, and touched her husband's throat, much as their son had done minutes earlier. "Astor."

The boy nodded, relief evident on his face. Marlin was here; she would take care of everything. She had already begun to roll up her sleeves, and her face showed no sign of panic.

"Go for the doctor. Take—" She took a deep breath. "You—what is your name?"

"Gerald," Darin replied softly. "He can't—can't speak."

"Gerald, then. Can you guard my boy through the warrens if he goes for the doctor?"

Gerald nodded grimly. He walked over to one of the bodies that lined the floor and retrieved a sword from its side. He started to pick up a shield, saw the broken circle etched there like a trail of flame, and cast it aside.

"Go," Marlin said, in a low urgent voice. "Hurry." Astor swallowed and nodded. He was out the door before Gerald had started to move. "You, Mika—can you help me move him?" She started to slide her hands under Verdor's still shoulders. Erin shook her head.

"Girl, get out of the way."

Erin stared mutely, her brows twisting in confusion as if she couldn't understand the language that Marlin spoke.

"Marlin," Darin said nervously, "she's not—she's not quite right. She . . ." He couldn't think of anything to say that would explain what he didn't understand himself.

Marlin's lips twisted; her eyes narrowed. "Get out of the way," she said, in a low even tone that made Darin's hair stand on end. "Let him go."

Erin clung more tightly. Marlin raised both hands to give Erin a shove. The innkeeper's wife was not trained to fight—Erin was. Darin bit his lip as Erin hit Marlin, hard, in the jaw; the innkeeper's wife fell back. When she rose, unsteadily, her lip was bleeding and her eyes were almost black.

"Dark Heart!" she swore. "Do you want to kill him?"

"He's dead!" Erin shouted back, baring her canines like an animal.

"He's not dead, you little fool, but you'll kill him yet!"

Erin looked up in confusion. Her eyes seemed to clear, but Darin could still see the madness in them, like liquid crystal brought to light. He pointed the staff again, but before he could draw upon its power, Bethany spoke.

No, Initiate. Not now. All I can do, I have done. This madness, this trap—she must find her own way out.

What if she can't?

Bethany had no answer. Darin's fingers bit into wood, but he stayed his hand. Without Bethany's aid and guidance, there was little else he could do.

"Alive?" Erin whispered.

Marlin darted forward in desperation and fear, but this time Erin only shrugged her off. Her eyes were wide and round; she looked young and fey—and dangerous.

"Dammit, Lorie! Please!" Her face was red, but even she could see now what Darin had tried to tell her. She swallowed, and her voice shook with anger when she spoke, but she kept the words simple, even. "Please. He needs my help." She turned to look at Darin, and he saw the fear struggling to the surface of her face. Marlin was strong, he'd seen evidence of it, but she was no match for Erin's mad strength.

"Oh," Erin said, in wonder. Her fingers came up, blood-stained and sticky, and fluttered at Verdor's throat like a moth near flame. Then they stilled suddenly, and the tears fell. "I *can* help him. I can." Before either Darin or Marlin could move, she swung her arm around and grabbed her sword. The light in her eyes was all brightness, a brilliant green glow that flashed outward like a beacon. Marlin skittered back, throwing her hands in front of her chest, a flesh shield that was useless.

"Erin, *don't!*"

The innkeeper's wife barely had voice for a scream before Erin did the unthinkable: she turned her blade point inward. Gritting her teeth, her mouth still clung to its fey smile. The blade sank into her chest and came out in a fountain of blood that rained down upon the unconscious innkeeper. She pitched forward, her hands jerking as they tried to grab on to Verdor.

Darin caught Marlin and held her as tightly as he could. The innkeeper's wife had no fight left; horror, and something that might have been pity, had robbed her of even words.

"Don't touch her now," Darin whispered, in a horror that echoed Marlin's. "Don't—she can't be touched." He pulled the older woman away, unable to tell whether it was her trembling he felt so strongly, or his own.

"Why?" Marlin whispered.

Darin put his arms around her, clutching the staff in his hands. He began to call upon Bethany, and this time received the answering warmth of her light. He kept Marlin's face turned away from Erin—but he himself could not help but watch. The light drew his eyes.

He didn't understand why she had done it, wasn't certain that madness hadn't driven her to take her life. But the light was glowing—surely there wouldn't be light if her death was all that she sought?

Lernan, please. Please . . .

And oh, God answered. For once, God answered. The light grew brighter and brighter, until Darin was forced to squint at the sight of it. He wondered, dimly, if Marlin would be able to see it. It grew, and for just an instant, Darin was in the gardens of House Darclan, beside a priestess whose power was, and would always be, beyond his.

She did not rise, nor did she raise her arms. Indeed she had not moved at all. But she was still the vessel of God. The light spilled outward, traveling, it seemed, along the river of her blood, to touch Verdor's still body. To sink into the wounds across it that still offered blood.

The light grew stronger, whiter, reaching outward to shadow the bar in Darin's vision. Marlin still trembled, her tears held in check only because the arms that held her were as young as her son's.

She couldn't see God's light. No one here could, save for Darin. Beneath the layers of fear and anticipation that enveloped him, he felt a strange type of pity for eyes that would not—could never—see the singular beauty of Lernan's healing light.

And then, even as he watched, the light dimmed and faded, hovering around Erin like a halo before seeping away into the ordinary. She had not moved. Her arms still clutched Verdor's bloodstained chest as if it were an anchor. There was silence a moment, almost too heavy to bear, and then once again the sound of weeping. Darin's throat grew dry.

At least Erin was alive.

He released Marlin, who spun around.

As if aware of the movement, Erin looked up, grimy red tears staining her cheeks. "I'm sorry," she said softly. "I—I shouldn't have tried to touch God. I swore."

Darin breathed a sigh of relief. The light, strange and fey, had gone out of her face. She looked haggard, disheveled, and dirty—but she was sane.

"Oh, Darin." She shook her head, her arms still holding Verdor. "He reminded me so much of—" Her hair flew up awkwardly as she discarded the sentence.

Darin started to speak and stopped, aware of the inadequacy of his words. She needed a comfort that he could not provide. If the Hand of God couldn't still her pain, what could he do? Something. Anything. He stumbled forward, reaching out to touch her shoulder.

But before he reached her, two arms wrapped themselves hesitantly around her torso. Verdor's arms.

* * *

I failed. I always fail. Biting her lip, she tried to bury her face in the wet apron that Verdor wore. *No. God failed me. God failed me.*

And then, she felt those arms *move.* They were shaky, but their grip was real, strong. Erin stopped breathing. She looked down suddenly, and saw the innkeeper's brown eyes, searching her face in concern. She started to speak, and then stopped as she heard a familiar, faint voice.

Great-granddaughter, your peace.

She had thought never to hear that voice again. "Why?" she asked, aware that Verdor's eyes were narrowing further. "Why? You betrayed us—betrayed me. Why have you helped me here?"

Erin, last of Elliath, you are to me what your line-mate Belfas was to you: a choice between two loves.

She flinched, began to speak in denial, and then looked down to see Verdor's very alive face.

I have chosen the harsh road and the harder love; I have sacrificed almost all. For hope; the hope of change. I accept your judgment, as you accepted Belfas'. But you are still my great-granddaughter, and we travel the same road, if you can see it.

She didn't want to think about what his words meant; not now. But she knew that he would leave her soon; his power was almost gone from her veins. "Thank you," she said softly, surprising herself.

"You're welcome," Verdor answered, as he struggled to sit. "What in the hells is going on here?"

chapter
eleven

"Lorie was fighting again, wasn't she?"

Marlin nodded quietly; stray wisps of peppered hair that had escaped her orderly pins struggled along her cheeks. "Hold still." She rolled her eyes as her husband tried valiantly to obey her dictate. The most he ever did was try—success was too much to hope for.

Sighing, she looked past his chest to the mirror at his back; that had been a costly conceit, but she was happy to have it at times like these. His chest was bare, and almost self-consciously she ran her fingers along the closed, pale length of one wound— the one that had almost killed him. Then she heard his gentle intake of breath and pressed her fingers to his lips. "Here. Put it on."

"Didn't catch much of it," Verdor said, as he pulled his head free of the unhemmed collar of the plain, dark tunic. "Those men in the bar—"

"I didn't see what happened." Marlin sighed. "Verdor, can you not stand still a moment?"

"Still?" he muttered. "I've done this before; you'll pierce me half a dozen times with those things." He glared at the pins that she held in her stout hands.

"I wouldn't if you'd stop twitching." As if to prove her words, she drove a pin through the swathe of cloth that she was fitting. She pricked herself and cursed none-too-gently while Verdor's smug smile made all the point that he dared.

"Where is Lorie, anyway?"

"In her room. Cleaning up, I'd imagine."

"She hurt?"

Marlin was silent again. Then she sighed and set her pins aside on a pitted table. "Yes," she answered quietly. "And no."

"Well?"

"Well what?"

"Which is it? Yes or no?"

"Both, I said." She turned away from her husband then, and raised her hands to her cheeks; they were cold.

"Marlin?" Verdor touched his wife's shoulder gently and turned her around. His eyes narrowed almost as much as hers had widened. "What's wrong?"

"I don't understand it. We thought—you'd both be dead. But she did something. And I don't know what." Marlin shook her head; more hair came loose, the motion was so fierce. "The half-wit brought her, and he can't explain her either. I've tried to get it out of him." She looked up and met her husband's eyes. Verdor, still as dense and alive as ever. Half-guiltily, she added, "They want to leave tomorrow, the four of them. I told 'em we'd give 'em what we could, but we don't have much."

"Marlin?"

"She brought you both back from death. And I want her to leave, Verdor, even though she could do that. She frightens me."

"Frightens you?" he said heartily. "Nothing frightens you—certainly no slip of a girl."

"You didn't clean up the dead."

They had both seen death before; they were no strangers to the violence that brought it. That Marlin was pale and this forthright spoke of things that Verdor knew he didn't want to hear.

"Who is she?" Marlin said suddenly.

"I don't know. But I'd wager that she's trouble for the Church, and that's fine by me." He smiled, trying to coerce a similar expression from his wife. "Anyone who is, is. Why do you think I put up with the half-wit?"

Marlin's smile was shaky, but it was there. Years of habit lent her the simple expression. "I don't know. I wouldn't." She swallowed, took a deep breath, and shook off the shadows. Almost. "She's—she's like the dead priests of Marantine, isn't she?" Before her husband could answer, she shook her head. "It's too big for us, love. We've done all we can."

"Too big?" He eyed the pins with resignation. "Aye, maybe it is. But we've done all we can, as you say. And maybe it'll count as a part of it yet.'' Leaning down, he tried to steal a kiss from his wife's pursed lips. He caught a pin instead, and grumbled.

Sleep unmakes experience, winding it into the fabric of dreams and memories so changed they become real.

In the shadows, beneath blankets thick enough to double her width, Erin slept, curled on her side, her cheek against plumped pillows. Her skin was smooth and dark, part of sleep's contours. No wrinkles creased her forehead, no frown tugged at her lips; seen this way, she could have been young again, with no travail of war, death, and broken promises to bind her to the living.

There were dreams, but no living nightmare; the bridge that straddled darkness and the waking world had been closed for one evening. The lingering presence of the Bright Heart kept fear and guilt at bay.

A fire burned low in the grate of the room, and the blinds shut out light from the street. The muted colors of faded furniture and curtains were shades of gray that might have belonged to a childhood long since outgrown.

The door to her room opened a crack; light filtered in, but so slowly it couldn't call her back from sleep. Verdor walked quietly in and held a small lamp to one side. Here, in the darkness and the peaceful quiet, he touched his chest with his free hand.

He knew more than he had cared to say to Marlin, because he knew that it would only upset her.

I helped you, he thought, as he straightened the covers very gently. *You repaid me.*

Many, many years ago, he had checked on his daughter's sleep in just such a way—but without the bitter alloy of loss and memory that he carried now.

You're going to leave us, aren't you, Lorie? She shifted slightly, and he put the lamp behind his back, blocking its soft light. *Just as well.*

But he waited for a few minutes, until she stirred again, because he was older and foolish with age. Because he wanted to hear her say it one more time, in darkness and sleepy need that had nothing to do with either of their lives.

''Father?''

''It's all right, lass,'' he whispered softly. ''Everything is safe.''

She didn't really wake. He knew she wouldn't remember this and was glad of it. He walked quietly to the door and then turned again.

"Lady of Mercy," he said almost hesitantly. "Will I ever know what really happened to my Caitlin?"

But she didn't answer; he didn't expect her to.

Lord Erliss of Mordechai was exhausted. He looked down at the report on his desk and frowned again; the frown had etched itself into the corners of his lips. At his right, a Sword waited his command; at his left, a slave waited to serve breakfast. He wanted food; his stomach gave a low growl, which embarrassed him. But business had to come first.

"Captain, are you certain of the accuracy of this report?"

"Absolutely," was the swift reply. "Lord Kellem was injured slightly, but managed to escape the Red Dog Inn in the warrens. He made his way home with an inefficient escort and has not stirred yet from his manse."

"And?"

"He was purportedly searching for a man known as Renar."

"We'd expected that," Erliss replied, trying to be composed and in control of the situation, as his cousin always was. "I expect Lord Kellem will return warren-side this afternoon with his house corps."

The captain nodded.

"And it looks as if we were right about the woman; from what you've managed to gather, the fighting was . . . similar to our last encounter. God's blood," he added, under his breath. "We can't afford to have her escape, and we can't afford to have her captured by another house." If she was, he might as well remain in this winter countryside; Malakar and its domain would no longer be safe.

The captain waited for orders in silence.

"You recruited mercenaries?"

"Sir. For three days hence."

Erliss ground his teeth. "They'll be wasted, then. We have no choice; we'll have to move." He began to rise, wondering if he would ever get a chance to eat, when a knock at the door interrupted him for the second time that morning. He nodded to the slave; the slave went.

When he returned, he returned with a Sword who had obviously made haste to arrive. The man knelt carefully at the edge of the carpet.

"There's no need to be so fastidious; the slaves will clean. What's so urgent?"

"The merchant caravan, sir."

"What of it?" Erliss spoke too quickly, and realizing this, he slowly resumed his seat.

"I think it's making preparations to leave the city, sir. There's activity in the compounds, and it seems to be at her direction."

It was the only good news that Erliss had received that morning. He allowed his pleasure to show for a moment before he returned to business. "Have our men ready to move as well—quickly. We have hours at best to prepare for our attack." He paused at the look on the captain's face. "You can be ready?"

"Lord."

"Good. Do so." Lord Erliss inclined his head slightly. "I will join you shortly. Have my horse readied." As the captain turned on heel and left, he gestured frantically at the slave. He had to eat, even though he suddenly doubted he had the stomach for it. Things had happened as he'd hoped—and planned—they'd just happened too quickly. He was in control.

Erin's companions were subdued and quiet when it came time for leaving. They ate the meal Marlin had cooked for them in somber silence. Trethar made a few sarcastic comments in Renar's direction, but even these were quiet barbs; both the thief and the mage had missed the fight entirely.

Darin winced as Renar seemed to absorb, rather than deflect, the older man's words. He frowned at Trethar, but the mage pointedly looked elsewhere as if to say, This man might be a king, but he's not *my* king.

Gerald was dressed for winter travel—and Darin guessed that the clothing itself must have come from Verdor. The sword hadn't, and Darin didn't ask because he didn't want to know that Renar had been slinking about the market again; the first trip had proved almost fatal.

Only Erin seemed unduly cheerful. She smiled often, laughing a little at Verdor's quiet comments. She ate well, relishing the food as if she'd just discovered flavor. Her clothing was new, but from the fit it was obvious that it had come from Marlin—a

Marlin who had absented herself lamely from the eating table
on the pretext of packing the last of the supplies for the travelers.

At the door—the back door—of the inn, Erin gave each of
those who'd come to say good-bye a quick hug. Marlin held
herself stiff, even though her arms mechanically returned the
embrace, but Astor whispered his thanks in her ear and hugged
her tightly.

Verdor swung her off her feet as if she were a child. "You
come back when you're finished, Lorie," he told her as he set
her down. "Come back. We'll miss you here." He smiled fondly
and tugged at her long, single braid. "You're about the only
decent thing that half-wit's ever brought to the Red Dog."

"Nobody else with any decency would come here," Renar
replied smartly. But he smiled for the first time since the Swords
had come.

Verdor took the hand that he offered and shook it soundly,
with a slightly malicious grin. "And you, half-wit. I'll see you
again, no doubt. And no doubt," he added, "you'll be trouble."

Renar nodded, trying to appear nonchalant as he massaged
the hand that Verdor had gripped. "I'm terribly sorry about the
bar," he said lamely.

"I'm only sorry you don't have the funds to cover the window," Verdor said. "Don't be sorry; it doesn't suit you." Then
he turned to Erin and hugged her tightly again. For a moment,
his chin rested on the top of her head. His eyes closed. It seemed
as if he wouldn't let go.

Smile, Initiate, Bethany said. *What he has done for the Sarillorn, no other could have done. He survived.*

I know, Darin replied. *He—he called her back.*

And she came. A good sign.

Renar led the way through the streets of the warren with an
ease that spoke of long association. He did, however, avoid all
alleys and shortcuts that might prove as disastrous as the last he
had taken, and Trethar followed his lead with only minimal
complaint. Darin was certain that at least part of the mage's tact
was enforced by the presence of Gerald, who, while not obviously there to protect Renar, nevertheless made a good shadow.

Discussion was nonexistent; both Erin and Renar were alert
and on the lookout, and if Erin was surprised by Renar's silence

and unusual look of purpose, she was too busy to comment. Although Erin and Renar were the slightest of the group in stature, they somehow seemed to be the most dangerous. Catlike, they stalked the shadows, twitching at any sign of unusual movement.

At length, they reached a section of the city that none but Renar had ever seen: the caravan compounds in the merchants' quarter. Erin turned to Renar and tapped him lightly on the shoulder as he came to a stop outside of its thickly barred gates.

"Yes?" He didn't turn to face her; instead he watched as men hooked horses to cover wagons. The wagons were themselves unusual; they had wheels, but an inch above where the wheels rested on the swept, frozen dirt were runners commonly seen on sleds.

"Is that the 'escape route' you spoke of?"

He nodded. "But I told them to be ready for us." His lips folded into a frown as misted air floated up to freeze on loose strands of hair.

"This is a merchants' caravan, isn't it?"

"Very clever, my lady. It's exactly that. And we are its most important cargo. Come on." And so saying, he reached between the bars very carefully and struggled with something that Erin couldn't see.

She heard the click, though, and stared at him.

He bowed. "I have to keep in practice," he said softly, with the hint of theatrical smile. "Why don't we find our savior?"

The merchant's guards were good enough; they noticed the gates begin their creaking roll open and were at once armed and ready. The horses nickered and were ignored as a tall man stepped forward. He was of an imposing build and wore a shirt of chain beneath a surcoat that was obviously designed for the cold. He wore no crest and no flag to designate him a house affiliate. Very few were the independent merchants who operated without house arms, house support, and house constraints.

"Hold it right there," he said quietly. "Luke—get Hildy."

Someone even taller than the guard leader grinned in response and disappeared into the stable. The second man also wore a chain shirt, but his surcoat, also naturally colored and without crest to face it, was decidedly less clean. The merchant obviously could afford to pay guards well.

"Really," Renar said, crossing his arms over his chest. "Is that sword absolutely necessary?"

The roll of the man's dark eyes told Erin clearly that he at least recognized Robert. Renar. She bit her lip and glanced sideways at her traveling companion, unable—or perhaps unwilling—to see him as a monarch.

And then she forgot him for a moment as a bundle shuffled into view.

"That's the merchant," Renar whispered quietly.

It was impossible to tell whether or not the merchant was male or female. Not that it mattered. The bundle stopped in front of the first man in chain as the man he'd called Luke pulled up the rear.

"Well, hello, Robert," the merchant said cheerily. Only then was Erin able to place her as a woman. She wore fur, and beneath the fur, a layer of wool covered her mouth and cheeks up to the lower edge of her eyes; a fur cap edged down to the top of her eyes. Her hands were mitten-covered, and her feet were either huge or, more likely, layered in socks so thick that they increased her boot size. "I hope you haven't had any more problems with my boys, dear."

"Hildy . . ." the guard in chain said, his tone of voice a combination of affection and warning.

"Men, then. But really, dear, you're all boys to me."

"Hildy."

"Just wait until you've had a chance to catch up a bit, Hamin. Now do be dear and don't interrupt me." She turned, or at least the scarf did, to face Renar. "Can't stand the cold," she said, and held out a mitten. "Now, what was I saying? Oh yes. Were the boys a little better behaved this time?"

The captain of the guards gave a sigh and rolled his eyes theatrically in her direction. He was not a young man, and his face showed the scars of his chosen profession; nothing about him looked even remotely boyish.

"Yes, rather, although it's quite clear that they recognized me; I don't know what this fuss with weapons was about," Renar replied, puffing his chest out slightly and glaring pointedly at Hamin. He bowed. "It's a pleasure to see you again."

"A pleasure, is it?" Hildy shook her head. "Well, it might be at that. But there's business to attend to." She looked past his shoulder; she was tall enough that this wasn't difficult. "These are your companions, then?"

"Indeed. Allow me to introduce—"

"That's all right, dear. We don't need to know their names. They match the description you gave; that's enough for now." She nodded to herself and turned back to Hamin. "Has the runner from Bordaril come through yet?"

"Yes, ma'am."

"And?"

"They aren't happy about the change of schedule." He shrugged. "But they'll have guards meet us before the north gate."

"Good," she said, nodding happily. She turned, and then turned back. "Robert, dear?"

"Yes?"

"You'll have to change the clothing you're wearing. It won't suit your role. I think we've got spare uniforms of sorts—put one on and try your best to blend in with the boys."

Renar's expression indicated clearly what he thought of that. So did Hamin's. They eyed each other with almost identical disdain.

"And you, sir," Hildy said to Trethar, "will be my resident cloth expert; your face looks old enough to have some useful experience behind it. The boy can join the men in pretending to be useful." Her eyes lit up as she saw Gerald, standing quietly behind Erin as if he were a guard of some efficacy. "And you, dear, will fit right in with the boys. I dare say you'll do us proud in that role. You will join them, won't you, dear?"

Gerald nodded, and then turned his gaze to Hamin. Their eyes met, and Hamin's narrowed softly before rounding out in surprise. "Gerald?" The giant remained silent—and still. "Gerald, is that you?"

He started forward, and Hildy caught him by the shoulder. Her grip, constrained as it was by a thick layer of sheepskin, was nonetheless very strong. "Hamin," she said, all lilt gone from her voice, "we ask no questions. Remember?"

Hamin nodded, but absently, as he turned to glance back at Renar. His eyes narrowed, but when they relaxed he once again wore a mask of bored indifference. What lay beyond that, no one asked.

Last, Hildy considered Erin; her gaze lingered there longest.

"You, young lady, you'll probably have to stay covered. And hide that sword, if you will. I'll probably claim you as a niece, or something along those lines." She sighed again. "I'd let you go with the boys, as you've more of the look about you than the young men, but it'd probably cause dissent at the gates. Either of them."

Erin nodded quietly.

"I've got your papers. You'll need them when we reach Dagothrin, but not before. Hamin, dear?"

"Yes, Hildy?"

"Do try not to be so boisterous with our guests, hmmm?"

"Ma'am."

Hildy executed a slow turn and made her way back to the wagons. Her voice, loud and low, could be heard clearly when she couldn't be seen as she directed her people in the finishing touches of the caravan's preparation for travel. Darin tried to ask Renar about the merchant, but he indicated quite clearly, if not loudly, that he didn't wish to speak of it here.

At last, when the wagons, with their runners, were loaded and ready to travel, Hildy called them into the caravans. For the first leg of the journey, she had Renar, Trethar, and Darin crowded into the supplies wagon. She told them that they wouldn't need to worry about the wagons being searched; the Bordaril passes, handed to gate guards that were also owned by Bordaril, ensured a clean exit from Verdann.

"But, boys," she added. "I expect you to behave yourselves. Don't argue, don't fight, and don't make a lot of noise. You'll embarrass the gate guards and get me into a small bit of trouble."

It became immediately clear that Hildy didn't drive her own wagons; she didn't, as she reiterated for perhaps the fourth time, like the cold. On the run back, she would take to the cab and direct the horses, but on the route there, she would take advantage of wagon room to hide from the wind and the open air.

"Well, dear," Hildy said, removing one of the three scarves she wore. "This is rather cozy."

Erin smiled; her cap and scarf were already in her lap.

"Don't keep such a distance from your aunt. Feel free to cuddle up." She indicated the wealth of furs that covered her body. "If you feel cold."

"Thank you—"

"Hildy."

"Thank you, Hildy." But Erin made no move to take advantage of the merchant's offer. "I—the cold doesn't really bother me."

"One of the advantages of being young." The older woman removed her mittens, and the gloves beneath, and then unraveled the last two scarves. Erin found herself face to face with a rounded, lined visage. But for all that she looked old, Erin had no doubt that Hildy was still quite active and healthy. "Of course, there are advantages to being old as well. They're just not as obvious to you youngsters." Hildy laughed again, her teeth gleaming in the muted light of the wagon. She leaned forward conspiratorially. "I've not done anything like this in five years."

Erin raised an eyebrow. "The Empire allowed you to trade with Culverne?"

"Pardon?"

"Uh—Dagothrin."

Hildy chuckled. "Marantine, dear." Her smile dimmed a moment as she searched Erin's face. "That's what the country was called, you know. And no, the Empire didn't officially sanction trade, but as you might know, Dagothrin has the best mines on the continent for precious metals, and not all the named houses were Church-affiliated. At the time. I believe Bordaril is, now."

"You brought goods into Dagothrin?"

"Goods, yes. And a cargo much like yourself." She frowned for a moment, her blue eyes narrowing as she stared off into the distance. Then she shrugged, and her massive shoulders shook the curtain of fur she wore. "Can't be helped, child. Things change, and if you can't adapt, you go out with the tide, so much flotsam and jetsam. Hildy always survives."

Erin didn't doubt it.

"I'll be in the city for at least a couple of weeks—four, I think—and I'll be staying in the merchant quarter. Not hard to find; not hard at all. You can ask for me, if you've got freedom of movement. You can send for me, if you don't." Hildy smiled and reached out with a bent hand. "I smell a new wind blowing, girl."

"You're taking a risk," Erin said softly, unsure of what else she could say.

"Yes. But that's the other trick to being a survivor. You've got to know when to take risks." Her eyes narrowed. "Are you sure you aren't feeling the cold a bit? You're shivering, girl."

"I'm fine," Erin said softly. "I—is this risk a good one?"

"It may be." Hildy sighed and looked away. "And to be honest, it may not be. But, child, to be truthful—and you can trust this, as it isn't about money—sometimes life is only worthwhile when the right kind of risks lie there waiting to be taken. Hope is the folly of humanity, as my granddam used to say, but we'd be dead of despair without it."

"Hope," Erin said softly. "But you might end up dead anyway."

"Well, now, aren't we the cheerful one? You just trust Hildy, young lady. I'll tell you when gloom-and-doom are the order of the day."

They met their guards at the gate, although Erin didn't see them until they alighted from the caravan at the first of the inns that would house them. Erin was given her own room, as was Trethar; Renar was expected to room with the caravan guards. He made no secret of how he felt about this, but wisely refrained from coming to blows with any of the attendant guards. Gerald made it clear, even without the use of words, that any fight Renar picked was his own to deal with; this, of course, was met with Renar's usual good grace. It was all an act—it had to be—but Darin still wondered how a grown man could pout so effectively.

"Sarillorn."

"Erin."

She smiled as the pale light that was somehow shadow resolved itself into two familiar bodies. The landscape curved away from her uneasily, roiling at her feet. She caught the hint of color lurking beneath the darkness of its surface, a deep metallic red, hard and cold.

As always, Belfas came first, a fine mist of light waiting upon form. He held out a hand in tentative greeting, just far enough out of her reach that she could not grasp it.

"Erin," he said again, softly.

"Belf."

"We haven't seen you in a long time."

"Days," she replied, and looked away for a moment. A hiss

of a sigh escaped his lips, curling around her ears. She shivered.
"Soon, Belfas. Soon, Carla, Rein, Teya. Soon." Belief, foreign
and welcome, lent strength and force to those words. She
clenched her hands and looked down at her translucent fingers.
"Where is Kandor?"

"Here, little one." He appeared beside Belfas, his light the
stronger light, his face the more peaceful countenance. His eyes,
luminescent, swept over her, returning to meet her steady gaze.
"You have found something that you lacked."

"Yes."

"What?"

"I don't know." She was afraid to question it or probe it too
deeply; this odd peace might prove to be fragile and easily lost.

"Tell me, Sarillorn, do you still seek death?"

She looked back at him, and then turned to Belfas. Mirroring
Kandor's gesture, she held out a slim hand, bringing it to within
an inch of Belfas' still face. His eyes were shadowed and pain
lurked just beneath their surface.

"I don't know," she said at last. "But death is the Lady I
must seek, or you will never leave this place."

"Yes." Kandor, gentle and peaceful when not at war, was
still an absolute; he had no lie in him, not even to comfort—the
Sarillorn understood this, even if Erin flinched. "Perhaps you
were better off before."

"No." She shook her head firmly, and strands of diaphanous
hair traced her cheeks. "I think I was a little mad."

"And do you now forgive God? Do you forgive the Lady?"

The intensity of Kandor's question caught and held her tongue.
The warmth that she had found faded into heat; the embers of
an anger that still burned, still hurt. "I swore blood-oath," she
reminded him softly.

He shrugged, signifying nothing. And he waited.

"Not the Lady," she said at last, gazing out into the endless
darkness. "Not yet. Not now."

"No? Ah well. Seeing you now, Sarillorn, seeing you at rest,
I do."

"You?" Beyond the one word, she could say no more. But
the thought that Kandor might harbor his own resentment, his
own anger, had never occurred to her. The Servants had been
all grace, all light, all servitude to God; if they had questioned
or felt anger or sorrow, she had never seen it.

Kandor smiled, although the smile was oddly stiff. "I was among the oldest of our number, Sarillorn. Yet even so I spent much of my time among the half bloods and the humans. I am Servant, yes, and to Lernan—but I am not immune to the effect of . . . affection. It eases my time, in this darkness, to know that you are more peaceful.

"By the will of God and the will of the Lady, you are the last of our children." The darkness held shadows that only Kandor could see; he gazed past her shoulder in silence before speaking again. "What will you do now?"

"We go to Culverne and its holdings. The patriarch of that line travels with me, as do three others."

"And there?"

"There's still resistance to the Malanthi rule in Culverne. We hope to contact it, to become part of it—and to use it."

"Go then, Sarillorn."

She nodded, feeling herself begin to slide away. "But I will come again."

In the morning, the snow was thin and completely white; the sun, untrammeled by clouds, made a winter desert of blinding light. The guards donned boots and snowshoes, and Erin was shuffled off to the wagons before she'd had a chance to strap what looked like flat baskets to her feet. Robert, Gerald, and Darin all seemed reasonably comfortable with them, as did both Hildy's guards and the guards of House Bordaril. Trethar disdained their use, but was spared any embarrassment by Hildy.

"At our age," she said severely, "we don't have to walk. Leave that to the boys, dear."

Trethar, beard frosted with frozen breath, looked dour. He was many things: mage, member of the brotherhood, teacher. He was not a "dear." But in the end, he chose to behave like any of the other men under Hildy's command; he followed the orders that were liberally wrapped in her mother's voice. Even the House Bordaril guards listened to her with only slight grimaces to show that they were used to a different master. It was obvious that most of them had traveled this route before. Both Erin and Darin kept as clear of them as possible without letting their previous experience with house guards show.

Still, Erin was nervous as she took to the wagons, and her

nerves, tightly strung, caused a shiver that had nothing to do with the cold.

It's the house guards, she told herself firmly.

Hildy, however, seemed oblivious to the reason behind the shudder, and Erin found herself wrapped in a shawl, two scarves, and two layers of mittens. Winter wear, as Hildy had said, was not in short supply, and if all of it was oversized, Erin couldn't see fit to point it out.

But when the wagons slid to a halt two hours from the inn, she threw off the woollen layers as if they were webs and reached for her sword before Hamin's face appeared between the canvas flap.

"Hildy," he said, in a low tense voice, "I think there's trouble ahead."

"Trouble?" Picking up Erin's castoffs, she held out a bundled hand, and Hamin helped her out, into the daylight. Erin followed, a tense and dangerous shadow.

The first thing she saw were the backs of the caravan escort; Hildy's in their plain winter wear, and the Bordaril guards in their crested livery. They had weapons ready; three had longbows, strung, with arrows nocked.

All this, Erin took in, in a warrior's glance; it had no time to register before her eyes were scanning the horizon. She cursed the snow, the light, and the conditions of the north that were so unfamiliar to her.

"There are men on the road, dear," Hildy said to Hamin.

"Yes," Erin replied, before Hamin had to think of something to say. "There are. I think about fifty." She took a breath and then exhaled it in a warm, wet cloud. "I don't see Church crests."

Hamin raised an eyebrow. "You've got good vision." He left Hildy's side and came around to stand at Erin's. "What else do you see?"

She squinted and muttered something dire about the sun. But as her eyes slowly adjusted themselves, she saw that at least one banner flew.

"Field of emerald green," she said, shading her eyes. "Gold; I think it's a crescent, curve up. I can't tell; we're too far away."

Hildy said something very, very unladylike.

"Hildy!" Hamin's jaw dropped.

"I'm sorry, dear," Hildy said. "But that's enough of a description." She shook her head. "I think we'd best pull back."

"It's Vanellon, isn't it?"

She nodded grimly.

"But they wouldn't dare—the last time they tried to launch trade war here, they were wiped out to a man, and they had to pay a sizable compensation to Bordaril."

"Yes, dear, we know that," she replied. "Get young Jenkins, please."

Young Jenkins was a man in his late thirties; he had served Bordaril for all of his adult life and had trained under their auspices for most of his youth. He wore three stripes and his age with equal dignity, and an odd sort of strength that might have been menacing in a different light followed the line of his brow and his dark eyes. He bowed to Hildy as he approached, but that was all the formality the situation allowed.

"Vanellon," he said tersely. She nodded. "Retreat?"

"I think it best, dear. We don't have the numbers or the strategic location that would make any other option wiser."

He nodded again, perfunctorily; it was clear to even Erin that he had no intention of pursuing any other course, regardless of what Hildy recommended. It was also obvious that he was angry; his lips were white around the edges, his eyes narrowed, and his jaw muscles twitched.

Hildy stepped aside and began to make ready to turn the wagons, and the horses, in the confines of the road. "I can't understand it," she muttered to herself. "They wouldn't dare do this unless something had changed."

And Erin felt it then; a sudden surge of power that made her bones ache with remembered pain.

chapter
twelve

"Off the road!" she shouted, already in motion. "Hildy!"
Hildy froze and then swung around to see Erin's body crest along the snow top. She took Erin's urgent command, and magnified it with the strength of her voice and her voice's imperative. No one in the caravan could escape the notice she gave. They fled, saving questions for later.

Hildy paused only long enough to cut the nearest horse from its straps; up and down the caravan, others had already made a similar decision. Then she, too, took to the dubious shelter that barren trees offered. She had no need to ask Erin why; the ground rumbled beneath her feet like a constrained giant.

Power crackled in the air, distorting vision in a visible, red aurora of light. The hair on Erin's neck, fine and soft, stood on end. Her skin tingled, and her teeth ached with a chill that had nothing to do with the winter.

She heard the screaming then, a thin wild note that pierced air and the barrier of distance with pathos and ease. Cursing, she pulled her sword.

A Karnar was on the field.

Just as he had been taught, Erliss bound his blood-power in a net around his dying sacrifice. He could see lines that reached from his fingers around the whole of the young man's body; they were red but bright, a fine, strong weave that tightened as Erliss concentrated. He traced each thread, each narrow line, and finally pushed.

Sweating, he held one hand aloft. The sacrificial blade gleamed red and silver as it met his palm; it bit, but did not

180

sting as it passed beyond his thin skein of flesh. The red robes—
an early gift from Vellen—that swirled around his arms and legs
were a flag; in a field of white, red dominated all.

Gently, almost nervously, he reached down and placed his
open wound against the throat of the dying man. Blood met
blood as Erliss joined the net he had made for God.

God answered. There were no words and no command, no
ceremony, and no grand welcome. Nevertheless, hand upon
death, Erliss felt the pulse of the Dark Heart as it became, for
moments, his own.

He rose, and those Swords that had attended him in the ritual
moved away like black-linked shadows.

Do not pull too much, Vellen had said. Erliss did not feel, at
this moment, that that was possible. Without care for archers,
he strode to the front of the assembled line and gazed down the
snow-covered road. There, casting tiny, fragile shadows, his
quarry began to flee. It was important that they not retreat.

For the first time in his life, he had no doubts at all about his
ability to stop them.

Darin knelt in the snow. His cheek brushed bark and branch,
growing red with little cuts.

"Darin, are you all right?"

Renar touched his shoulder gingerly, and Darin spun around,
Bethany clutched and levered as if to strike. He stopped himself,
or Bethany stopped him—he wasn't sure which. Shaking, he
tried to look out to the road.

Darin.

I know. He bit his lip, while he listened for the shouts of
Bordaril guards as they gave and took their orders.

"What is it?" Renar said, speaking more sharply than he had
ever done.

"P-Priest." Darin swallowed. "A priest is—is with them."
The road trembled again, and Darin rose, seeking safety in the
thick of the woods.

"How in the hells can you see that from here?" Renar said,
his forehead creased. "Even I can't—" the rest of the sentence
was lost as the ground began to buckle like simple, white linen,
folding slowly into itself.

Initiate, Bethany said, her voice no less harsh than Renar's
had been. *Ward.*

* * *

Erin cursed again; she felt the folding of the earth and knew that the Karnar had seen to it that the wagons, at least, could make no passage back. She felt red-fire in the ground beneath her feet, a distant pain, and protected herself from it with the power of Line Elliath. Green light shimmered on the surface of her skin as white light struggled to fruition.

She knew what had to be done, and knew—again and always—that she could not be the one to do it. Daring the edge of the road and the hill that was forming out of snow and twisting dirt, she gazed out at the enemy.

Not one armed man had made any move toward them. They waited the outcome of their Karnar's attack. Just as she would have done, had their positions been reversed.

Darin reached down for the simple dagger he carried as the ground attempted to prevent his action. Snow, like white earth, split and separated; trees loomed above like crippled limbs. He thought of fire—but not the flames of Trethar's magic.

Darin.

Shaking, he righted himself, thinking of priests and the Dark Heart and slavery—whispers of death and the fear of it. Bethany's voice was an urgent harmony to his gestures, as the knife came free.. He hesitated a moment, and then it came back: the True Ward.

He missed his palm, the first time. He tried to tell himself that it was the cold that caused the trembling, not the fear that the ward required. A distant scream of panic lit up like an aural flare; it lingered so close to his ears that he might have voiced it.

And then his blood, steaming slightly, graced the snow; he felt the sting of cold steel before he dropped the knife. He wouldn't find it again, he was certain of that. It didn't matter.

His hands crossed his chest in the Circle. His eyes grew green and bright and shining; he couldn't see them, and Renar, who could, could not appreciate the first sign of God's grace and the hope that it brought.

Darin felt Lernan's power as it flowed beneath his skin and raised his hands high before he realized that he didn't know what to do with it.

Initiate.

When had Bethany fallen? He didn't remember dropping her, and he began to scramble around at his feet as the ground threatened to shift again. *Bethany?*

Take me up.

I can't! I—

"Patriarch." Darin jumped back in surprise, and Renar shoved Bethany's cold, smooth form into his hands. "You were looking for this?"

He didn't take the time to offer thanks.

Now. Touch the ground, Darin. Touch it. You will know what to do—and I will help. This man is Karnari; his power is, I think, greater than yours.

Darin touched the ground; snow melted against his hands, but he didn't notice the cold; against the barrier of his fingers, he felt red-fire *snap*.

Erin felt it, too. Her ears, attuned to the red and the white in a way that even Darin's would never be, heard the distant roar of power as the two blood-magics clashed beneath her feet. She dropped her head a moment, realizing what must have happened; her lips moved in a prayer of thanks before she raised her eyes to scan the northern road. Now, the enemy would have to come to them.

Erliss felt it the moment it hit. The ground, which had seemed an extension of his will and his desire, suddenly fought back, pushing the fingers of the Dark Heart's power away. He had expected it—he told himself this as he bent himself to the task.

"Lord?"

Through gritted teeth, he shook his head, his lips turned up in a silent snarl. The Swords watched and waited his command.

"Darin?"

"Not now."

Renar touched his shoulder. "Darin," he said, softly but no less urgently, "we have to know—will the roads hold?"

We? Darin looked up and saw one of the House Bordaril guards standing stiff at Renar's side. His face was bruised, and a trickle of blood trailed down his jaw, drying in the cool wind. "I don't—I don't know. I think so."

Renar and Captain Jenkins exchanged a look. Jenkins nodded grimly. "We'll start a retreat. Can you move?"

"No," Darin replied, struggling with the word.

"Guard his back, then," the Bordaril captain said. "You'll know when to move."

"I will," Renar answered softly. He settled back against a lopsided tree and watched as the wind made moving shadows of low-hanging branches.

"Lord!"

Erliss glanced up; sweat beaded his forehead although the air was biting in its chill. His eyes, red, shone with God's power; the Sword that had interrupted him so urgently fought the urge to take a step back. Erliss said nothing.

"You asked to be informed of the enemy disposition. They're retreating."

Erliss bent his power—his will—to the road; he felt the white shields of his ancient enemy give without breaking. Frustrated, he almost lashed out with the Dark Heart's granted magic—but he held himself in long enough to let the Sword's words penetrate.

He had two choices: He could continue to contest the stone and frozen dirt that he had hoped to use to achieve a painless victory—or he could order his Swords, and the guards of Vanellon, into combat. He had always been taught not to choose in haste—but here, he had no choice.

Darin suddenly collapsed into the snow. The movement was so sudden and so complete that it caught Renar unaware; before he could cross the scant distance between them, Darin looked up, shaking snow from his face.

"It's gone," he said.

"What's gone?"

"The red. It's gone."

Renar clapped him on the back and caught his jacket to prevent him from sprawling, again, in the uneven snow.

"No," Darin said, grabbing the thief's wrists, "you don't understand. I didn't do it—it just stopped."

"Just stopped?" Renar's eyes narrowed, and then widened. He turned lightly in the snow and vanished over a newly created hill's shelf. Darin had time to collect Bethany and gain his feet before Renar returned.

"It's time to retreat," Renar said quietly. "No—not that way. Off the road, Darin."

"But what about Erin?"

"Now," Renar said urgently.. "The Lady can take care of herself."

Erin heard the horses scant seconds before she saw them. She didn't take the time to warn Captain Jenkins, Hamin, or Hildy— she didn't need to. Hamin's brief curse, and Jenkin's obscenity, made it perfectly clear that they, too, could see their danger.

"They'll pay for this," Jenkins whispered, just before he began to bark out orders to his men.

"Great," Hamin replied. "They'll pay. But we won't be around to see it."

"Hamin!" Hildy's voice sounded.

Hamin turned, half in guilt. "Yes?"

"We don't need a chief morale officer, dear. Luke, pay attention to the roads. Where are Robert and Darin?"

"Someplace safer than here."

Erin might have complained about the chatter, but even over it, Luke and Hamin were in motion. More of Hildy's guards came to the fore, to stand loosely beside their Bordaril counterparts.

"Ma'am?"

She shook herself as a younger, crested soldier spoke. "Yes?" She responded.

"You'd best get behind the line. We're fighting in retreat, but you and Hildy can probably get clear."

The absurdity of having a guard of any house defend her— possibly die for her—made Erin wince. The world had grown strange and impossible in the past three centuries.

"Ma'am?"

She looked down at her blade—the bright sword that the Lady of Elliath had crafted for Gallin's use. "No," she said softly. "I don't think that would be wise."

"Dear?" Hildy's voice was sharper than the young guard's.

I'm sorry, Hildy, Erin thought, as she turned her back on the merchant's unspoken command and joined Hamin and Luke, *but this is the life I know best. And these are the enemies I've always fought.*

"Hildy, dammit! Get *out* of here!"

The wagons were pushed into the road's center; they formed an awkward and easily moved barricade behind which Hildy's men—and Erin—grouped. The horses that carried the charge this far began to slow in their pace. Foot soldiers would not be far behind.

Erin cast a small orb of light past the range of her vision. Seconds later, it guttered like a candle in a storm. She cursed.

"Lady?"

"Karnar's here," she replied, without looking up to see who had interrupted her concentration. A word that was easily less genteel than her own moved back through the ranks like a wave. She spun to see Hamin's pale face. "He's mine, if he's anyone's. Trust him to me."

So saying, she pulled back her shield arm, dropped her shield, and gestured in a wide, doubled arc. Her blade caught the light and reflected it back tenfold.

Hamin stopped, caught by the hard angle of her jaw and the long, thick line of the braid that cut her back. Her skin was pale, and her eyes were hard, almost metallic, as they shone green. Something about her was familiar—something about her reminded him of Marantine.

When the pillar of white-fire suddenly leapt to life beyond the wagon barrier, he suddenly stopped breathing, caught in the hints and shadows of the memories of his youth.

"The Church," he said softly, eyes wide. "It's not the king they're after—it's you they want."

She didn't reply. But a scream did—followed by an eerie, lambent red that enveloped the treetops, a counter to her first strike.

"Mine," she whispered again, softly, as she bent to retrieve her shield. No one gainsaid her.

Renar cursed softly; the words formed a cloud of mist, rather than sound. In the snow, under the clear and cloudless skies, two sets of tracks made obvious both their retreat and their direction.

This alone would not have caused his consternation. The

quarrel that had lodged three feet to the right, still quivering in the sudden silence, did. It was very unlike either the Swords or the house forces to use something as simple and inelegant as a crossbow. It was very unlike either to stop and track two people who had obviously deserted before a major battle.

But of course there had to be exceptions. He tried very hard not to dwell on the reasons for those. His hands were cold as he fumbled for a weapon that lent itself to throwing. They were colder when he readied it and peered out from behind the tree he had chosen for cover. He couldn't see Darin at all and couldn't afford to take the time for more than a cursory glance.

Ah. There—the branches were quivering counter to the breeze.

The wagons, of course, stopped no one for long; Vanellon soldiery and their Church counterparts came streaming in on the flanks, green and gold, black and red.

"Lady!" Hamin shouted. His tone made clear what he wanted to say; time deprived him of the chance to be more clear.

Dispassionately, she wondered how competent Hildy's men were. And then she had no time to wonder, for which she was almost thankful. The black and the red were upon her, and were it not for the intangible weight of experience, she might have been sixteen again, starting out fresh and untried in the summer fields of Elliath.

Remember: This is for real. You cannot step out of a circle and be safe; you cannot call the fight. The time for games is past.

Telvar. The man who had had the teaching, and the command, of her early skills. His words came back, as they almost always did in battle.

But, she thought as she parried the first strike of the day, he was wrong. It was very like a game—and each contestant, each combatant, bore the marks of his training; the style, the attack and defense, of past masters, and of past warriors. Here, on fields of dirt and snow, or wheat or forest or plain, they would test, and be tested—and those that won, lived.

If some part of her was dimly aware that life was more than simple survival, she forgot it; she denied it. Light blazed down the lines of her face, calling the Swords to battle.

And all there witnessed the terrible grandeur, the icy beauty,

that Erin herself could never know and never see—the vision of
the Sarillorn of Elliath upon the field of blood-war.

Before Renar could even aim, the tree erupted in a skein of
fire and smoke. He heard screams that died slowly; winter bark
crackled and blackened in harmony. The dagger that he held
found its sheath as he sagged briefly against his own tree and
closed his eyes.

Fire came again; he saw it reflected around the shadows at
his feet, and felt its heat at his back. He heard another tree wither
and die beneath the screams of burned flesh. He counted softly
to himself, and when he heard the fifth tree fall, he peered out
into the lengthening, unnatural silence.

"Old man?" he whispered softly.

There was no answer. He listened, and caught the sound of
heaving breath, a single person's. He waited; nothing happened.
"Old man?" Quietly, he stepped out and began to scan the
forest.

He saw only Darin. "Boy?"

Darin turned slowly at the sound of his voice. "Yes?"

Renar started to ask about Trethar, and then stopped, seeing
the pallor of Darin's face. Seeing—and suddenly understanding.
He stepped forward, unmindful of snow and blackened ash and
caught Darin's shoulders.

"You didn't have to—" His voice caught and broke. He saw
a young man before him, his only connection to childhood a
dearth of years. "I was supposed to guard your back, remember?"

"You take orders from House Bordaril?"

"No." Stung, Renar let his hands fall to the sides. Darin
turned away, searching the smoking ruins of human bodies and
dead trees. Searching, finding—and remembering.

"You don't like to kill any more than I do," Darin said quietly, drawing Bethany to his chest as if to gain security from
her. "You can't do it for me. I'm—I'm the patriarch."

Before Renar could speak, he saw the tears glisten down Darin's cheeks. He approached Darin again, sliding an arm across
his shoulders as a comrade might. "And I," he said, watching
what Darin watched, and seeing in it no different light, "am the
king."

* * *

Erin discovered, too quickly, that the House Vanellon soldiers were nonblooded. She called light; it barely touched their eyes. More, she could do—but it was unwise at best, when they had the advantage of numbers, to throw away the last vestiges of her power to affect them. She remained in the odd half circle that Luke and Hamin formed at her flanks, drawing on their abilities and their own lack of blood to balance her battle skills.

It was not so strange; after all, she had been the first to accept the gray-kin into her growing army—the first to train them and to accept their oaths of allegiance to Elliath. She knew how to best make use of their steady and imperturbable strength in the face of the red-fires that pocked the fields of war.

She used it now, retreating in time to cast her shields and summon the Greater Ward, with the Sarillorn's power behind it. She could not see her enemy clearly; not with normal vision. But she was aware of him, as he was of her.

How much longer can you keep this up? She bit her lip, and changed her grip on her sword as Hamin, too, fell back. As she parried a blow from the side, she grimaced; there was no room to dodge or roll without compromising either of her two companions.

Red-fire flared up, seeking purchase against her skin. How long? Longer, she feared, than she could.

Trethar, where in the hells are you?

"There," Renar said softly, as his head sunk back below the embankment. His eyes were clear and unblinking, but Darin could clearly see the sallow circles that ringed them. He brushed his hair out of his eyes, and turned.

Darin could hear the din of swordplay clearly. Orders cut the silence, falling into cacophony before either he or Renar could understand them, let alone decide which side they had issued from.

"They've used the wagons to block the cavalry charge. There are no horses." Renar crawled up the snow-covered ground again and turned to look over his shoulder. "Are you ready?"

"Ready."

"Let's go, then."

The fire that suddenly fanned out like a sheet across the forest was no blood-magic; Erin knew it before she heard the concerted intake of breath from friend and foe alike. She was a warrior; she took advantage of the momentary distraction to end the closest threat.

The fires faded, and with them, the red-fire attacks. Erin could clearly hear the tenor of relayed orders shift. Her lips turned up in a smile that never reached her eyes; instead of remaining on the defensive, she sprang suddenly forward like a cat unleashed. She heard Hamin's single-word curse and Luke's descriptive four words, before she left the comfort of their ranks—and the road.

The Karnar had moved—quickly—to retreat. She didn't want to lose him.

She didn't want to give him the chance to surrender.

Erliss of Mordechai stumbled as the snow beneath his feet turned into slush. He cursed and waved his Swords on, glancing nervously over his shoulder. Something had gone wrong, but he did not understand what.

The fires, obviously magical, that were unblessed by either Bright Heart or Dark, were known to him; they belonged to Lord Vellen of Damion, and no other. Had Vellen somehow betrayed them?

He shook his head, trying to free himself from the weight of the thought. Vellen had nothing to gain if he died. Nothing. But betrayal for political reasons beyond the ken of a liege was not unknown. It worried him, and he had no time to worry; at any moment, white-fire or mage-fire could consume him if he let his guard slip. He kept his shields up with words and gestures and hurried for the horses that now seemed impossibly far away.

He never really considered the danger of a normal, un-sheathed dagger. And when he did, his consideration lasted for mere minutes—as did his life.

When Erin finally tracked her quarry down, she knew that he was gone; his light had flickered and dimmed even as she ran, forsaking the expedient of cover.

His black robe lay snow-sodden and sprawled against the ground; the smoking ruins of what must have been his honor guard were scattered beside charred trees.

She swallowed bitterly and let her own light dwindle and die, until she was only another swordsman on the field.

"Lady."

She turned at the sound of the voice. Renar stepped quietly out from behind a blackened oak. He bowed; his hair trailed his cheeks.

"Good work." Her voice was terse and noncommittal.

He said nothing, nothing at all; instead he stared at her face as if clearly reading the disappointment she tried—and failed—not to show.

"Where's Trethar?" she said, after a moment's pause.

"Isn't he with you?"

"No. He's—" And then she stopped. "Darin?" She gestured at the fallen.

Renar nodded. "Your war, Lady, is also the patriarch's. And my own."

"Where is he? Is he whole?"

Renar nodded again. "But he's not the soldiers we are. He's claimed a few moments of private time. He'll join us at the wagons; I believe the battle is over."

"I never thought of you," Erin said, as she turned and called the compass spell, "as much of a soldier."

"And I never thought of you," he replied, as his eyes followed the swaying line of her warrior's braid, "as much of a killer."

"I didn't kill him," Erin said, stung. But she froze, suddenly aware of the red patina that stained her sword and her tunic with its little glow of death.

"No." They both knew what he meant. He met her eyes, and saw them, sunken and hollow. "It's always easier," he offered at last, "when you feel these things yourself; seeing them in other people reveals just how ugly they are."

She narrowed her eyes, confused, and stopped herself from sliding into a sudden, sharp valley. "I wanted to kill him because he was their leader."

"In honesty?" He offered her a hand, and withdrew it when she turned away. Slowly, and with more grace than Erin had ever shown, he leaped across the open divide, his cape trailing him like a plume of velvet smoke.

"Not—not completely." She didn't understand how anyone could sport such an impractical item of clothing and hoped sincerely that he would fall and break a limb.

Renar nodded. "I like to kill them, too," he said softly, and when he offered her a hand the second time, she took it. "I've killed a total of four of the Karnari over the space of the last five years. It's never been enough." He grimaced as he discovered that she was deceptively heavy. "I want Vellen, you see. And I want Duke Jordan of Marantine. Of *Illan*." He spit, clearing his mouth of even the hint of the word. "But I know why—I want them to suffer. I want to see them die. I want them to know who it was that killed them—and why. Yourself, Lady?"

Stunned by his honesty, Erin shook her head, unable to offer him less, but unable to match him.

"Do you know where Darin is?" he suddenly asked, swerving in conversation so sharply, Erin again shook her head. "He's mourning the dead. All of the dead."

She stopped then. "Renar—I'll meet you at the wagons as well."

He bowed, as if her sudden stiffness was completely natural. His words cast more of a shadow than he did; Erin watched his back grow smaller and more distant as she stood in the sun-warmed chill. Her hands began to tremble, and she looked down at them, wondering, suddenly, who she was and why she was not the person that might once, like Darin, have mourned.

Trethar had been injured when the priest had twisted the road; he had felt the tremor of the earth beneath the wagons, but had not moved quickly enough to escape the canvas-covered confines.

Darin discovered his mentor under Hildy's gentle—and loud—ministrations. She was putting the finishing touches on a makeshift sling that hooked around Trethar's forearm on one end and his neck on the other.

Trethar was pale, and obviously in some pain. But he smiled as Darin came into view. "Darin."

"Are you all right?" Darin rushed to stand at Trethar's side.

The brown-robed mage grimaced. "No. But I'm told I'll live. You're pale," he added, reaching out to clasp Darin's shoulder.

"We won."

"We know that, dear," Hildy broke in. "Trethar, do sit still for just another minute. The wagons are almost ready to move, and I'll need the boys to help me lay you out."

"I'm not a corpse yet, Hildy," he replied with a wry smile. He lifted his arm gingerly. "But I'm not young, either." "No," she answered, as she put her hands firmly on his shoulders to bar him from standing. She looked at Darin's silent face and shook her head. "I don't imagine many of us are, anymore. Darin, dear—go tell the boys that we're ready to move. Help them with the fallen if you can."

He nodded and started to leave before her voice brought him up short.

"And tell Hamin that we'll take our dead, as usual."

It was not Darin, but Erin, who offered the comfort and healing of the Bright Heart. She did so without ceremony, and indeed, often without notice. "I'm a doctor," she would say, if anyone asked. Only a few did.

With a touch, and little flare of light that only she could see, she killed infections, stopped bleeding, and eased pain. For one or two of the young men, she brought the peace of death; there was no other mercy she could grant. And then, exhausted, she helped Hamin, Luke, and the rest of Hildy's guards gather their dead.

"We can't leave 'em here," Hamin said, his face tight and angular. "We'll break ground in the city and bury 'em there." He looked up at the sun; it had reached its zenith. "But Vanellon'll pay for this."

"We all will," Erin said, in a whisper so quiet that Hamin missed it entirely.

interlude

He writhed in the darkness of memory, silent now, although the cry bloomed within him like a second, ruptured heart. Black air dissolved and reformed in a cacophony of motion, an unsteady welter of deep shadow, that conformed to him whether he willed it or not. He knew himself to be delirious, even here—especially here.

For in the wave and murmur of the Dark Heart's hand, he could see her face and hear her voice, although she could be found in nothing at all that surrounded him. Nothing. The memory of a Servant was endless and perfect, and try as he might to turn from it, it followed, dogging him, wounding him with the perfection of her tears and her deep, bitter anger.

Sara . . .

The Dark Heart's laughter matched his loss, equally silent and equally felt. He did not know how long he had been here— but he was not Sargoth and had not studied any other plane of refuge. There was the human world, replete with its stench of mortality and loss, and there was the womb of the Dark Heart. Neither place held comfort for him, but here at least he had thought to escape her image, her anger, and her hatred.

The very air swam in mocking denial.

"No, Lord. I am well aware that that is not your way." It was useless for him to try to hide the bitterness of his words; it was not the words that betrayed him or laid him open to his Lord's enjoyment. Rather, it was what the humans and their half-sired brethren so primitively called blood.

Stefanos, your gift to me has no likeness.

His Lord laughed loud and long, the hiss of it lingering in the

194

tremor of the ground, the movement of air, and the boiling of what lay between.

Stefanos did not reply.

His Lord laughed again, and Stefanos felt that laughter running through him, an alien, living thing. Yet still, through it all, Sara watched him with her accusation writ large across her pale face.

Stefanos knew that his own laughter was a pale echo of all that the Dark Heart was. The darkness was too vast, too strange, for even the First Sundered's comprehension; Stefanos still bore the faintest trace of the taint of his Enemy.

No. No Light exists here. None that I do not control. Not even the taint in you.

Stefanos was still First Servant. He stood, grimly, if that had meaning here. "You could not, Lord. I am no mere mortal to be thus controlled—even by you."

You are of the Darkness. Through you, my hand holds the gray world. There was silence then. There was ethereal darkness, blood older than life stirring. *I could take the gray world from you, First of my Servants.*

The landscape grew quiet, touched and twisted only by the anger of the First of the Sundered.

"Only try, Lord. Try, and there will be no half-breed priests left to grace your marble altars. Combined, they still cannot stand against me, and they have less power now than they did when they first tried to do so."

Perhaps, Stefanos. To add interest to this, I will warn you of one thing: You are not the only one to whom Sargoth has shown his pathways.

Stefanos did not reply. A small part of his mind told him to render his Lord a very Pyrrhic victory; the Dark Heart's was the greater power, and therefore the greater majesty. But none of his Servants accepted defeat easily, no matter that it was a given, and Stefanos had always been first among his number. For the sake of his hollow Empire, he had lost Sara. This, the Dark Heart knew well.

And if he had paid so dear a price for the Empire, he would keep it.

No one had ever seen the Dark Heart's smile, but all of his Servants had felt its echo at one time or another in their long battle. Stefanos felt it now.

The Dark Heart could hear the unspoken determination that was fueled by the loveliest of griefs. Such a gift. Yet great as that gift had been, the Dark Heart had been shown a way to make it greater still.

The Second of his Servants had given him that path. He did not know if his First would survive it; nor did he care. Never in the time since his awakening had he played so large a part in the affairs of the outer world. He flexed one muscle and felt, for an instant, all of creation twisting and dying in his hand. Pleased, he continued to watch and to plan.

chapter
thirteen

The city. It was an intricate man-made mountain, capped with the subtle colors of winter and the gray of a bleak sky.

What was its name? From the top of the graduated hill, Darin stopped to stare. It had always been just *the city* to any who mentioned it, the sound of the words crisp and clear in case any idle listener should wonder.

"Dagothrin," Renar said, touching Darin's shoulder lightly.

"Dagothrin." The word sounded strange as it passed his lips. After a second, he realized why: It was empty, hollow. "The city."

"Yes."

Darin had never approached it from this gate before; he'd only traveled south twice. No, it had been three times. His throat went dry as he pushed the thought away.

"It—it looks the same."

"From here, yes." Renar's lips curled. "Gerald looks the same as well."

I don't, Darin thought. But he said nothing, looking down at his right arm. The scar was hidden under layers of clothing that kept the winter chill at bay. "What are we going to do, Renar?"

"We?" Renar replied, trying to capture lightness. He failed. "I don't know what you and the Lady must do." His face grew still, remote. "I am going to kill a man." Bethany shifted in Darin's grip, but before Darin could speak, Renar said, "Don't get religious on me. It won't be the first time I've done it."

Darin was silent.

"Never mind. We've got to get there first, and when we do, we've got to find a place to stay. We can't stay with Hildy, and

197

the equivalent of the Red Dog burned down in the fires years ago.''

Gerald, silent in movement as well as speech, placed a hand firmly on his monarch's shoulder. Renar shrugged it off, glancing back in anger. "Enough, Gerald. Just let it be.''

But Gerald shook his head firmly, and after a moment, made it clear that his intent was not to lecture. He pointed to the caravan, tracing the road it followed to the city—and beyond. Then he touched his chest.

For a moment, Renar stared at his friend, his eyes narrowed. Then he sighed and nodded. "Take a horse, all right?''

Gerald nodded and left.

"Where is he going?''

"Not to Dagothrin,'' was the moody response.

Initiate, Bethany added, just as Darin drew breath to speak again, *there are some things it is better not to know. We are not safe, yet.*

A sharp word cut the sleep away. Darin stirred uneasily and then shot upward; Erin's roll lay empty. It was dark in the tent, but flickering orange told Darin that the fire was still alight. He shook his head, drawing his coat tightly around himself, before he emerged from the bedroll.

Very reluctantly, and no less cautiously, Darin pushed the flaps of the small tent aside.

"—no less suicidal than what you plan!''

"Lady, for your own sake, I—''

"And you can stop calling me that! I'm no child when it comes to the necessities of war!''

"I've never even implied—''

Darin pulled himself back into the tent. With an angry snort, he pulled his vacant boots from under the bedroll and stuffed his feet into them. Then, cursing, he removed them and put them on the correct feet.

At least, he thought, *Trethar isn't with them.*

"—don't just assassinate the governing ruler of an imperial province and blithely walk out!''

"No more than you assassinate a Lord of the Lesser Cabal and do the same!''

Erin met Renar's shout—and it was a shout—with a blistering

glare. Darin was afraid she was going to hit him; her fists were clenched tightly at her sides, and they were shaking.

"I've got a method of walking out again. Can you say the same?"

"What method could possibly dispose of the Swords of the damned Church?" He followed the direction of her clenched fist. Frowned. "Lady, you are *not* an army."

You haven't seen her fight, Renar. But looking at her, her fingers furiously tapping her sword hilt, he wondered. There was no madness behind the honest anger she showed, and he couldn't guess at how much of her battle prowess had been skill and how much insanity.

He bit his lip, glad that they had chosen to camp at the furthest remove from the Bordaril escort. He didn't understand why they were both being so loud.

"Lady."

"Robert."

"There's something you aren't telling me, isn't there?"

Erin laughed. Of all sounds, it was the one that Darin expected least. "Something *I'm* not telling *you?*"

"I believe that was what I said."

She laughed again. "When we first met, what were you running from?"

"I might ask you the same if you'd do me the grace of taking me seriously."

"After all the work you do to make sure I—or anyone, for that matter—don't?"

He was silent a moment, deciding. "From the Church." He shrugged fluidly, his chest beginning to jut forward in his normal speaking posture. His face took on the mold of long-suffering arrogance so familiar to Erin.

Darin believed him anyway.

So did Erin.

"Why?"

"Pardon?"

"Why were you running from the Church?"

His mouth formed a pout of distaste. "If you must know, Lady, certain members of the Church hierarchy and I had something of a misunderstanding. I thought it best to flee the capital for more southerly climes until the dust had settled." He paused, raised an eyebrow, and struck a pose that was at once indolent and arrogant.

Erin said nothing, but she met his eyes squarely as he opened his mouth. He shut it again and shook his head with a bitter smile. In a completely even voice, he said, "It is the truth, you know."

She did not reply, and after a moment, he turned away and continued. His voice changed, as did his posture; he slid his hands under his arms and did not look back. "I assassinated two of the Greater Cabal."

"Two?" Her eyes wide, Erin shook her head softly.

"Two of his faction; they war, even among themselves. Especially among themselves. I would have killed him, but he's heavily guarded. I did what damage I could." He spun around suddenly, eyes swallowing darkness.

"Renar?"

"Yes, Lady?" His voice alone asked for the silence and peace that his words would not.

Erin ignored it. "How were you discovered?"

"Discovered?"

"How did they know it was you?"

"Lady." His face, bare of any pretense, was a stranger's to her. He seemed a winter thing; chill and frozen and pale. "I told you: I wanted to make him acknowledge me. To cause him harm and to make him realize who had done it, and why. I made no attempt to hide my identity." His face was stark and impenetrable, a wall of stone. "If not for the vaunted, publicized, and undeniable truth of Vellen's cursed magical abilities, I would have killed him long ago."

"Renar, who are you?" Her voice was muted, even gentle.

Renar did not answer the question that she asked. But he did answer. "Who am I? Renar of Dagothrin. Prince Renar of Maran, and of Marantine. Youngest brother to Gregory, the man who would have been king in these lands. Did you see the height of our walls? Centuries ago, they were built for us by the strongest of the Servants—the Lady of Elliath—that they might stand against the malice of the Dark Heart and his Servants. I don't know why. I don't care. They were my home."

"They fell."

"Yes." He turned again, restlessly pacing the confines of the cage that night made—night, and Erin's watchful eyes. "But from within. Had the Servants of the Enemy themselves been present, they couldn't have breached those walls—or so we were taught.

"Why else did Marantine stand when all other kingdoms had fallen? For years—years!—we defied the Church. Slaves escaped to our lands, and those of the Empire who had the mind to fight it and the cunning to pass through enemy territory. The enemy waited, and in vain.

"Or so we thought." He put his hands behind his back and locked them, trembling, perhaps due to cold. Bitterly, he began again.

"I was always a trial to him. My mother, perhaps, understood me better—we, she and I, were trained by the same hand, and if she was my superior, she had less chance to practice."

It was moments before Erin realized that he spoke of his father and his family.

"I was the youngest of four—far from the throne, a peace offering to my grandfather. I went everywhere, throughout all of our lands into Veriloth itself. I never practiced my craft in my own country. Why should I have? We had enemies in plenty. I was brash. Arrogant. I let my name be known. Why do a deed if not to receive credit for it?" He laughed. The sound cut Darin deeply. "And they credited much to me. Bards—the few that still survive—storytellers, common people.

"My—the king eventually heard of this. I believe that at first, it amused him. But then our nobility began to suffer unexplained and expert thefts. That amused him not at all. We traded many harsh words over it, but there was no proof that it was I, so it remained an embarrassment to the crown. I often found myself with duties that kept me well out of Dagothrin.

"Do you wish to hear more?"

Erin stepped forward, all anger drained out of her by the flow of too many honest words from a man who rarely gave voice to them. She reached out to touch his shoulder; he pulled away.

"Outside of Dagothrin, a man can learn many things. And perhaps, in another country, that many might even be of use. I drifted south, to Verdann. I met Verdor and his sweetheart there and spent some months watching her pin him down. Then, I went south again. I found myself in Malakar.

"It's not much changed; grand, glorious buildings, statues depicting any number of Church victories, a marketplace that puts anything else to shame—and the Church complex, a huge set of buildings that dwarf anything else in the city. The priests plan their agendas from within its walls.

"I made friends among the merchants there—very, very few, but friends nonetheless. And through those connections, in a roundabout way, I found that the members of the Greater Cabal had started to refer to themselves as the Lords of the Broken Circle. I thought it hubristic, but I was younger. My curiosity forced me to find out exactly what they were planning."

His hands swung around, forming two fists. "I learned. I went home directly and discovered that those thefts credited to me had had their price. I told them all—my mother, the king, my brothers. My mother, I think, might have been swayed to believe me." He gave another laugh, another bark of pain and oscillated breath. "But she was in the grip of an unusual illness. She died two weeks after I arrived."

"Renar—"

"I did the foolish thing. I accused the Duke of Melgrant of duplicity in a public forum. He was my uncle, Lady. Family in Marantine is important—you must understand that." His breath came out in mist and wreathed his face. "I accused him of selling Marantine to the Empire in exchange for the rulership of her. He was damnably clever; he'd seen it coming all along, and he'd made his own provisions. The thefts, the whispers, the ear of the king—even the death of my mother—all these things to force my hand. I was younger, then. I lost all control."

She did not ask him what he had attempted to do; she knew.

"The king disowned me, publicly. He had no choice; there were a half-dozen witnesses who were willing to condemn me for assaulting the duke with an intent to injure. I couldn't stay. I didn't want to."

Darin thought for a minute that Renar might cry; his face was frozen in a balance between rage and tears. But gradually the wrinkles thinned into a mask again. Only the voice showed emotion.

"And now Duke Jordan of Melgrant serves Veriloth by sitting upon the throne of the governor. The lap that held us as children holds the scepter of Marantine."

He turned away. "I wish I could say that I always hated him. I wish I could tell you that I never trusted him. I can't.

"But I will kill him."

Erin spoke softly, then. "Understood, Renar. But afterward, what will you do?"

He shrugged. "Afterward? If there is one, I shall wait and see."

"And the throne?"

"What of it?"

She shook her head, letting the matter drop. "We each have our allotted tasks, you and I. Go to the governor. I will go to the priest—to the Lord of the Lesser Cabal. And I will show him that the Circle has not yet been broken." She drew her sword suddenly, and the night's darkness was broken by harsh light.

"Lady—" Renar stopped speaking. His eyes met hers, and he found in them a hardness that equaled his own. Lady Erin of Elliath had chosen for herself the path of the warrior and walked it yet.

"Who are you?" he asked softly.

"Erin," she replied. Her lips closed in a firm line as she watched him. "Two lines stand allied with you, the rightful monarch of Marantine. Darin is the patriarch of Culverne, although I suspect you know this well."

"And you, Lady?"

"The Sarillorn of Elliath."

He did not even blink an eye. "Not the matriarch?"

"No. I am the last of my line."

"And not more?"

She met his eyes and slowly brought her sword down. A great wariness seemed to take her, and with obvious effort, she put it aside. "You are braver than I, Renar. Yes, there is more, but I choose not to speak of it. I cannot."

He stared at her a moment, and then spoke again. "Lady, if you enter the temple, do you think, in truth, that you will leave it again?"

She made no answer, absorbed in the sheathing of her weapon.

"Erin?"

"I don't know."

Without a word, Darin retreated to the safety of his tent. He didn't know how either of his friends intended to accomplish their goals—but at least they had them.

What was he going to do in the city?

* * *

When the Lord of the Lesser Cabal received news of a visitor from Malakar, his feelings were mixed. Born of House Cossandara, he was the second son of the reigning lord and had entered the Church's service at a tender age. He had lived most of his life within the confines of the capital, forging a political alliance with a high priest that had endured until that high priest had become the Lord of the Greater Cabal.

And three short years after the completion of that goal, Lord Vellen of Damion had exiled him to Illan. Illan, the only province of the Empire that was not fully civilized and that had these cursed, cold winters without the full amenities that a man of Marak's station had grown accustomed to.

The slave—one brought with him from his house—waited patiently in posture against the carpeted floor. If she had positioned herself rather too close to the fire, Marak was not predisposed to notice; had he, he would have been forced to discipline her in some way, and the slaves that might be called upon to replace her were notoriously ill-disciplined and poorly trained.

That had changed somewhat since he had first arrived and would no doubt change again over time. He had almost learned to be patient.

"Very well," he said quietly. "Send him in."

"Lord." She rose quickly and silently, and he watched her leave the room, all grace and all proper deportment.

When the messenger entered the study, Marak's eyes widened a fraction before he schooled his face. The man was obviously a Sword by his armor, but the fact that he was disheveled and obviously breathing hard lent urgency to his presence. Marak gestured carelessly at a chair, but the Sword shook his head firmly. He dropped to one knee on the carpet and bowed his head.

"High Priest," he said softly, his breath harsh. "I have a message to deliver to you."

"From who?"

The Sword did not answer with words; instead, he reached into the folds of his surcoat and brought out a flattened parchment roll. Red wax, heated and molded into a seal, was all the identification Lord Marak could have asked for.

He cursed the trembling of his hand as he reached for the

scroll. Although the edges of the seal had cracked due to rough handling, the body of its round, flat face was intact; no other eyes would read the missive. He drew a breath, unaware that he held it, and broke the wax.

Usually, in matters of the Church, Vellen chose to have acolytes take dictation and return a completed message for his signature and seal; not this time. The distinctive, bold strokes of Vellen's hand made clear that the request contained therein was urgent. Marak read it carefully, thoroughly; his eyes glanced over the letters again and again, as if to try to absorb what lay beyond the words in the writer's thoughts.

At last he looked up; the Sword still knelt upon the carpet, much as the slave had done. It was almost as if he knew what the message he had carried contained.

"Rise," he said softly. He clapped his hands, and the slave that ran his household was there in an instant; she had to work to make her subservience more pronounced and obvious than the Sword's. But she managed.

"Your answer?" the Sword asked, making no move to comply with the Lord of the Lesser Cabal's permission.

"You shall carry it," Marak said softly. "But it will take time. Rise."

This time, the Sword did as bid, planting his feet firmly against the pile in order not to sway.

"See to him," Marak added, sparing a glance at the slave. "Make a guest room ready and have a meal prepared." He smiled almost apologetically to his new guest. "I'm afraid that I won't be able to join you; I have business to conduct in light of this message. If you would care to follow my slave, she will see to your needs."

The Sword nodded stiffly—he was too exhausted for grace or show. Marak watched, with concealed amusement, as his slave, and Lord Vellen's servant, exited the study together. When he was alone, he allowed all that he felt to brighten his face.

Prince Renar of Marantine, the message had said, *is even now returned to Illan. Stop him, and all who travel with him, and I will see that your service in the province comes to an end—and your service in the capital begins.*

If you do not fail me in this, I will cede to House Cossandara the trade routes that Wintare once commanded; the alliance between Damion and Cossandara will be sealed by your ascension to the ranks of the Karnari.

You have only failed me once, old friend, and I did not mete out the punishment that that merited because of all that had passed between us. I have not forgotten.

Send word with my rider; I will wait in Malakar for any news of your endeavor.

The curtains had been drawn in disdain of the garish light of day; fires burned away the chill of the winter snows. The mahogany table in the great room of Lord Marak's manse gleamed in well-oiled perfection and cast back a reflection of each of the thirteen members of the Lesser Cabal of Illan.

High-backed wing chairs, with burgundy velvet cushions and armrests, had been neatly and evenly spaced along the perimeter of the oval table. All of the chairs were now occupied by the lords and ladies of the Church and the families that served as houses in the province. The two finest chairs, set apart at either end, were occupied by the two men who claimed to be the most influential in the province.

Lord Marak looked calmly and directly across the table at the visage of Duke Jordan of Maran—governor of Illan and member of the Lesser Cabal. In any other province, the Lord of the Lesser Cabal ruled; not here—not yet. On both the left and right, the duke was flanked by two of his palace guards; they stood at perfect, even admirable, attention in dress armor and surcoats of gold-tinged blue. Jordan's eyes, pale gray, narrowed.

Lord Marak raised his hand for silence, but as usual it was the unsubtle clearing of Duke Jordan's throat that caught and held the cabal's attention. The simple circlet of worked gold that cut his forehead commanded obedience from the families.

"Marak," Jordan said, his voice low and even, "this is a hastily called meeting; I had to interrupt somewhat urgent business, and I have little time. Why did you call us here?"

"My home," Marak answered, in a slightly higher but no less even voice, "is more secure than the council chambers in the palace, Your Honor. And I have news that I wish to contain within the Lesser Cabal—it may affect us all."

Dallis of Handerness raised a pale brow and tilted his head in a manner just shy of insolence. "Indeed, Marak, we had assumed as much." He cast a sideways glance at the duke, who caught it, frowned, and returned a slight, but perceptible, shake of the head. The two men were almost of an age. They were both nearing fifty, and in the prime of their power and the stations they had contrived to achieve. They were allies, and not uneasy in the alliance, as might have been the case had they been Veriloth-bred.

"Dallis," another member said softly, "please allow the high priest to continue."

Had any other spoken, Marak would have counted these words in his favor. But the shock of her voice unnerved him. Verena of Cosgrove was the only priest-designate on the Lesser Cabal who happened to be a woman. In and of itself, it was not completely unusual; women sometimes served the ranks of the Lesser Cabal, although they did not ascend to the Greater.

But Lady Verena, with her dark brown hair and her sharp, angular face, was not possessed of the character that Marak expected in a woman. She was as like to poison an enemy—a kill particularly used by the gentle sex—as to draw the dagger she wore openly at her thigh and cut through his chest. She practiced no veil of modest power, no subtle manipulation, unless particularly hard pressed—and even then, the menace in her carefree smile and her jaunty, friendly laugh was so strong it was tangible.

Fennis of Handerness reached out and caught her hand. She tensed, and he released it immediately, but his annoyance was plain. His father, who carried the line, was not to be corrected by a Cosgrove who did not even hold the title.

Were there not the subtle interplay of politics between those who had come from Malakar—Priests Jerred, Correlan, Altain, Corten, and Sental—and those who had always called this city home, the families would no doubt resort to a more open method of solving their conflicts. They did not.

"Very well," Marak said, nodding quietly. "I have just received word—from a source that I will not even question the veracity of—that Prince Renar of Marantine will soon return to Dagothrin." His breath filled the silence as he paused to let the words sink in. "He will arrive in a matter of days. I believe we can apprehend him at the gates."

Whispers filled the room, some close enough to be heard by the priest, and some meant for the duke's ear. Neither of the two men spoke next.

"No," Verena said softly, raising a hand and smiling with just one corner of her mouth.

"Oh?" Fennis said, before anyone could stop him. "Do you still consider Prince Renar a Cosgrove?"

His words fell like full challenge in the room; all eyes turned first to him, and then to Verena, to wait for her reply.

"No, Fennis dear," Verena replied. "He was never a Cosgrove; that was made clear by Lord Cosgrove when my aunt chose to join Maran." Fennis opened his mouth to reply, and Verena raised a hand, almost snapping her fingers in the air. "But unlike yourself, Cosgroves are not famed for being . . . premature."

"Fennis!" Dallis said sharply; his son subsided angrily, choking back a reply. "Lady Verena?"

She nodded. "We could trap him at the gates—if he enters as you expect him to; I would not count on it. Or, we could prepare more carefully and more cunningly. There is still resistance to our rule in the city, even now. There is still the ragtag little underground that the fires didn't claim."

"They've caused us no trouble for years."

"Talk to Shiarin's merchant guard!" Verena snapped back. "Talk to ours!" But she subsided, as if the anger were an uneasily worn mask. "He'll make contacts here; he has to. If we know he is coming, we'll be able to see where he goes and who offers him aid. These people we can deal with at our leisure, and without giving warning."

"I am not certain," Marak said at last, "that this course of action is wise."

Lady Verena swiveled her head and stared down the point of her nose at the elder man. "Oh?" she asked, in a voice that was too soft. "But, Lord Marak, in your two attempts to take control of this situation, you have failed the Lesser Cabal twice."

Marak's eyes suddenly silvered. Two of his compatriots drew sharp breath and involuntarily moved back from the table; their chairs scuffed along the carpet, teetering dangerously.

If Verena tensed at all, it went unnoticed; she met the sudden pupilless sheen of his eyes as if they were just mirrors in which she could better study the hard lines of her reflection.

"Lord Marak," Duke Jordan said, interrupting yet another obvious power struggle. "Enough. What Cosgrove suggests makes eminent sense to me. The prince was always rather brash and arrogant—and if reports from the south are true, he remains so. Let him come, let him seek contacts and aid, and let our people be prepared to take action in one concerted móvement.'' Before Lord Marak had a chance to reply, the duke rose. ''And now, I have business to attend to. On the morrow, we may formulate the exact methods by which we will counter Renar's intrusion; for today, have the gates watched. That is all.''

The family representatives rose as well, pushing their chairs back, and bowing at the duke's passage. Verena smiled politely at Lord Marak's obvious dislike and trailed her ruler's exit.

Marak hated the Lesser Cabal in Illan with a passion that bordered on youthful indulgence. Not a youth, he kept it firmly under control. He did not dare to openly defy the duke; not yet. It was clear that the families that held power gave more of their allegiance to the duke than to the Church—and those houses that had started relocation in the intemperate climes of the north had not yet gained a strong political foothold.

But he prayed that he would not have to wait until they did.

The wagon lurched to a stop at the gates embedded in the great walls that surrounded Dagothrin. Erin could see them long before she approached, but it was not their size that caught and held her attention. It was the gentle glow that had been the signature of all of the Lady of Elliath's work. Gallin's sword had been an artisan's work—but it paled in comparison to this monument of stone, steel, and wood.

Why did you choose to wall this city, Lady? Why this city and not our holdings?

She did not ask. Instead she began to pay more attention to the guards that had ordered the wagons to a full stop and now made their way over to inspect them.

''Pardon, ma'am,'' one man said, and Erin realized he was speaking to her. ''You'll have to step down for a moment while we check the wagons.''

She nodded meekly and followed his directions, doing her best to stay out of his way.

''What's that, then?''

She stopped as a frown crossed his face, turning it ugly. She looked down, as he did, and flushed. ''It's a—a sword, sir.''

''I can see that. Why are you carrying it?''

She tensed, keeping her hand away from the hilt with an

effort. To her relief, the man did not ask to see it. On the other hand, the Bordaril guards were also in force, and while they cooperated with the city guards, it was clearly not out of respect for anything but custom.

"Come, come, Captain," Hildy said, although the man was clearly not a captain. "You know the problems merchants have had with banditry these last few years; it's not as if the Church— or the governor—has had much success in dealing with them, for all of their promises to us. We can't possibly take too many precautions—and you've seen the girl yourself. Quite pretty." Hildy flipped through a sheaf of papers that rustled and slid against the wool of heavy mittens. "Here. It's all here. I've permission to arm my own guards. Bears the insignia of—"

"I know, ma'am," the guard replied, in a tight, curt voice. "I've seen them already." He turned to stare at Erin again, weighing his choices, and then abruptly deciding. "Keep it bonded in the city, girl, and don't go wandering away from your quarters carrying it. Weapons are strictly prohibited for civilians; if you've a need to go armed in the city, you'd best get another set of papers to carry with you."

Erin nodded, relaxing.

In another half an hour, Hildy's cargo had been cleared. The gates were opened, and the wagons, preceded by Hildy's guards, entered the city. The guards had obviously been through this gate before, for they led the wagons into the heart of the city without asking for directions. Eventually they approached a series of large, tall buildings. From the sounds that permeated the thick canvas of the wagon, Erin could only assume that other merchants made winter treks to Dagothrin. Only when the wagons came to a halt again did Hildy speak.

"You'll know where I am, Erin. Remember me if you need help."

"You've helped us more than you—"

Hildy raised a heavily covered hand. "Wait an hour here, and then you'd best be on your way."

"Thank you, Hildy."

The older woman caught Erin's hand and gripped it tightly through her mittened fingers. She said nothing, but none of her meaning was lost through lack of words.

* * *

"Right." Renar paced in a tight circle. "Are we ready, then?"

"Renar, you've asked this—"

"Yes," Erin said, picking up her pack for the tenth time, as she cut off Trethar's growing annoyance.

Renar nodded and peered out of the dirty window. He cursed and went back to his pacing. "Why are the guards out in such numbers?"

It was a rhetorical question; Trethar had already tried answering it twice a mere half an hour before. Nor would Renar tell them where they were going; he thought it too much of a risk. He had already gone out once, on his own, and his return had been unexpected and hastily accomplished; he would not explain where he had gone, nor why he had entered from the back roof.

To Erin, it was clear that he had managed to evade someone who had followed him; it was also clear that to gain the advantage of that, speed was of the essence. It did not seem as clear to Trethar, who had argued it for a full fifteen minutes before giving up in suspicion and disgust.

Darin took the opportunity to peer, yet again, out of one grimy window.

It doesn't look much different.

No, Initiate. Conquered cities change slowly if the battle to take them is finished quickly. But there are differences.

He sighed, his fingers caressing the hardwood sill.

"Right. Are you ready?"

Pulled out of his reveries, Darin nodded. Erin picked up her pack again. There was more cursing.

Renar pursued this ritual until the streets were at last clear of guards that Darin was almost certain were mythical. Then the prince stepped quickly out of the large building, gesturing for the others to follow. Darin went first, followed by Trethar. Erin hung slightly back, her hands fluttering above the one weapon she was certain of.

The streets were empty. Renar navigated them with the ease of one who is in a familiar house. He walked in the tracks left by horses and wagons, skirting new snow; his companions took care to follow his lead. Twice, they were forced to backtrack while they listened to the ominous sound of clanking armor. But the guards never met them; as a guide, Renar ensured that. He did not speak at all, making his desire known with brief, curt gestures. Seeing him, Darin could almost believe that everything else he had ever shown them was an act: he was efficient, and the expression in his eyes was cold and dark.

The streets began to get larger and cleaner; the buildings became more grand and obviously better kept up. Packed dirt and cobbled stone gave way to lawn, and lawn to sweeping grounds that lay under a blanket of white, behind iron gates. Renar stopped in front of one of these.

"Here," he said softly, his face turned to one side. It was the first word he had spoken since they'd left the merchant quarter. He walked quickly up to the gates and inserted an arm between the bars. Erin thought it odd that such a manor would have no guards, but offered no comment. The gates creaked; Renar pushed them to one side and stepped forward, motioning the others to follow.

"Welcome," he whispered, "to House Brownbur."

"Brownbur?" Darin's eyebrows rose.

"No, he wasn't born with the name. I believe that he was required to choose one to establish his house. He's wily; he's managed to survive the takeover almost intact. He holds more land than previously and has wider trade routes. Most of the southern-based merchants don't choose to travel this far to the north; many won't even come as far as Verdann."

"Isn't a brownbur a weasel?"

"Yes." Renar smiled. "Yes. It's the choice of the name that brings us here. He's an old friend, and as I've said, wily. Anything that can be survived, he'll survive. Much of what I know, I learned from him."

"He'd have to be intelligent to have survived the fall of the city."

"Or immoral."

"Trethar, please."

As they approached the front of the manor, the doors swung open. A balding head peered nervously out at the group. It nodded quickly, and Renar stepped into the house, followed by his companions.

"Hello, Anders."

"And yourself, Your Grace." The man gave a clumsy bow. "Not the best of circumstances to see you in."

"Nor, one hopes, the worst. Is he awake, pray tell?"

"Aye," a melodious, deep voice said. "Awake and waiting your pleasure."

Darin spun first and gave a nervous smile. Lord Brownbur did, in some ways, resemble the namesake he had chosen; his face was triangular and pointed, his front teeth protruded prominently in his small jaw, and his nose, straight and short, rounded out the picture.

"These are the three I received word of, then?"

Word? Darin thought, but asked nothing.

"No, sorry. I had to leave those three at the gates."

"A man in your position," Lord Brownbur said, with a smile that took the sting from his words, "can't afford to be so snide."

Renar shrugged. "It depends, Lord Brownbur, on the audience, wouldn't you agree?"

The man began to laugh. "Lord, is it?" He walked over to Renar, still chuckling, and offered one smooth hand. "Brownbur, is it?" Then, instantly, he sobered. "Aye, I suppose it is now. But come, Renar, don't insult a man in his own home. You know my name."

"If I recall correctly, you insulted several people in their own homes, and on more than one occasion. But very well; Tiras is shorter than Lord Brownbur and slightly more bearable. Come, let me introduce you to my companions."

But Tiras, gray head bowed slightly, had already walked over to Darin. He looked down at the youth, his gaze traveling to the staff strapped along his back, drawn like a moth to the fires.

"Aye," he said quietly. He bent at the knees with a grace that belied the age he wore, and Darin was reminded that this was a friend of Renar's. Another actor, perhaps; certainly one who didn't give much away. "The staff that you carry is yours?"

Darin nodded.

"Then, Patriarch of Culverne, you and I need no introductions. I am ever at your service." He straightened up and then bowed elegantly and formally.

"Or as much as you ever were," Renar added caustically. "Do you think that you can get on without offending *this* patriarch?"

Tiras shot Renar a withering glare that turned into a smile at the last moment. "That much at least. But maybe more." His hand smoothed the wave of gray that covered his forehead. "I've aged, as you'll notice, and not perhaps as gracefully as I might once have. Things change, boy. Don't forget it." He bowed, again, to Darin. "I had heard that the line had fallen."

"I remain." On impulse, Darin pulled the staff from its strap and rested its tip gently on the ground.

"So I see. And maybe not the last of the line either, if you survive the years. But who are your companions? The buffoon I know quite well; he was and is the most embarrassing of my students, but also the most brilliant. Who are the other two?"

"This is Trethar of the brotherhood. He's a—"

"I also teach." Trethar interrupted Darin with a subtle, dismissive wave; it was not lost upon Tiras.

"The name of your order is unfamiliar to me. Your business in Dagothrin?"

Trethar nodded slightly in Darin's direction. "My student."

"I see. And the lovely young lady?"

"Erin, sir." She stepped forward. "My business in Dagothrin is the other half of Renar's."

"I see. Well, as Renar has kindly thought not to inform me of what *his* business here actually is, perhaps we had best leave it at that for the moment. Anders."

"Sir."

"Did you bother to prepare guest rooms in the basement?"

"Sir."

"Good. Show our guests to their quarters, make sure they're settled, and then return here. I've a mind to see about food. And baths." He wrinkled his nose in distaste. It was exactly the same expression that Renar often used.

"Sir."

Erin circled Renar warily. His expression, a jaunty, arrogant half smile, hadn't faltered once. He was at home here, surrounded by four stone walls and a roof that was low and gray, and he thought to take advantage of the fact.

"Come, Lady." He twisted his wrist, bringing wooden sword around in a circle that ended with a stylistic flourish.

Erin snorted. She'd already hit him twice, although both blows, half-deflected, had only glanced off his shoulders. Still, he was better than she might have thought, given his sloppy stance and the lackadaisical way he held his weapon.

She frowned slightly, ignoring the throb at her wrist. *Be honest, Erin. He's much better than you thought.*

"Do you know what your problem is, Lady?" The sword danced up again, and Erin steadied herself. Renar was light, and wore no armor—he had been trained to count on flexibility and speed, just as she had. "You don't talk enough. Sessions like this can rapidly become boring—" He slashed downward in a sudden, low arc. The dull thud of wood against wood punctuated his half sentence. "—without intelligent conversation. I'm certain you're capable of it."

She lunged before the last word trailed off, the point of her sword aimed for the center of his chest. He pulled back, blocked low—and somehow succeeded.

He opened his mouth to speak, and she was at him again, wood flying everywhere.

I'll give you boring.

Sweat sheened their foreheads as they slashed, stabbed, and parried. Neither counted on exhaustion to defeat the other first— but Renar did not speak again. His face lost its amused distance, taking on the grim determination of the woman he faced.

Erin discovered that Renar was very, very good at feinting; even the usually subconscious clues as to movement and direction were misdirections. She held her own against him, but it was a near thing. Not since Telvar the weaponsmaster had she been so tested—in Elliath.

For an instant, she froze. Her fingers locked around the hilt of her sword. Renar's next blow connected viciously with her side; he had long since passed the point of gentle testing. She fell to the floor, bringing up her own weapon automatically as Renar lowered his.

"Erin?"

She shook her head, gritting her teeth. Slowly, she forced herself to her feet.

"Erin, is something wrong?"

She shook herself again, defiantly. Her sword came up. "No." She brought it around, two-handed, a wild maneuver that was not meant to connect. It didn't.

"Erin, perhaps"—block—"we should recess a moment."

Slash. "No." She was breathing heavily, her face flushed.

"What is going on here?"

Erin and Renar broke apart, taking large steps out of each other's range without pausing to think. Renar reddened slightly.

"Tiras."

The older man stood in the open door, something very like a frown coloring his precise features. "What exactly do you think you're doing?"

"Practicing?"

Tiras came through the door, shutting it behind him. "Practicing?" He waved a fist in Renar's face. Clenched between his curled fingers was a roll of vellum.

"Yes, sir."

"With *that*? Have you forgotten *everything* I've taught you, or are you just being selective?" He shook his fist again, then looked at the scroll. "Hells."

Erin bowed. "Please forgive us if we've caused you any trouble, sir. It was my suggestion."

"Aye." Tiras didn't take his eyes off Renar. "But you wouldn't have found the drill room without his help. Remind me the next time I take a pupil. Blindfolds."

"Any student of yours would eventually discover all the layout of this place." Renar smiled.

"Any good one. I believe you were just finishing up? Good," he said pointedly, before anyone could speak. "You've only been keeping us for an hour and a half now."

"And hour and a—"

"Remember? Two past noon in the north conference room?"

Erin walked over to the wall and set her sword aside. She ached, and her breath came heavily; her side would be a mass of purple flesh in the morning. But for all that, she felt good. Renar was a competent test of skill; a worthy opponent.

"—and there aren't any windows, Tiras. Now come, be a good host."

Tiras snorted. "And you'd just bathed. Renar, you've become positively uncivilized since last I saw you."

It was rolled out in front of them, edges furling slightly against old mahogany. To Erin and Trethar it was a map—a good, clear one, but still just a map. To Darin and Renar, as they leaned intently over it, it was more.

Each black line, crinkled in the center where Tiras had so carelessly gripped it, each name, each significant building, came together to form the cells of a body.

The white surface of vellum was scarred with red, where Tiras had carefully marked out the changes that had occurred since the fall: The royal library had been gutted and was now inhabited by the Church; the palace was the home now of the man who had betrayed Dagothrin and ruled her in the Empire's stead; the Leaflet and the Iron Horse were both burned to the ground in the riots.

"What are these?"

Tiras looked at Renar carefully, noting his former pupil's calm, serene face, and nodded slightly in approval. "New row of buildings. Slaver's guild here; brothel here."

Renar said nothing for a moment, eyes tracing thick, ugly red lines. "Terrela's?"

A shadow crossed Tiras' face. "No," he said quietly. "She died in the first of the riots. The first night of fires."

"Riot?" Renar laughed grimly. "You couldn't get her to leave her brothel—not without a good show of arms, or a good deal of money." He did not acknowledge the grimace of pain that crossed Tiras' face. In truth, it surprised him. His former teacher had never been given to displays of emotion, no matter how slight. Or rather, had never been given to genuine ones.

He looked back down at the map. He noted the position of Tiras' house, marked more for the information of his companions than for himself. He traced the web between this manor and the royal palace with a finger that shook.

"Aye," Tiras said softly. "A simple run."

"Well guarded?"

"The palace is." The older man shrugged. "It shouldn't matter to you."

Renar started to smile, but the expression faltered, half-formed; for a moment, Gerald's visage flashed across his vision: silent, mutilated tongue hidden firmly beneath clenched lips.

"Most of the old guard is gone," Tiras continued, "either banditing in the hills or dead. Some remain, thinking it better to serve one of Maran blood, even if that one brought the fall of Marantine."

"And you?"

Tiras shrugged. "I serve myself, Renar. Always."

Darin listened to them as they continued to speak. Erin interrupted with a question; Tiras answered. Trethar asked another, to which Tiras also responded. For a moment it didn't matter. He could see Dagothrin sprawled out like a corpse before him, made thin and flat by parchment and frail markings.

Five years. For five years she had labored under slavery perhaps only a little more gentle than his own had been. He reached blindly and firmly backward. His fingers gripped the staff of Culverne tightly as he drew Bethany, letting her tip rest against plush crimson carpet.

As he lifted her, his sleeve rolled back and he saw the brand; white relief against the paleness of his skin. He could see the scar of House Damion's symbol blurred by age and growth, but still visible. He could see the lines of its patterns, and for just a moment, they were inroads, bridges, the lines of a miniature city.

His eyes turned back to the map that lay stretched against the table top.

Dagothrin. The city. *They left you alive.*

Only Erin's eyes could pick up the faint glow that suddenly surrounded Darin. It spread from his hands, as if the staff were on fire, and slowly haloed his body. It was green, but it was not gentle, and it grew brighter.

Darin flexed his arm, and then, instead of letting the sleeve roll down as he almost always did, he raised both his arm, and Bethany, so that the scar was fully revealed above his head.

They left us alive.

They made a mistake.

Erin stopped speaking in mid-sentence and Tiras gave her a slightly anxious look as her eyes widened and her breath caught. The room, in her sight, was bathed in a sudden, brilliant, green—a green so pale, it was almost white. The staff no longer had the appearance of smooth wood; it was glowing—it was unmistakably the voice of a founder of a line.

And Darin, her young Darin, wielded the fire. At that moment, the boy he had been was gone forever; the pale nimbus of light burned him away and left only the Line Culverne. Erin dropped to one knee, bowing her head.

Only then did Darin fully see her.

"What is going on?" Tiras' voice rang oddly hollow; his words were distant and muted.

"Erin?" To his surprise, his own voice was distant. He became aware of the staff above his head, and lowered it slowly groundward. But he did not blush, and he was not embarrassed. "Erin?"

Erin raised her face. The light of Culverne caught the contours of purpose that tightened her jaw. "Grandfather of Culverne. Line Elliath stands against shadow at your side."

Darin couldn't see his reflection in her eyes; she was too far away. But he felt it in the tremor of her voice.

Is this, he thought, *how I see you, Lady?*

But he made no comment, afraid to break the moment of his anger. He was the patriarch of Culverne—last of his line or no— and Dagothrin was part of his line's care.

One way or the other, he meant to staunch the flow of her blood.

chapter
fourteen

The city was miles away, and no sign of its civilization marred the winter landscape. Gerald's breath billowed frequently in the air as he made his way toward the encampment that sprawled against snow in a shaky, gray web. His hands shook, partly from the chill and partly from the news that he carried. He looked down into his pockets to see that the papers he carried had not been dislodged. He had done so every few miles.

Tenting, row upon row, was punctuated by the smoke of small fires. A few horses, hair grown long around the ankles, gathered in the northernmost portion of the camp. Gerald counted the number of tents to himself, then shook his head. It was bad, but it was no more than he'd expected.

He approached more cautiously, slowing down for the first time in his journey.

"Halt!"

A smile touched his lips even as his feet froze in place. He couldn't see the archers, but he knew they were present.

He waited, and the wait was rewarded by the sight of four men. Each wore chain, although the chain itself was in disrepair even from this distance. Two carried crossbows, readied and aimed.

General Lorrence stepped forward. He was old, older than Gerald, his face a bearded gray mass. This wing of the resistance owed their survival to the man's tactics.

Gerald smiled the more broadly as Lorrence approached. He held out both hands, more to show the lack of weapons than in greeting.

It wasn't necessary. Lorrence's eyes drew into a tight squint and then sprung open.

"Gerald?"

Gerald nodded.

"Bright Heart. We'd heard your unit had fallen. What happened?" Lorrence stepped forward, hand outstretched, and Gerald gripped it tightly.

It was good to be home, more so because he'd been certain he would never see it again.

"Gerald?"

Lorrence received the shy, pained smile that Gerald used in place of speech. The giant shook his head softly, and touched his lips.

Lorrence laughed. "We're secure here."

Gerald shook his head again. Very slowly, he reached down into his pocket and pulled out the papers that he had carried so carefully. He handed them to the captain.

"What are they?"

Gerald said nothing.

The first piece of paper fluttered in the wind that had already grown more chill. Night was coming quickly.

"You were captured," Lorrence said tersely. He didn't look up, sparing Gerald the pity that flashed briefly in his dark eyes. Instead, he shuffled the sheet to the back and continued to read.

Only when he had finished reading, and rereading, the written words did he pause.

"The prince," he said softly.

Gerald nodded.

"You'd best come back to camp, then." Lorrence nodded to the three men, who had relaxed only marginally since first approaching Gerald. They lowered their bows.

"You do realize it's a crazy idea?"

Gerald nodded again, his eyes shining.

"Then again, the young prince never had a sane one. And if we'd listened the first time . . . well, you know it." His hands were also shaking. "But it might work. Let me think on it. In the morning, we'll talk."

The smile that Gerald gave was humorless, but not grim; a fey wildness was growing like light in his eyes.

* * *

"Verena, this is madness." Lord Cosgrove stood, back to his granddaughter, face to the flickering fire. He held a crystal glass in his hand, but although he had gone to the effort of pouring for himself, he didn't drink. Light glanced off his face, and shadow nestled in the lines age had made there; Lord Cosgrove was not a young man. His oldest son, Bretnor, was not young either, if it came to that—and Verena, directly in line for the family estates and their control, had much in common with both of them.

"Madness?" she asked, her voice low and breezy. "Why do you say that? We have everything that we need. We know who Renar arrived with."

"Do you know where he stays?"

She shrugged; velvet brushed against velvet as she availed herself of the brandy that did not seem to suit her grandfather. "We will, soon enough."

At this, Lord Stenton Cosgrove did spin. "You've lost him already?"

Stung, she narrowed her eyes. "I didn't have the luxury of following him myself, if you recall."

He said nothing for a moment, then turned away. "And you ask why I call it madness." The wall caught more of his words than she did, but his tone was enough to make her bristle.

"We know who he'll seek—who he'll have to seek. I'll catch him yet, and we'll have an end to this, Stent."

At this, a faint smile hovered in place around the older man's lips. "That's the duke speaking, Verena. Take care; he is not so old and foolish as you think. If there is a victory here that he can claim, he will; it won't be to our benefit."

She shrugged and turned a pleasant smile against her grandfather's skeptical one. "Did I not tell you, Lord Cosgrove?"

"Don't Lord Cosgrove me, girl. You know very well that you haven't told me anything that would sway my opinion yet."

"Ah. Well—do pick up your drink, this is cause for celebration—Lord Makkarin of Maran has started to pay court to me." Her smile deepened as she watched his face. It was true; he had. And she intended to let him pursue her until she chose to firm up that alliance by a marriage of some sort. But she regretted that she could not tell her grandfather all of the truth: She knew well where Renar was staying and knew with whom.

But she did not trust Lord Cosgrove completely to react in a proper manner; his actions in the past had been suspect.

* * *

"Do the two of you never stop?"

Renar gave a grim smile and put up his "weapon." He bowed, arm extending with a flourish.

Erin laughed. "Idiot."

"Why is it that life constantly shows me that familiarity does indeed breed contempt?"

Tiras, hand on doorframe, dignified the comment with a grimace. It was a sight with which, over the last five days, both Renar and Erin had become familiar.

"Why is it that life constantly shows me that my students invariably turn out to be a classless lot?"

Erin walked over to the wall and placed her sword down. She brushed strands of matted hair off her forehead and took a deep breath.

"Of all places—the drill room." Tiras didn't bother to enter. "I do have other rooms for use in the house. An elegant boudoir for visiting ladies. The baths. The dining room; the gallery. Each of those costs me much more time and pride than this one." He gave a pained frown. "Renar, in all the years you professed to be a student of mine, nothing short of threats of torture could bring you to this place. Then, I would have been overjoyed."

"Instead of underjoyed?" Renar joined Erin at the wall, laying down his wooden stick neatly beside her own.

"A good fight, Lady."

She smiled; she couldn't help it. It had been a good session. No hesitancy had marred her aim; no memories had come to dull the edge of her concentration. And Renar, fighting with dagger and sword, had given her much to mull over. Elliath had always favored the single weapon approach, perhaps wrongly so if Renar's skill could be duplicated.

"Gods, Renar, you stink."

"Really? How kind of you to say so." He bowed sarcastically. It amazed Erin that such grace could be put to such use.

"I'll be visiting your vaunted baths in a moment, Tiras. I trust you had a reason for interrupting us?"

"In fact, it is not I that brings the news."

Renar was instantly serious. "What news?"

"Perhaps you should come upstairs and see for yourself." His hands caught Renar's before they made their way to his

shoulders. "Come, lad. Don't try that on me in my own home.
I'm old, yes, but not decrepit."

"What news, Tiras?"

"Come."

Tiras whirled, and Renar was at his back so quickly it seemed
that they would collide. Erin followed at a more discreet distance. They walked the narrow stone hallway without comment
and entered the sunlight that flooded down the stairwell.

"Tiras . . ."

"Come, Renar. Don't let your impatience show—not even
here. You'll get out of practice."

Erin smiled. She could literally hear her comrade grinding
his teeth. She reached out and touched his shoulder gently. He
stopped for a moment at the feel of her hand. Straightening, he
turned around and met her eyes.

In six days they had come farther than in the six weeks before
it. They were not friends, not yet, but allies. Trusted allies.

"Side with him, will you?" he whispered. "During tomorrow's session, Lady, I shall have to show you the error of your
ways." But he smiled, and she felt the tension ease somewhat.

They walked up the stairs together and followed Tiras into
the meeting room closest to the front doors. There, sitting
sprawled in one of three large chairs, was a lean man in a plain,
worn cloak. His boots, folded and creased, were still gleaming
with snow. A large brown hood hid the face that bowed itself
into two cupped hands.

"This man is here to speak with you." Tiras bowed formally.
"He said it was most urgent."

The man's head shot up. His hands fell away, revealing a
gaunt, scarred face. Perhaps in another time it might have been
handsome.

Renar met the brown eyes without flinching. "Kramer."

The man stared for a moment more. Then his eyes, if possible, grew wider. He darted out of the chair, pulling himself to
his feet. His knees bent shakily, one touching the carpet inches
away from Renar's feet.

Erin saw the stiffening of Renar's back. Once again she
reached out to touch him, but pulled short at the last minute;
this was not hers to ease or resolve; this pain he would have to
face as steadily as did the man before him.

She walked the length of the room to stand by Tiras' side.

The older man did not seem to notice; his eyes watched Renar with an intensity that Erin could not understand. More was there than just concern; more than respect.

"You may rise."

The man looked up. "It's true." His voice was a shaky wisp of air.

"Aye, Kramer." Renar's lips dared a smile that never quite touched his eyes. "You came with news? Rise and deliver it."

The man did as bid, gaining his feet slowly. Every movement spoke of exhaustion. "Lieutenant Kramer reporting, sir."

"At ease, Lieutenant."

The man nodded. His hand dove into his cloak, and after struggling with it a moment, he pulled something out of an inner pocket. He unfurled it with great care, his hands shaking as he did.

"Identification, sir."

Renar looked down at the patch of cloth the man held. Gold against blue; the wreath and lynx glinting where a stray beam of light managed to hit it. The crest of the royal guard.

"None but our number would carry it." He looked away. "It's—it was changed at the order of the traitor. Those that serve him do not wear these colors."

Renar was silent a moment, his eyes closed. He drew himself up to his full height—which was perhaps a half foot less than that of the man who faced him.

"Carry it a little longer, Lieutenant. You have done better by it than many of your ancestors could have hoped to."

The weary face looked down at Renar. Erin saw the man's lips lift in a smile, one that started slowly and spread. Seeing the expression, she revised her estimate of his age down by ten years.

"What word do you bring?"

"Gerald reached us with your message, my Lord. We can have our—your men here in two weeks."

"Barring storms?"

"Barring nothing."

"Numbers?"

The younger man flinched slightly. "Not more than a hundred."

"So few?" Renar murmured, mostly to himself. "Never

mind, Lieutenant Kramer. A hundred is more than I've any right to expect.''

Yes, but a hundred won't even make one gate . . .

"Come." He shook himself. "You've traveled some distance, and at good speed. Take the time to refresh yourself while I gather my allies. We've a decision to reach before you depart again.''

Lieutenant Kramer, cleaner and visibly more tense than he had been upon first meeting Renar, sat in a corner of the rectangular conference table. Arrayed before him were the five upon whom what was left of the royal guard would take its final risk, for better or worse. He looked at them carefully. An old man, almost obscured by the dark robes he wore, sat aside, his face a set study of annoyance. A youth stood beside him, dressed much as a farmer, with a grim set to his jaw that belied his apparent age. The boy's eyes kept returning to the map of Dagothrin that lay pinned to the table, before struggling away again to rest on one of his companions. Not that the lieutenant could blame him—the woman's sharp, long features, while too strong to be pretty, were definitely striking. He glanced down at the sword by her side, wondering if she could actually wield it, or if circumstance alone forced her to bear it. There were no scars to mark the fairness of her skin, so he was certain that she had never seen battle.

This, he thought bitterly, *is what the Empire has forced us to—the use of women, children, and the aged.*

To comfort himself, he turned his attention to Prince Renar and the aptly named Lord Brownbur. The latter had lent what aid he could to the resistance—without risking himself, of course. These two at least he trusted to be prepared for what lay ahead.

"All of the gates are defended with equal numbers. More runners are placed on the northern one, but they won't add to fighting strength." Tiras' fingers rapped the four gates on the map for the benefit of those unfamiliar with Dagothrin.

Renar nodded.

"On our side in this fact: Any attack will be unexpected." Tiras stopped to massage a kink out of his neck. "On their side, though, the walls are still the walls.''

"They've been breached once.''

"Aye—but technically no. The southern gates were thrown open."

Renar's face darkened. "And will have to be again, although I'm not sure if I favor the south."

They spoke on, and the lieutenant felt his heart sinking. A thousand men might stand some chance of entering the city, but only a slim one—and at that, only if you didn't believe the legend of the Lady of Elliath and her ageless protection. A hundred would provide target practice for the Swords' archers, a diversion from the monotony of guarding the walls.

No, he thought, gritting his teeth. *He would not have returned without some plan. I'll trust him.*

Renar sighed.

"Then we're decided. Whichever gate we choose, to stand any chance we *must* be able to open them from within."

Tiras nodded.

As a man, they both turned to look at Trethar. It became obvious to Lieutenant Kramer that they had had this discussion before and were replaying it for his benefit. It was clear that they had some plan in mind and had decided all but the finer points of their action.

Which fact seemed to make the old man testy. "What?"

"Old man, I know we've perhaps not made the best of traveling companions, but—"

"Not the best?" Trethar snorted. "I believe this is the first time I've heard you understate anything. Do continue."

"Trethar," Renar said, with obvious effort, "we need the help of the skills you learned with your brotherhood. They've not been witnessed by many here, and it may give us the edge that we need."

Trethar snorted again. "The gate that you need."

"The gate, then."

"Where will the Lady and my student be?"

Erin looked up slowly, taking her eyes away from the map. "I do not know where Darin will be. I will be here." Her finger came slowly and steadily down to rest against the largest red outline on the map.

Trethar's eyebrows shot up. "There?" He rubbed his eyes and stood up, leaning over the map. "Rubbish! That's the Church!"

Erin nodded.

"And who will accompany you?"

"I will," Darin said softly.

"You?" Trethar's eyes grew larger. He looked vaguely comical, his exaggeration so great that it seemed almost a farcical act. Darin felt a hint of anger. Without hesitation he pulled out the staff of Culverne and set its point on the ground before him.

"Yes. Me."

"And who else?"

There was silence at the table. Only Kramer's was the silence of confusion.

"The two of you alone?"

Erin had turned to stare at Darin. She saw two things clearly: his age and his station.

You can't take him. He's barely adult.

No. He is *adult. He is the patriarch of Culverne—and Marantine is his domain. He goes, and does, what he must for the good of his line. I've no right to deny him that choice.*

He can't fight, except with the power of the staff. He has no skill in combat—you've seen that.

Have I? She shuddered, remembering the distant smell of charred flesh and the brief glimpse of blackened bone.

He is the Grandfather of his line. We fight as the lines have always fought the darkness—together.

She nodded quietly in Trethar's direction.

Trethar snorted a third time.

"That settles it, then. You and your friend will have to find some way to liberate your gate. I shall go to keep watch over these two."

Darin was strongly annoyed, but also slightly relieved. Trethar's power was much greater than his—although his was growing—and he was likely to be of more help to Erin should they make it into the church. He started to speak, and then caught the quiet look that passed between Renar and Tiras.

When he opened his mouth, the words that came out of them surprised even him. "No. We, Erin and I, have our own fight and our own battle—the Church of the Enemy is the domain of the lines."

Lieutenant Kramer's jaw fell a few inches. Darin didn't notice.

"Don't say it, Trethar, please. If I could wield the power you've taught me half as well as you, I'd go to the gate. And if

you won't, I must go, but that"—and he lifted his staff high—
"is not my first responsibility. The altars of the Enemy are being
blooded in this city—in the city that was the domain, and still
is, of my line."

Once again he felt the gentle glow of Bethany's approbation.
He lowered her almost hesitantly, a youth again for a second.

"We all have to do what we must."

Trethar's mouth remained open as Renar and Tiras looked
first at Darin, and then at him. When it shut, it shut with a
definitive snap; the old man was not happy.

"I don't think we can take the city without you at the gate,"
Erin said softly. "And without that, all the work Darin and I
do—all the work that Renar and Tiras do—will be worthless."

"My Lord, may I speak?"

Renar looked momentarily surprised. He'd forgotten the presence of young Kramer. He nodded.

Kramer bowed to Trethar. "I do not know what brotherhood
is spoken of, elder. But if you have a skill that my Lord believes
is necessary, then I enjoin my plea to his. Help us regain our
city."

Trethar slapped his wrinkled brow with a slightly curled fist.
He threw a dark look at Erin, and a darker one at Darin. Neither
could compare with the glance he cast at Renar.

"Done, then. Done, all right? Now can we talk of something
else?"

But Kramer had not finished. He rose steadily and walked
over to where Darin stood. There he bowed, as low and as
reverent a bow as any he would give to Renar.

"Patriarch of Culverne." *I thought him just a boy.* He felt no
embarrassment at the oversight. He saw, in half a way, that it
was the truth. But he saw, in the boy's face and the way his
hands gripped the staff he held, the pride and the strength of the
former, fallen, matriarch.

"I never thought to see you again."

Darin nodded, mostly to hide the sudden blush of shyness
that took his face. Among friends, among comrades, it was easy
to shed and bear the light of the line; he could be certain that
their approbation would never overcome their judgment. But this
man, this lieutenant of a disbanded army, he was different, as
Gervin had been different. The light in his eyes, fervent and full
of the strength of hope, reminded Darin of everything that the

patriarch should be. It reminded him of all the things that he was not.

"With your aid, with your return at the side of my Lord, we are certain to succeed."

"More certain, perhaps, than we thought," Tiras murmured.

"My Lord?"

Tiras did not reply. "Darin," he said softly. "Lines?"

For a moment Darin stared in confusion, and then he blanched. He swung round to glance guiltily at Erin.

Slowly she shook her head from side to side, her gaze both measured and reassuring.

"Lines."

Tiras met her eyes. "Lady, the rest of the lines—"

"I am the last of my line; there will be no others." She lifted her hand to forestall Renar's comment. Their days together in the drill room made this clear to him.

"Landros?" Tiras asked, mentally revising his estimate of her age upward. He did so with some annoyance. He was not a man used to making errors of judgment.

She faced him, closed her eyes a moment, and drew a gentle breath, sifting through the memories that were always too close. Belfas. Carla. Rein. Teya . . . so many that she had loved were dead or damned. And yet there were still those that she could love and could help. She had already made her choice. What was left but to acknowledge it?

"Not Landros, Tiras." As Darin had drawn his staff, so now did Erin draw her blade. It shone in the room more fiercely than sunlight alone could explain. "Elliath."

"Elliath? But that's impossible—you'd—"

"The statue." Renar said, his eyes wide and dark. "The statue in the marketplace of Verdann. The statue in the capital."

She raised an eyebrow at Renar's words.

"The Lady of Mercy."

Again confusion darkened her eyes. "Lady of—"

Mercy.

For a moment she saw it again: the pavilion in Rennath, hung with banners of black and red, shadowed by Swords and the countless civilians who had somehow survived the trek to the city to plead their case before *the Lady of Mercy.*

And her dark, grim, beautiful Lord.

She saw the hope in their anonymous eyes, inextricably bound with their fear as they stepped forward, encouraged by her smile, her presence, or the vague rumors of her powers.

But more clearly than that, she saw Stefanos, robed against the daylight that threatened him less and less. She saw the faint hint of a smile hover around his lips as she listened to the claimants; she saw his nod as she passed her judgment and he let it stand; she felt for a moment the cool circle of his arms when she succumbed to the stress of the inevitable fact that she couldn't change the world overnight.

Sara . . .

It had been a while since she had remembered him so.

"Erin?"

Darin's outline wavered before her eyes. She realized only then that she was near to tears. She quickly sheathed the sword that trembled in her hands.

"Please," she said in a rush, "continue a moment without me. I've—I've left something in my rooms."

The door shut solidly behind her. She leaned back into it a moment. Tears trickled slowly from the corners of her eyes.

Where is the warrior now? she demanded, her throat too swollen to voice her anger. *Where is your resolve?* For a moment, the shadows of night threatened her; she felt a hint—the day's echo—of his pain and his desire.

And Erin knew it fully as her own.

We are judged by actions; by actions and not need. She swallowed, running her palms, hard, against her eyes; smearing tears and memories into an angry blur. She breathed, harshly, deeply, fighting for control. And because she had come this far, through so much shadow, she won.

Even through the thick closed doors of the meeting room, voices carried into the hall.

How long have I been gone?

She shook her head, feeling the stiffness of skin where unchecked tears had dried. She tried a smile on, quirking the corners of her lips upward.

You, she thought, *you're going to try to save the world?* Shaking her head, she opened the door and entered the room.

The conversation died around her.

She walked over to Darin, opened her arms, and hugged him before he could think of moving. Releasing him, she turned to face Renar and Tiras.

"Did you find what you were looking for, Lady?"

She nodded. "I am Erin, Sarillorn of the Line Elliath. I was trained in the arts of combat and war—to fight against those who serve the Enemy—many hundreds of years ago. No, Renar, I cannot explain all—let it be enough to know that I stand here ready to do everything I can to help."

"And are you then the Lady of Mercy that so many pray to and wait for?"

"I don't know." She bowed her head a moment, weighing her words. "These statues that you mentioned—I've never seen them. But . . . there were some who called me that."

"And were you the Dark Lord's Lady?" His voice was low, intent. She could almost see the sword in his hand; she could almost feel him circling.

She was reminded of a cold, winter evening on a stretch of ill-used road, when he had offered her honesty. She could not offer him less now, but she could not explain what she barely understood herself. She nodded.

"Lady." He bowed very formally.

She knew the tone and the resonances of it well; she had grown up in Elliath using just that word, in just that way. "Don't call me that." Stiffness crept into the words; she couldn't stop it.

He looked up, eyes flashing. "What must I do then, Lady? You've just said yourself that you're centuries old; that you've returned now—when the Dark Heart rules the world. What am I to think of one who makes such a claim? You've not aged, even I can guess that, and you've power, skill—what am I supposed to think of you?" He pulled away from her abruptly. "You are revered, Lady, by slaves and commoners across the Empire. Some go hungry for a day to bring secret offerings to your statues. You are part of their myth, their legend."

He was angry; everyone else stood in shock. She circled him without the benefit of sword or the blank gray walls of the drill room, angry herself. "What have I done to merit that myth or that legend? Lived? Survived? Have I freed those who—who worship me? Their prayers are given to stone, damn it, and by stone received!"

"Oh?" He stepped free of the table and chairs and walked over to meet her; an invisible circle, drawn over the intricate, hand-knotted rug, contained them both. "Then why are you here, now, when the shadow is darkest?"

She had no answer. But, angry, the lack didn't stop her from making one. "How in the hells should I know? Maybe there's a fate beyond the Lady of Mercy's ken."

"Or maybe," he said, his voice softer but in no wise gentle, "only love will stop the Lord of the Empire."

She drew her breath so sharply everyone heard it. And then, instead of anger, she turned upon Renar the bitterest of smiles. She stepped back, well away from him, and out of their imaginary circle. "It is not love I offer, *Majesty*," she said, as she rested her palm against the hilt of her sword, "it's war. We can fight each other, or we can fight our enemies."

He took a step forward cautiously. He stared again at the tangled hair that framed her face. Then he smiled, an odd sort of a smile—part bitter, part self-deprecating, part conspiratorial.

"I'm sorry," he said, just as he often did after a grueling session in which less of his skin was bruised than hers. "I wish you'd told me earlier."

"I didn't trust you," she answered, and looked away.

"And you do now?"

"Yes. Or maybe I finally think I can trust myself."

"Good. We're touched to hear that."

They both turned to Tiras, so used to his interruptions that they automatically fell silent.

"Now that you've got that sorted out, can we get back to the matter at hand? Your time is being measured in days here, not years."

They smiled at each other awkwardly and returned to the table.

Two hours later, Lieutenant Kramer left the residence, a much happier man than when he had arrived. Impossible though it seemed, he kept the shine out of his eyes and the spring out of his step. He kept his head bowed in a stance of dejection.

He tried to capture the fear of risk—for they would all be taking the risk of their lives—and the fear of loss, but both eluded him. For the first time in five years, the struggle seemed completely worthwhile. Now he knew why he had not stayed behind, why he had not sold his service to the Lord of the "province" as so many of his compatriots had chosen to do. The powers that the old man, Trethar, had chosen to show still caused the hairs on the back of his neck to stand on end—but they were as nothing to the other three things he had learned.

The king—the rightful king—had returned, for better or worse, to Dagothrin and Marantine. The patriarch of Culverne was somehow miraculously alive, although all knew a night-walker of the Enemy had come in force to see the line destroyed. And both of these men had accepted his pledge of allegiance.

But more than that, the line of the Lady walked again in the world, bearing a sword of Light that the Enemy and his Servants must run from, or be destroyed by.

True, they were only four—but with four such as these, the lieutenant was certain the tide had turned. Who would dare to stand against them? Let him make it back to Captain Lorrence safely—*Ah, Lernan, even with only breath enough to tell them my news*—and the pain and loss of five years would be repaid in full.

chapter
fifteen

Tiras paced the length of his conference room, crushing soft pile
with the force of his step. Rings glittered, sparkling blue and
green in the hint of sunlight, as he paused to straighten the
immaculate curtains; he had once loved rubies, yes, even after
Marantine had become Illan. But that was before the Night of
Fires, and he could no longer bear to have them on his person
or in his sight. The curtains swayed to ground, and he resumed
the aimless rhythmic walk that threatened his carpet.

"A hundred men. A hundred might do if they were already
in the city, already prepared, and if they could strike at exactly
the right moment."

Erin sighed. "We know that, Tiras. But we've scarce time to
send exact words back to those men as it is; we'd appreciate
some sort of help."

"Or anything," Renar drawled, "that even approximated it,
coming from you." Bitterness was there, a mix to the flavor of
the words that could not be separated from them.

Tiras shut his eyes. They'd been at this for the better part of
the morning, and any answer that they could come up with in-
volved Renar's men already being on the *inside* of the walls.

Erin massaged her neck. "If there's a riot, or something very
like it, will that pull the palace guards out?"

"All three hundred? Not very likely." Tiras shrugged. "And
those that remained would all be active. State of emergency, that
sort of thing. No, you've got to move *fast*; you've got to be there
before word of your presence reaches the palace."

"Aye." Renar nodded. "But that word will have to be
watched for, and we can't do it alone."

235

He walked over to the slit windows of the room, pulled the curtain aside, and glanced out. Snow, light and crisp, was blanketing the ground. It was a common enough sight in Dagothrin. *Bright Heart, curse those riots.* The fires had robbed him of nearly anyone who might have come to his aid. Almost anyone with the strength to stand by their convictions had fallen in them. That left him the men and women most like Tiras, willing to bend without breaking, willing to bow. They had chosen their lives in trade for their beliefs, and he wasn't certain that he had enough to offer them to make the liberation of Dagothrin as important to them as living was.

He grimaced; he knew the type well.

Was it not his own?

Maybe it was a bad choice. He let his forehead rest against the coolness of stone. *I'm a thief, not a hero. Not a king. I can only lead these men so far because they want to be led.*

"Renar?"

He looked up, stiffening the lines of his face. Erin had walked to his side so quietly that he hadn't been aware that she moved at all. It was a bad sign, that, to be so unaware here, at the heart of Dagothrin.

"It seemed a good idea," he said, because the silence was suddenly uncomfortable. "To come here. To kill the governor. To kill Uncle Jordan."

"It was." She touched his shoulder, her palm flat against him. "It *is*."

"Is it?" He looked away. Her eyes were too green. He felt uncomfortable with this reminder of her heritage; she was his comrade now, and he wanted no separation between them. Yet he felt the warmth of her touch as something preternatural, something welcome. "I fear that I've begun to give credence to the tales they tell about me.

"Those men—they're the last. If they fall, no more will come, no more will stand. The Empire will be completely unquestioned."

"Not forever." The words surprised him. "It can't last forever, even if it outlasts us." They surprised Erin as well, although it was she who had spoken them.

"Why not? What makes you think that?" Those words, suddenly too small for the width and the light of her eyes, died into stillness and watchfulness. He heard her hope, and wanted to give it the strength of a belief he wasn't certain he had. Yet the facts remained, and they were a chill her touch did not lessen. "But a hundred men—what can we do with a hundred? If a hundred could accomplish the liberation of Marantine, don't you think it would have happened in the last five years?" His fist slammed into the wall. "More than that died in the riots." "But they didn't have you. They didn't have the patriarch of Culverne. They didn't have the Sarillorn of Elliath. They didn't have whatever Trethar is trying so hard to teach Darin."

"They didn't have me, if it comes to that," Tiras said. It sounded as if he made a confession and an offer of penitence more than a pledge of aid or belief. His voice was tired, heavy, the defeat in his words so deceptively soft. He took a seat and sagged against the armrests, bracing himself, strengthening himself.

"I can think of ten. Ten who might, in their own way, be able and willing to help. No—don't look relieved yet. They may be dead. They may have left Dagothrin. They may be with the resistance. I've heard little of them since the riots." He smiled grimly. "But I know that they weren't among the fallen."

"Ten is still better than five, especially if they've been in Dagothrin all this time. Any idea as to where they might be?" Renar didn't ask who; he knew that Tiras would not yet answer.

Tiras frowned. "None," he said. "I was watched, carefully. Your uncle doesn't trust me much. But I'm a merchant family, and my connections are needed if this city isn't to fall into disuse. He doesn't risk killing me if I don't risk being a justifiable target. And that means no connections. None."

Renar looked at him flatly. "I don't believe you."

Tiras' smile was the first genuine one of the day. "I do believe, pupil, that that's a compliment. I get them so rarely that I shall have to savor it. But later."

Leaning down, he removed a piece of paper. "Nothing definite here."

Renar nodded. He looked at the first item on the neatly printed grocery list, deciphered it, and began to head out of the room.

"Renar?"

He turned.

"Do you go alone?" Erin's eyes were light, almost painful to look into.

"I know the city well, Lady." He bowed. "I think it best."

"But I'm an able guard, an able swordsman. I can move near as quickly and silently as you."

He looked at her, and then above her head a moment. "Why not?" he said at last. "This is as much your battle as mine."

Darin's head ached. His arms were sore. His legs were sore. His back felt permanently cricked.

Given that, the lessons with Trethar had gone very well that day. He went to Erin's rooms, found them empty, and began to wander the mansion in search of her.

He found Tiras instead.

The older man was very finely dressed. Lace cuffs and a ruffled shirt hid beneath a black velvet jacket. Gold was worked into it, and it looked genuine.

"Yes, Darin?" Tiras said mildly. The servant brought his cloak and murmured something about the carriage. "May I help you?"

"I—I'm looking for Erin. Or Renar."

"Ah, well. I suppose I cannot be of assistance after all." He fastened the clasp of the cloak and stepped gingerly into very finely worked boots. "I am off for the day on matters of some import. If you're hungry at all, you might talk to Anders; I'm sure he can fix you something."

"Sir," Anders replied.

"But have you seen them?"

"Some time earlier this morning. I don't exactly remember the last place I saw them, but I imagine they'll be around soon enough. Sorry that I don't have more time to speak, lad."

Darin clenched his teeth. He was certain that Renar had learned everything he knew from Tiras. He was also certain that although Tiras knew where they'd gone, he wasn't willing to share the information. About that, at least, he was right.

Erin watched Renar's stiff back. They had avoided the infrequent patrols of the wealthy quarter without much difficulty, although both found the snow upon the ground a nuisance. No tread, no matter how light, could pass and leave no trace here.

She was surprised at his silence. It was not merely the silence of movement, not the silence of shadows, but rather the silence of grimness. He wore it heavily, and it fit the lines of his face, lending him age and an anger that time had not quelled.

She thought she might understand how he felt. To walk in the ruins of Elliath would be more of an agony than that which Renar showed. This had been his home.

Of that, at least, there was no doubt. He moved with purpose and economy, never once stopping to ascertain direction or street. He didn't tell her where they were going, and she didn't ask.

But please, Renar, no shortcuts.

Erin looked up at the buildings that grew taller. It was sunny, or it had been when they started, but it made no difference here; no trace of light pervaded the shadows that the tenements cast upon the blanketed ground.

I lived for four years in a city, she thought. *Four years, and I never saw this. How much else did I miss?* Her shoulders drew inward, as if to avoid the touch of darkness. She looked at Renar, who walked as if he knew this part of town well. She wondered what else he knew and what else he had seen.

She gained no answer, but she followed him as he made his way into the streets that had already grown narrow.

He stopped outside of one building that looked no different from those surrounding it on all sides. It was tall, as were its neighbors, and in the same state of repair. Perhaps, had it been made of stone, it might have shown time less poorly, but perhaps its occupants could afford little better than wood.

He entered the front door, and Erin followed.

In the hall Renar relaxed slightly.

"It isn't much," he whispered. "But it has its uses."

She blushed, wondering if all her thoughts were as transparent. But he had already turned and resumed his pace, reaching the end of the hall and mounting the stairs before he thought to look back.

She shook her head. He nodded.

It was almost like being in the unit again; like scouting ahead with Deirdre. But there were no warriors to back them here, no priests to report to, and no time set for their safe return.

Renar stopped at last in front of the third door on the north side of the narrow hall. It was a well-fitted door, one that shut firmly enough to allow no hint of light, or life, to show through the cracks.

He knocked at it, almost continuously, his knuckles beating out a gentle pattern that changed too quickly for Erin to catch all of.

But she heard, clearly, the shuffling that came from behind the door.

"Someone's in," she whispered.

Renar didn't notice. He waited, counting, and then began his drum against the wood again, this time in a different tempo.

The door opened a crack. Even its hinges were well kept; they gave no protesting creak as a head peered out.

The man was balding; his hair ringed his head just above his ears, breaking at either temple. He looked cautiously at Renar, and markedly more so at Erin, before allowing the door to swing fully open into neatly kept quarters. A single lamp burned on a warped, thin table; one old chair sat overlooking the street to one side of a barred window. There were boots in the tiny vestibule, the only sign that someone lived here.

Renar stepped in, and Erin followed him. The door was firmly and quietly shut behind them.

"Renar," the man said, bowing. No surprise at all was expressed; no disbelief, no jubilation. Like his apartment, the man's face was carefully empty.

"Lianar." Renar held out a hand.

The older hand gripped the younger hand firmly, and then fell away. "You look well."

"You look terrible."

Lianar smiled for the first time. "Still a Cosgrove, eh?"

"If you're still serving them."

"Yes," Lianar said softly. He waved toward two chairs. Renar shook his head.

"We haven't the time to stay."

"Ah. Message, then?"

Renar nodded.

"And?"

"I wish an audience with Lord Cosgrove. If he is willing, it must take place within a three-day."

Lianar nodded. He gestured, his fingers brushing his chin.

Renar smiled wearily. "Of course. Erin?"

"Yes?"

"Come. We've more to see in this quarter yet."

She looked back at Lianar, who hardly seemed to have moved at all. Then, shaking her head, she followed Renar out into the corridor.

"Who was he?" she asked, her voice pitched low.

"Was? He is Lianar; he serves the Cosgrove merchants in this quarter."

"And Lord Cosgrove?"

Renar was silent a moment before answering.

"My grandfather."

She swallowed. "Was this wise, then?"

"Wise?" He started to speak, and then shook his head; he knew well what her concerns were—in her position, he, too, would have been worried. As he was. "No. But my grandfather will not betray me without first offering me a chance to speak."

"He's a Lord of Illan, isn't he?"

"Yes." He lifted his hand stiffly, palm angled toward her lips. She fell silent.

The list that Tiras had penned saw the light briefly before Renar returned it to the inner pocket of his jacket. His breath, a heavy sigh, frosted the air around his face. His eyes were lost in that mist for a moment.

Erin touched his shoulder. She'd done it often enough in the last few days that she'd made a place for herself there. The prince did not pull away.

"A horse," she mouthed. "Pulling a carriage." She nodded toward the alley.

Renar only smiled. "I'd give much for your hearing, Lady." He looked up at the sun; it was still high enough. "Come." He walked forward into the street.

Erin shook her head and followed, her eyes sweeping the empty street. There was too much that she didn't understand about being in this city—about being, truly, in any city. Her hand brushed her sword hilt as she waited; the sound of the horse drew nearer.

From around the farthest corner her eye could see, she caught sight of it. It was dark, but flashes of white touched its chest and forelegs. Air left a cloud past its nostrils as it pulled against a wooden carriage. The carriage was not a fine one, and seeing this, she relaxed.

Renar raised his arm.

"What are you doing?" Erin asked.

"Hailing a cab," he replied, his voice wry. "Haven't you seen it done before?"

His arm went up and down in a fluid motion.

Erin shrank inward as the cab rolled, slowly, to a stop.

The man behind the reins looked down at them, his eyes the only thing visible between the layers of wool that covered his face. They widened.

"Where're you going?" he said loudly.

"We're staying in the lower quarter." Renar walked to the carriage door.

"Lower quarter's a big place," the man replied. "And I'm almost off-duty as it is."

"Really?" The door swung open. "Well, then, we shall be careful not to take you too far out of your way. Lady?" He held out a hand.

Erin looked dubiously at the inside of the carriage and then at the driver's seat. The latter looked far more comfortable.

"Lady?" Renar said again.

She sighed and clambered up through the open door, thinking that a new word had to be invented for something so small and awkward. She settled against the wooden bench that creaked beneath her weight and wondered how on earth two people were meant to ride in the cabin. Not comfortably, that was certain.

Renar joined her, lurching into a wall as the cab began to move. He grimaced and began to straighten out the crumpled folds of his jacket while his elbows jogged against the wood.

"Where are we going?"

"To the yards, I think."

"Yards?"

"Never mind. I can't hear you over these wheels, but you'll find out soon enough." He grimaced. "If we survive the ride. Borins never used to be this horrible a driver."

What am I doing here? Erin thought, when the bumps didn't provide enough of a distraction. *I should have trusted that Renar would avoid trouble. He doesn't need* me.

She glanced around at the buildings that raced past. It wasn't like being in the forest, and it wasn't like being in Rennath. If Rennath had been shadows, those shadows still had the feel of life about them.

At least they had when Stefanos rode at her side.

She bit her lip, and her teeth pierced it as the carriage ran over something. She didn't want to think of him. Not here, not now. The decision had already been made. But it was impossible not to; his face hovered at the corner of her eyes, wearing the human profile that he had almost always chosen.

She stared blindly out of the window again, refusing to turn at the memory. She was unsure whether she refused because she didn't want to face it, or because she didn't want to know he wasn't there.

The cab rolled to a stop. Erin shook her head, cleared her eyes, and tried to smile at Renar.

He looked at her oddly before touching the handle of the door. He waited until she shook her head before shaking his own and leaving.

The smell of the yards was enough of a distraction. The smell, and the three armed men that waited beside a large, wooden building. They didn't look friendly, and they didn't look clean, but they obviously had enough money to arm and armor themselves reasonably well.

Erin reached for her own sword and Renar caught her hand. She looked down at his fingers and he immediately removed them. They stood a moment, staring at each other.

"Not here," Renar said at last.

She nodded uneasily. She tried a smile and was surprised to find that it held.

"Do you know them?"

"Them? Not likely." He pulled his shoulders back until he looked every bit the proud peacock. "Does it matter?"

Her smile widened. "If I'd half your ability—"

"You'd have rather a lot more bruises or scars." But his own cheeks dimpled. "Do let me handle these ruffians, lady." With a flourish of movement that could almost be called a bow, he turned, hat in hand.

Erin thought his head must be getting rather cold. She followed, looking as demure as possible, until she bumped into his back. Then she wondered, as she blushed, how anyone could possibly walk with their face constantly turned toward the ground.

"Good day to you all, my good men."

The guard in the lead crossed his arms. "What's your business?" he asked, his voice soured by boredom and chill.

"Business?" Renar asked. "Ah. I see you are men with strong dedication to duty, so I shall force myself to dispense with idle pleasantries."

"Good."

"Really, my dear man, don't you think that you might at least struggle with a friendly smile? My companion and I have come all the way down to the yards, at considerable discomfort and inconvenience to ourselves, and I believe we are owed at least that. It's common decency."

The guard snorted and took a step forward, one large hand outstretched.

Renar's surprised little hop did nothing to rescue the collar of his jacket. He managed a rather good imitation of a fish out of water as the guard yanked him almost off his feet.

Erin's eyes went to the other two guards. They were watching their leader and Renar with a trace of amused contempt, but their stance had relaxed.

"Easy with him," the cab driver said, appearing from behind the heaving flanks of his horses. It was as much of an interruption as he cared to make, however, as he began to lead his horses to the large building that served as their stall.

"Be careful with that!" Renar shouted. "Good heavens, do you realize how much a jacket of this style is *worth*?" He took a breath, stopped, and then added, "Well, no, I don't suppose you would."

"No, he probably wouldn't."

Erin's head jerked to the side, and she felt a mix of embarrassment and respect for Renar. Even she had been taken with his spectacle, so much so that she had forgotten to keep her tentative watch.

A man had stepped out of the building. It was obvious that the noise that Renar had made had attracted his attention; he wasn't dressed for the cold. A light jacket, unbuttoned, had been thrown on over a large sweat-stained tunic that was so thick it looked almost like burlap.

He was a thin man, almost wiry, which made the effect of the clothing even more unfortunate. Nor was he young, although the graying line of his hair had not receded. The line of his brows were drawn tightly together.

"Duram?"

The guard closest to the door shrugged. "Just came down with Borins."

"Stretch?"

"Wouldn't answer my questions."

"I was attempting to answer this rather rude man's question," Renar said. His cheeks were quite red, and his eyes were almost circular. "He didn't give me even the chance to do so before beginning his assault."

The third guard snorted. " 'Assault,' is it?" The quick shake of his head made his opinion of that quite clear.

"I see. Well, best release him, then."

"Release him?"

"That's what I said. Problem with some of the words?"

"You're the boss."

Renar's little yell came a moment before he hit the ground.

It didn't impress the thin man who appeared to be in charge. "Well, don't just sit there yowling. Get up. Get in. It's a damn sight colder out here than it is inside."

"But my *jacket*!"

Erin shook her head and slid her hands under Renar's armpits. With a little heave, she pulled him to his feet. "Come on," she said. "You heard the man."

Renar continued to mutter to himself, throwing a disdainful glance at each of the guards as Erin guided him in through the doors. Only when they closed did he stop, but his face was still red with annoyance.

The man brushed sturdy hands through the short length of his hair. "Bright Heart, Renar. Don't you ever stop?" The lines of a perpetual scowl gave way reluctantly, but his smile was weary and shadowed.

"Every now and then. But I forget myself. Erin, this is Morgan, the owner of this illustrious pit. Morgan, this is Erin."

" 'Pit'?" The smile deepened.

"Yard. Whatever you call it."

Morgan's hand was already out. Erin took it firmly, shook

it, and let it drop; the yard owner was obviously not paying any attention to her.

Morgan's hand then spun around and slapped Renar lightly on the shoulder. "What are you doing back?" It was a simple question, but unease colored the words and weighted them with suspicion.

"Freezing."

Morgan laughed. "Right. My study."

"How can you have a study in a place like this?"

"Nobody bothers me here." He raised an eyebrow. "Almost nobody." The tread of his steps in the empty building came more quickly. "I take it you met no guards?"

"No one followed us, no. Not the way Borins drives." Renar walked into the door that Morgan held open. "No one looks for us here; not yet. I believe word will come soon, so time *is* of the essence."

"And in your case that means what can be said by a normal man in a minute will only take twenty instead of an hour."

"Very droll."

Morgan's chair scraped across the floor as he pulled it free of the sparse and simple desk and sat lightly on its edge. Erin wondered that he sat at all; he seemed to rest an inch or two above the seat at any time. His face, taut with tension, was the only part of him that remained still. "What have you come for?"

"I—we—need your help." Renar looked around for another chair, frowned when it became clear that there wasn't one, and continued to speak. "There isn't a driver in the city that knows it as well as you do."

"Not any more."

Renar's lips turned down a fraction of a second. He nodded, almost grim.

"We stay out of the way." It was as much an explanation as Morgan could give. "The merchants that'll come this far north have a use for us, so we've been left pretty much on our own." He shrugged as heavily as Renar had frowned. "Taxes are higher."

For a moment he looked like the building he owned; worn with use and care, empty except for a flicker of lamplight and a sheaf of accounts on a weathered desk. "I do as I'm able. I've sent money down Kaarel's way, and I've sent the odd message, the odd warning.''

Renar's body trembled slightly. ''You've seen Kaarel, then?''

''Not myself, not much. Too risky.'' He seemed to shrink further. ''Too risky, after the riots. After the fires.'' He glanced over his shoulder, although the room's solitary window was boarded up. ''It's good to see you, Renar, but I'll be honest. Can't help you much.

''You seen the city? They burned the Tin Canteen to the ground; they took out the Wayward Son.''

Renar nodded.

''Cospatric's about, in the lower city. Wily man, but bitter now; it took a lot of years to build up the wreck of the Tin Canteen. Merilee—Merilee died in the fires. Her and her son.'' He seemed lost for a moment in the words and the images they conjured, too private, and too near. Then he raised his head. ''What can I do for you?''

It was as much a plea as he could make. And at any other time, Renar would have heeded it; he understood it very well.

''Maybe die.'' Stark words. Erin glanced at Renar to be sure that it was his lips that had passed them. ''Maybe not. But you know the city, and we'll have need of your knowledge.''

''For what?''

Renar smiled. ''One way or the other, I'm here to stay. Upon the throne, or beneath the ground, I've returned to Dagothrin. To Marantine.

''I would, of course, prefer to be on the throne. But there are a few things that stand in the way.'' He paused to allow Morgan to comment, and then kicked himself mentally; Morgan would speak only after he'd heard what Renar had to offer. That was his way. ''We've got to bring men through the south city gates.'' He lifted his hand as Morgan's brows approached the line of his hair. ''Don't ask how; that isn't your problem. But assume that we manage it. We still have to get them to the palace, as quickly as possible.'' He turned and began to pace the length of the shadowed room. ''We have to get them there before warning can be sounded.''

''Horsed?''

"Some. Not many."

"How many?"

Renar's lips pressed together in a tight line. He did not answer.

Morgan nodded stiffly in approval and walked over to a cabinet against the north wall. Like the room, it was old and dark; Erin wondered if anything other than cobwebs would be found within. But the cab owner was familiar with what little he retained; his hands pulled out a large rolled map.

With care he began to unfurl it. "South gates?"

Renar took a breath, closed his eyes, and shook his head. "North."

"Ah. Harder than the south."

"Not as carefully patrolled." There was more to it, of course, but Morgan was not a stupid man; he didn't demand a better explanation.

"Right." Black lines with fine, faded writing covered the desk. It was like Tiras' map, but infinitely more detailed. Morgan's finger began to move from the north gate to the city's heart: the palace. "Best route here. But here"—his hand paused— "you've got a plethora of city guards. They never stop the patrols. And some of them have brains about 'em—most likely they'd arrow for the palace."

Renar nodded, leaning over the map until his shadow touched its farthest end. He reached out and caught Morgan's hand.

"Cospatric, you said?"

"Aye."

"Morgan."

The old man shook his head almost fiercely. "You ask a lot, Renar. I took a risk when I got you out of the city—but that was years ago. Things change." The map seemed to suddenly devour his entire attention; his eyes flickered over its surface. His breath was so shallow it was almost nonexistent.

Renar waited. It was all that was left him to do.

"You had to come back, didn't you?" Morgan said softly. He didn't look up. "You couldn't stay away and cause trouble at a distance—you had to come here.

"My wife's still alive. My boy's a free man, looking to take over this business. I've got grandchildren." He lowered his head. "We've had to be so careful. I can't ask them to throw that away for a fool's game."

Renar nodded stiffly. "No. We'd best head out, then. But, Morgan—don't tell them unless they ask?"

Morgan swallowed. Nodded. "That much, I can do."

Renar walked out of the room, Erin close at hand.

"Hey, Renar?"

"Yes?" He turned a little too quickly; hope caught in his throat.

"Here." Morgan held out a thick roll of vellum—the map that had been his pride and joy. "It's got your routing information. You should be able to follow it. Dotted lines are the heavily patrolled routes." In the poor light, Morgan's eyes were shining just a little too brightly. He looked away as Renar reached for the map.

"Morgan, I—"

"It's not free. You'll have to do me a favor or two in return—and when you're finished, that map comes back. Understood?"

"Yes."

"Good. I've a few things to deliver in the merchant's quarter. Borins'll take you there." He caught the frame of his door and held it with whitening fingers. "Best I can do," he said quietly.

"It's help," Renar answered. "And I'll remember it."

"Best go easy here, master."

Renar nodded as he stepped out of the cab. "I will, Borins. But I think, for now, we're safe."

Borins nodded and began to tug at the reins. "I hope we'll be seeing more of you. Morgan's in a better mood than he's been in these past five years. I could near hear him yellin' from the gates."

The prince of Dagothrin winced.

"Pay some mind to him—he knows his business."

"It would be impossible," Renar said pertly, "*not* to pay mind to him, as you say. Now off. I'll take over from here." He hefted the pack at his shoulder. He took a step forward, experimenting with the weight. He stumbled slightly, but when Erin reached out to steady him she found him stable. His face, pale, was cast groundward.

"We need help," he whispered quietly, almost to himself. "And we—I—have no right to expect it."

"Renar?" Erin looked at the house with some misgiving. It

was squat, small, and far too gray—but for all that, it seemed in good repair. There was a small amount of traffic in the street; the snow was muddy and well traveled over.

"That's our destination." Renar murmured, leveling his shoulders.

"Are we still in the lower quarter?"

"Merchant quarter," he replied, as he approached the door. "It's a guesthouse. Belongs to one of the three lines that Lord Tiber Beaton sponsors."

"Noble?"

"Yes. But of Marantine still, if he can harbor Kaarel."

"If he knows of it."

"He's sharp enough; he must know. And it gives me hope. Nine of the fifteen families perished in the first riot. Six of the fifteen capitulated—Tiras tells me five now have 'priests' on the council. But Tiber Beaton has none. As of yet." He knocked sharply on the door. "He owns the mines; he knows their workings. He was a friend of my uncle's, once."

"And now?"

The door swung open before Renar could answer. An elderly woman peered out from beneath a dustcap. She smiled almost timidly as she took in Renar's garb. Her plain brown dress folded into a clumsy bow.

"Yes, Lord, may I help you?"

"If it please you, I've come to speak with Master Jorgen. Tell him I've come to iron out the last clauses in our contract of the sixteenth."

"At once, Lord. Would you care to wait inside?"

"It is a bit chilly without."

The woman took a step back from the door, and Renar stepped in. Erin followed quickly and caught a sharp, worried glance from the old woman before it melted into a tame smile.

She wandered away down the hall and around a corner as Renar deposited the pack. It hit the floor with an authoritative thud. "This is heavy!" he whispered.

"I offered to carry it."

"If we have to do this again, I'll most certainly take you up on the offer. Manners should not extend further than the limits of my back, after all."

Erin smiled.

"You know, Erin dear, you look like a cat when you do that."

She opened her mouth to reply, and the serving woman reappeared.

"Master Jorgen will see you now, sir."

"Ah. Very good, then."

"I'll lead the way."

Renar nodded again and began to follow the woman down the hall and around the corner. Erin noted that the walls were not so plain as the outside of the house; little flashes of color caught her eyes as she walked by paintings, a portrait or two, and a large oval mirror.

For an elderly woman, the servant walked briskly; almost too much so. There was a nervous gait to her steps and a tension in the slope of her shoulders. Still, away from the streets and the press of buildings, Erin felt comfortable here; there was a sense of home about it.

"Just beyond the doors, Lord."

"Thank you, uh—"

"Clora." The woman curtsied.

Renar opened the door.

Erin saw a face framed by the corner his neck and shoulder made. The man was about Renar's age, his eyes the type of blue that often turns by a trick of the light, and his hair was light-colored and closely cropped. He stood taller than the prince. Most men did.

The smile that touched the stranger's face said many things at once: relief, recognition, surprise—friendship. Erin stepped a little to one side to get a better view of him. She wasn't sure where he and Renar had come to know each other, for this man didn't have the look of the nobility. All that he wore was eminently practical, and his hands had a callused look of labor about them, just as hers once had.

She smiled as her movement caught his eye, and he returned the smile. She liked him.

"Renar," he said, and held out a hand.

Renar took it and shook it warmly. "Kaarel. I always told you," he said, "that your years of antimonarchist press would bring you to a sorry end."

Kaarel's smile didn't falter. "It isn't over yet."

"The *Leaflet* was destroyed in the riot."

"The press was."

"Is Ruth—"

"Clora's been sent to fetch her. I thought—Clora's description was very good." It took Erin a moment to realize that the peculiar expression Kaarel suddenly adopted was in imitation of Renar.

Renar's laughter told her that it hadn't taken him that long. He smiled. "You don't look much different."

"Five years, Renar, more or less. Did you think I'd be bald?"

"And fat." He shook his head. "And bitter. You're right, old friend. The *Leaflet*'s still alive." He took a step forward, held out his arms, and stopped when the door burst open.

A small woman walked into the room. She bounced in, really, for her feet, which were as diminutive as the rest of her, hardly seemed to touch the ground at all. There were lines around her eyes and lines that ringed her mouth, but even these seemed youthful, caught as they were by a brilliant smile.

"Renar!"

He had barely enough time to turn, but his arms, already outstretched, caught her full weight and lifted her off the ground as her own arms wrapped themselves around his neck.

"Ruth." The word was quiet. Erin lost sight of Renar's eyes for a moment as he bowed his head. When he raised it again, his eyes were filmed slightly, and the smile on his face was one she had never seen there.

"Careful, Renar. It took a lot of work to find that wife. You can find your own if you want one."

Ruth laughed. It was a high sound, a young one. And it was out of place in Dagothrin. "A lot of work on whose part?"

Out of place? Erin thought, as Renar's smile grew mischievous. He looked younger, less grim. Her own lips turned slightly in a half smile, like an echo from some other time.

We're at war, Telvar. Does it mean we can't be human?

She shook her head, hearing the sounds of a sudden shriek of laughter.

She remembered Telvar's reply. *Erin, you, myself, your mother, the Grandfather—we aren't human. Not in the way you mean. We can't afford to be frivolous; can't afford to let our guard down when the price is more than just our own lives. When the war is over, maybe then.*

Telvar was lost to the war, lost centuries ago. Erin hoped that across the Bridge, he had found the time that they had fought for.

But she looked at Renar as he flirted—flirted!—with Kaarel's wife. She watched the way Ruth's eyes rolled as she played at straightening out his collar. And she caught the look of mock anger that lined Kaarel's brow.

She wanted to join them. The sword at her side, hard and cold, felt suddenly out of place. They continued to talk, forgetting her for the moment, and forgetting the war that had brought them here.

This was what Renar needed. He was her ally, he was no less determined to have an end here than she, and no less committed—but he needed a reminder that all had not been destroyed. Or did he? Maybe it was only a ghost of her own sudden longing, a desire to be part of their warmth.

But blood separated them. The blood of the Lady. The blood of the Light.

Was the Light cold before the awakening, Kedry?

Was the Dark cold?

Did they really not feel as we feel, think as we think?

We have changed, little Erin. But the Light is still in us, and it makes us—different. A little different.

But how different? Erin moved away to rest against a wall and watch, to absorb the warmth here, even if it wasn't directly offered to her.

Renar shook his head.

". . . still the most beautiful woman in the world."

Ruth was blushing.

"Except, maybe, for little Kayly. But I suppose she isn't all that little anymore. Where is she, Ruth?"

Everything froze as the words left Renar's lips.

Kaarel's head went down quietly, the light of his blue eyes shut out by trembling lids.

Ruth looked down at her hands as they rested, suddenly, against the fabric of her stilling skirt.

Last, Renar's eyes closed. Tight, this time. The smile was gone from his face, its lines melting into a more familiar sorrow and weight.

Ruth tried to smile. But her eyes were more red now than brown.

"It wasn't the war, Renar," she said in a rush, said to take some of the guilt from his face, even if it couldn't extract the pain. Even now, caught in pain of her own, she offered this. Erin didn't know how she spoke, but the rest of her words wouldn't come. Her bond-mate spoke quietly, to fill the heavy silence with explanation.

"We all survived the first and second 'riots.' When the troops came in and gutted Serry block, a few of us had had prior warning."

Renar looked at Kaarel.

"Kayly was with us. She was fine, then. But wintering was hard. At the beginning, no family, even the sympathetic, could aid us. There was too much caution on the part of the new government and the Church.

"We survived, but Kayly—" Kaarel looked away for a moment, his voice catching. "The winter was very hard."

They stood in silence.

Erin moved, then. Even if pain hadn't called her, she would have done so. The few minutes of laughter, the moments of joy and friendship, had left their lingering warmth. And it was suddenly important to her that they not die completely. Bringing back that warmth seemed more important than the fear of being an unwanted interference, more important than the feeling that she didn't belong here.

She walked past Renar to Ruth and caught shoulders that trembled. Her lips started to move, but the words, too awkward, wouldn't come.

Instead, she let her power flow outward in a warm, wide band. Light touched them both.

Ruth surrendered her tears.

"I'm sorry," she said. "I—It's been years, and we don't blame you, Renar. It wasn't your fault. I just—"

Erin continued to hold her. Seeing, through the light, the release of pain.

"She—" Her chin tilted upward, her eyes finding the ceiling. "She asked about you. She wanted to know when you were coming back." Her teeth found her lip.

The light kept glowing.

"We tried to explain, but she never really understood it. She was certain you were—you were coming." She tried to laugh, even though it caught in her throat. "And she was right. She would have been impossible when she found out how right she was.'' Then she looked at Erin.

Erin let her go, giving her shoulders a little squeeze that she hoped conveyed what she was afraid to say.

Ruth stood alone as the light faded.

No, Erin thought. *We aren't so different.* The blood that was barrier could also be bridge.

She looked up at Renar and found he was staring at her.

chapter
sixteen

There was no light here but that of lamps and eyes; no sounds but breath drawn into lungs not yet tested. Renar wore his silence like a bruise as he looked at the diminutive woman who circled the ground, confined by some invisible pattern that only she could see on the drill room's plain floor.

Ruth lingered in his vision, a ghost beside Erin, and, like her, deceptively small. He compared the two: necessary warmth against tempering flame. He had seen Erin, had known what she was capable of—had he not felt it himself?—yet he had never thought she could be of aid to Ruth, or to any mother, wife, or woman who was not a warrior in the traditional sense.

"Thank you."

Erin looked down at the wooden sword in her hands. "You won't after we've finished here."

"Won't? Ah. Thank you, you mean." He picked up his own practice blade in the silence. "Getting a little arrogant, aren't you? It's considered a serious character flaw in these parts, Lady—but I shall do my utmost to correct it."

Erin laughed, the sound coming from the back of her throat. "Shall we stop the chatter?"

Renar lunged.

"Darin, you aren't paying enough attention."

Darin sighed, and turned to face Trethar.

"How often must I tell you that this is important? You *must* be able to concentrate. And you must be able to control." Trethar, looking at least as tired as his student, ran his forearm

256

across his cheek. "Your life, and the lives of those around you, will depend on it. Trust me."

Darin nodded automatically. He didn't bother to tell Trethar that he felt too numb to open even the tiniest of gates. He'd already tried it five times, and if it hadn't worked for any one of them, it wouldn't work now.

"Fire is the easiest of the gates to open—but it is not the only one. We learn a new one, while we have time."

A nod again.

"Try once more. Look at the quill."

Every line of that damned quill was completely familiar.

"Now. Close your eyes, but remember the feel of it. You've almost got the gate; I want to feel you open it and lift the quill."

Obediently, Darin closed his eyes, leaning slightly against the warmth of Trethar's palms as they rested their tendrils of magic against his shoulders.

A few minutes later, Trethar gave up in disgust. Darin was asleep.

The sun had set hours ago. Renar tended almost absently to the oil in the single lamp of the study; it was burning low. Light caught his image and cast it against the wall in a long, thin shadow that made no struggle.

The strongest light gathered against the vellum of the city map. Several areas had been marked and countermarked by at least three different quills; Renar was no longer sure which marks were his own.

His eyes trailed the streets to the north gate and then followed them back to the palace.

Uncle Jordan.

His fists curled around the silent words and the images they conjured. Royal picnics, birthday parties, dinners, affairs of state—all attended by the duke, his uncle. A hint of velvet trailed across his cheek and brow like fire—how often had he hugged that man, sat in his lap, or listened to his endless, dynamic tales? His childhood became, for a moment, the sum of cupidity and naïveté, made so by the treachery of one man.

The one man who lived when all others lay, by his actions, in unquiet graves.

On the map, the palace was a flat set of lines, neatly and tidily drawn. Those lines bore no relation to the home that he had known so many years ago. Or to the man that had taken it for the service of the Empire at such a high cost to Marantine.

It was quiet in the study, but the shadows held the hush of a crowd made suddenly aware that the executioner's blade could fall. Tomorrow—or today, when the sun rose—he would speak with the Lord of Cosgrove.

He should sleep now. He would not get a chance later, and it was imperative that his mind be clear and fresh to the challenge. The lamplight deepened his frown.

"Renar?"

A second light entered the study. Renar's brows rose a fraction as he saw whose hand held the lamp.

"Lady." He bowed. "You should be asleep."

"Yes." She walked to the table and set the lamp down against the map's surface. "I tried."

It was true; even now she wore the bedrobes provided by Tiras. He gazed at her in the low light, thinking that she looked very small without the weight of her sword by her side. It was rare indeed when he saw her without it.

He looked at the map again, but this time he followed the route to the royal library: the home of the priests. This far, they would come together.

"You can't sleep either?"

"No, Lady. But I admit that I have not tried." He stretched, trying to ease the tension from his neck and shoulders.

Her silence waited upon him, as it often did.

Renar frowned again. "It's the meeting tomorrow. It weighs on my mind." His eyes turned away from hers, for he found them too bright, too green. They always shone so when he was at his worst, and instead of a comfort, it was a reminder. "I would almost rather fight the battle proper than go to meet Lord Cosgrove."

"Why?"

Such a simple question. How to answer it as simply?

Cosgrove has a priest upon the city council. One of the thirteen.

He shook his head. No.

Lord Cosgrove knows what the cost to Marantine has been, and yet of the fifteen families, he was first among those to acquiesce.

He smiled bitterly. *The Cosgroves have always been survi-*

vors, have they not? Had the Cosgroves not acquiesced in some form, would they not have met the fate of the nine who resisted?

"Because," he said at last, "Lord Cosgrove was my mother's father. He is no stupid man. He must know that the duke arranged her death. Yet still he serves. Still."

Erin walked over to Renar, reaching out to touch his shoulder gently. "Do you fear him?"

"Fear him?" He considered it, but briefly. "No."

"No?"

"No. I was the youngest of four children, as far from the crown as any born into my family could be. My mother raised me as a Cosgrove. I summered with the family until I was sixteen. I had the training that she had had.

"And Lord Cosgrove would do nothing, directly, to harm his family or its members."

He pulled away from the light touch of her hand, almost mistrusting it. "Gregory hated it. Hennet was less difficult, and Reynalan, for all that she was a spiteful sister"—here he smiled—"found it amusing. The training, I mean.

"My mother had pride—a Cosgrove's pride. Her marriage meant that she had to disavow her family; her father—my grandfather—did not approve. I was the wreath of peace passed between them, many years later."

He looked up at Erin. "She was his youngest. I know that he loved her very much. But he did nothing to find justice for her death. And I—I have done what little I can. I do not want to meet him on the morrow. And I do not think we can do this without his aid."

"Maybe," Erin said softly, "he did what he could to preserve his family for the future. For *this* future." Even as she said it, she knew that she was speaking not only to Renar, but the ghosts of her own dead people. "Had he stood against the invaders in the beginning, he wouldn't be here to aid us."

Renar's laugh was harsh and bitter, so different from the laughter that Ruth and Kaarel had evoked earlier the same day. "Erin, Lady, the lines might have had some such pure motives had they ever sought such a surrender—and they have not, at least not in the histories that I was taught. Do not think of my grandfather in a similar such light; you do not know him as I do.

"If, on the morrow, I cannot convince him of our greater chance of success, he will be of no use to us at all."

Again, her silence came, but there was no waiting in it. She looked down at the lamp, picked it up, and walked to the door. There she stopped, framed by it, almost dwarfed by it.

"Renar?"

"Lady."

"Did you love him very much?"

From anyone else, the question might have been cruel. But her voice was so open and low, that the hint of fear in it carried. He could not be offended by it.

"Yes."

She nodded, as if to herself, but stood in the doorway a moment longer. "Love was like that with the lines as well."

Before he could ask her what she meant, she was gone.

They met Lianar in the lower city. They were prompt, as was the servant of Cosgrove. He supplied them with both clothing and carriage.

"Thank you, Lianar."

The old man nodded quietly, almost uneasily. "It's a rough homecoming, young master."

"But I am home." There was more in those words than in hours of talk. Lianar was used to this from the Cosgroves. He nodded stiffly, turned, and then turned again, off-beat, and somehow off-stride.

"Young master? I offer you a word of caution. Mistrust your cousin, Verena." And then he was gone.

The carriage was marked as merchant's, but Renar did not recognize the emblem upon the doors. It was large, and the seats were well cushioned; the doors, unlike those of Borins' cab, were large and more easily maneuvered. He guided Erin up the step and nodded to the coachman before entering himself.

"Remember," he told her quietly, "if you are asked to wait, wait. Within the house itself we need fear no harm."

Erin nodded; it was the fourth time that Renar had said this. She wondered if it was because he only half believed it himself. But she still had her sword; it was too long to be easily hidden, although the cloak covered it well when she walked. If necessary, she would use it.

Borins was indeed a terrible driver, at least if the ride here was anything to judge by. Either that or the stones and holes in the road had been miraculously repaired in the last three days. She watched the buildings roll by beyond Renar's stiff profile. On impulse, she reached out and caught his hand.

To her surprise, he returned the grip tightly instead of withdrawing.

Tenements became houses; houses became manors with large iron gates and guardhouses. In spite of herself, Erin pulled back as far as the cushions would allow.

The carriage eventually turned up the long roadway to a large, stone edifice. Guards stopped it; Erin could see them move into, and out of, sight. She heard muffled words and then the guards returned to their posts, satisfied. She let herself breathe again.

Renar smiled at her, but the expression was brittle. When the carriage rolled to a stop, he opened the door without waiting for the footman, and walked around to the other side to allow Erin to leave.

"This, Lady, is the Cosgrove Manor."

Guards waited at the front of the building. They looked relaxed, but they were well equipped.

"This way, sir," one said briskly.

"No time to view the grounds themselves, then. Perhaps later." He offered an arm, and she took it. Both were trembling.

But she looked as she walked through the arches that led to the courtyard. They were high and grand, reminiscent of the great hall of Elliath, but newer and perhaps a little less clean. She felt dwarfed by the architecture, as no doubt some planner had intended.

So intent was she on the heights, that she nearly tripped when Renar stopped abruptly—stopped in front of a carved insignia in the flagstones.

"Bright Heart," Renar said, through teeth that were suddenly clenched. "Not this, too."

Erin closed her eyes, but not before seeing. The stones were blooded. Cosgrove was a house of the Empire.

She glanced at Renar out of the corner of her eye. He stood very stiffly, his face a pleasant blank, his shoulders slightly back. For the first time in Erin's sight, he looked every inch the man he was: a prince of Marantine, returning home. She preferred the man she had come to know.

The guards made no comment; indeed they seemed not to

have heard Renar's unfortunate words or the anger inherent in them. They were well trained; Cosgrove as a house must still have money.

The doors opened for them; they were wide double doors. The hall looked down upon them as they made their silent progress beneath its molded ceiling. Color was evident everywhere, but it was tasteful; tapestries lined the walls, and flowers—in winter, yet—stood in burnished vases before the evenly spaced mirrors. A hint of fragrance told Erin they had been freshly laid out.

They passed another set of double doors, these simple and dark. A candle flickered beneath a glass sphere on either side. It was for decoration, really, as the sunlight was strong enough to cast out shadows even as they progressed.

At last the guards stopped outside of a more modest door. Two guards, in like uniform, nodded and opened it.

Renar went through without comment, and Erin followed, brushing lightly against one of the men. No one sought to stop her, and she was grateful for it; to wait outside while Renar faced his grandfather alone would have been very hard indeed.

The walls of the room were tall and lined with shelves. Row upon row of leather-bound books dominated the scene; there was even a ladder on small wheels to allow access to them.

At the farthest end of the room was a large, plain desk. Behind it sat a man, the only other person in this library. He was older, his hair streaked with gray. Once it might have been black, but it was hard to tell. His brow was one long line of peppered hair that dovetailed in the center. He rose in silence to greet them.

The Grandfather of Elliath had never looked so forbidding.

"So," he said softly, the word crisp and clear. "It's true, then."

Renar said nothing.

"Come. There are chairs; take them." Lord Cosgrove waited until both Erin and Renar were seated. Then he smiled, and his smile was the winter of age. "It has been a long time, Renar."

"Indeed, Lord Cosgrove. Long enough that much has changed within the family's grounds."

"Much has changed within Dagothrin."

"Yes." Renar looked at the polished surface of the desk. It

trapped his grandfather's reflection, but softened the lines. "How is Lady Lisbeth?"

"Well."

"And Lord Bretnor?"

"Also well."

There was silence again, with its sharp little teeth and its towering walls between the kin.

"Lady Verena?"

"She is well." Lord Cosgrove leaned back in his chair, his eyes never leaving his grandson's face.

"And does she enjoy her new duties?"

At this, the older man smiled, his lips drawing up momentarily. It aged his face.

"She serves the family's interests. As always."

Erin watched them both, the young man and the old one. There was a resemblance in their faces, but she wasn't sure whether it was due to blood ties or to the expression that each wore. They were wary; they belonged in the training circle, not in the stately library of a noble family. They circled each other with words, testing, feinting.

And with words, she thought, the older Cosgrove was the more capable. He did not have Renar's anger—or Renar's pain.

Yet it was the older man who spoke first.

"Renar, why have you come?"

"This was my home, Lord Cosgrove," the prince replied. "Am I not welcome to return to it?"

It was the older man who rose first.

"You are welcome here, as always." His eyes were dark. "And as always, when you are here, you are considered to be of Cosgrove, and not Maran." He turned to the window, showing Renar the breadth of his shirted back. He wore no jacket and no crested finery—his presence alone conveyed his power. "The matters of the crown are not the matters of Cosgrove. Has this not always been the case?"

Without his grandfather's eyes to goad him, Renar seemed to shrink at the words. But he did not rise, and he did not look at Erin. This was the old quadrille, this was a dance he should well know by now.

But he had not expected that it would be his grandfather who would take the first step to set it in motion.

"Who is your companion? I see that she bears a sword—is she a southern guard?"

"She is Lady Erin," he replied. "She has come this distance to aid me."

"In what undertaking?"

"The one that I have chosen, Grandfather." He paused, weary suddenly. The blood in the carved grooves of the flagstones had left their stain on more than stone. "Does Verena serve the Church in its ceremonies, or only in its politics?"

"She serves the family." There was a hint of anger here, an echo of Renar's edged words.

"And not the new crown?"

"The crown is dead, Renar."

"My mother is dead."

"Yes." Cold, cold word.

Erin jumped forward slightly and then gripped the armrests of her chair firmly. They were alike, these two. Their anger and their pain—both jumped to the same pulse, the same beat.

Renar, why did you say that? She looked at his closed face, wondering if he was even sure himself.

"Why have you come?"

"I have come for your aid." He stopped, weighing his words. "We seek to return the crown of Marantine to the line of Maran."

"And you seek my aid?" Lord Cosgrove turned then, his arms behind his back. He chuckled; it was a black, bitter sound. "Perhaps you really are more of a Maran than a Cosgrove. Did you not hear me, boy? The crown is dead, and Maran with it." He held out one hand; it was as steady as Renar. "Come as a Cosgrove, Renar. Or leave."

Renar rose, shedding the walls of his chair for the first time. He looked stiffly at Erin. He nodded as she stood, watching her gather her cloak more tightly around her shoulders. He walked, rigid and graceless, to the door and then stopped.

"Is that what you told my mother?" he asked, his voice very low. He did not wait for a response. Instead, he reached for the handle of the door. "Then I fear I must give you, measure for measure, her answer.

"There is no peace between us; you have the things that she paid for with her life. Lady?"

Erin shook her head. "Renar," she whispered, and turned to

look at the Lord of Cosgrove. His face, like Renar's, was set and final.

She saw the two of them clearly, more clearly than they saw themselves. Taking a deep breath, she took a step away from Renar.

"Lord Cosgrove." Her voice was a bell that rang crisply and left its echo in their uncomfortable silence. "Renar's mother was your youngest, wasn't she?"

He nodded. It was the only sign he gave that indicated he was listening. His eyes, black and hooded, rested upon his kin.

"Was she like him?"

"He has her looks." The words were grudging. "And some of her ways. Stubborn."

"As are you."

His smile could have cut.

"Renar is of Maran; of Marantine," Erin continued.

The smile vanished.

"But he is of Cosgrove as well, else he wouldn't have survived this far."

"Erin." Renar was grim. "Come; this does neither of us any good; it tells us nothing new."

"You loved your daughter," Erin continued, paying no attention to Renar's curt command. "And you loved your grandson. You raised them both." She waited, wondering what this stern lord would say.

"Yes." He closed his eyes. "Yes."

Without thinking, she took two steps toward him before forcing herself to stand. His call was strong.

"Do not turn that love inward; it was never meant to be a weapon." Again, again she realized even as she spoke that it was not just to Lord Cosgrove that the words applied. "Help us."

She wanted to touch him with Elliath's power. She wanted to, but held her ground. Let this choice come from him, let it be for him. Anything mortal had some of the light within it.

And some of the dark.

"Lady," he began, and his voice was ice. "My daughter Mara died when she left these walls. The queen, Maralan, was born in her stead. She sought no advice from me, no counsel." His hands came down to touch their reflection on the desk. His head was bowed; Erin caught a flicker of movement in the lines of the desk.

When he looked up, he was old. "It was a Maran edict.

"I would have had her choose otherwise. There were many who would have been glad of an alliance with Cosgrove." He turned suddenly. "But she would have her *fool* of a husband."

"She loved him," Renar said, bristling.

"And he loved himself," Lord Cosgrove replied tightly. "She was a Cosgrove—she saw the tide turn." Hands became fists. "She tried to tell him. *You* tried. And in trying, you were dismissed from the family you tell me you want to reinstate."

"That isn't fair," Renar said, feeling young and foolish, as he did so rarely now that his childhood was past. His colors rose, reddening his cheeks. His hands mirrored his grandfather's.

"Fair! What is 'fair'?" Lord Cosgrove said, as he stepped forward around the desk. "The king was the author of his own misfortune—his stupidity cost Marantine everything!"

"Everything?" Renar's voice rose. "Did his stupidity cost the life of the person whose blood stains the family crest?" He, too, stepped forward. "Or was it your cowardice?" He closed his eyes, and his voice dropped suddenly. "Was it ours?"

The door to the library opened suddenly, and two guards stepped in, weapons drawn.

Both men turned to stare at them.

"Lord," one began, "we heard shouting."

"Get out!"

From their reaction, Erin knew that they had never seen him so raw in his anger. They all but jumped back through the door.

He knew it as well. His height seemed to dwindle as he struggled for control.

"How do you know?" Renar asked softly. "How do you know what she knew? How do you know that she tried to sway my father?"

Lord Cosgrove reached out suddenly and both of his hands folded themselves around Renar's collars; only then did Erin realize how close together the two stood. He was the taller and larger man; it was almost a matter of ease to lift Renar off his feet.

Erin's nails bit into the palms of her hands as she watched

them. Like the Cosgrove guards, she knew this was no time to interfere. And like them, she wanted to.

"You did nothing, either." Lord Cosgrove said. He released Renar suddenly, to resume the battle for self-control.

"I know." It was as much an admission of guilt as either was willing to make.

Erin wondered who the queen of Marantine had been and how she would have felt to see these two, son and father, as she came between them.

"I have lost one child to Maran," Lord Cosgrove said. "I did what I could to ensure that I would never lose another." He walked back to his desk and sat down heavily. "She came here. She came to ask my aid. She had her suspicions of Duke Jordan, even then." He closed his eyes, remembering.

A weary smile touched his lips. "You are not like your mother," he said softly. "She was always different; not a Cosgrove, not at heart. You have more of us in you than she."

Renar said nothing.

"She told me. Demanded my aid. We argued. We never argued so much when she was young." He bowed his head. "I sent my agents out. I watched for word. They heard nothing, saw nothing.

"And then you came back, and your father disowned you. Two months later, Marantine fell. The riots followed. We lost many in them. Duke Jordan took governorship. We made our pledges.

"Verena volunteered for the council." He ran his hand over his eyes. "The Church made its rules clear. The stones are blooded here by quarters.

"But the family survives."

"Grandfather . . ."

"I never thought you would come back." The old man rose. "Better that you stayed away. In safety; you were good at that. Tiras always said you were his best.

"Why have you come? You have no hope of restoring what was destroyed."

Very starkly, Renar replied. "To kill Jordan."

"To be king?"

"No," Renar whispered. "To kill him." He drew breath. It hurt. "To kill him. For Maran. For Marantine. For my mother."

"As Cosgrove should have done."

"I didn't say that."

"You didn't have to."

Silence again, the silence of two separate struggles. "She was my youngest." Lord Cosgrove smiled again, almost ghostlike. "The youngest are always the most wayward." He drew himself up, and his eyes glittered. For a moment he wavered, and then his face stiffened, shutting out vulnerability and doubt. Wordless, he lifted his arm and his shaking hand pointed to the doors.

Erin bowed her head; she lost sight of their pain through her own, unexpectedly. To come so close . . . As Renar turned, she glanced back once and then began to follow the isolated prince.

And then Lord Cosgrove spoke, his voice a whisper. "Renar, hold. I am grown old and foolish, but I must know. How will you kill him?"

Renar's eyes widened before they closed, and when they did, his lashes were moist. But he offered no tears. "Stent," he said, in so quiet a voice that Erin almost missed it. He stood and walked in a blind teeter to where Lord Cosgrove sat.

"Re." His grandfather held out a hand.

Then they both straightened out, aware of their dignity, and aware of the woman who watched. It was habit; she was not of the family, and weakness such as this was a family matter.

Almost apologetically, Renar turned to Erin. His eyes were red-rimmed, but no tears escaped them.

"Stenton Cosgrove," he said. "All of his friends called him Stent—and I wanted to be as important as I thought they were."

They returned to their seats, and in earnest began to tell Lord Cosgrove the minutiae of their plans. It took a pitifully short time.

"That's idiotic!" Lord Stenton Cosgrove's face was red. "I have never in my life heard such drivel!"

"It may be 'idiotic,' but it's the only chance we have!" his grandson shot back. "Unless you have troops to aid us, and I haven't noticed many with your colors in the street!"

Erin sighed. She had been sighing for the better part of two hours. Lord Stenton Cosgrove had a very brittle method of exhaustive questioning. He was known for his sharpness for very real reason.

"Lord Cosgrove," she began.

"*If* you have this so-called mage, and *if* his powers are up to the attack on the gate, it still has to be opened."

Renar nodded grimly.

"Have you thought on that?"

He nodded again.

"Details?"

"Later."

Lord Cosgrove snorted; he knew prevarication when he heard it, being a master of the art himself. Then he turned and gave Erin an appraising glance. "So while Re is off on his fool's errand, blithely entering the palace and equally blithely asking all three hundred of the royal guards to kindly get out of his way while he kills Jordan," he paused for breath, "you will be knocking cheerily on the church's doors and asking the Swords to step aside while you kill the priests?"

"I won't be alone, either."

"Ah, yes. You'll be with the patriarch of Culverne."

She bristled at the tone of the words. "Yes."

"No."

They both turned to stare at Lord Cosgrove. His word was completely final.

Renar sighed. "Stent, I'll be using the underground."

Stenton Cosgrove raised one eyebrow.

"Underground?"

"My mother built a few tunnels in her spare time." His smile was bitter. "I played in them. I learned to use my skills there. I'm not so stupid as to walk up to doors at the head of my army."

"That's the first intelligent thing I've heard you say so far." He raised his head thoughtfully. "Tunnels?"

"Emergencies."

"Mara." He shook his head and leaned over the desk to drum his fingers against the table. He, too, had a map; not so fine a one as Renar had procured, but clear enough to tell the tale. "This route?"

"Morgan's suggestion."

"This route, then. But it's heavily patrolled."

"By city guards. Most of them don't have official uniforms anymore; Tiras tells me they're responsible for their own."

Stenton Cosgrove smiled. "Yes." He stood, walked over and rapped at the library door. It opened instantly. "Get the captain. Send him in."

"Yes, sir."

The door closed swiftly. Booted steps echoed in the hall.

"There is one other family that we might wish to speak with," Lord Cosgrove said, as he rested his chin atop his steepled fingers.

"Beaton."

Lord Cosgrove nodded. "Tiber. He's living on the political edge as it is, but he still maintains a large group of family guards. For his merchant lines."

"Would he help? He and Jordan were once close."

"You and Jordan were once close," Lord Cosgrove said darkly. No other explanation was offered. Or needed. "He may attempt to negotiate concessions if you succeed."

"Such as?"

"Marriage is the most probable."

Renar cringed.

His grandfather smiled. "Merchanting territories. Tax concessions. Land—the land of the nine that fell is still in Jordan's keeping."

"And?"

"You can get away with the land concessions." His eyes were twinkling. "But he's likely to press for marriage at a later point in time. If you succeed." The smile vanished. "Now. The gates. It takes half an hour to open them—and you won't have it."

"Speak to Lord Beaton," Erin said crisply. "We—we might have a method of opening the gates."

"Oh?"

"The details . . . haven't been worked out yet." She was painfully aware of Renar's raised eyebrow as his gaze fell against her profile.

He nodded. "How long do we have?"

We. Erin smiled. "A week for the message to travel out of the city and back."

"Let me speak with Verena, then. She rooms here; I'll send a message via Lianar."

They rose, and the doors to the library swung open.

Renar stopped dead.

Stenton was smiling broadly.

"Captain Cospatric, I believe you've met my grandson?"

* * *

Outside of the manor, Renar paused in front of the blooded stones. He murmured something, bowed, and then turned to Erin.

"Lady?"

She took his offered arm and they waited for the carriage to be brought round to the front.

There was only one more place to go, and that would wait until after they had eaten.

"I'm coming, I'm coming!" Hildy fastened the belt of her housecoat tight around her solid girth. She strode down the steps that creaked beneath her, her expression thunderous. Corden, her oldest servant, quickly made way for her; he pitied anyone—be they Sword or guard—who earned her wrath.

"Can't even let an old woman get any sleep. I've a word or two to say to them," she muttered as she reached the bottom of the stairs. "Where are they?"

"Front door, ma'am."

"Haven't answered it yet, have you?"

Corden shook his head slowly. "Didn't recognize them."

The annoying knock came again, and Hildy grabbed the handle of the door, yanking it open.

"What on—" She stopped, the redness of her face diminishing. Then, her lips turned up in a smile of recognition; her eyes brightened, and thoughts of sleep and irritation left them.

"Hildy," Erin said, extending a hesitant hand. "Might we enter?"

Hildy rubbed her eyes once, and then nodded to Corden. "Put some tea on—or would you like something stronger?"

"Tea would be wonderful."

"Something stronger."

Erin turned around as Renar stepped into Hildy's view. Hildy couldn't see the younger woman's face; it was aimed at Renar.

"Tea would be acceptable."

Erin sighed, and stepped quickly into the house. She followed Hildy into a small sitting room—one that had no windows to the outside world.

"Take a chair, dear—or do you not have the time to sit for a bit?"

"We've the time," Renar replied. "Guard patrols around this area are rather frequent at this time of night."

Hildy nodded. "Well, then. Don't stand on my account, dear; Corden will be along in a moment with an extra chair."

"I will certainly not sit while a lady is forced to stand." He bowed. "Do be seated, madame. I shall wait for Corden."

Not one to remain uncomfortable for longer than politeness decreed, Hildy took a chair and pulled it up beside Erin. She gave the younger woman an encouraging smile, which was returned cautiously.

Corden arrived with tea—and was sent away for the promised third chair. He arrived with this, looking somewhat more tired.

"Thank you, Corden. Back to bed with you, dear—you look as if you could use it."

Corden looked pointedly at both of Hildy's guests.

"No, dear, I think they're fine. And I can handle myself if it comes down to that."

Corden looked more pointedly at the sword at Erin's side.

"To bed, dear. Now."

With a shrug that was more eloquent than words, Corden surrendered. He turned and walked out of the room. Erin very much doubted that he would get any sleeping done at all while they were there.

"Much better. Cream, dear, or sugar?"

Erin shook her head. "No thank you."

"And you?"

"Both."

As soon as the tea was placed in front of them, Erin leaned forward. Hildy settled back into her chair with a satisfied smile, her face attentive.

"Hildy—when you helped us to get into the city, you said that we might call on you if we needed any help."

"Aye, dear. I believe that's what I said." She took a sip of tea and then set the cup aside. "And you've come for my help, have you?" She clapped her hands together. "How exciting!"

Renar rolled his eyes and gave Erin a very arch "I told you so" look. She ignored it.

After a moment, Hildy sat back, her eyes still bright, but her face much more sober. "It's serious business, isn't it?"

Erin nodded.

"And in any other situation—even in this one, if the truth were told," Renar put in, "we'd not have come to you for it."

"That serious?"

Erin nodded again.

"Let's have it, then."

"You said you would be leaving the city in two to four weeks."

"Aye. And you want me to take someone out with me? I can do it, dear, but there doesn't seem to be much place to take them to, if you understand what I'm saying." Hildy looked mildly disappointed.

"We want you to take someone with you, yes—but we want you to leave him at the gate."

"At the gates, dear?"

"What the young lady is trying so poorly to say is this: We need the north gates open long enough for approximately a hundred armed men to come charging through. Opening the gates is a time-consuming procedure—and unfortunately, our man at the gate won't be able to do it alone—he's going to have to keep an eye out for the garrison. The only way we can have the gate opened to our advantage is if those set to guard it follow their usual procedure. Needless to say, they wouldn't do it for us."

"North gate?" Hildy rubbed her chin a minute. "Garrison's stronger there. Why north?"

"Not the gate I would have chosen, but we've no choice." Renar shrugged it aside. "The risk to you, and there is a risk, is that you must keep your caravan midway between the gates so they can't be easily closed. It wouldn't be necessary, but you know as well as I that closing the gates to Dagothrin is much simpler than opening them."

Hildy frowned. "That's a risk, all right. I've not many men, although I'll grant you that all of them can fight."

"I wish I could tell you that they won't be called on to do it. I can't. But your caravan, and one or two other incidents, will be the signal for—"

"All of it, Renar," Erin said curtly.

He glanced at Erin, and set his lips in a thin line.

Her frown was equally tense, but it didn't last beyond her sigh. "Hildy, we need the north gate; you'll be our signal to those who wait to enter. There are a hundred men, maybe more."

"Ah. The resistance, then." Hildy was silent and thoughtful, her brow furrowed, her eyes on the far wall. After a moment, she picked up her cup of cooling tea and sipped it reflectively. "I'll have to think on it. It's a risk."

Renar threw another look at Erin, and she stood quietly.

"Madame"—he bowed—"there is no reason why you have to accompany your caravan."

China hit wood with a sharp clunk. Tea sloshed out of cup to splash table. "Young man." Hildy stood. "I'll thank you not to ever suggest that I'd send my people into a danger I wouldn't face myself."

Renar bowed. "My apologies. I was considering your safety."

"Not a pretty excuse." She sat down again. "Aren't you going to stay and finish your tea?"

"We've much to do to be prepared—and if your help cannot be counted on, we've others to seek."

It was a lie, and her expression told him that she knew it well; such exaggerations were not uncommon in her profession. They regarded each other carefully a moment, and Renar began to speak again.

"We cannot offer you much, but if we should succeed, I can promise you a large portion of monetary—ouch!"

"Let you do the talking," Erin muttered, giving him a less-than-friendly shove back into his seat while he massaged his shin.

"Aye." Hildy nodded, taking another sip of tea. "I don't know why you let him do it, dear, but at least you've the sense that he obviously doesn't. Money indeed." She smiled. "You've got my curiosity piqued, I'll give you that. Money."

Erin watched the old woman, and then picked up her own cup. She was smiling. "We need the gate," she said, ignoring the glare that Renar was almost certainly directing at her, "because we need to get the men into the city. There aren't enough of them on their own, but with the help of one or two highly placed people, we intend to take the palace."

Hildy smiled encouragingly at Erin, who continued.

"We believe we can wrest it away from the governor and the priests that form his council. But speed and time are of the essence—and we can't do it without your help. We've a way to take care of the garrison, but no way to open the gates—without you."

Renar was sputtering quietly. He was used to being ignored, true, but only when he had decided on it.

"Well. Well, then. I have to think a moment."

"Will you help us?"

"Help?" She sighed. "Youth is always so impatient. I was talking to myself there. But help you? Of course I will." She looked suddenly at Renar, and then sighed. It was very theatrical.

"But you know, dear, they don't make royalty like they used to."

Renar froze for a moment.

"Time was when royalty knew how to be polite." She began to chuckle, and Erin, her heart slowly starting again, joined in. She started to speak, and Hildy caught her hand.

"No, dear. It isn't necessary. Why know more than I have to know? I'll talk it over with the boys."

Tiras stood in his bathrobe, holding a light aloft in the long hallway. Shadows flickered across his stark face, lending it a gauntness that the day normally hid.

The side door creaked once, and he stepped forward.

For an instant the lamplight caught Renar in strict relief, back against wall and face tilted into darkness. He straightened immediately, planting his feet firmly apart.

"It's only me," Tiras said softly. "Did you find what you searched for?"

Renar bowed his head. Tiras mirrored the gesture a moment and then gestured with the lamp.

Together they walked up the stairs and into Tiras' small study. The door closed softly behind them.

Lamps were lit, giving the room a warm glow. Renar fitted his mouth with a smile; Tiras did the same.

"Five of the ten, Tiras."

"Better than we'd hoped."

"Yes." Renar's smile wavered and he turned abruptly away from the source of light in front of him.

"Renar," Tiras said quietly, "you were, in many ways, the best of my students. Your mother's equal." He shook his head. "In some ways, you were my worst. But it's because of this that you're here; because of it, I'm willing to help."

"Don't. Don't say it." He looked up. Tiras had always de-

spised any acknowledgment of pain. Knowing this, Renar did
what he could to hold on to his facial expression. "I know."

"No—no, you don't." Tiras gave a bitter chuckle. "If you
listened to everything I've tried to teach you, would you be
manning an attack on the royal palace with little over a hundred
men?"

Renar stared at the desk. "Five of the ten, Tiras. The rest
perished in 'rioting' because they could not sell what they believed in."

"I know." As if from a great distance, he continued to speak.
"We argued about it, Terrela and I. Long arguments; real
ones. She was not, in the end, a cunning woman—nor a subtle
one. She knew only her own business well.

"Aye, we argued. We fought for two weeks. In the end, she
threw me out. She would not listen to me. Would not believe
that in this, there was a power greater than her own."

Renar listened quietly.

"I went out that night—the Night of Fires. I went out into the
streets, among the Swords and guards. I thought I might somehow find her; somehow change her mind." He laughed hol-
lowly. "Wouldn't have done any good, and I knew it. She was
infamous by that time; if any had escaped, she could not have
been among them. The Swords had their orders.

"I killed a few for her on the way back. A few?" He laughed
again and turned away from his student, hiding his face a moment. "Every one I could get my hands on."

Renar said nothing. There was nothing he could say that would
not acknowledge what Tiras was feeling.

"They used her to blood the stones of the Church."

Then Renar, too, turned away.

"I know what you're feeling, Your Highness. If I'd been willing to help—if I'd been there . . . But it's a trap, and a foolish
one. Five remain, and those five will aid us as they can." He
reached over and suddenly damped the wick of the lamp. "And
we'll win. We'll remember."

The shadows freed them and comforted them.

Lady Verena sat in the comfort of her rooms; she had retreated there after a grueling session with her grandfather, Lord
Cosgrove, in a mood that was less than pleasant.

Lord Cosgrove was no fool; he had had the presence of mind

to reveal his plans to her alone of all their family. But those plans bordered on lunacy. She wondered what he had been thinking, to make them, or to agree to them, when it put the whole of the family at near-inconceivable risk. She had restrained herself enough to nod in near-silent agreement after her initial show of shock—and that seemed to mollify the old man somewhat, but she was not now certain that he wouldn't have her watched, or have her actions monitored.

His lack of faith both amused her and irritated her greatly; one day, the family would be in her keeping—did he think she would be fool enough to allow anyone to risk it rashly? It was more than time to take matters into her own hands.

The hour that had passed, with the comforts of a particularly strong snifter of brandy, had mellowed that mood enough that she had the presence of mind to write. The quill in her hand didn't shake at all.

HRH Duke Jordan of Illan,

My scouts have located Renar of Maran. They have discovered who his contacts are and where those contacts can be found. For this reason, I consider it expedient to request a summoning of the Lesser Cabal at your earliest convenience.

Your servant,
Lady Verena of Cosgrove.

chapter
seventeen

An inch above the ground the quill cast a wavering shadow.

"Good. Very good. Keep it steady."

Darin didn't answer; even the effort of listening threatened the tenuous hold he had on both gate and feather. The warm tickle of sweat rolling down his cheeks made him wonder how he could be suffering from physical exertion when he'd barely moved a muscle in the last two hours.

The quill floated gently to floor before he realized his mistake. Trethar's frown had already turned thunderous.

"Is that your idea of *concentration*?" he shouted, the last word more of an epithet than his cursing.

"No, sir." Darin said softly.

A knock at the door spared him the rest of the lecture that was sure to follow. Almost gratefully, he rose to answer it.

"Darin?"

"Erin!"

She laughed at the look on his face. "We've got a meeting. Can you come?"

Darin nodded before Trethar could answer.

"So soon?" Trethar murmured.

"Soon? It's been almost four days since you've sequestered yourselves away here."

"Four days." The tone of his voice told her what he thought of them. "Ah, well. Let's get this over with quickly, then." He rose as well, looking more annoyed than tired.

"Where have you been?" Darin whispered as Erin threw an arm around his shoulder.

"All over Dagothrin. Several times."

"Is everything all right?"

She nodded. "Better than we thought. How are the lessons?" She glanced at the strained lines of his face and changed the subject. "We've planned the route into the city. We've a decent chance of getting to our destinations in one piece."

"Who'd you talk to?"

"Save it for the meeting." She stopped then and hugged him. The faint hint of new sweat lingered as she pulled back. "It's good to see you."

His smile was shy.

"So. There you have it. Hildy, the merchant who brought us in, will leave slightly early, and by the north gates. She's due in to the mines." Renar glanced at Erin.

Tiras nodded.

"Trethar will travel in the wagons, at least as far as the gate. Erin and Darin will wait about a hundred yards from the gate, and they'll go as far as the royal library"—he could not bring himself to call it a church—"with the men who make it through."

"Tiras and I will start our entry into the palace proper at that point."

"Timing?" Erin asked softly; it was still a point that made her nervous.

Renar shrugged. "We'll chance it, Lady." He began to roll up the map. "When the men have gone past Kevler Road, Ruth and Kaarel will start to hang notices in the area; let's hope what they say will prove true."

"When do we send word?"

"This eve. We have one more word to wait upon."

They started to rise, and Anders opened the door.

"Sir?" he said to Tiras.

"What?"

"There are three men who are here; they ask an audience with you."

"Tell them that I'm indisposed at the moment."

"Sir."

"Indisposed?" came a voice from the hall. It was familiar. "The hells you are."

Erin shook her head as both Darin and Trethar tensed. Darin relaxed slowly; Trethar grew more agitated.

Anders, however, looked more annoyed than worried as he swung around.

Lord Stenton Cosgrove, attired in distinctly flamboyant clothing, pushed past the manservant and entered the room.

"Stent," Tiras said curtly. "What are you doing here?"

"I might ask the same of you, but I won't waste the question, as I already know the answer." He smiled, nodded at Erin, looked carefully over Darin, and raised an eyebrow at Trethar. "Patriarch?" he asked.

Trethar's frown deepened.

"Uh, no, sir." Darin said softly. He stepped forward, self-consciously putting the staff of Culverne between himself and Lord Cosgrove's astonished glance. "I am."

"You? Gods, Renar!" He shook his head and turned to the door. "Come on in!" he shouted.

Anders' face was almost purple. "Sir, I really must insist—"

Cospatric entered the room, followed quickly by an older man in similar uniform. Erin didn't recognize him.

Tiras and Renar did.

"Lord Beaton!"

"Tiber!"

Stenton Cosgrove took the time to enjoy himself immensely; it was a small luxury, and it could be afforded.

"In Cosgrove colors," Lord Beaton said. He bowed, his mouth turned in an ironic study of a smile. "I've taken temporary leave of any sense I once had."

He rose, and Erin took the opportunity to study his face. He was an older man, perhaps not quite so old as Stenton Cosgrove, but the years had etched themselves more heavily into the lines of his face. His eyes were deep-set, and Erin thought them each a different color, one green and one brown. In the light it was hard to tell. Pride was there, and a certain sternness that spoke of concealed anger.

"Lord Beaton," Renar said, this time more quietly. "This is a risk, is it not?"

"It is." He looked around the room. "It is indeed, Your Majesty." Here he bowed, and this time the bow was low. "But I had to see for myself; only a fool trusts the word of a Cosgrove to stand on its own."

"You wound us," Stenton said. But he smiled.

"Trust you to take that as a compliment." Tiber's voice was

wry. He spoke again to Renar. "Stent says that you've a plan to take back Marantine."

Renar nodded.

"We've already wasted time bargaining," Lord Cosgrove said. "We won't waste more."

A flash of mild annoyance crossed Lord Beaton's face and then subsided. "As you say."

"You're bargaining for Maran?" Renar said to his grandfather.

"Maran has never been known for its ability in that quarter." A challenge there.

Renar refused to take it. "Which lands?"

"Sennet."

"Ah." Renar smiled darkly. "Those lands are currently in Jordan's keeping. Done."

The three men nodded in unison; formal acknowledgment. Usually there would be some celebratory drink and the drawing of contracts—but in this place and time, the nod would suffice.

"Cospatric?" Lord Cosgrove said, stepping back to let his captain speak.

"Lord Beaton's offered the use of his family guards. We've four of the clothier's guild on hand to construct a few uniforms."

"How many men?" Renar said, unable to stop his eyes from widening with unexpected hope.

"Eight patrols of eight. We'll guard your route from the front, Renar. We'll pull up the back as you pass us."

Sixty-four men. Renar turned to Lord Beaton. He knew how important it was to be a king, to act the part. And because he knew it, he did not, and could not, speak. But his expression was eloquent. Sixty-four men, all trained, all hidden—it was more than he had thought to ask for, except perhaps from the Hearts in his dreams.

"Don't look at me like that," Lord Beaton said softly, angrily. That anger was strong and supple; it turned inward painfully. "I've served as long as the other five, but perhaps a little less well. I hear you were in the merchant's quarter."

"Yes. And for them, I thank you."

"Don't thank me. Win."

Something in those words spoke of loss. No one asked, and Lord Beaton volunteered nothing.

Tiras was already busy unfurling the map. "Shall we begin this again?"

It was Cospatric who nodded, coming forward with his hand already beneath his chin in a reflexive gesture of thought. "Eight patrols," he murmured to himself as a frown grew. "That's a fair stretch of territory. Does it have to be that route?"

"Speed over subterfuge in this case, wouldn't you agree?"

He thought about it, but it was clear that he had already done so for some time. He nodded. The nod was grim. "The men'll wear small flashes to distinguish our patrols from theirs. I hope we don't lose many."

Renar closed his eyes, then swallowed. He opened his eyes. "Right. This is the plan."

Cospatric listened, wincing in two places, and he glanced at Erin and the patriarch of Culverne.

"No, Renar," Stenton said softly. "The last part of your plan bears changing, but it means your messenger has no leeway."

"Speak plainly."

"Very well. Verena and I have talked long about this. There was a council meeting that was to take place in three weeks, two days."

Renar frowned. "Too late."

"It will now take place in ten days. The full council. In the palace's grand chamber."

Renar's eyes grew wide. "How—"

"It's foolish to split the three of you—or four, if you plan to take old Tiras." He smiled, and then continued briskly. "Your targets will all be in one place."

"But how—"

"If you fail," Lord Cosgrove said, allowing his grandson no words, "we will all perish. Every single one of your contacts, every single one of your allies."

Lord Beaton nodded quietly; his smile reminded everyone of the gallows. "A guarantee of good faith," he explained. No one needed the explanation.

"But—"

"Verena knows exactly where you've been and why; she will offer this information to the council on that evening. If you fail in your attack, Cosgrove will still continue, in one fashion or another. I'm sorry," he had the grace to add, "but . . . it's the family."

"Stent . . ."

"You've no choice in the timing; you *must* attack that eve. Lady Verena has called the meeting on a matter of some urgency: you see, she's received inside word that Prince Renar of Marantine plans his attack in just under three weeks, with the mobilization of the last of the resistance." His smile was most unpleasant. "At the meeting she will give them her information, and they will discuss the best method of dealing with him."

Renar laughed, then. The laugh was loud and long.

"Stent, this is the best thing you've ever done." He looked to Erin, his eyes alight. "Lady, this truly is our battle, then. From start to finish."

"Indeed," Stenton interjected. "But it had best be the right finish. Verena has been trained by Tiras. He'll vouch for her. She'll hold her hand until you've made your way to the council."

Renar nodded, sobered. "Tell her, Stent. Tell her that Jordan is mine."

"You're a Cosgrove, Renar. He's ours," his grandfather whispered softly. "Ours, at last." He held out a hand, and Renar shook it.

Lord Beaton took a step toward the door. "Cospatric?"

The man in question nodded. "We've got a lot of work to do if we're to pull our troops together." He saluted Renar; it was crisp but less than perfect. "When this is over, I want my inn back."

Renar nodded.

"And I want you to keep out of it for the first few months. I can't take another one of the brawls you start while I'm rebuilding. Got that?"

Renar shook his hand firmly.

"Do you do that everywhere?" Erin whispered.

"Not on purpose." He shook his head. "Gentlemen."

"We'll see you on the front," Lord Beaton said.

As Renar looked askance, he added, "I'll be with one of the patrols."

He was risking everything, then. Everything.

"You didn't bargain well enough, if you only get the Sennet lands out of this."

"I'll get what I want," Lord Beaton replied. His voice was cold and hard. "This is the true fight; the true test. This is what we've needed." He straightened himself out. He was not a tall man, but neither was he short. In all eyes there, he stood very tall indeed.

"Ten days, then."

"Ten days."

Only one task remained: informing the renegade palace guards of the plan and timing of their arrival. Word was sent through Cosgrove. The messenger left, with writs and papers, through the south gate. It would take him time to double round, avoiding the eyes of the city's walls.

It was time well spent.

The messenger was a young man. Once it had been his intention to apply for the palace guard, to serve the king and Marantine in its stand against the Empire.

Instead, he had found himself faced with the loss of king and kingdom, and his dreams were burned to ground in the second night of fires.

Out of the ashes, those dreams had been reborn.

Oh, the armor he wore bore no crest and no colors, the horse that he rode belonged to no royal cavalry unit. But the message he carried held all of those things. Words on paper, about acquisitions and territories, in which the right eyes would find the right words.

The king had come. The line had come.

Against such two, the Empire must surely fail.

And he had been chosen for the task that would finally set it all in motion.

It was hard to carry himself with anything but righteous pride. It was hard to pass the gates of the city and the guards that served the traitor without issuing the challenge that should have been issued five years before.

For the sake of the king, he did all of that.

For the sake of the king, he would do more.

The ten days passed slowly.

Renar practiced caution as if it were religion. He knew that Lady Verena's message to the council would have already set in motion the rudiments of full-scale alert.

But Dagothrin was his city; he knew it as well as a Cosgrove could—or better. He avoided the city guard patrols with ease borne of long practice. He melted from sight before he left Tiras' manor and returned without being seen. Of this he could be certain.

He visited his grandfather's house three times. Each time he stopped at the flagstones; each time he bowed there. Whether they had been willing or no, he granted both his respect and his pain to those whose blood browned the stones.

Cosgrove itself was in a small uproar; he had never seen the like within its stately walls. Oh, there had been noise, yes, and shouting—neither Lisbeth or Stenton had ever been particularly quiet when cordoned off with family—but never had there been this quiver of excitement.

It was not good spirits, exactly; there was too much that was angry, even vicious, about it. But it was hope for change, hope for victory, both of which had been unlooked for. Hope was a gift, one that blood would be spilled to obtain, but no less precious for all that—the shame of survival, kept hidden for so long, might in one swift stroke be broken. And be justified.

Cospatric drilled his men in the courtyard; this was not unusual, as Stenton hastened to inform his grandson. What was unusual was the presence of the uncrowned king.

Renar sighed as he did his inspection at Lord Cosgrove's behest. He sighed even more deeply as one or two of the younger men made haste to draw their swords and lay them at his feet, as if they were tempered hearts. He felt his grandfather's mild frown and knew that even should they succeed, Maran and Cosgrove would have some struggle between them yet. But Lord Cosgrove did not discipline these guards of Cosgrove for their impulsive actions.

Renar spoke to these men seldom, and he measured his words, surprised at how difficult it had become. No flowery speech would serve him here as it had done in the past, and he could no longer seek comfort in the guise of the half-witted buffoon. These men were going to fight for him. Many would die. He owed them a leader that they would be proud to follow.

He paid as much of that debt as he could, thinking bitterly of how much better Gregory would have been.

Ah, Uncle, he thought, and the word was a curse, *that, too, you will pay for.*

"When it's over," he would say to Cospatric, "I'll want a good drink."

Cospatric would laugh, as he did only when they were alone.
"Not at my inn."

The tide was turning.

Darin summoned fire. He let it burn, red and ugly, before his
eyes. The practice room, when not in use by Erin and Renar,
contained the flame and hid it from prying eyes.

Only Trethar watched, commenting, encouraging, or dispar-
aging. His words, his gentle, almost-imperceptible hands upon
Darin's shoulders, became a counterpoint to the rhythm of
struggle and power.

Ten days. Ten days, and they would have to make their stand.
Darin let fire expand; letting the tingle flow down his arms and
into the open space before him. Would ten days be enough?

Would the tenth day finally pay for all?

For if Renar was to regain a throne, Darin was to remake a
line. Culverne must rise as well.

He worked as the days melted by in the heat of his unnatural
blaze. He worked as the quill drifted horizontally across still air.
And he worked to bring a flash of lightning into the air without
the clouds and thunder that presaged it in nature.

"Don't worry, Darin. You'll be ready."

Darin nodded grimly. What other choice had he?

Only for Erin did the ten days drag by.

She practiced in the drill room in isolation, choosing to spend
her time there instead of at Renar's side. Hours passed, warping
and twisting themselves in her perception into minutes or days.
She worked tirelessly, but the work called the ghosts of the past.

Telvar stood at her shoulder, the brisk shout of his annoyance
ringing in her ears. Deirdre stood in the circle in front of her,
her face a grim set of determined lines that Erin had forgotten
she knew so well. The Grandfather came to visit, to watch
as she progressed.

She fought for them, for all of her dead. But the living haunted
her as well.

Stefanos.

Memory was her enemy now. Without Renar or Darin to
anchor her to the present, the past lived in all its dark splendor,
growing steadily stronger as each dawn moved inevitably into

darkness. She did not dream; she walked—and every step, fought against, struggled with, and ultimately denied, sought to bring her to the side of the Lord of the Empire. She did not think she had the ability to face him again.

But the road had strengthened her; Ruth had shown her the beginning of what might be a new life, a new position. Renar, quirky, loud, and unpredictable, had shown her a face that she had not thought to see: pain, fear, and vulnerability. Somehow, knowing that these things lived within him, her own ghosts became less daunting. But only a little.

And memory would not, in her chosen isolation, be denied. What she was came out of all that she had once been: and all that she had been cried out for reckoning.

She was in the drill room, in darkness. No windows let prying eyes watch; no windows let light in. Here, shadows reigned; here, memories refused to be dislodged.

Stefanos.

Sara.

She walked over to the wall and picked up her practice sword, hefting it easily in her right hand. Spinning lightly on her feet, she lunged forward, piercing empty air. She could almost feel Renar sidestepping and slid abruptly to the left so he could not take advantage of her overextension.

Lady of Mercy.

She struck again, her body tighter and more controlled. Dancing across the floor, the sword cut the air in a complex series of moves, outlined by the flow of light that was her power, called unknowing in the shadows of her internal battle.

He had seen her thus, recognizing, as she did not, the supple beauty of his Enemy's hand.

Sarillorn.

Why?

Sword skittered off the wall, nearly overbalancing her; Renar's block was absent.

Why had he kept her alive over the centuries? Why had he decided to wake her at all?

Sweat ran down her forehead in place of the tears she would not shed. No weakness was allowed in combat; if it had to be shown at all, it would wait until battle's end. If there was an end. Telvar's training held her without demanding acknowledgment, but what must not be shown could still be felt.

Why why why

why did you break your word, Stefanos?

With a strangled cry she threw the sword across the room, stepping out of the circle, paying her weaponsmaster his due. Her arms swung outward and up in a wide arc. There was precision to their wildness as they bent in unison to write a pattern across her chest.

Light flared, circling her feet and climbing upward—light, white and green, the power and peace of her heritage.

Why did I trust you?

White obscured her vision, and she held herself completely still in its circle. Because she had her answer. Even now she knew the answer.

I loved you.

I loved as much as I could.

He stood then, before her, his shadow long and cold, the gaunt lines of his jaw and cheekbones free from the grace of illusion. His eyes, crimson a moment, and then pure black, opened upon her. Limned in darkness of memory and anger, his arms spread wide and ringed with the ugliest of red, he waited.

His face, now expressionless, was turned toward her.

He wards, she thought, and waited.

But his arms made no further movement; they hung wide on either side as if suspended.

She waited still, as if this sharp and clear a memory could finally answer her. But when words came, they were not his.

Love is our greatest strength. And often our most terrible weakness. But without it, what choice but darkness?

It was an old line, a Lernari teaching homily, uttered so often, and by so many, that it was thankfully faceless.

The memory image of Stefanos was not.

She thought that this was how she had first truly seen him, a finger of the enemy, lit with the Enemy's fire and the Enemy's destruction and pain. But no; his face held no expression that spoke of Malthan—just perhaps the hint of his pride.

She took a step forward, and the light parted to make way for her feet. It was just a step, but now he was closer, larger.

She did not forget Belfas, or his pain, or her own at his loss. But even so she stepped forward again, raising one arm.

The image held true.

"Stefanos." Another step. "Hate is your greatest strength; the hatred of the Dark Heart for the Light. And often it is your kin's most terrible weakness—do you remember the loss on the field of Kallen because the Karnari there could not contain his God's great hatred?"

This ghost of his memory made no answer, and she edged forward again, beyond feeling foolish. She knew, on some level, that she was alone—but she did not feel it. There was something that had to be said.

"But without it, without this hatred—" He was so very close now. The tears began; without the accoutrements of battle, she had no control over them. "What choice but Light?"

She brought her hands up to touch his face, now no longer chill and distant. His arms swept downward, so familiar even here and now—

And she stood alone in a gray empty stone room. Memory played its tricks even now. Memory and time. But even alone, she heard the echo of his voice; it cut her deeply before it ebbed into stillness.

Sarillorn. I loved you as much as I was able.

Belfas' face flashed before her, bloodstained and almost life-less. The bodies of her line-mates, heaped like refuse, acted as kindling on the muted heart of her anger; the tears that traced her cheeks burned.

For a moment she froze and her anger raged outward, the color of it red. Red.

No.

No.

It was my choice. My *choice, too.*

She saw it clearly. Her anger, her hatred—guilt turned out-ward. *Our greatest weakness.*

But now she saw the pavilion again; saw those walk free by her judgment and his command, who otherwise would have perished.

Our greatest strength.

The red burned into ashes. She felt the loss no less clearly, but now it was a clean thing, sharp as new blade.

Sara.

I loved you.

I never wanted to lose you to anything—not even time.

As she thought it, she could hear the low, smooth utterance of his voice, a harmony or melody to hers. She held herself, cradling her upper body with her arms. If loss had a rhythm, she swayed to it. She understood now why he had committed his crime, and the full understanding brought her, at last, a measure of peace.

Through both the weakness and the strength, she had somehow become real to him; too real to lose to the course of time. He had given her everything that he could, for all that the giving struggled so harshly against his nature. Perhaps this, this is for what the Lady had hoped, and for what Lernan had hoped.

The thought of the Lady was still painful to her. If Stefanos had deceived her through misguided love, deception was still a large part of his nature—yet only once had he lied to her. The Lady had no such excuse.

Some part of her mind tried to argue with this: Deception was no part of the Lady of Elliath, and for no reason would she have forced herself to it against her very nature. Perhaps the deception had extracted as dear a price as the love that Stefanos had offered. Perhaps, but the argument held little sway; it was too new.

For if this was indeed the Lady's hope, then that hope had failed.

Erin faced the fact squarely. She felt pain, but not the half-crazed frenzy that had driven her this far. Stefanos loved her, but he was what he was—Ruler of the Empire. During the centuries that she had slept, the changes she had wrought had not stopped him from destroying her kin and the rest of the seven lines; it had not stopped him from enslaving the last of the free kingdoms.

Perhaps the Lady had hoped that Erin might return to him; live out the slow centuries in the hope of seeing the First of Malthan truly leave his God. But the Lady, immortal, could not know the pain of whole generations born into slavery and dying without ever knowing what freedom truly meant. Erin was not the Lady, to feel so little.

Very gently she unsheathed her sword and watched its mesmerizing glow.

If I'd known what you intended, Lord, would I have let you be destroyed?

She lifted the sword slowly, as she asked the question honestly for the first time. Without the fury, without the pain of betrayal, no answer came.

And even that felt whole.

"I *am* the Sarillorn of Elliath." She had not been sure until this moment. She loved him; he loved her—but they still remained true to what they were. She was Lernari. He was older and more fell. Between them, in private, all laws changed, but the world and the war remained too insistent for either to ignore or walk away from. The Dark Heart and the Light Heart still beat out their asynchronous rhythm.

"I swore the warrior's oath—to fight against the Enemy until either of our deaths. In a moment of anger, I swore blood-pledge, and now in a moment of peace, I renew it. What I can do to free these lands, I must do." She lowered her sword.

But she prayed, for the first time in months. She prayed that she would never have to face Stefanos on any ground that she chose for battle.

The nights were hardest. Awake, she thought of him. Asleep . . .

The mists rolled in, black and thick, uneven, unknowing and cold. She walked within them, surrounded on all sides. Darkness was a constant, but little else was. Not here.

The pain—his pain—had dimmed, although the call of it was strong. She wanted to be free of it, but it mirrored her own.

Yes. She could see that now.

"Little one."

"Kandor." She slowed, waiting.

He came. A glow, almost human in form if not substance.

"Is—is Belfas here?"

"He is."

"Belf?"

Her former line-mate came at her call. He had always come, when he could hear her. "Erin?"

It hurt, suddenly. She had not thought to feel this here, where her own pain should have had no voice compared to the grief and anger of her line-mates. "Belf . . ."

She reached out to touch him. She felt the power flow outward and pushed it almost fiercely. Let it go. Let it leave her. When it was all gone, she would be human.

Between her arms, he took form and shape. If she could have seen his face, she would have wept. But his arms, as they grew solid, closed around her; they stood, two ghosts, in the comfort of a long lost past.

"We're going to fight the war, Belf," she whispered.

"Which war?" His shadow voice was low. His chin rested against the top of her head. When had he gotten so tall? Had she missed it?

"Against the Empire. Against him."

"Erin . . ."

"We're going to overthrow the governor; we're going to win back Culverne. We're going to . . ."

She could not look up. She imagined that she could smell him, and thought that he hadn't washed in days. She opened her mouth to say it, and then stopped.

"I'm afraid." It was a whisper; it was the truest thing that had left her lips so far. She tried to pull back; she had never said that to him before. Not when he was alive. She had always been the strong one.

He knew it, too. "You were never afraid before."

"No. Not . . . not never." Her head wavered from side to side—weak denial.

"It's all right, Erin. To be afraid."

"If I don't have courage, what else do I have?" She wanted to shout it. She couldn't—not here.

It was Kandor, not Belfas, who answered. "Love, Sarillorn."

"Everyone I've ever loved has died."

"Everyone?" Kandor's question was soft—and still unanswerable. "Sarillorn, everything changes, everything grows. Even you cannot be proof against it."

She didn't understand what he was saying. But his voice was soothing, almost comforting.

"Don't hate me anymore," she said quietly. "Even if I deserve it, even if you have every right."

Belfas said nothing at all, but his grip seemed to tighten; in the darkness it was hard to feel warmth. She stood there until the last of her light ebbed away. And when the dawn came, the feel of his arms lingered about her, the smallest trace of the Elliath that had been her home.

"Where is Erin?"

Tiras frowned. "The training rooms. The one the two of you practice in. She comes up for meals; other than that, she puts a full day's hours in."

"Why?" Renar's frown was an echo of his teacher's. "How much can she practice on her own?"

"I don't know. But whatever it is, she can do it for nine solid days."

Renar nodded and began to walk away. Tiras tapped his shoulder lightly.

"Renar?"

"I should have taken her with me," the prince answered curtly. He knew his worry showed, and it irritated him. "I shouldn't have left her alone."

"I think you may be right."

No lights burned in the training room.

Renar held the lamp aloft as the soft glow of the lit hall passed between his feet and over his shoulders.

"Erin?"

Ah. There. But no wooden sword trembled in her hands; the one she held aloft was bright, sharp steel. It glowed. Her power? Sweat glinted where it lay in fine beads against her skin. If not for that, he might have mistaken her for a spirit trapped on this side of the Bridge.

Erin dodged, the first step of an inimical dance. She parried some invisible ghost. She lunged, skirting stone by a fraction of an inch.

He wondered what personal demons she fought in this darkness. He wondered if she was winning.

"Erin," he said, his voice louder.

She turned, her eyes wide. And green. And glowing faintly, no trick of the light.

For a moment, her eyes widened and her mouth grew round. He almost whirled to look over his shoulder, so clear was her stare. But then she shook herself and seemed to dwindle.

"Renar."

He walked into the room and set the lamp down on the bench. Everything grew soft by its light, even the lines of her face. Shadows leaped about them both as the wick flickered. These were familiar somehow.

"What time is it?" she asked, her voice peculiarly flat.

"Past dinner, Erin. Have you eaten?"

She thought about it. Nodded unsurely.

"Are you all right?"

She nodded again. Swallowed. "It isn't—it isn't time yet, is it?"

He shook his head and watched as she slid her sword into its scabbard. He was suddenly certain that scabbard hadn't left her side in the past nine days.

"What are you practicing?"

She smiled sadly. "What I know." Light flared, white-fire gone wild. "All of it."

Something in the way her voice sank brought back an image, but it was not of Erin.

Kayly glanced at him; it was dark outside, and her parents had stayed late at the *Leaflet*. She was young, perhaps five, although memory played tricks with her age. Her hair was long and fine, something for her face to hide behind when she was embarrassed or upset.

But now, she was neither. She gazed out into the streets; they were poorly lit.

"What are they made of?"

"Glass."

"Is the fire glass, too?"

"No."

"Why doesn't it go out? There's no wood."

"These lamps are oil. It's a liquid, and it burns slowly. Like the one on the desk."

"I want to see out."

He lifted her, not noticing her weight at all. *You'll understand it all, Kayly. Just give it a little time, and you'll be out there, too.* The thought saddened him.

But he remembered the way she levered herself up on his shoulders to get a better view of the empty streets; the memory was precious. He had wondered what she could see in them that would hold her attention so long, when little else did.

Moths. Moths against the glass of the street lamp. He had told her they were cold. He hadn't wanted to tell her the truth. But he hadn't expected that she would run, suddenly, to the door to let them in. The world she saw was always new to her, a place to be at home in, and lost in.

As Erin was lost in it.

"Erin," he said gently, "put the sword aside."

"Pardon?"

"Lay it aside a moment."

"Why?"

"Because you've trained enough for the day. There isn't much more you can do, and I can't join you at the moment." He walked over to her and very gently began to unbuckle the scabbard.

She lifted her arms, making no move to help him, but none to hinder either. In the light of day, she would never have done this. But the shadows held a promise of privacy and escape from the light.

"Why are you fighting in the darkness?"

"I can see."

He didn't ask what. Instead he walked over to the bench and laid the sword down beside the flickering lamp. She started toward it and then stopped as he shook his head. "Time enough for fighting tomorrow. The next time you wear it, it will be in earnest."

"I don't understand."

"I know."

"We've got so little time—"

"I know." He walked toward her and very gently placed his hands on her shoulders. "What was life like, with the Line Elliath?"

She shrugged. "It was like life."

"What did you do?"

She shrugged again, feeling the pressure of his hands. "I don't know."

"When you were younger?"

"I took my lessons."

"Where?"

"Why are you asking me this?"

"Because I know so little of your life, Erin." He could hardly see her face at all, although her hair had been pulled back and tightly bound with copper wire. A swath of shadow hid all but the most prominent of her features. "Where?"

"In the south wing of the great hall."

"What did you learn?"

"History." She sighed heavily, to make clear that she answered only to humor him. "Genesis. The beginning of the wars. We learned of Gallin and his fall and what his fall gave us. Learned of the Twelve of the Enemy and their plans and their methods of fighting." Her eyes met his, asking permission to stop.

"And?"

"Renar, what difference does it make?"

"And?"

"We learned to use our powers. How to draw light enough to see by, how to draw light that normal eyes might see, if we had the power. Some of us learned to memory-walk"— here she drew breath too sharply and struggled to steady herself—"and some to heal; some learned to hold the fire of the line." She took another breath, a more even one. "We learned to fight. To use the sword, and the bow, if we had the strength for it. I didn't. We spent hours in the drill, with different weaponsmasters."

"And?"

"The Lesser Ward. The Greater Ward." She bit her lip and looked away. "The True Ward." She thought he might press her and wondered what she would say if he did. He surprised her.

"Did you learn to sing?"

"*Sing?*"

"Ah. No. Did you learn any musical instruments?"
She shook her head dumbly.

"Did you read any poetry? Did you write it?"

"No. And no. Why are you asking this?"

"Numbers. Did you learn those?"

"Yes."

"Did you learn to—"

"Renar!" She pulled away, lifting her hands the way they did to stop each other in drill.

He did not accept her surrender. "Erin, Lady, did you ever learn to do anything other than fight the war?"

"Anything other than—" Her eyes widened and caught

flecks of lamplight, blurring and then sharpening as his meaning, veiled by seemingly pointless questions, was suddenly made clear. "Renar, the war never stopped! When did we have the time?"

His eyes were dark.

The tears started before Erin could stop them, and it frightened her because she hadn't any idea why she was crying. She stumbled backward into darkness. She called the light, called it as a shield.

"I'm sorry," the prince whispered. His face was ringed by a warmth he couldn't see. "Maybe you didn't have the time. Not then.

"But tonight, Erin, we have that time."

"*Tonight?*" Her voice was a shriek; all her control had ebbed away in the shadows. "We're going to do battle in the morning!" She choked on the words and the anger that remained just beyond her comprehension. "We don't have the time to waste!"

"We have the time."

"I don't understand you! This is *your* city, these are *your* people! How can you talk about anything but war at a time like this?"

"Because, Erin"—he stepped forward, stalking her—"*my* people as you call them, know war—but they know why they'll fight it, too. They have a life—a *life*—based on living. Not on death. Not on killing. And it's a life that they want back."

She couldn't speak. Her throat was too swollen, too tight. He caught her then, and without another word pulled her close, as he once had Kayly.

She was trembling, and it wasn't with fear, yet fear was there beneath the wild anger that Renar had somehow invoked. No red-fire had summoned her light, but she fought now, as surely, as desperately, as she had ever been forced to do.

"We did it for you!" she shouted in fury, the velvet of his jacket catching the noise before her voice broke. "We did it so you could *have* a life! That's what the light means! That's what it means."

"I'm sorry." He couldn't curl down protectively around her; they were of a height. "But we don't ask it anymore,

Erin. You don't have to fight the darkness for us—fight it with us. Fight it the way we sometimes fight it when we just live.'' He wiped the tears away as they fell.

And she looked at him, as his fingers brushed her cheeks. That look, seen across the faces of so many children, no matter what they might later become, contained her whole face, her whole thought.

"I don't know how," she whispered.

"I know." He cupped her face gently in his hands. "I know. That's why I came." He took a breath and exhaled the softest of breezes against her brow.

"Have you ever been in—" He felt her shudder and cut the question short. If she hadn't reminded him so much of a child, he might have stopped speaking altogether. But he saw her in darkness, alone. The road to Verdann had nearly swallowed her; the road to the palace was no longer one he was willing to let her walk alone. Now, he knew more of who she was and of what she could do. He thought of Ruth and the tentative, half-abashed way that Erin had approached her—as if the comfort she offered might not be good enough, might be rejected.

"Erin." His voice was light, the way only a forced voice can be. "Can you dance?"

"D-Dance?"

"Dance."

"No."

"I used to dance. I was good at it—and it was one of the few things I could share with someone else. I won't drill with you tonight. Will you dance with me?"

"I don't know how."

"I can teach you now." It wasn't true—the dances at which he excelled had taken months of work, years of lessons. But what was true was the fact that it was one of the two things he could share with her. The other was war.

"We don't have any music."

He might have cried at the sound of that voice had he been any other man. "We don't need it. Not yet." He held up her arms, just so. Held out his own, a cradle around her. "Have you seen this done?"

"Y-Yes."

"Don't worry, then. You know that dancing is just so

much footwork. I've seen you move when you fight; this should be easier.'' He moved his right foot forward and ran into hers. Shook his head. "Sorry."

"What do I do?"

"You move your left foot back. Then your right to the side, then pull your left to your right."

More awkwardly than he could have imagined, she did as he said. He stepped back, couching his instruction in a low voice. "That's it. Just keep that up."

"I'll hit the wall."

"Start here. I'll tell you what to do about the wall in a minute."

She was stiff as she looked down at her feet, and he knew he wouldn't have nearly enough time to talk of posture, grace, elegance. It didn't matter.

In the darkness, he began to hum.

"What are you singing?"

"The 'Spring of Marantine,' " he answered. "It isn't a song that one normally sings—and I make a very poor orchestra. But if you don't mind, I think we can make do."

She began to move again, her feet slowly taking up the rhythm as she grew more confident.

"Now," he said, as he approached, "let me lead you. Keep that movement and follow me." He caught her again, his stance superior to hers; he held her rigidly, compensating with his experience for her lack.

He began his wordless hum anew as he moved across the room. The voice that had been one of his mother's joys was full and vibrant, if wordless; it never once strayed from the tune that it seemed to carry without effort.

What is war, without this to fight for? He said nothing. *Come, Lady. Do as we do.*

He thought he might never again have a partner such as Erin; he thought that maybe in this dance, he was at his finest, with his feet moving madly to avoid crushing hers and his arcs and sweeps out of time, out of step.

And when he caught the hint of the tentative smile she offered, he knew he was right. He pulled her close then, loving her, accepting her gift. He, too, had been long away from life.

chapter
eighteen

"Hildy, do you know what you're doing?"

"Now, dear, you've asked me that four times today."

"And you haven't answered once."

"No, Hamin, I don't suppose I have." She shrugged. "Well, then, no. No, I don't."

Hamin was too tense to give her his usual theatrical sigh. *Just make sure the wagons don't move.* It was not unlike Hildy to come up with odd commands, but this one was the strangest he had ever received; he knew it would be the most dangerous, precisely because Hildy refused to give him any details. He'd already spoken with his men and hoped that his anxiety had not somehow transmitted itself to them.

And of course, there was now no time left for dialogue. Action, whatever that action might be, was all that was left them.

They approached the north gates; the walls grew above them, towering in sharp, pale relief against the too-bright sky. Very few were the people out on the roads at this time; the sun was sinking, and with dusk came the cold. Hamin's breath came out in a plume of fog that was the very mirror of his thoughts: murky, heavy, and lingering.

He signaled a stop to the caravan, although the wagons were, at any rate, coming to an automatic stop; the gates were closed, and the horses couldn't go much further. The guards at the gate, looking very much as bored as they felt, perked up a little as the wagons rolled to a standstill.

Hildy pulled out her papers in a curt, businesslike way. Firmly clutching them in heavy mittens, she walked over to the guard at the closed gate. He took them and began to leaf through them almost casually.

"Short stay," he muttered, nodding to the four men behind him. He was familiar enough with the Brownbur crest on the documents; they meant trouble for him if he offered any but the barest of inspections—but Hildy had never caused any difficulty, and for that reason, a cursory inspection didn't hurt his pride. His men were fairly quick, though, and after a few moments, the gates began to creak open.

"Early for you, isn't it, Hildy?" he asked, with the cheery wave that had become perfunctory between them.

The merchant, heavily bundled as always, jerked to a stop, and then turned back to wave. It was a good thing, this day, that Hildy wore scarves and hats; they hid her sudden twist of lips. Her breath was weak before she straightened out and walked back to her wagon. She usually liked to ride in the center—but this time she had chosen the tail end of the caravan.

The wagons began to lurch slowly forward, horses pulling easily at the lighter weight. She regretted, briefly, that she hadn't had the time to load them down. Maybe it was better; less could be lost if things got "messy."

The first wagon came through, followed by the second. Hildy peered out, seeing the looming arches of the massive gate approach. They were thick, these walls, and pale gray. But it was the gates that worried her; heavy iron, hinged in place by mechanisms that were meant to close in a hurry. Never mind thinking about it, though. She was committed. She gave a brief glance back into the wagon and nodded as the horses continued to pull.

Mittened hands grabbed the reins, counting the preternaturally loud click of hooves against stone.

Three. Two. One.

She yanked the reins back as hard as she could; the horses brought their heads up and whinnied in protest. The wagon rolled to a lurching stop, midway between the gates. Hamin, dear Hamin, acted immediately, bringing his men to surround the wagon.

There was a moment of silence, and then the guard at the gate came forward, waving them on. He spoke, but the word was lost.

Trethar came *through* the side of the wagon. Tarp flashed briefly as flame struck it and passed through it as if it were air.

The guard had time to raise his eyebrows before a column of living flame engulfed him.

Hildy closed her eyes.

She opened them when shouting overcame the sound of choked-off screams. Trethar stood at the back of the wagon now, clear of the arched gateway. Old, she had thought him; her age at least. But now, standing straight and tall, he had the strength and seeming of youth gathered about him. His arms swept up in a wide, smooth arc. His face, tilted upward, was calm, almost tranquil. He opened his mouth, moving it around words that Hildy could not catch. She shivered. His eyes were silver. They flashed as he spoke.

Red and black had been the colors that Hildy had always associated with power, with death. They were gone now; she could not remember them clearly. Silver remained, underlined by the sudden screams high above her. She was grateful that the arch protected her from seeing what went on above; the one guard had been enough.

Trethar's face was lined in a gentle pink glow.

From the left and the right, a large group of guards erupted, swords drawn. Their livery was city garrison; Hildy recognized it.

They made a line for Trethar.

"Stop them!" she cried, her voice so harsh and so urgent that it sounded foreign to her ears.

Hamin hesitated a moment, and in that time, one of the guards wheeled round to see them blocking the gate. He started to wave them aside, and then his mouth fell open.

"Over here!" he shouted, and half the group broke away, the barest hint of relief on their faces. "Clear the gates!" They rushed forward past him as he shouted another set of orders.

Hildy turned to look outward, beyond the city.

She heard a sharp crashing, as if of thunder, but didn't turn back.

Men were coming. Some twenty were mounted, and more were on foot. She thought one carried a banner, but they were still too far off for her to be sure.

Never mind.

"Trethar!" she shouted, her voice cutting above the sound of clashing metal. "Trethar! The gates! Watch the men on the gates!"

She wasn't certain that he heard her. She could barely see him through the curtain of flame he'd erected. But his head turned slowly, arms dancing delicately. The flame cleared as he spoke again.

Silver glowed, but less harshly than it had before. Hildy caught sight of the brief bolt that started in front of him and shot outward.

Lightning.

She wondered if there was anything that he couldn't do. Then she stopped thinking about it at all. The horsed men were upon the gates, weapons raised. Farther behind them, the rest continued on foot, not slackening the pace they had set for themselves.

The city was their goal.

She closed her eyes again as she caught sight of the banner. It was nearer now; close enough to be read, to be clung to with eyes and more. Her lips curled into a hint of smile, her cheeks dimpling against the light scarf she wore. The king. They came for the king.

The guards saw the same thing. They began to back out of the arch, some holding their ground, some breaking.

"*Hildy!* What do you think—Damn it!" Hamin neatly blocked the wild swing of a retreating sword. "Not at my age, Hildy!" But he advanced as quickly and as cautiously as he dared. Why on earth had he not insisted that she remain behind? "Get back inside the wagon!"

Hildy shook her head and reached for the reins of the horses. She was tense, but only a little—no time to worry now about a stray weapon. Quietly, but with visible determination, she dragged the horses off the road, timing her retreat to coincide with the arrival of the forefront of the king's army.

Once or twice before, she'd been caught in a bandit raid; she told herself this over and over again when the clash of steel against steel rang out, impossibly crisp and impossibly close. Thank the Bright Heart the horses were good. She led, they followed.

She heard the thunder, saw the flash of lightning, and shivered. It disturbed her more than fire; fire had always been a thing of man. Lightning was a force that no human should ever control.

The first of the horsemen passed her, spear raised. She turned, knowing her wagon was safe. The spear found a target, albeit only a leg. She closed her eyes then. In words of battle there was glory, honor, and strength. She preferred mere words; they couldn't capture the splash of crimson; the sight of severed flesh, the shouting, or the occasional scream, choked off in midcry.

I'll never understand, she thought, as she half raised her hands to cover her ears, *you women who choose to fight for your rights to honor in battle.* The hands stopped. She forced her eyes open, hating the weakness that kept them shut.

Do I not understand? She looked at her wagon, at the strips of cloth hanging from one side. She wondered what had ripped it.

For strength, her eyes caught the king's banner and held it. It rippled in the air in the hands of a youth who bore it so painfully proudly. Men surrounded him, weapons drawn. Protecting the standard. The group pushed forward, through the open gates. In minutes there was no one to stop them. Still she stared, struggling between tears and a fierce, hard smile. Both won.

"Hildy."

"Yes, dear?" Years had given her this habit of speech; she had never before been so grateful to habit. She turned to look at Hamin. He was bleeding; something had grazed his cheek. She looked away and caught sight of his sword. Bleeding as well.

Hamin waited patiently. He had seen Hildy like this on two occasions before. It was one of the reasons he followed her.

"Dear?"

"Yes, Hildy. It's over."

She nodded, drawing herself up. "Well, then. We'd best see to the wagons, hadn't we?" She smiled, the smile faltering before it had properly started. She hadn't seen the expression on Hamin's face very clearly at first. Tears did that. Tears and age.

"Those men," she said quietly, turning to her horses. "They'll march on the castle?"

"Yes."

"Did you recognize any of them, dear?"

"Some, Hildy." He walked over to the horses and caught their reins in his free hand. She covered it with a mitten.

"Hamin, you swore no oath to me. I never did hold with that sort of thing." It was his turn to be silent. "I didn't take you in because you had nowhere to go. You were trained with the royal guards. I knew the value of that, and I've never been disappointed. You owe me nothing."

"Hildy, we both know that isn't the—"

"Go with them. Go if you feel it will help. They're here, but there aren't many of them."

He straightened then and drew a deep breath. He opened his mouth to ask her.

"Yes, dear. Take your men with you as well, if they want to follow." She clutched his hand tightly, which was hard given what she was wearing. "But, dear?"

"Hildy?"

"Do give them a choice, won't you?"

He nodded. He knew what their choice would be.

So did Hildy.

"Hildy, if we survive this, we'll—"

"Wait until then, Hamin. Come back if your vow of allegiance allows it." She smiled, shaking her head. "It's a foible of mine, choosing men who know the value of a word given. Now go. Don't waste your time or energy on an old woman when the castle awaits you."

She would have asked him for a hug, but she knew him well. So she waited until he had gone, and then began to lead her wagons back into the city.

"My mother built it." Renar looked down into the forlorn well. "My mother." Sunlight cast its shadows upon the snow that lined the rock; those shadows were long and dark.

"Aye," Tiras said softly.

"You knew of it." It was not a question.

"I found her the people she needed. Fast. Quiet." He smiled. "We renovated her quarters. I'm not sure the king was pleased."

"It depended on the expense." Renar leaped up onto snow-covered stone.

"She covered it."

"Did she ever tell him?"

"No, lad. You, me. Perhaps one or two others. Don't blame her—it wouldn't have saved your father or your brothers. They hadn't the skill to use either entrance or exit."

"Rope?"

"Here." Erin began to untwine the large bundle she carried.

"Not yet. You and Darin will need it. And maybe Tiras, if his quips about aging are to be believed." He began to carefully clear away snow, his fingers finding purchase in the well's wall. He lowered himself slowly.

They watched his descent in silence. Darin leaned over the well's edge to get a better view; snow melted against his hands and water dripped down the rock side like tears.

"Careful," Tiras said. "You don't know the way of it, boy."

Darin nodded, but continued to watch.

A third of the way down, Renar stopped. Suspended somehow by his feet and one hand, he began to search the wall's surface. His hand slipped once, but the expected cursing did not come. He righted himself, continuing in silence.

Why doesn't he use the rope?

Darin had the sense not to ask the question aloud. Neither Tiras nor Erin seemed concerned—perhaps they knew better than he the skills that Renar possessed. Or perhaps they had both had experience that automatically accepted risk. He didn't know. He watched.

Renar's hands brushed the surface three times before coming to rest.

"Got it."

He climbed further down and rested his cheek against the rock. His fingers seemed to twitch, once, twice, three times. He smiled. Very slowly, the wall before him began to give way, falling inward as if hinged.

Above, Tiras rewarded his former student with one smile. "Your mother's son."

Renar crawled back out of the well. If he heard Tiras' comment, there was no sign of it; his face was as the well—cold and hard. "Rope."

This time, he didn't stop Erin from unraveling it.

"Darin first."

She nodded, and began to make a loop with a loose knot.

"You see it?" Renar asked softly.

Darin nodded. He lifted his arms, and Erin dropped the rope around them. Renar helped him up to the well's edge.

"We'll lower you slowly. When you hit the entrance, swing your feet in. Are you all right?"

He nodded again. His gloved hands gripped the rope rather tightly.

He kept his feet still as he was lowered carefully down to the edge of the door that Renar had opened. Inside, all was dark, shadowed dimly by what little light made its way beyond the mouth. Darin's fingers gripped the side of the door and he hauled himself in. The ground beneath his feet was rocky but firm.

"In?"

The voice rang oddly in the confines of the walls.

"Yes," he called back up; the word bounced against the walls as if caught there. He began to struggle his way out of the rope, careful not to lose his staff in the process.

Erin came down next, followed by Tiras, who surprisingly chose to use the rope.

"It isn't all humor." He smiled at Darin's stare. He tossed the rope out and fumbled in his pack a moment before drawing out a light. He waved them further into the tunnel and waited for Renar.

"From here it's fairly easy. There are two pits—let Renar or I lead. Don't panic at anything you see or feel. Where is he?"

The rope clunked to the ground.

"Here." Renar gave a fluid bow. "I see your patience is eroding, Tiras."

"On mission," the older man said gruffly. "Close it."

"As good as done, dear teacher." The door creaked slowly shut, and the sunlight vanished.

Erin murmured; in the torchlight Darin could see her hands dance slightly in the air. Light.

If he couldn't master the spell, he could still see its effects. It shimmered around her, dancing outward in waves that put the torch to shame. Nonetheless Tiras held it high as he passed it to his student. It was a reminder to Darin that vision was not always a thing to be taken for granted.

Renar bowed. "Lady?"

She smiled and stepped out of his way.

"Follow me, please. I realize it isn't much of a hall, but you will, I trust, forgive the lack of hospitality and allow me to make it up to you in the future."

"Most certainly." She bowed in return, allowing him to pass. They made a single file of life in the blackness as they followed him.

A young man turned over the blackened corpse with the toe of a worn boot. His face was pale; his lips were set tightly together. Yet although he blanched, it was clear that he had seen this effect before. The two nights of fire had burned more than the physical; their images were indelible patches of memory and loss.

"Did you get them all?"

Trethar nodded at the older man, a commander of some sort. He had never studied enough of army regulations to know what rank the man was, nor did he particularly care.

"Good." General Lorrence started to bark out his orders with the energy and verve of a much-younger man. Then he stopped.

The young man continued to stare at the bodies.

"Carson!"

"Sir." Training and its imperative were deeply rooted; they permeated more than memory, becoming as reflexive as breath. Almost gratefully, the young man joined the troops that had already started to move. They were headed to the castle. He thought of that, thought of how they had lost Marantine; what did it matter if they regained her in like fashion?

It helped, but only a little.

"Careful."

Erin drew closer to Renar's still back.

"Pit?" she asked softly.

He nodded and handed her the torch. "Hold it here; stay as close to the edge as possible."

She nodded, although his face was turned away from her. She put out one hand, gripped uneven rock tightly, and leaned forward. She alone could sustain enough light for Renar and Tiras to see by, but she chose to conserve her power for the fight ahead. This was Renar's ground and she trusted him on it, no matter how treacherous it might seem.

With a grimace, he took the end of the hemp between his teeth, gesturing for Erin to let it out. He scrambled along the side of the pit with a surety that spoke of years of experience. The pit was not smooth, just sudden; it was hardly a challenge for him at all.

But it brought back memories. It made him feel, for a moment, young again. He could feel his mother's presence just ahead of him, could hear Tiras' less-than-gentle coaching from behind. He shook his head to clear it. No game this, no practice session after which he might rest and feel slightly proud. He

was here on business—business which should have called him
years ago.

He pulled himself out of the other side of the pit, gripping the
rope firmly in both hands. "Lady, do you have it?"

"Yes."

"Good. Darin."

Darin took a hesitant step forward. Wells, pits—why did everything always have to include such a drastic fall?

"Slide the rope under your arms. Use your feet where you
can to push you across it. And don't worry about it; the fall isn't
too far."

Darin slid the rope around his arms and lowered himself into
the pit. He heard Erin grunt slightly as the rope went taut, but
both ends held.

Not that far? No, of course not. He gritted his teeth as his
feet clambered shakily at the stone wall without finding purchase there. *Just far enough to easily kill a man.* He said nothing, realizing that Renar didn't know that he could see—or in
this case, not see—the bottom of the pit by the light Erin cast.

He edged himself across, hands trembling with the tightness
of what little grip he could find.

Renar caught him and hauled him up.

"Good, Darin. Very good. Given time we might make—"

"Renar."

"Ah, Lady. Very well. Your turn."

She handed the rope to Tiras, who nodded as he took it.

Erin crossed more surely than Darin had. She didn't make
the mistake of looking down, and her feet found nooks to rest
in as she moved. Years of Telvar's training had given her this.
But her throat was dry, and her eyes were almost closed.

Don't look. Don't look down.

Tiras crossed last, bringing the rope with him.

"One more," Renar whispered to Darin. "One more and
then the trouble starts."

Cospatric stood grimly, his eyes on the north wall. They widened, becoming dark spheres as the flares went up. He had never
seen flares like them; they were brief, bright—and human-
shaped.

"Sir?"

He nodded grimly. "Petian?"

"Sir?"

"Take time to breathe."

The young man blushed, then nodded.

"You all remember what I told you—the blue flashes are *our* men, not theirs. Don't attack a patrol wearing them."

"Sir." They all thought it so obvious.

He looked at them and shook his head. Not one of them had had any real experience on the front; they were too young at the time. He wanted to be able to drill into their heads how easily mistakes could be made and how costly those mistakes could be.

He didn't. They wouldn't believe it could happen to them, and worse, if they did they might hesitate at the wrong moment—and lose more than eight friendly lives.

"Keep an eye out for the runners. Let's go."

They heard the rumble in the streets long before they saw the coach; they saw the patches of snow drawn in and spit out by spinning wheels on the main thoroughfare. Cospatric tensed, but his guards walked in proper formation. There was nothing out of place here, nothing worthy of note.

But then the carriage drew to a stop; the horses were reined in short, and their flanks heaved. Lantern glow cut the streets and the cobbled stone as a thin man swung out of a side door, his hands out in supplication or surrender.

"Cospatric!"

"Morgan?"

"No one else!"

"But I'd heard—"

"We don't have time for gossip, idiot! Borins and Feltham are behind me. Pile in and quick—you've got a route ahead to get to a mite more quickly than foot'll take you."

Cospatric gave the word, surprised; he wanted to say something to Morgan, but he hadn't the time. Which was probably best for both men; neither were given to open displays of anything but ire and annoyance.

Lord Beaton drew his sword from his scabbard. It glinted dully; there was little enough light on the streets. He looked at those he would lead and nodded, satisfied. Above their boots, little flashes of blue could be seen. He hoped them brilliant enough to be distinguished before fighting was joined.

It had been Cospatric's idea. But they were Beaton colors.

"Sir?"

He nodded grimly, letting the pain of five years past come to life—it had never really died. He had nursed it, had chosen the humiliation of survival for the meager hope that some day he might live to see justice. His only son, body unrecovered, had fed the fires. His closest friend held the leash upon which the Church roamed.

But tonight—tonight he would lay it all to rest.

Footsteps came crashing up the cobbled stone. His smile was ice as he stepped into the streets. There would be battle here. Finally.

Ruth looked at the ink stains on her apron and sighed. She knew there were traces of black on her chin and cheeks. Never scratch an itch when printing by hand. Never.

She looked up, caught the concentration on her husband's face, and smiled down at the words he was printing over and over and over again.

Prince Renar of Marantine has returned to his kingdom in victory.

He came back, Kayly. You were right. Her eyes grew watery, and she shook her head fiercely.

Tomorrow she would cry. Tonight she would work.

"Run now, run to the castle—give the sentries as little time as possible to raise the alarm!"

The city was alive with the sounds of booted feet. What few people there were along the walkways scattered before the presence of armed men; experience had taught them that much.

The streets opened up before the army as if in welcome. It was their city in the silence. They traveled from lower quarter to merchants' quarter and from there to the manors that lined the streets.

Those streets seemed near empty. Never mind; if they wanted a fight, a fight was theirs at the end of the road.

Like a wave they came to the outer walls of the castle proper. A sense of familiarity brushed across the men who had spent so many of their years on the other side of these walls. The gates were closed. Up above, they could hear the sounds of horns calling; the alarm was being raised while they stood outside.

"The gates!" Lorrence cried, waving a sword with mailed arm. Men rushed forward then, holding a makeshift battering ram. People cleared a path to make way for their passing.

"*Hold!*" Trethar's voice carried above the sounds of muted whispers and shuffling feet. Had there been din of war, it would have carried anyway. Or so those that heard it felt.

"We've no time to hold," Lorrence answered brusquely. That he answered at all was a testament to the power of Trethar's voice; already time was slipping away. The barracks would be emptied to the alarm in minutes—and against the whole of the new royal guard they counted as a passing threat, no more.

"Time enough," Trethar answered. He walked almost majestically up to the gates. He raised his head a moment, and a stream of hard, white light flashed upward. Whatever he had hit fell back, the sound of mail against ground unmistakable.

Those holding the battering ram moved at his gesture.

"This will be the last of it, Captain."

General Lorrence looked slightly annoyed, but held his peace. Anyone who might have corrected Trethar's assumption of rank did not speak and the moment passed as the mage lifted both of his arms in a sudden rush.

The air around him seemed to spark and burn in a haze of different colors. Breeze blew the strands of hair away from his upturned face, his silver eyes.

His mouth opened around a few syllables; his arms wavered slightly in the air. They drew back from him. He didn't notice.

As his arms sliced cleanly through air and fire, as his mouth barked out one sharp, crystal syllable, a brilliant light cut the air. It headed unerring toward its target—the gate and the wall that held it.

In the momentary blindness that took the unwary, the sight of the gate was lost. But the sound it made as it exploded was not. Wood, iron, and stone gave a deafening roar and tumbled inward like tinkling glass.

Trethar slumped forward, knees almost giving under his weight. He looked up to see the carnage his magics had wrought, and a small smile hovered around his wrinkled lips.

"Aye, Captain," he said into the hollow silence, "that's the last of it. But a work. Quite a work."

As if his words were a trigger, the men began to head for the ruined wall like a single bolt. They converged upon the grounds they had once guarded, and little was left to stop them; beneath the ruins of rubble a stray limb could be seen here and there. They paid little attention.

"Now comes the test," Lorrence said, calling to his men. "Play your part as agreed. Corrin, take your sixty and head immediately to the barracks."

"Sir!"

"The rest of you, follow me. We work toward the chamber of the governing council."

They flowed past like water, weapons out and ready.

Unremarked on, Trethar followed behind them. He had served as promised, but he was still curious to see how the rest of the play unfolded.

Tiras held his place beside his student, lending both light and encouragement. Twenty feet below, Erin and Darin waited, shunning the darkness with Lernari light.

Erin's arm rested gently on the shoulders of her companion. He could feel the constant trembling in it and was surprised to find that he himself was not shaking.

"Damn this thing!"

Darin winced.

"Renar—"

"No, I can do it. You've never seen it in operation."

The words had a hollow ring to them when they reached the two that waited. Darin counted the seconds, unsure whether he counted accurately, but unable to stop. It kept him from wondering if Trethar was still alive, and from wondering if any of those guards loyal to Renar had even made it to the castle.

Damn. He'd lost count again. He started over and heard Renar give a short, sharp sound. He glanced up.

Erin smiled. "I think—"

"Got it!"

From above, the dimmest of lights filtered down to touch their upturned faces. It was real light, not blood-light. Darin wanted to shout for joy—he hated these dark, cold tunnels.

Anticipating him, Erin gently touched his lips with her fingers. Both Renar and Tiras scrambled up, and, after a few tense seconds, lowered the rope back down into the pit. Erin caught it and made a slipknot of it.

"Ready?" she asked softly as she pushed it down around Darin's arms.

He nodded, and she gave the top of the rope an urgent tug.

Soon. Soon they would be free to act.

Tiras shed his winter garments with a silence and a speed that defied his age. Renar did the same. Both men wore light, smooth clothing that allowed for easy movement without the hindrance of bulk. They fumbled a moment with pockets, and then straightened out.

It was odd to watch them mirroring each other's actions so closely. But Darin could believe, as he struggled out of his jacket and two layers of sweater, that Renar had indeed been among the best of the older man's students. There was a precision about his movements, an economy of action, that spoke of skill and experience. He pulled the staff out of its sling with a soft smile.

Bethany glowed a faint green.

Initiate.

Bethany. He held the staff out a moment in front of his small chest.

Let us not be parted again until the battle is done.

Darin nodded, allowing the word *battle* to sink in.

Renar crossed the carpeted floor, moving quietly to the door.

"Back ways?" Erin whispered.

He paused for a moment, considering. Then he shook his head. "No. Too often used, too well known. My father was not as apt a concealer of ways as my mother. And besides, the tunnels do not lead directly to the chamber; we would be no better off with their use." He touched the door, and then turned back. "Your sword, Lady."

"Too obvious."

He winced slightly, remembering its biting glow. He wished that his mother could have requested private chambers with a view to the outside; at least that way he would know how much success—or failure—his people had had.

They were close enough to the Lesser Cabal's chambers now; there was no suitable or subtle way to approach them. The halls were too well-lit—lavishly so—but with good reason. "Your sword," he repeated.

She hesitated a moment before unsheathing it.

She was right, Darin thought, as he looked at the naked blade. No one would be able to miss it. And if Renar thought it didn't matter . . . He gripped his staff more firmly.

"Tiras?"

A hint of a smile flashed in the darkness. Tiras gave a low, smooth bow, and then knelt at the door. He worked quickly, and in absolute silence.

"Back."

Both Erin and Darin followed Renar's command, as did Renar himself.

Tiras stood—a motion so graceful and fluid he seemed to be jointless, seamless—and threw the doors open.

For an instant, in the light that flooded like sudden dawn into the room, Erin could make out the glint of black metal on either side of the door. She thought it to be chain, but it didn't matter; the forms clattered noisily to the ground an instant after Tiras bolted out the door.

"Now!" Renar said, running forward.

She leaped out the door, closely following the light pad of Renar's steps against stone.

Darin's speed matched neither of theirs, but he ran. As he cleared the door, he closed his eyes briefly, knowing what lay to either side of it. It was perhaps the last chance he would have to allow for squeamishness.

It was too much to hope that the hall would be somehow deserted. It wasn't. What was odd was the way it was full; men in armor running to and from a large hall that branched to the left of the one they were running down.

"Damn," Renar said, loudly enough that it carried. "We're late!"

He drew a sword as a group of six men came down the hall toward them.

"The attackers have penetrated the castle!" The voice was one of mixed confusion, anger, and despair.

Six pairs of eyes bore down on Renar. In none of them was the glimmer of recognition that he'd been faintly praying for.

"I've the back!" Erin cried, and pivoted lightly on one foot. Darin skidded to the right to avoid the point of the blade she held at ready. He turned, less neatly than she had done, to stand beside her.

If magic is a weapon, Darin, it must most closely resemble the readied bow.

He kept his grip on Bethany as a detachment of six men came rushing toward him.

It's always better not to close in battle, boy. Let them come to you—but don't *be foolish enough to let them reach you.*

But they were coming so quickly . . .

Erin shoved him slightly to the side, jarring him out of his state of shock. She took a quick step, brandishing her blade as if it were a ward made for battle. It created a lattice of light across the air, burning the afterimage into the eyes of any who watched.

The guards, damn them, were good. The presence of the sword didn't phase them or in any way halt their progress. But the sword-work of the woman who wielded it did. Blood came, an answer to the call of her blade.

The sight of it galvanized Darin.

He swept his arms back and cleared the momentary panic out of his thoughts.

Don't close your eyes, Darin. You have to be able to use your ability in combat—and no one fights blindly.

He shut out Trethar's teaching. Too much was happening, and too quickly, for him to be able to do otherwise. Later, he would have time to wonder how Erin had ever learned to ignore the sounds and smells of close combat.

In the darkness behind his eyes, the gate formed. He kept it small, remembering what had happened the last time he had just called power—and knowing that he would have to hoard his resources.

The tingle that rushed down his arms and the back of his neck told him all he needed to know. His eyes snapped open to the sight of wordless combat, his ears once again hearing the crash and clatter of metal.

Fire snaked outward, giddy in the small freedom that Darin permitted it. It caught a guard in its lethal embrace.

Darin forced himself to watch.

Power like this, at a distance, could be too heady, too impersonal. The fire burned its grip of destruction into his mind. He wanted to see, wanted to remember just how horrible a thing it was.

He did.

The flame moved onward, straining against the control he exerted. He held it through the strength of his revulsion. The death that Erin offered was an easy one, a pleasant one, compared to this. He stopped wondering how she could do what she did. He refused to start wondering how he could.

And then it was over, for the moment. Erin's cheek was grazed; blood beaded as it tried to get through the slight scratch another sword had managed to put there.

She, too, looked at the dead that surrounded her. She bowed once, her face hidden. But when she spoke, her voice was steady and cool. "Renar?"

"We're ready."

Darin turned to see Tiras and Renar near the bend in the hall. Their dead, unlike his, lay almost peacefully where they had fallen.

"Not a pretty sight, Darin," Tiras said softly. His eyes, always cloaked and distant, had grown cold. "This—fire, it interests me. Where did you learn it?"

Renar caught his former master's shoulder in a firm grip, and the older man turned. "Enough, Tiras. You recognized his office. The riot and the burning took place when he was too young to act in it."

Tiras forced himself to relax. He had heard about the old man's power and had accepted Renar's claim that it could be utilized to take the gate—but he had never *seen* it displayed. And if Darin was so minor a power compared to his master . . . He felt a momentary pang of shame—to be so obvious in front of a student and two strangers! To hide it, he spoke again.

"Are there others who can wield so mighty a gift?" His voice, soft, was the cat's voice.

"Tiras!" Renar said.

"At least three." Darin replied.

"Those three?"

"My teacher, the high priest, and—and one other."

"Tiras," Renar said again, a warning note in his voice.

"My apologies, student." There was just a little emphasis on the last word, which was not lost on Renar. The hand that held the old man was withdrawn. "It is not my way—nor should it be yours—to trust too easily."

"Trust now," was Renar's clipped reply. "It's rather too late to do otherwise.'' He turned. ''We've lost enough time to questions.''

''True.'' Tiras straightened. ''But the council has undoubtedly been alerted. Shall we, my lord?'' He bowed.

Renar raised an eyebrow, then nodded briefly.

As one person, they turned to the large double doors at the end of the hallway. The doors were grand; they conveyed, by their inlaid work and large brass handles, the majesty that was contained behind them. Those doors were firmly sealed shut, as always—but there were no guards outside of them. It could only be hoped that the two that should have been posted there were among the fallen.

''Come,'' Renar said softly.

Together they walked to the end of the hall.

chapter
nineteen

Trethar was thankful that he had enough power left to take advantage of the shadowed halls to mask his presence. Fighting developed a ferocity he'd rarely seen as they progressed inward through the castle. He carried no weapons for such a man-to-man confrontation; he'd never taken the time to see to their proper use.

He winced as one of the guards—hard to tell which side he fought on—fell. In the poorer light the blood was an inky stain that welled along the base of his throat. The sight of it was almost hypnotic.

He shook himself, drawing back; he was dangerously tired, but he forced himself to think of other things. They had made progress. He'd caught a glimpse of the floor plans that Tiras had so carefully drawn up; they lay open to his sharp memory as if they were now in front of him. He hoped that he was not too late.

Renar gripped the large handle of the left door in both hands. Erin, sword reluctantly sheathed, did the same with the right door. Tiras stood ten feet back, taut as a strung wire. He nodded.

Even before the doors were fully open, he began to run at them, his feet light and soundless on stone.

Darin, flush against the right wall, caught a glimpse of the inner chamber as Tiras tucked his chin in and went into a roll along the ground inches before he passed through the door.

Two bright lengths of steel cut the air where his chest should have been. They clattered ineffectively against each other as

319

Tiras gained his feet and threw his arms back in a perfect, semi-circular arc.

The audacity of his entrance took twelve of the thirteen who sat around the long, large table by surprise. The Lesser Cabal of Illan gaped at his black-clad form a moment in silence.

''Your 'Majesty.' '' Tiras gave a low, easy bow.

The two men at the doors crumpled, almost unnoticed. As their armored bodies slid partially into the doorframe, Darin could see that they were Swords. The black and red crest on their surcoats buckled and folded, mere cloth without life to give the office strength and fear.

Erin nodded, and together she and Darin stepped into the room to stand just behind Renar.

At the head of the long table, in a chair with a high, velvet-lined back, sat a man with a circlet across his brow. Darin had never seen him before, but knew the trappings of office well: the sceptre and the crown of Maran. Along the sides of the table, robed in black, with the red of the broken circle as crests, sat several men. These, too, Darin knew, although he had never seen them before in his life: they were high priests and priests, none of them Karnari. Seven had come to their feet at the interruption; five remained seated. He looked at those five, saw two women, and wondered which one was Lady Verena. Whichever she was, she showed no sign of recognition.

Along each wall, weapons drawn and readied, stood six Swords. A further six waited behind the king's chair.

From the high seat at the end of the large, heavy table, Duke Jordan of Illan inclined his head. If there was surprise in his eyes, it was buried in their glittering darkness; his lips turned up in the pale ghost of a smile.

''Tiras. How unexpected and how very disappointing. But at least we will have an end to it; this little subversion has lingered too long.'' And he turned his head to glance at his nephew.

''Ah, Uncle, precipitous as always.'' Renar stepped further into the room.

''Renar,'' he said, his voice a little louder, but no less even. ''I was always rather fond of you.''

''A peculiar way to show affection, Uncle.''

''Is it? Marantine was doomed to fall, whether sooner or later, it doesn't matter. The Empire and the Church were omnipresent and near omnipotent. What I did preserves Maran much more effectively than any of your father's plans.''

"Doomed to fall?" Renar spit to the side; his cheeks were flushed, but his face remained near expressionless. "The walls were made by the Lady of Elliath; had *we* endured, they would have.''

"And you believe that? Fool. You are not so perceptive as I once might have hoped." He raised a hand in a gesture of command. "I saw a new power, Renar; I saw it and realized that it was greater than the old, dying magics.''

Two more of the priests abandoned their chairs.

"Jordan."

The king turned to face the only priest that had not yet taken to his feet. "And I fear, my dear nephew, that you will come to believe in its strength. As I did. Remember the fires." His eyes, dark, left his nephew's. "I would like you to meet Lord Marak of Cossandara.

"Come, do not be petty. We've business which needs attention, and mere family squabbles should not interfere." The man turned to raise an eyebrow at one of the women. "Lady Verena, it appears that your 'warning' has come late." Voice icy, he added, "But we will deal with the question of you as we will deal with *him*.''

She bowed her head, her hair a tightly drawn dark mass. When she raised it again, an enigmatic smile hovered at her lips. "Ah, Marak, ever the optimist. My warning, if you had chosen to support me, would have come on time." Pale, she bowed to her cousin. "Renar of Maran. It's been years, cousin. Perhaps it would have been wiser had you stayed away." But her voice held no regret; instead, it trembled with fierceness.

"You!" a pale, dark-haired young man said. "You betrayed us!"

"I?" Verena smiled. She leaned, almost languid, into the tabletop; the edge of her braid skirted its polished reflection as she contemplated its surface. And then her smile hardened, sharpened; it turned from catlike to something inexplicably human and vicious. Fennis of Handerness barely had time to widen his eyes before her dagger found its perfect, quiet mark. "Very well," she said, as shouting erupted around the table. "I have.''

Renar stared at his cousin in shock as she twisted the dagger before drawing it free. As if aware of his gaze, she turned, and although other voices drowned out her words, he read her lips clearly.

"I can't always be upstaged, little cousin. Don't fail!"

Darin began to call the fire.

If he had thought the sight of priests might upset his concentration, he had been wrong. Each of these black-robed men had held the power of life and death for so many, so long—but they had no hold over him. He was no longer a slave, to stand and fall at their whim; he was patriarch of Culverne; he was free—and he was irrevocably their enemy, in a position of what little strength he could muster.

He had just a few seconds to react when the eyes of the seated priest turned steel gray.

I saw a new power, Renar.

Suddenly, everything was too clear.

Renar leaped out of the way as a pillar of fire erupted through the floor that he'd been standing on.

"Run, nephew, it does no good—this is a special flame; it follows where you go! You weren't here for the fires, were you? Guards!" The Swords bridled at so common a term, and they hesitated for a moment. "Take the rest!" Only a moment, though. They knew a threat when they saw it and could only stand on formality so long before taking necessary action.

Out of the corner of one eye, Darin caught the raised glow of Erin's sword. It swept through the air in a pattern familiar to him. He turned to see Tiras standing almost immobile as he stared into the living pillar.

Fire. The Night of Fires, the two nights, took the old master's senses as he stared, unnoticed, at the priest. He had his answers at last.

White-fire exploded on the table. Somebody screamed; Darin was not sure who, and didn't take the time to look. His gate was open; the power willing.

A second pillar of flame burst into being. It moved toward the first, a sluggish column of red. There was life in the room; life to burn, life to extinguish. To meet flame instead was not its goal.

Beads of sweat formed on Darin's forehead as he struggled to control what he had summoned forth.

Fire touched fire, molding itself into one entity. Darin bit back a cry of shock as his arms began to tingle. The pillar moved toward him now, Renar forgotten. He tried to force it back, focusing the strength of his will upon it. It slowed perceptibly. It didn't stop moving.

Shaken, he took a step back toward the doorway. He tried again to control the fire. He tried to separate what he had called from what it had joined. The flames inched steadily closer.

No! He bit his lip on the word, trying to force it to become reality.

A whisper of laughter, distant and dry as the rustle of leaves, echoed clearly over the din of the noise in the room.

Yes.

He looked up then; his vision misted. He had never really tried to see out of power-touched eyes before this. He had always had eyes for the fire alone; the fire that glowed so brilliantly and warmly.

Everything was blurred, the edges of forms, both living and inanimate, tinged in a faint haze. He could make out bodies, see faces and weapons, as if from a great distance. Only one thing other than the fire was completely clear: the priest seated at the end of the table closest to him. He was younger than Trethar. His hair was white with shocks of dark black in both beard and brows. And his eyes were silvered glowing orbs.

Etched into the hard, cold lines of the man's mouth was a frosty smile. "I don't know where you learned this, boy."

The fire moved again, cutting inches away from the distance between Darin and death.

"It appears I won't have the chance to find out."

Again the fire slithered forward.

It ended this way. Darin felt bitterness forming a knot at the base of his throat. *We've lost.*

The city was already the domain of the Church. The people, killed or cowed, would offer less and less resistance. The men that had come at Renar's behest would be slaughtered. And the last of the lines, Elliath and Culverne, would meet their end and give truth to the lie of the broken red circle that glittered in mockery along the front of the priest's robes.

No! Shutting his eyes, he threw his hands out in a gesture of denial and anger.

The fire stopped.

The priest stood, his unpleasant frown a relief from the darkness of his smile. The frown grew.

Darin widened the gate in his mind, and the single column flared, its light intensifying as its height did. And then he began to *push*.

The fire started to slide an inch above the stone floor toward the priest.

The column burned more brightly again, if it was possible, and came to a lurching halt.

The older man's brow was now etched with the deep furrows of effort. He gestured, a grand, sweeping motion. The pillar of flame touched the high, arched ceiling. But even when it began to move toward Darin again, the priest showed no satisfaction. His face glistened with sweat.

Darin had never seen a priest sweat before, certainly not like this. And he knew why the man did. He had never before seen so large a fire summoned forth—the cost of controlling it would be far too large a risk.

He bit his lip, felt his teeth breach skin, and tasted the salty tang of his own blood.

The fire crackled, looming larger before him. Larger and closer.

What choice did he have?

He caught the edges of his own gate in a wild mental grip and tore.

CRACK.

Power surged through him. Fire boiled along his veins, the warmth too sudden and too sharp.

He could not see the face of the priest, the widening of eyes, or the way he scrambled up on the tabletop. And he was glad of it.

"No!" A voice, thin and tinny, but loud. *"He's mine!"*

But fire surged forward, unstoppable now, unshakable.

The priest had the time for one loud cry before the fire scorched the flesh from his throat.

The resistance was gone. The fire belonged only to Darin. And he was very, very tired.

"Darin!"

Initiate!

There was another scream, shorter this time. The smell of burned flesh clogged his nostrils.

"They've gotten this far." There was evident relief in both the voice and the face of General Lorrence. Sweat ran down the

lines of a perpetual frown, and blood crusted his cheek where
the line of his helmet had been struck, hard.

Trethar took advantage of the momentary halt to examine the
fallen bodies. Three men lay dead of sword wounds—efficient,
single strokes. The fourth had been cut twice. The Lady's
work, then. He smiled softly.

Two corpses had been charred and blackened.

Darin had also survived this far.

The men took a deep breath and began to move forward,
more caution evident now than during the rest of their struggle.

Close to the bend of the large hall lay several more of the
palace guards. They were dead, three apparently unmarked. Nowhere was there a sign of Renar or Tiras.

"This is it," Lorrence said softly, halting his men once again
before they turned down the final hall. He surveyed the number
that remained; the ferocity of the fight had taken its toll.
Twenty—twenty, the prime of the royal guard were left. "Protect your king."

There were grim nods, silent ones. No need to give such a
command here—for this purpose had they fought so viciously
and fiercely. Perhaps, should any survive this, they would have
time to consider just how ferociously they had fought—and how
unfairly they had killed. But not now.

Lorrence, being untrue to his rank, took the bend first.

"Bright Heart!" he shouted.

The rest of the men rushed forward, with Trethar very close
to the lead. The doors to the governing council's chambers had
been flung open. This they expected.

Nothing prepared them for the flaming pillar that seemed to
stretch from the ground to the ceiling itself.

Trethar sagged against a wall. Outlined by the ugly glare of
heat and fire, he recognized the tight, still form of his pupil.

"God curse you, boy," he murmured almost dispassionately.
"I am spent." He was angry, but there was no point in showing
his anger at having come so far in his plans, just to have them
cut so surely from beneath him by one of his own!

The leader took a deep breath and raised his sword. "Follow," he said. His voice was shaky, but command was there
nonetheless. And his followers, every last one of them, were—
truly, if the prince was still alive—royal guards. They obeyed.

* * *

"Darin!"

He heard another scream.

Erin's hand gripped his shoulder tightly. He tried to shake her off, but found he had no strength for it. As they had once before, his knees locked—it was the only reason his legs still supported him.

The fire, he thought nonsensically. *The fire is mine.*

He watched it, mesmerized by the pulsating patterns that lurked just beneath its fluid surface. Why had he never seen the fire's beauty before?

Something stung his cheek, and he turned listlessly in the direction it came from. He could see the indistinct form that stood beside him. The lines of the face blurred, becoming more and more indistinguishable. Only the fire was real.

Initiate.

He raised his head almost blindly, eyes still chained to the summoned element.

Darin. Darin—return.

He recognized the voice. Darin opened his mouth as if to answer. No sound passed his lips; no sound could cut above the suddenly glorious screams of the dying.

Beth . . . Bethany . . .

Darin, Initiate, Patriarch—you must stop this summoning or you will kill the people you have come to aid!

Kill?

Yessssss

Killing is

Fiiiiiiire

Killing is

DARIN!

The shout resounded through him. For a moment the indistinct grew more real; gray and colorless shapes took on familiar form.

Renar leaped out of the way of the fire, rolling beneath the large table. The table vanished beneath the onslaught of flame. Another woman, black robed, dodged away as a chair was consumed, moving with such grace and surety that he knew she was no true priest.

RENAR!

Yesssssssss

The sibilant whisper echoed through him and set his arms and legs tingling. It was the only thing he could feel.

He recognized it now: it was the voice of the fire.

Never before had it been so clear—never before had it felt so . . . welcome.

"No!"

He felt the harsh croak against the back of his throat. Remembered suddenly why he had come.

Yessssssss

Oh God, Oh Light Heart, Lernan

He forced the sagging strength of his will outward, trying to harness the fire that he had set in motion. It seemed to hesitate a moment.

Fiiiiiire

Burrrrrrrn

He struggled out of the chain of its thought, if something so primitive could be called thought.

How—HOW?

Slowly the fire inched forward. The scream that followed resonated through him like music.

Shuddering, he tried to restrain it. He felt the cords of his will draw the fire in. And, miraculously, he held it.

But Lernan, God, he was so tired . . .

There seemed to be no answer. He could not now open yet a larger gate to stop the flow of flame. He had done it once, and it had succeeded, only to bring him to this.

No. Wait.

Frantically he clutched at the thought.

He had done it before. It *had* succeeded.

The death of the priest ended the priest's summoning; with no conduit, the part of the flame directed against him ceased to be. Death had closed the enemy gate. Death.

But God, dear God, he had seen the death by flame too many times to want it for himself. The flame struggled against his will; he knew he would lose; it was only a matter of time. And the loss—the loss meant the death of everything he had come this far to achieve.

He had no energy to scream or gibber; no energy to cry. He had only enough to make the choice he had been raised to make.

With the last of his control, he brought the flame home.

* * *

"Darin! Darin—stop the fire!" Erin shook him with a grip that should have been bruising. There was no response. She saw the sweat glisten on his forehead and saw the glazed look in his eyes. She slapped him once. He responded like a rigid china doll. Her raised hand stopped the automatic backswing; she thought that if she hit him again, she might break him.

Renar was dodging the pillar of flame that moved so inexorably through everything in the room. She tightened her grip in despair. The council was scattered across the room among the Swords. She did not think that any were still alive. Moments ago, that might have been considered a victory.

"No . . ."

Turning, she saw the faint motion of Darin's lips. The word itself was barely audible, even to her ears.

Dear God, Darin—Darin, please . . .

He couldn't hear her. She felt his body tremble beneath her hand. She threw her sword to the floor, hearing it clang against the stone without bothering to find out where it had fallen. It was useless now; against the fire it had no effect.

She caught Darin with both hands and shook him again.

There was no result.

She heard Renar swear—his voice was the only one in the room that was both audible and free of hysteria.

Releasing Darin, she whirled around in time to see the council table dissolve.

"Renar!" she shouted, but he had already rolled out from beneath the table. The fire continued its pursuit. Renar was flagging. He could not keep up this frantic pace for much longer—minutes perhaps. It was not his endurance that impressed her. It was the way he stayed a foot from the fire's reach. He held the fire's attention by choice; of all the people trapped here, his training gave him the edge and experience necessary to flee to safety.

And then the fire hesitated. It inched forward before coming to a complete halt. Quivering, it stood in the center of the room, the table forming a black mantle of ash around it.

A sigh of relief passed her lips, and she let go of Darin's shoulders before it died.

Her mouth froze. Relief disappeared as the flame began to move once again. There was no mistaking the direction it traveled in.

Frantic, she grabbed Darin and dragged him backward, out of the long hall. His arms lashed outward feebly, thudding gently against her shoulders.

"Me . . ." he whispered. His face was etched with strain and fear.

Erin looked over his head; felt the strands of matted hair beneath her chin. The fire was still coming. She pulled him back another few feet.

A hand caught her back.

"Let him be, Lady!"

She turned her head, arms still locked tightly around Darin. Trethar stood directly behind her.

"The fire—"

"The fire will burn forever if he cannot send it back—and he can't."

"What—what do you mean?"

"Lady." Trethar's voice was softer but no less urgent. "He has called the flame into being. He serves as a conduit for it. If he survives, the flame will destroy us all before moving out into the city. Do you not think the boy understands this? The choice he makes is the only one he can make if we are to survive. You must let him continue—he will not be able to hold the flame for much longer."

"Hold the—" If it were possible, Erin's face grew paler. Almost gently she set Darin down against one wall.

Bright Heart. Her fingers curled into tight fists. *He intends— he means—*

The fire gave her no space to think clearly. It moved, pulled by Darin's will, across the stone floor.

She scrambled at her belt a moment before pulling out a dagger.

Trethar nodded grimly. "Yes, Lady. The death will be kinder." But he turned away from her then, eyes upon the floor. This loss he had not intended, and failure was bitter to him.

Without hesitation, she drew the edge of the dagger across her hand. It cut more deeply than she meant. With a soft curse, she threw it forward, where it passed harmlessly into flame— and was consumed.

She had no time to almost kill herself. Not if she was to save Darin's life. The flame's caress brought death too quickly and too suddenly.

But she had never, *never* been able to call upon God at will. She had never been adult.

Panic gripped her even as she brought her arms up in full circle. She lost the ability to breathe.

If God denied her now—if she could not reach His hand, Darin would perish.

And so, standing behind her young friend, would she.

Before she could think, she retreated backward a step.

I'll die. Images of blackened corpses filled her inner vision. Her feet, with a will of their own, pulled her further back from the moving column.

I'll die, too.

For an instant the stone walls melted into canvas, darkened by night. She felt supplies all around her; she heard the clashing of swords and the screams of her people.

She was terrified. She didn't want to die.

Please, please, God, don't let them find me. Don't let them—

She had been so desperately afraid of death—of pain—of the power of the Enemy's Servant. She had wanted to run, but her legs would not carry her—would not even unfurl. She had dreamed of the large, stone hall of her ancestors, of running through the cloisters, of her friends and their plans and goals.

She hadn't wanted it to end there by the Dark Ceremonies.

Oh God, I don't want to die

I don't want to die. Like ice it touched her.

But I—I deserve—I—

I deserve to die.

She took a deep breath, steadying herself, as the fear sent adrenaline through her veins.

She took another breath, deeper, fuller. The child met the woman then, each bearing twin fears. Those fears were evenly matched, and she, suspended between them.

The fire drew closer.

Of all the strange things that could come to her then, she heard music, a hum of breath against her cheek. There was a sweep of velvet, of warm arms and movement.

Life. The life she had never had. Given in a few moments as a tantalizing hint of possible futures.

I don't want to die.

Renar. Darin. Tiras. Trethar. Verdor. Lord Cosgrove. Ruth.

Kaarel. Their faces surrounded her in the cold silence. They had their plans, each of them—as she had hers. And she wanted to live. To live to see them grow to fruition. To live to see each of them fulfilled and at peace.

To be at peace herself.

Peace.

The canvas faded. The stone hall surrounded her. The fire was less than a foot away.

Her arms swept down, one elegant, trembling motion. She felt the fear twist at her mind as she forced her feet forward—and she accepted it. She accepted Erin at twelve. She accepted the death, the pain, and the war that she was only another soldier in. Finally, she accepted herself.

Her hand found Darin's shoulder as the fire engulfed them both. She screamed once—a shattering cry that the crackle around her swallowed.

I'm burning—I'm burning God I'm—

Burning.

White, brilliant, warm.

The Hand of God held her. She held Darin.

Great-granddaughter. I am with you, at last, by your call.

God's blood flowed through her; she could not contain it, nor did she try. His healing held the fire at bay, surrounding Darin with a nimbus of light that only she could see. Her head flew back, and she let out a single, wordless cry that held all joy, all triumph.

She felt His approbation, His gentleness, and the faint hint of His hope.

I am here, I have always been here . . .

I understand. She drew Darin in more closely. His eyes fluttered open, and he stared in bewilderment at the face of the fire. He threw up his arms to cover his face, and she hugged him tightly.

His arms came down in slow wonderment. He looked at his hands, turned them over, and touched his cheeks, pinching them.

His eyes widened. He tried to jump to his feet and hit Erin's chin with the top of his head. He could *move*. He could think.

He could feel the edges of his ragged gate in the dark corner of his mind. The fire struggled against him; he could feel this, too, and was glad.

Fiiiiiiiire

No. Enough.

His grip was firm and sure. No exhaustion marred his determination. What he called, he controlled. He gave the word that was the law of will, and the fire began to diminish.

Erin watched as the fire moved. It left no ash in its wake; no charred body. She hugged Darin tightly again.

She understood.

To want death, to hope for death—that was not the province of the Heart of Light. The darkness of death was all she had wanted; and that part of her He could not touch. Only when it was physical—only when her mind could no longer hold that desire—could she rest in His hand as her kindred did.

But to want *life*; to want life and all that that implied—that was His; that was what He could speak to and understand.

Not the fear of living. The fear of dying.

She smiled, and as the curtain of flame opened, she threw up one arm.

I am Sarillorn of Elliath still; I am your initiate at last. Let me bring your peace and power to Dagothrin.

White light flared outward as the last of the fire disappeared. Glowing, radiant, it traveled from its source like the ripples on still water touched by wind.

And those touched by it felt, for a moment, renewed. They couldn't know why, for their eyes could not perceive its passage. But they were heartened.

All, that is, save one.

Erin turned at the sound of a harsh, ugly cry—of a pain both powerful and repellant.

Malanthi. Her hands came up, releasing Darin. She had no weapon now but the fading power of God. Against Malanthi that was enough.

But it was not a priest she faced.

Huddled against a wall four feet away, was a shadowed figure. Darkness, like a cloak, touched his face and hands; a black robe swirled around his bent body.

She froze.

"Boy," the shadow said.

Darin's hands almost let go of Bethany. He recognized the voice. He recognized the figure using it. He shook his head in confusion, unwilling to use either of the two names.

"Sargoth." Erin's voice was soft; there was no question in it.

"Sarillorn."

"But—"

"Boy, the game is bigger than either of you." Sibilant hissing issued forth. Erin recognized it as the Servant's laughter. The Servant's form wavered slightly in the air. Black became brown; the hooded face a familiar wrinkled visage. "You know better than to summon more power than you can control."

Darin shook his head in stunned silence.

Trethar vanished like discarded clothing as the Servant drew himself to full height.

"You surprise me, Lady." He bowed. "The Old Power is strong in you. I did not realize you had it; you have never used it until now. A mistake on my part. I dislike error. I shall not give you the grace of repeating this one."

Darin raised his staff in trembling hands.

"Let me explain." Knowledge, to the Second of the Sundered, was power; and power, he displayed, as any of his kin might: with pride, with a savagery of its own. "The daylight only harms the Servant who touches the Dark Heart. I traveled with you like any other . . . half-breed." Disdain curled his lip. "Only we two, the First and the Second, have ever walked without the power of God behind us. And only I have ever done so with that knowledge.

"You drove him from our Lord," Sargoth added. "Be pleased, little half-breed." He raised a hand. "No, boy. Once again, I must grant you the smaller victory. And once again, I look forward to meeting you in the future." Laughter, harsh and sibilant, filled the gutted hall.

White-fire passed through the air where Sargoth had been standing. He was gone.

"I don't understand."

Erin put one arm around Darin's shoulder. She was physically exhausted. "No. I don't, either."

"Why did he teach me—"

"Darin—"

"What if I'm—"

"Darin."

He stopped speaking.

Initiate.

Bethany?

You bear no taint of darkness. Your blood would not allow it. Be comforted if you can.

But he was a—

Friend? He has his own plan—the Second of the Sundered was always known for that. If you trusted him, do not regret it— his teachings were your victory here—and perhaps your victory for the city.

Yes—but why would he help us? Why, when the Enemy is against everything we stand for?

I do not know. But do not worry.

Darin felt cold. Bethany was not following her own advice.

He turned, leaning against Erin, his throat too tight for words. For an instant, he felt the warmth of hands upon his shoulders; the whisper of trust within his ears; and the tingle of power in the back of his mind.

I trusted him.

Bethany said nothing; there was nothing she could say.

Renar was standing in what remained of the council chamber. He was covered in black ash; it was hard to distinguish him between bruises and soot. But his face was quirked in a smile. There was youth in it; there was some hint of optimism and hope. He had not accomplished all that he had set out to; his uncle had died by the hands of fire and not by his. But perhaps it was better that way. He glanced around at the men—his men— as they followed his command. He was home.

Home.

He thought of the countless times he'd abandoned her to seek adventure and infamy within the Empire's vast border. He would never, *never*, take her for granted again.

"Darin. Lady." He bowed formally. "We did it."

He was all grace, all formality, even covered as he was in sweat and ash. His shirt was torn at cuff, collar, and shoulder. Darin waited for Renar to comment on it, but the king, for once, did not notice the state of his clothing.

It was just as well. But Darin thought, with the slightest hint of whimsy, that he might miss the Renar that had been. He smiled and returned the bow of his monarch.

Renar darted forward suddenly, lifting Darin off his feet and spinning him round in circles, rank forgotten.

"We did it!"

"Dignity, student. For a king, dignity is crucial." Tiras said, dusting black ash off black shirt.

"Then he won't make much of a king," Verena drawled. "I don't suppose you have any interest in a queen, instead?" Verena tossed a dagger, sticky with blood, into the air. She caught it as it tumbled down and smiled. "No? Ah well. I don't love politics, young cousin.

"But in my own way, I loved Marantine. I was ashamed of our grandfather—but perhaps we will have peace."

Renar, looking at the sharp smile on his cousin's angular face, felt a twinge of sympathy for Lord Stenton Cosgrove.

Erin looked around. Several of Renar's men were doing their best to clean the hall, and if they noticed the mad prance their uncrowned king was doing, it didn't show on their faces.

"Say"—Renar put Darin down—"where's the old man?"

The cries rolled like waves through the streets, spanning cobbled stone and packed dirt alike.

Wind passed the black-inked papers that had been placed at nearly every corner on every building. The ink was dry, but only barely.

For those who lacked the education to read, the king's crest gleamed against parchment. It wasn't fancy—neither Ruth nor Kaarel had had the time to embellish—but the simple lines of stag and eagle beneath crossed swords said more than enough.

Those cries grew from whispers and tears, from shock and disbelief—and occasionally from anger. Even in Dagothrin there were many who had already claimed the Empire's interests as their own.

They would not do so for long; Renar's men would see to that. They walked through the streets, searching.

Four days had passed since the fall of the governor; it had been four days since the roll had been called and the army of Marantine began to be invested with what young blood remained.

Cospatric did not yet get his wish to return to a comfortable retirement, but he was philosophical—it had been a tad boring. He did, however, refuse the rank of a commissioned officer, preferring, in his own words, a "more useful position."

Lord Beaton and Lord Cosgrove, with Tiras as both aide and

adjudicator, began the process of 'advising' the king on disposition of crown lands. Lord Stenton Cosgrove found to his chagrin that Renar was indeed of *both* families; he bargained hard, and gave away much less than either Lord looked for.

But on the tide of the renewal of Marantine, both Lords allowed their generosity to show; they supported Renar.

Which was good; he needed it.

Darin had little time for marvel or for victory—as the patriarch of Culverne, he was besieged on all sides by nobility, merchants, and even common people. It was difficult, as most of the people chose to defer to a rank that he didn't fully understand—his own. But he talked, less and less hesitantly, as they spoke about rebuilding Culverne.

He also oversaw the dismantling of the four churches of the Dark Heart, and it was with particular joy that he blessed the grounds and reclaimed the land for his people.

Erin spent the four days in the palace infirmary. She tended to the injured with the skill of her mother and found peace in it—as did those who felt her link with the Bright Heart.

One man in particular caught her attention: Gerald of the royal guards.

For him she pulled all of her power, and as much of God's as she could touch. Her hands found the side of his face, as he watched in bemusement.

She smiled, and he returned it, catching her tiny hands in his for a moment.

When she withdrew, he was whole.

"I don't know why you bothered," Renar said from the doorway. His eyes were shining brightly. "He never talked much anyway."

She gave him a dirty look; such jokes were in poor taste, especially here, but Gerald laughed broadly. And then nearly choked.

"Lady," Gerald said softly. His eyes widened further.

"Sarillorn," she said, gently disregarding his shock and his awe.

She knew that word would grow from here; it had already started. But it didn't matter. If the word brought hope, it meant a healing of a different type, and it couldn't be bad. Not now, not so soon after victory.

"Are you finished here, Erin?" Renar nodded at Gerald, who remained dumbstruck, hands already reaching for his mouth. "I told you. Most men would at least test the use of their tongue after something like this."

Gerald, stubborn or in shock, proved that he was not most men.

Erin shook her head and smiled a little tiredly. "Yes. I think—I think I am finished with the infirmary for at least today. Are you finished with your council?"

He snorted, rubbing his forehead with the sides of his hand. "Finished with, or finished by?"

"With. But never mind; you look exhausted and that's answer enough."

"You're one to talk, although I suppose you look as lovely as usual."

As usual. She laughed, looking ruefully at the russet stains of blood on her robes. She rose, leaving the chair that she had placed beside Gerald.

"Shall we leave off our plans for the evening?"

He took her hand firmly in his, bowed over it, and then offered her his arm.

She really didn't want to take it; he was attired in rich and regal wear, and she felt so dirty. But his look was insistent, and she sighed as linen touched velvet.

"Our plans," Renar answered softly, "are what has kept me going throughout the abysmal stretch of an interminable day."

She laughed, and the laughter surprised them both.

Together they left the infirmary and began their ascent to the king's chambers.

And there, in the warmth of lamplight, above the celebrations of Dagothrin, they began their halting dance.

epilogue

"First of Malthan."

Stefanos started to turn. He stopped, realizing where he was. The laws of the physical did not bind him in the hand of the Dark Heart.

"Second," he said, bitterly.

Sargoth was silent a moment. The shadows parted, allowing his presence to loom large above the changing landscape.

"Emotion, Stefanos. Here. Only you would be so bold."

"Only I? I think not, Second of the Sundered. You are here. You are never anywhere without reason. Speak your piece. I will listen." Around him the chaotic landscape wrinkled and tremored.

Again there was a hesitation.

"Sargoth, speak or leave."

The warning in the First's voice was impossible to ignore. "As you wish. It is—different here, is it not?"

"It is dark." Stefanos replied neutrally.

"Dark . . ." Sargoth gave the equivalent of a shrug. "Perhaps. Perhaps." The mist congealed. "First of the Sundered, allow me to be bold."

"Allow it?" Bitterness again, underlined with a hint of dark amusement.

"When do you think to return to the mortal plane?"

"In time."

"Ah."

Silence, while the shapes twisted and altered asynchronously. Sargoth began again. "Very well First among us. But I felt I

338

should tell you that time, as you call it, may be of the essence.
For you.''

"What do you mean?" There was a sharp suspicion, barely
concealed in Stephanos' question.

"Illan has fallen. Your old enemy, the city of Dagothrin, has
restored itself. Marantine stands again.''

Silence.

"There are rumors, in the mortal plane, that an army will
ride on Verdann.''

Silence again; the silence before thunder. In a cold, even
voice Stephanos began to speak. "Sargoth, if your hand is in
this, I will see that there is another Second before a mortal day's
end. Do you understand this?"

"You are the First," Sargoth replied. Sibilance. A hint of the
Dark Heart's laughter. The mist twisted suddenly; the sharp,
oily landscape convoluted in a blur of ugly color.

"I will return. The Empire is *mine*."

Where there had been two, one stood alone.

The Dark Heart twisted yet again.

"Lord.''

Second of my Servants.

"It is done. The woman and the boy are now a threat to him,
where once they were fugitives. He will take to mortal fields
against them; I will make certain that he does not know their
identity. It is his hand that will destroy them.''

The hand of darkness closed tightly around Sargoth.

The Dark Heart was pleased.